A SECRET AFFAIR

POWER OF A WOMAN

BARBARA TAYLOR BRADFORD

A SECRET AFFAIR

POWER OF A WOMAN

HarperCollins*Publishers*

This omnibus edition published in 1998 by HarperCollins*Publishers*

HarperCollins*Publishers*
77–85 Fulham Palace Road,
Hammersmith, London W6 8JB

A Secret Affair
Power Of A Woman

Barbara Taylor Bradford asserts the moral right to
be identified as the author of this work

ISBN 0 261 67142 1

Printed and bound in Great Britain by
Creative Print and Design (Wales), Ebbw Vale

As always, for Bob,
with all my love

1

He was closing the small padlock on his duffle bag when a deafening explosion brought his head up swiftly. He listened acutely, with accustomed practice, fully expecting to hear another bomb exploding. But there was nothing. Only silence.

Bill Fitzgerald, chief foreign correspondent for CNS, the American cable news network, put on his flak jacket and rushed out of the room.

Tearing down the stairs and into the large atrium, he crossed it and left the Holiday Inn through a back door. The front entrance, which faced Sniper Alley, as it was called, had not been used since the beginning of the war. It was too dangerous.

Glancing up, Bill's eyes scanned the sky. It was a soft, cerulean blue, filled with recumbent white clouds but otherwise empty. There were no warplanes in sight.

An armored Land Rover came barreling down the street where he was standing and skidded to a stop next to him.

The driver was a British journalist, Geoffrey Jackson, an old friend, who worked for the *Daily Mail.* "The explosion came from over there," Geoffrey said. "That direction." He gestured ahead, and asked, "Want a lift?"

"Sure do, thanks, Geoff," Bill replied and hopped into the Land Rover.

As they raced along the street, Bill wondered what had caused the explosion, then said aloud to Geoffrey, "It was more than likely a bomb lobbed into Sarajevo by the Serbs in the hills, don't you think?"

"Absolutely," Geoffrey agreed. "They're well entrenched up there, and let's face it, they never stop attacking the city. The way they are sniping at civilians is getting to me. *I* don't want to die from a stray rifle shot covering this bloody war."

"Me neither."

"Where's your crew?" Geoffrey asked as he drove on, peering through the windscreen intently, looking for signs of trouble, praying to avoid it.

"They went out earlier, to reconnoiter, while I was packing my bags. We're supposed to leave Sarajevo today. For a week's relaxation and rest in Italy."

"Lucky sods!" Geoffrey laughed. "Can I carry your bags?"

Bill laughed with him. "Sure, come with us, why don't you?"

"If only, mate, if only."

A few minutes later Geoffrey was pulling up near an open marketplace. "This is where the damn thing fell," the British journalist said, his jolly face suddenly turning grim. "Bleeding Serbs, won't they ever stop killing Bosnian civilians? They're fucking gangsters, that's all they are."

"You know. I know. Every journalist in the Balkans knows. But does the Western alliance know?"

"Bunch of idiots, if you ask me," Geoffrey answered and parked the Land Rover. He and Bill jumped out.

"Thanks for the ride," Bill said. "See you later. I've got to find my crew."

"Yeah. See you, Bill." Geoffrey disappeared into the mêlée.

Bill followed him.

Chaos reigned.

Women and children were running amok; fires burned everywhere. He was assaulted by a cacophony of sounds . . . loud rumblings as several buildings disintegrated into piles of rubble; the screams of terrified women and children; the moans of the wounded and the dying; the keening of mothers hunched over their children, who lay dead in the marketplace.

Bill clambered over the half-demolished wall of a house and jumped down into another area of the marketplace. Glancing around, his heart tightened at the human carnage. It was horrific.

He had covered the war in the Balkans for a long time, on and off for almost three years now; it was brutal, a savage war, and still he did not understand why America turned the other cheek, behaved as if it were not happening. That was something quite incomprehensible to him.

A cold chill swept through him, and his step faltered for a moment as he walked past a young woman sobbing and cradling her lifeless child in her arms, the child's blood spilling onto the dark earth.

He closed his eyes for a split second, steadied himself before walking on. He was a foreign correspondent *and* a war correspondent, and it was his job to bring the news to the people. He could not permit emotion to get in the way of his reporting or his judgment; he could never become involved with the events he was covering. He had to be impartial. But sometimes, goddamnit, he couldn't help getting involved. It got to him occasionally . . . the pain, the human suffering. And it was always the innocent who were the most hurt.

As he moved around the perimeter of the marketplace, his eyes took in everything . . . the burning buildings, the destruction, the weary, defeated people, the wounded. He shuddered, then coughed. The air was foul, filled with thick black smoke, the smell of burning rubber, the stench of death. He drew to a halt, and his eyes swept the area yet again, looking for his crew. He was certain they had heard the explosion and were now here. They had to be somewhere in the crowd.

Finally, he spotted them.

His cameraman, Mike Williams, and Joe Alonzo, his soundman, were right in the thick of it, feverishly filming, along with other television crews and photographers who must have arrived on the scene immediately.

Running over to join the CNS crew, Bill shouted above the din, "What the hell happened here? Another bomb?"

"A mortar shell," Joe answered, swinging his eyes to meet Bill's. "There must be twenty or thirty dead."

"Probably more," Mike added without turning, zooming his lens toward two dazed-looking young children covered in blood and clinging to each other in terror. "The marketplace was real busy..." Mike stopped the camera, grimaced as he looked over at Bill. "A lot of women and children were here. They got caught. This is a real pisser."

"Oh, Jesus," Bill said.

Joe said, "The mortar shell made one helluva crater."

Bill looked over at it, and said softly, in a hard voice,

"The Serbs had to know the marketplace would be busy. This is an atrocity."

"Yes. Another one," Mike remarked dryly. "But we've come to expect that, haven't we?"

Bill nodded, and he and Mike exchanged knowing looks.

"Wholesale slaughter of civilians—" Bill began and stopped abruptly, biting his lip. Mike and Joe had heard it all before, so why bother to repeat himself? Still, he knew he would do so later, when he did his telecast to the States. He wouldn't be able to stop himself.

There was a sudden flurry of additional activity at the far side of the marketplace. Ambulances were driving into the area, followed by armored personnel carriers manned by UN troops, and several official UN cars, all trying to find places to park.

"Here they come, better late than never," Joe muttered in an acerbic tone. "There's not much they can do. Except cart off the wounded. Bury the dead."

Bill made no response. His brain was whirling, words and phrases racing through his head as he prepared his story in his mind. He wanted his telecast to be graphic, moving, vivid and hard-hitting.

"I guess we're not going to get our R & R after all," Mike said, a brow lifting. "We won't be leaving today, will we, Bill?"

Bill roused himself from his concentration. "No, we can't leave, Mike. We have to cover the aftermath of this, and there's bound to be one ... of some kind. If Clinton and the other Western leaders don't do something drastic, something especially meaningful, there's bound to be a public outcry."

"So be it," Mike said. "We stay."

"They'll do nothing," Joe grumbled. "They've all been derelict in their duty. They've let the Serbs get away with murder, and right from the beginning."

Bill nodded in agreement. Joe was only voicing what every journalist and television newsman in Bosnia knew only too well. Turning to Mike, he asked, "How much footage do we have so far?"

"A lot. Joe and I were practically the first in the marketplace, seconds after the mortar shell went off. We were in the jeep, just around the corner when it happened. I started filming at once. It's pretty bloody, gory stuff, Bill."

"*Gruesome*," Joe added emphatically.

Bill said, "It must be shown." Then, looking at Mike, he went on quickly, "I'd like you to find a place where we can film my spot, if possible one that's highly dramatic."

"You got it, Bill. When do you want to start rolling the tape?"

"In about ten minutes. I'm going to go over there first, talk to some of those UN people clustered near the ambulances, see what else I can find out."

"Okay, and I'll do a rekky, look for a good spot," Mike assured him.

William Patrick Fitzgerald was a renowned newsman, the undoubted star at Cable News Systems, noted for his measured, accurate, but hard-hitting reports from the world's battlefields and troublespots.

His fair coloring and clean-cut, boyish good looks belied his thirty-three years, and his tough demeanor stood him in great stead in front of the television camera.

He had earnest blue eyes and a warm smile that bespoke his sincerity, and integrity was implicit in his nature. These qualities underscored his genuine believability, were part of his huge success on television. Because he had this enormous credibility, people trusted him, had confidence in him. They paid attention to his words, listened to everything he had to say, and took him very seriously.

It was not for nothing that CNS treasured him and other networks coveted him. Offers for his services were always being made to his agent; Bill turned them all down. He was not interested in other networks. Loyalty was another one of his strong suits, and he had no desire to leave CNS, where he had worked for eight years.

Some time later he stood in front of the grim backdrop of burning houses in the marketplace, and his sincerity seemed more pronounced than ever. He spoke somber words in a well-modulated voice, as always following the old journalistic rule of thumb: *Who, when, where, what,* and *how,* which had been taught to him by his father, a respected newspaperman until his death five years ago.

"Thirty-seven civilians were killed and many others wounded today when a mortar shell exploded in a busy marketplace in Sarajevo," Bill began. "The mortar was fired by the Serbian army entrenched in the hills surrounding this battle-torn city. It was an obscene act of aggression against innocent, unarmed people, many of them women and children. UN forces, who quickly arrived on the scene immediately after the bombing, are calling it an atrocity, one that cannot be overlooked by President Clinton and the leaders of the Western alliance. UN officials are already saying that the Serbs must be forced to understand that these acts of extreme violence are unwarranted, unconscionable, and unacceptable. One UN official pointed out that the Serbs are endangering the peace talks."

After giving further details of the bombing, and doing a short commentary to run with the footage of the carnage, Bill brought his daily news report to a close.

Stepping away from the camera after his ten minutes were up, he waited until the equipment was turned off. Then he glanced from Mike to Joe and said quietly, "What I couldn't say was that that UN major I was talking to earlier says there *has* to be some sort of retaliation, intervention by the West. He says it's inevitable now. Public anger is growing."

Joe and Mike stared at Bill doubtfully.

It was Joe who spoke, sounding entirely unconvinced.

"I've heard that before," he said and shook his head sadly. "I guess this disgusting war has turned me into a cynic, Billy boy. Nothing's going to happen, you'll see . . . it'll be status quo . . ."

But as it turned out, Joe Alonzo was wrong. The leaders of the Western alliance in Washington, London, and Paris had no choice but to take serious steps to stop the Serbs in their systematic slaughter of Bosnian civilians, or risk being the focus of public outrage and anger in their own countries.

Just two days after the mortar shell exploded in the marketplace, the alliance sent in NATO warplanes to attack the Serbian army in the hills of Sarajevo.

It was August 30, 1995. The bombing began in earnest that day, and it was the biggest attack of the war. There were more than 3,500 sorties in the short space of two weeks, and even Tomahawk Cruise missiles were launched in the assault.

At the end of three weeks, the Serbians had begun to back down, withdrawing their heavy weaponry from the Sarajevo hills at the edge of the city, and making sounds about peace negotiations.

Because of the NATO attack and later developments, Bill Fitzgerald and the CNS crew remained in Bosnia, their week of rest and relaxation in Italy postponed indefinitely.

"But we don't really care, do we?" Bill said one evening when the three of them sat at a large table in the communal dining room of the Holiday Inn.

"No, of course we don't," Mike answered. "I mean, who cares about missing a week in Amalfi, relaxing with a couple of beautiful girls. Nobody would *mind* missing that, certainly not I. Or Joe." He shrugged. "After all, who gives a damn about sun, sea, and sex. And wonderful pasta."

Bill chuckled.

So did Joe, who said, "Me, for one. I give a damn." He grinned at the cameraman, who was his best buddy, then addressed Bill quietly. "I was certainly looking forward to our trip. And you were fixated about Venice, Bill, come on, admit it."

"Yes, it's true, I was. And I plan to make it to Venice soon. Maybe in the next month or two."

It was late September and relatively quiet out on the streets of Sarajevo; the fighting was less intense, with only sporadic sniping and fewer forays into the city on the part of the bloodthirsty Serbs. The entire foreign press corps were fully aware that the intense NATO retaliation had worked far better in curbing the Serbs than the words of appeasement the West had been uttering thus far.

Bill said, "I think things *are* going to ease up here, and very soon."

From their expressions, Mike and Joe were obviously disbelieving, and they did not respond.

Looking at his colleagues intently, Bill added, "With a little luck, this war should end soon."

Joe, ever the cynic, ever the pessimist, shot back, "Want to bet?"

"No, I don't," Bill replied swiftly. "You can never really tell what's going to happen with the Serbs. They talk out of both sides of their mouths."

"And shoot from the hip with both hands. Always fast on the draw, the fucking maniacs," Joe exclaimed.

"They started this war and they're only going to end it when it suits them. When they get what they want."

"Which is most of Bosnia, if not, indeed, all of it," Bill said. "This war's always been about territorial greed, as well as power, racial bigotry and ethnic cleansing."

"Greed, power, and hatred, a pretty potent combination," Mike murmured.

The cameraman glanced at his plate of food, his expression glum. He grimaced and put down his fork; his nose curled in distaste. "The soup was watery and tasteless, now this meat is greasy and tasteless. Jeez, this damn curfew has been getting to me more than ever lately. I hate having to eat here every night. I wish we could find somewhere else."

"There's nowhere else to eat in Sarajevo, nowhere that's any better, and you know we can't go out at night anyway," Bill reminded him. "Besides, it's difficult driving without any streetlights." Bill stopped, sat back in his chair, suddenly feeling worried about Mike and Joe. They rarely complained about anything; lately they had done nothing but complain to him. He couldn't say he blamed them. Living conditions in Bosnia never improved, only got worse. He thought of the line he had heard when he first came to the Balkans at the outset of the conflict. It had been told to him by a reporter from a French news magazine and he had never forgotten it: *A day in Bosnia is like a week anywhere else; a week is like a month, a month is like a year.* And it was true. The country was wearing and wearying. It killed the soul, drained the spirit, and damaged the psyche. He was itching to get out himself, just as Mike and Joe were.

"It's not much of a menu, I'll grant you that," Joe suddenly said, and laughed hollowly. "It's always the same crummy food every night, that's the problem."

"Most people are starving in Bosnia," Bill began and decided not to continue along these lines.

All of a sudden Mike sat up straighter and announced, "Personally, I aim to be in the good old U.S. of A. in November, come hell or high water. I plan to be out on Long Island for Thanksgiving if it's the last thing I ever do. I want to be with my mom and dad, my kid brother and sister. It's been too long since I've seen them. I'm certainly not going to be in this godforsaken place, that's for sure."

"I know what you mean, old buddy," Joe said. "Me . . . I'd like to be in New Jersey for *my* turkey dinner. With my folks. I don't want to spend Thanksgiving in Bosnia either. Screw that!" Joe threw Bill a pointed look, and finished with, "Let's tell Jack Clayton we want out, Billy boy."

"Sure, I'll do it tomorrow. No problem. I'm positive

our grateful and adoring news editor will understand your feelings, and Mike's, and mine. He'll tell us to hop a plane to Paris, any plane we can get, and to hell with the expense, and then board the first Concorde out of Paris to New York. Pronto, pronto. Sure, he'll tell us to do that."

"Sarcasm has never been your forte, Bill," Mike remarked with an engaging grin, then went on: "But very seriously, talk to Jack tomorrow. Our rest period is long overdue. Originally, we were supposed to have it in July, then it got shifted to August, and finally it was canceled altogether. We haven't been out of Bosnia, except for a few long weekends in Hungary, for *three months*. I happen to think that we've all reached the end of our individual bits of rope."

"Could be we have. And you're right, Mike, so is Joe. Our R & R has been postponed for too long now. We're all edgy. Look, the peace talks are about to start in Dayton in October. That's only a few days away. Things ought to be relatively quiet here during that period, so I can't see that there would be any problems. Jack'll just have to send in another news team, should anything serious erupt when we're gone."

"There could easily be trouble," Mike remarked in a thoughtful tone. "Just because the peace talks are on doesn't mean that the guns will be silent. Not here. Anything goes."

"Only too true," Joe agreed. "Let's not hold our collective breath on that one."

"I know Jack's a tough news editor, but he is fair. He'll agree to this. Don't forget, *we* elected to stay when the NATO bombs started falling at the end of August. Jack was very appreciative that we did." Bill paused, thought quickly, and made a sudden decision. "Let's plan on getting out of here in a week. How does that sound, guys? Okay with you?"

Mike and Joe stared at him, dumbfounded. Then they grinned and exclaimed in unison, "*Okay!*"

2

The light in the piazza was silvery, the sky leaden, frosty. A faint mist rising from the lagoon and the many canals swathed everything in a veil of gray on this cold winter's afternoon.

Bill Fitzgerald walked slowly across St. Mark's Square, not caring about the weather in the least. There had been too many abortive attempts on his part to get to Venice, and he was glad he had finally made it.

It was a relief to be here after life in the battlefields of Bosnia; also a relief that the tides and the winds were cooperating and Venice was not flooded, as it frequently was at this time of year. Even if it had been, he wouldn't have cared about that either. The Venetians always managed very well when the city lay under water, so why shouldn't he?

He had been coming here whenever possible for the past few years. It was relatively easy to get to Venice from most cities in Europe, which was where he invariably was, on foreign assignment for his network. And even after only a couple of days here he always felt considerably refreshed, lighter in spirit and uplifted.

La Serenissima, the Venetians called it, this city of churches and palaces floating on water, blazing with color and liquid light, brimming with treasures of art and architecture. Bill thought it was one of the most intriguing and evocative places in the world, its aspects bound to delight even the most jaundiced eye.

On his first visit twelve years ago, he had spent a great deal of time in many of those churches and palaces, gazing at the breathtaking paintings by Titian, Tintoretto, Veronese, Tiepolo, and Canaletto. These masterpieces touched his soul with their incomparable beauty and, thereafter, the Venetian school of painting was one of his favorites.

He had always wished he could paint, but he was not in the least gifted in that respect. His only talent was with words.

"He's kissed the Blarney Stone, that one," his maternal grandmother, Bronagh Kelly, used to say when he was growing up. "True," his mother would agree. "That's his gift, a way with words. And he writes like an angel. We must remember that the pen is mightier than the sword."

Bill was an only child. He had spent a lot of time with adults when he was young, and his lovely Irish grandmother, in particular, was a favorite of his. He had been especially attached to her.

When he was little she had held him spellbound with her stories of leprechauns, lucky shamrocks, and pots of gold at the end of the rainbow. Bronagh had left Ireland with her parents and a younger brother when she was eight, and had grown up in Boston. It was here that she had met and married his grandfather, a lawyer named Kevin Kelly.

"I was born in 1905, and what a birth it was, Billy!" she would exclaim. "I came into this world at the stroke of midnight on the twelfth of June in the middle of the most violent thunderstorm," she'd tell him. "And me darlin' mama said it was a bad omen, that storm." She always embellished the details of her birth with every retelling, obviously enjoying his rapt expression and widening eyes. "And indeed it's been a stormy life I've lived ever since, Billy," she would add, with a huge laugh, which led him to believe she had relished her stormy life.

His wife, Sylvie, had loved Grandma Bronagh as much as he had, and the two had become very close over the years. His grandmother had been a true Celt, spiritual, mystical, and a little fey. Sylvie had shared these traits, been very much like her in many ways.

His only regret, whenever he came back to Venice,

was that he had not brought Sylvie here before she died. They had put it off and put it off, and suddenly, unexpectedly, it was too late. Sylvie was gone. Who could have known that she would die like that? In childbirth, of all things in this day and age. "Eclampsia" it was called; it began with seizures and ended in coma and death.

Losing Sylvie was the worst thing that ever happened to him. She had been too young to die, only twenty-six. His grief had overwhelmed him; he had been inconsolable for a long time. In the end, he had managed to come to grips with it, throwing himself into work in an effort to keep that grief in check and at bay.

As he went toward the Basilica, his thoughts were still centered on Sylvie. She had died in 1989; the baby, a little girl, had lived. She was called Helena, the name he and Sylvie had chosen. Now six years old, she was the spitting image of her mother, an adorable creature who entranced everyone she met.

Certainly she was a great joy to him. Whenever he felt depressed and disturbed by the rottenness of the world, he had only to conjure up her face and instantly he felt better. She made life worth living, his beautiful child.

A fleeting smile crossed Bill's face, touched his eyes

when he thought of her. Because his job as a foreign correspondent took him all over the world, she lived with his mother in New York. Fortunately, he saw her frequently and the time they spent together was genuinely meaningful. She was a good little girl, spirited, intelligent and not too spoiled, although his mother did dote on her only grandchild.

He had just spent two weeks in Manhattan with them, after covering the start of the Bosnia peace talks in Ohio. He would go back again in December, to celebrate Christmas at his mother's apartment in the East Sixties. When he wasn't in the middle of a battlefield or covering a major story in some far-flung corner of the globe, Bill made a point of being with "my best girls," as he called them. There was nowhere else he wanted to be, especially on important occasions and holidays.

But this week in Venice was his time for himself. He needed it badly, needed to put himself back together after his three-month stint in Bosnia-Herzegovina. Bill felt diminished by the conflict he had witnessed in the Balkans, and he was depleted, weary of war, of the destruction and the killing.

He wanted to forget. Not that he ever really would forget any of it. Who could? But he might at least be able to diffuse some of those horrifying images, still so vivid, that had left such a terrible scar on his mind.

His best friend, Francis Peterson, a war correspondent for *Time* magazine, believed that none of the
newsmen would ever be able to expunge the violent
images of Bosnia. "They're trapped in our minds like
flies trapped in amber, there for all time," Frankie kept
saying, and Bill agreed with him. All of them had seen
too much savagery; its imprint *was* indelible.

Francis and Bill had met at Columbia University's
School of Journalism in 1980, and they had been fast
friends ever since. They were often covering the same
wars, the same stories, but even when they were not,
and were in different parts of the world, they stayed in
constant touch.

Francis was currently assigned to Beirut, but he
would be arriving in Venice in an hour or two, and they
would spend a few days together. Later in the week,
Frankie would fly to New York to celebrate his father's
seventieth birthday.

Bill was glad his old friend was able to join him.
They were exceptionally close, shared the same interests
and understood each other well, were usually on the
same wavelength.

Suddenly Bill realized he was the only person in St.
Mark's Square, alone except for flocks of pigeons. The
birds flew around him, soaring up above the Basilica.
Usually the square was the center of animation in Venice,

teeming with people, mostly tourists from all over the world. Now he was its solitary occupant, and as he glanced about it seemed odd to him, strangely surreal.

As he continued to walk, he became aware for the first time of the unique paving in the piazza. In the past when he had strolled here, there had been hundreds and hundreds of pairs of feet covering it, obviously the reason he had never noticed it before now.

His eyes followed the flow of the pattern: flat gray stones covering most of the square, balanced on either side by narrow white marble bands set in classical motifs. At once he was struck by the way the motifs directed the eye and the feet toward the basilica. No accident, he thought, walking on. When he came to the church, he did not go inside. Instead, he turned right and went down the Piazzetta San Marco, which led to the water's edge.

For a long time Bill stood looking out across the lagoon. Sky and sea merged to become a vast expanse of muted gray, which soon began to take on the look of dull chrome in the lowering afternoon light.

It was so peaceful here it was hard to believe that just across the Adriatic Sea a bloody war still raged. Nothing ever changes really, Bill thought as he turned away from the water at last. The world is the same as it's always been, full of monsters, full of evil. We've learned nothing over the centuries. We're no more civilized now than we were in the Dark Ages. Man's monstrosities boggled his mind.

Hunching deeper into his trench coat, Bill Fitzgerald retraced his steps across the empty square. He began to hurry now as dusk descended, making for the Gritti Palace, where he always stayed. He loved its old-fashioned charm, comfort, and elegance.

The rain started as a drizzle but quickly turned into a steady downpour. Bill, increasing his pace, was almost running as he approached the side street where the front entrance to the Hotel Gritti Palace was located.

He sprinted around the corner of the street at a breakneck pace and collided with another person also moving swiftly. It was a woman. As her large-brimmed cream felt hat and her umbrella went sailing into the air, he reached out and grabbed hold of her shoulders to prevent her from falling.

Steadying himself, and her, he exclaimed, "Excuse me! I'm so sorry," and found himself staring into a pair of startled silvery-gray eyes. In Italian, he added, "*Scusa! Scusa!*"

She responded in English. "It's all right, honestly," and disentangling herself from his tight grip she ran after her hat, which was blowing down the street.

He followed her, outran her, caught the hat, picked

up the umbrella wedged against the gutter, and brought them both back to her. "I apologize again," he said.

Nodding, she took the hat and the umbrella from him. "I'm fine, really." She glanced at the hat. "And this isn't any the worse for wear either." She shook it and grimaced. "Just a *bit* splattered with mud. Oh well, never mind. Who cares? It was never my favorite hat anyway."

"I'm a clumsy fool, barreling around the corner like that. It wasn't very smart of me. Are you sure you're all right?" he asked in concern, unexpectedly loathe to let her go.

She proffered him a faint smile, slapped the hat on top of her dark curls, and sidled away from him, saying, "Thanks again."

He stood rooted to the spot as if paralyzed, watching her walk off when he wanted desperately to detain her, to talk to her, even invite her for a drink. He opened his mouth. No words came out. Seemingly, he had lost his voice, not to mention his nerve.

Suddenly he galvanized himself. Almost running up the street after her, he shouted, "Can I buy you a new hat?"

Without pausing, she called over her shoulder, "It's not necessary, thanks for offering, though."

"It's the least I can do," he cried. "I've ruined that one."

She stopped for a moment and shook her head. "No, really, the hat doesn't matter. 'Bye."

"Please slow down. I'd like to talk to you."

"Sorry, I can't. I'm late." She glided on, swung around the corner.

Bill hurried after her.

It was then that he saw the man coming toward her, waving and smiling broadly.

The woman increased her pace, waving back and exclaiming in Italian, "Giovanni, *come sta?*"

A moment later she was holding her umbrella high over her head so that the man she had called Giovanni could properly embrace her.

Disappointment surged through him. Immediately, Bill turned away, rounded the corner, and went down the street toward the Gritti Palace. He could not help wondering who she was. Certainly she was the most stunning woman he'd seen in a long time. Those luminous silver eyes set in a pale, piquant face, the head of tumbling dark curls, the elegant way she carried herself. She was beautiful, really, in a gamine sort of way. It was just his luck that she was apparently already spoken for. He would have liked to get to know her better.

3

They met in the bar of the legendary Gritti Palace, which faced the Grand Canal.

"It's great to see you, Francis Xavier!" Bill exclaimed, "Just great that you could make it." He enveloped his best friend in a bear hug.

As they drew apart after their rough, masculine embrace, Frank said, "And likewise, William Patrick. It's been too long this time around. I've missed you."

"So have I—missed you."

Still grinning at each other, they both ordered single malt scotch from the hovering waiter and sat down at a small table near the window.

"A lot of wars have been getting in the way," Frank went on, "and we seem to have been covering different ones of late."

"More's the pity we haven't seen the same action."

They exchanged knowing looks for a long moment, remembering the tough situations they had encountered together and had shared. Genuinely close since journalism school, the two men, who were not only friends but colleagues, understood each other on a very fundamental level. And each worried about the other's well-being. They had a great deal in common, always had had—a love of truth and the need to find it, traits which made them superlative newsmen; diligence, honesty, and a zest for adventure. Yet, despite the latter, both were cautious, fully aware of the dangers involved in their work. Whether together or alone on assignments, they always endeavored to minimize the risks they took in order to get the story.

Their drinks arrived, and after they'd clinked glasses, Frank said, "There's no way I'll go back to Bosnia, Bill."

"I know. And I don't blame you. I've sort of had it myself. How is it in Beirut?"

"Fairly quiet. At the moment, anyway. Things are improving, getting more normal, relatively speaking, of course. I don't think it will ever be the Paris of the Middle East again, but the city's perking up. Good shops are opening, and the big hotels are functioning on a more efficient basis."

"Hezbollah's still lurking, though."

"You bet! We have to live with the threat of terrorism around the clock. But *you* know that." Frank lifted his broad shoulders in a light shrug, his dark eyes narrowing. "Terrorism is more prevalent than ever. Everywhere in the world. The bastards are all over the place."

Bill nodded, took a sip of his drink, and leaned back in the chair, enjoying being with Francis Peterson.

Frank said, with a wide smile, "Let's change the subject, get to something more worthwhile. How's my little Helena?"

"Not so little, she's grown a tad. Which reminds me . . ." As he spoke Bill pulled out his wallet, removed a photograph, and handed it to Frank. "Your goddaughter wanted you to have this. She sends you hugs and kisses."

Frank stared at the picture Bill had just handed him. He smiled. "She's the most adorable kid, Billy, you're so lucky. I see she's still got that Botticelli look about her . . . positively angelic."

"To look at, yes, but she's mischievous, a bit of a scamp, my mother says." Bill grinned. "But then who wants a perfect kid?"

"A perfect kid, if there is such a thing, would be insufferable. How's Dru?" he asked, putting the photograph in his own wallet.

"Pretty good, thanks. You know my mother, Frankie, full of piss and vinegar and energy, and as loving of heart as she ever was. She sends you her love, by the way."

"When you speak to her, give her mine. Better still, I'll call her myself when I get to Manhattan, to say hello.

Incidentally, I'm sorry I couldn't get home when you were there. I had a really tough deadline for my piece on Lebanon. There was just no way I could take off at that time."

"I understood."

Frank went on, "I gather you weren't particularly impressed with the peace talks in Dayton."

Bill shook his head. "I wasn't. The Serbs are a diabolical bunch. Gangsters. They're never going to agree to a proper and *fair* peace treaty with the Bosnians, you'll see. As for all this UN talk about prosecuting some of the Serbs as war criminals, you can forget it. I assure you it will never happen. They're never going to get those butchers to the Hague to stand trial, for one thing. Just take my word for it. The Serbs are going to get away with their crimes."

"Tragic though it is, you're probably right, Bill."

"It's just wishful thinking on the part of the UN."

"I agree."

A small silence fell between them.

The two men sipped their drinks quietly, lost for a moment in their own thoughts.

They were a good-looking pair, both of them clean-cut and collegiate in their appearance. Any casual observer would have known immediately that they were Americans.

Frank was as dark as Bill was fair. He prided himself on being third-generation Irish-American, and Black Irish at that. He had a shock of dark hair, black eyes, and a fresh complexion. Like Bill, he was thirty-three, and currently single. His marriage to a television foreign correspondent, Pat Rackwell, one of the rising stars of her network, had foundered on the rocks of her career four years ago.

Fortunately they had had no children, and the divorce had been amicable enough. Whenever they ran into each other on a story, they pooled their information, their resources, and tried to be helpful whenever they could. Very frequently they had dinner together when they were in the same foreign city.

Breaking the silence, Bill said, "I heard a nasty comment about us the other day."

"Back in New York?"

"Yes."

"What was it?"

"That we're war junkies, you and I. That we love danger, love being in the thick of it, and that that's what gives us our jollies. We're characterized as being extremely reckless. A bad example."

Frank threw back his head and roared. "Who cares what people think! I bet it was one of your competitors at another network who made *those* lousy comments."

"As a matter of fact, it wasn't. It was one of the guys at CNS."

"Aha! He wants your job, William!"

"Yeah, he probably does." Bill hesitated for a second, then gave Frank a piercing look. "Do you think the odds *are* against us? That we will get killed one day, when we're covering a war in some godforsaken place?"

Frank was reflective. After a second he murmured, "So many journalists have lost their lives . . ." He let his voice trail off; his expression remained thoughtful.

"But we won't lose ours. I just feel it in my bones!" Bill asserted, his voice positive all of a sudden.

"You're absolutely right, it's just not in the cards. Anyway, you're bulletproof."

Bill chuckled.

"Furthermore, you're my lucky charm."

Bill cut in swiftly, saying, "Except that I'm not always with you these days, Frankie."

"True enough, just wish you were. We've had some experiences in the past, shared some highs and lows, haven't we? Remember the Panama Invasion?"

"How could I forget it? December of 1989. Sylvie had only been dead a few months, and I was so grief-stricken I didn't care what happened to me, didn't give a damn whether I lived or died."

"But you did care about me," Frank said in a low

voice, staring at his friend with sudden intensity. "I wouldn't be sitting here tonight if it hadn't been for you, Bill, you saved my life."

"You'd have done the same for me."

"Of course I would! But don't ever forget that I've always been very grateful."

"And so has the female population of . . . whatever city you're living in at the moment."

Frank grinned at his friend, said facetiously, "Aw shucks, Billy, don't start that again. I'm not the only newsman who likes a bit of female company occasionally. And what about you? You're not so shy with the girls either."

"There haven't been many women around lately, I'm afraid, not where I've been."

Frank nodded. "Sarajevo's hardly the place for a romantic interlude."

Bill confided, "Heard another thing in New York, Francis Xavier."

"Oh, yeah, and what's that? It obviously has something to do with me, from the tone of your voice."

"Sure does. Rumor has it you're suffering from a terminal Don Juan complex."

Frankie chuckled and went on chuckling. He was highly amused.

Bill smiled, feeling comfortable, relaxed, and more

at ease with himself than he had been for a long time. He knew that with Frank in Venice, for a few days he would be able to shake his depression, dispel the horrific images of war, and recharge his batteries completely.

Now Bill motioned to the waiter, ordered two more drinks, and said, "It's not such a bad reputation to have, when you think about it. After all no man can be a Don Juan unless women are interested in him."

"Only too true. As they say, it takes two to tango. By the way, I ran into Elsa in Beirut a few weeks ago."

"Elsa?" Bill frowned, looking puzzled.

"Don't tell me you've forgotten Elsa Mastrelli, our guardian angel from Baghdad."

"*That* Elsa! Oh, my God, how is she?"

"The same. Still covering wars for her Italian news magazine, still playing Florence Nightingale, ministering angel, and earth mother all rolled into one. At least, so I've been told."

"She was really great. Is she still as attractive?"

"Yes. Well, slight correction necessary here. Elsa has matured, looks more interesting, more experienced, even a bit war-weary, tired. But yes, she's still a knockout, a good-looking woman with a lot of savoir faire. In other words, she's grown up. We had a quick drink at the Commodore and reminisced about Baghdad."

"That was one hell of a time in our lives, Frankie!" Bill exclaimed animatedly. "My God, I'll never forget it . . . January of 1991. Only four years ago, but it seems so much longer, don't you think?"

"It sure does. We took some real chances, Billy, in those days."

"We were only twenty-nine. And very daring."

"Also very stupid, if you ask me." Frank threw Bill a pointed look. "No story's worth dying for."

"No, it isn't. But we didn't even think about dying, let's face it. And our Baghdad coverage made both our careers. Weren't we lucky that CNS was the only television network allowed to stay on in Baghdad? And that you and Elsa were the only print journalists given permission to stay on with us to cover the Gulf War?"

"All thanks to you and that enterprising producer of yours, Blain Lovett. What happened to him, is he still with CNS?"

"No, he went to NBC, then moved over to CBS. He's still there, doing very well, but no longer going out on foreign assignments. By choice, I guess."

"He was great, the way he networked. What a wheeler-dealer he was."

Bill grinned, remembering his former producer. "He had his act down pat, making his important contacts before the war started. Long before. And the Iraqis loved his schmoozing. He charmed a lot of them well before the conflict began and so they favored him. And we were home free when holy hell finally did break loose."

"I'll never forget the day he told you that our Iraqi minders were letting CNS bring in all that television equipment from Jordan," Frank said. "Including that satellite phone. I, for one, was flabbergasted."

"So was I, Frankie, and where would we have been without it? That phone was our only link to the outside world, and CNS was the only network getting coverage out for the world to hear and see."

"It did wonders for CNS, pushed them to the top of the pile in live news coverage in particular. And actually, Billy, we were fortunate to come out of that debacle alive, all things considered, and all those direct hits the hotel took. And there was Elsa, what a terrific little trooper she was . . . "

Frank paused as he realized that he had lost Bill's attention. "What's wrong?" he asked.

"Nothing."

"Something's wrong. You're not listening to me. And you have the strangest expression on your face."

Bill turned to Frank. "I don't want you to look now, but it's that woman over there. At the other side of the bar. Did you see her come in?"

"How could I fail to miss her? She's the only other person here except us. So, what about her?"

"I almost knocked her over earlier today. Collided with her this afternoon as I barreled around the corner, on my way back to the hotel. I chased her hat."

"*Chased her hat?*"

"Oh never mind, and don't look at me like that."

"Like what?"

"As if I'm nutty."

"Well, you are a bit crazy, Billy, and so am I, thank God. Life's too damned hard not to be slightly crazy from time to time. How else are we going to deal with all the stress and tension? Anyway, what about this woman?"

"I was very taken with her this afternoon. I wanted to get to know her better."

"I can't say I blame you. She's interesting-looking. Is she Italian?"

"I don't think so, even though she looks as if she might be. I'm pretty sure she's an American, certainly she sounds it. Anyway, her hat flew off as we collided, so I ran after it. I also ran after her as she thanked me and walked off. I wanted to invite her to have a drink with me. It's funny, Frankie, but I didn't want her to go."

"Why didn't you ask her to have a drink?"

"I tried to, but she was hurrying, almost running. I

was right behind her, and so naturally I saw her with the man she was meeting. Just my luck that she's involved with someone. For all I know he might even have been her husband. I watched them embrace. Still, I must admit I've thought about her for the past few hours, off and on."

"There's only one thing to do."

"What's that?"

"Go over and invite her to have a drink with us," Frank suggested. "You'll get the lay of the land pretty quickly."

"I guess you're right." As he spoke, Bill pushed himself to his feet and strode across the bar, walking in a direct line toward the young woman.

She looked up from a notebook she was holding and smiled when she saw him. "Hi!" she said, sounding friendly.

"Since you wouldn't let me buy you a new hat, could I at least buy you a drink?" Bill began. "My friend and I would love you to join us for . . . drinks *and* dinner."

"That's really nice of you both, but I can't. I'm waiting for a friend. I have a previous engagement," she explained.

Bill looked crestfallen. "Just my luck, er, er, our luck. Well . . ." His voice trailed off and he half turned to go, and then he swung around to face her again. "You're an American, aren't you?"

"Yes, I am. From New York."

"So am I."

"I know."

"My name's Bill—"

"Fitzgerald," she supplied, eyeing him, looking suddenly amused. "I know who you are; in fact, I watch your newscasts all the time, Mr. Fitzgerald."

"Call me Bill."

"All right."

"And you are?"

"Vanessa Stewart." She thrust out her hand.

Leaning forward, Bill took hold of it, and shook it. He discovered he did not want to let it go. "I have a great idea," he said and finally released her hand.

"You do?" She raised a dark brow and her large silver-gray eyes were quizzical as they focused on him intently.

Bracing his hands against the back of the chair and leaning forward, drawing closer to her, Bill said, "We must be the only three Americans in Venice at the moment, so we *must* spend tomorrow together."

"*Tomorrow?*" Her brows drew together. "Why tomorrow?"

"It's Thanksgiving."

"Oh, my God, I'd forgotten."

39

"Well, it is. Thursday, November the twenty-third. And it would be a crime if the only three Yanks in Venice didn't celebrate this most American of all holidays together. Join me and my friend, Francis Peterson of *Time*. Come on, what do you say?"

"Very well, I'll join you, but only on one condition."

"What's the condition? Shoot."

"That we have a proper Thanksgiving dinner with turkey and all the traditional trimmings."

Bill's face lit up in the most engaging way, and he grinned boyishly. "You've got a deal!" he declared.

She smiled up at him. "Then I'll be happy to come, thank you very much. Shall we meet here in the bar?"

"Good idea. Champagne first, and then on to our turkey dinner with all the trimmings. What time?"

"Seven. Is that all right?"

"Perfect." From the corner of his eye Bill saw the Italian, Giovanni, entering the bar. He inclined his head and politely took his leave. Moving away from her table swiftly, he retraced his steps across the room.

Frank had been watching Bill alertly, and now he said, "What happened?"

"She can't join us tonight. For obvious reasons. The Italian is on the scene again."

"Is that him over there now? The guy she met this afternoon?"

"Yes. Giovanni. However, she has agreed to have dinner with us tomorrow night."

Frank looked impressed. "That *is* an accomplishment, old buddy. How did you do it?"

"I reminded her that it's Thanksgiving, pointed out that we were more than likely the only three Americans in Venice, and added that it would be a crime if we didn't celebrate the holiday together."

"And she agreed?"

"On one condition."

"And what's that?"

"A turkey dinner. She wants a traditional Thanksgiving meal with all the usual trimmings."

"You didn't promise it, did you?"

"Sure I did. Why are you looking skeptical, Francis?"

"Where the hell do you think you're going to find a turkey? In Venice, of all places, for God's sake! This is pasta land, Billy."

"I know, and don't worry. Just trust me."

"But Bill, a *turkey*—"

"Did I ever let you down in Baghdad? Who's the one who always managed to find the most delectable stuff in that war-torn city ... from Johnnie Walker to cans of corned beef."

"Well, you were pretty good," Frank admitted, grinning.

"I know what I'm doing," Bill remarked. "I booked us a table at Harry's Bar tonight. And we'll go there again tomorrow. Everyone from Arrigo Cipriani, the owner, and the maître d' to the youngest busboy knows me well. Please believe me, Harry's Bar will make us a real American Thanksgiving dinner. They'll get a turkey, no matter what. After all, the mainland's not far away."

"I know better than to argue with *you*, Billy. And what's the lady's name?"

"Vanessa Stewart. She's from New York. She knew who I was."

Frank threw him an amused look. "Good God, don't sound so surprised, Bill. The whole of America knows who you are. Your face is in their living rooms every day of the week."

4

"Do you think she's stood us up?" Frank said the following evening. He and Bill were sitting in the bar of the Gritti Palace, waiting for Vanessa Stewart to arrive. He glanced at his watch. "It's twenty past seven."

"Stood *us* up! *Never*," Bill answered in a jocular tone, with a quick laugh. "Two dashing war correspondents like us. Good Lord, Frankie, don't you know by now that we're irresistible?"

When Frank merely threw him a sharp look and made an exasperated noise, Bill added in a more sober tone, "But seriously, I don't think she's the type to do that."

"What makes you so sure?"

"I just am, trust me on this," Bill replied firmly. "I thought she seemed like a serious person yesterday, and although we spoke only briefly, I detected something in her, an air of breeding. I know she would have phoned us here by now if she weren't coming, to make some sort of polite excuse. I sensed that she was not flaky, not the flighty kind at all."

"If you say so. And I guess it's a woman's prerogative to be late," Frank responded. Then he and Bill exchanged swift looks and promptly sprang to their feet as Vanessa Stewart appeared in the doorway of the bar. She hurried in, gliding forward at a rapid pace.

The young woman, who was of medium height and slender, wore a burgundy-colored outfit made of crushed velvet and carried a matching wool coat. The narrow velvet pants were paired with a loose, tunic top, which, with its square neckline and long sleeves cut wide at the cuffs, had a medieval look about it. Strands of amethyst-and-ruby-colored glass beads were twisted into a choker around her neck, and small gold medallions gleamed at her ears.

Both men wore admiring expressions as she drew to a standstill in front of them, a look of concern on her face.

"Sorry I'm so late," she said in an apologetic voice, shaking her head. "So rude of me, but it was unavoidable. I was delayed at a meeting this afternoon. When I got back to the hotel it was late and I had to change. I didn't want to lose any more time by calling you in the bar. I thought it best just to dress and hurry down."

"Are you staying here?" Frank said.

"Yes, I am."

"It's not a problem," Bill exclaimed, wanting to put

her at ease. Smiling warmly, he went on, "Vanessa, I'd like to introduce you to my friend Francis Peterson of *Time* magazine. And Frankie, this is Vanessa Stewart."

"It's very nice to meet you," Vanessa said, shaking Frank's outstretched hand.

"And I you," the journalist answered, offering her a welcoming smile, thinking how personable she was and how attractive, in an offbeat way. Bill had described her to him as being gamine, and it was true, she did have a roguish, saucy kind of charm. With her huge gray eyes in that small, piquant face and her short, curly, dark hair she looked very young and vulnerable. She reminded him of someone, someone he couldn't quite place.

Vanessa put her coat on a chair and sat down.

Bill said, "Would you like a glass of champagne or do you prefer something else?"

"Oh, champagne's lovely, thank you." She settled back in the chair and crossed her long legs.

Champagne was poured, and after they had all clinked glasses Bill said, with unconcealed curiosity, "You mentioned you were delayed in a meeting. So are you here on business?"

"Yes, I am." Vanessa cleared her throat, and went on, "I'm a designer. Of glass. I get most of it blown here. On Murano, to be exact. So I'm coming and going all the time."

"Are you a New Yorker?" Frank asked.

"Yes. I was born there."

"Do you live in Manhattan?"

She nodded. "In the East Fifties."

"Good old New York," Frank murmured. "There's nowhere else like it in the whole world."

Bill said, "What kind of glass do you design?"

"Vases, fancy bottles, big plaques and plates, decorative objects mostly, things to put on display. But I also make jewelry, like these beads." She touched the choker on her neck and explained, "But mostly I create objects for the home. Last year Neiman Marcus launched a line of mine, which I designed exclusively for them, and it's been a big success. That's why I'm here right now, to supervise the new collection."

"Oh, so it's currently being made, is it?" Bill said.

"Yes, at one of the oldest glass foundries on Murano. There's nothing like Venetian glass, in my opinion anyway. I think it's the best in the world."

"Where did you study in the States?" Frank probed.

"The Rhode Island School of Design, but also here in Venice. I did a graduate course for a year."

"So you lived in Venice!" Bill exclaimed. "How I envy you. I love this city."

"So do I." Vanessa's face took on a glow; she smiled at him. "La Serenissima . . . the Serene Republic, and it's so aptly named, isn't it? I always feel truly content here, peaceful, yet very alive. Venice is a state of being, I think."

Bill looked at her closely. He knew exactly what she meant about Venice. Struck by her openness, he nodded, returned her smile, and found himself staring into her luminous gray eyes. He averted his face, picked up his drink, and took a quick swallow. He felt suddenly self-conscious of his awareness of her, of his sexual attraction to her.

Frank, conscious of Bill's sudden discomfort, said, "And tell me, Vanessa, where do you normally spend Thanksgiving?"

"With my mother, if we happen to be in the same place. And sometimes with my father, if Mom's away. It depends on the circumstances."

"You make it sound as if your mother travels a lot," Frank remarked, raising a brow questioningly.

"She does."

"For pleasure or business?" he asked, still probing.

"Her work."

"And what does your mother do?"

"She's an actress."

"In the theater?"

Bill sipped his champagne, leaning back in the chair, listening, thinking that Frankie was asking too many questions. But at the same time he wanted to hear her answers. She intrigued him in a way no woman had for the longest time.

"Oh, yes, my mother works in the theater, and in films," Vanessa said.

"Would we know her?" Bill leaned forward, focused his attention on her.

Vanessa laughed. "I think so. My mother is Valentina Maddox."

"Is she really!" Bill cried. "Well, now that I know who she is I must admit you have the look of her, a very strong resemblance, in fact."

Frank said, "And Audrey Hepburn many years ago, when she was in *Sabrina.* That's who you reminded *me* of when you first walked in. Hasn't anybody ever told you that you look like her?"

Vanessa was still laughing. She nodded.

Frank now asked, "Aren't your parents divorced?"

"Yes. But they're still friends, and they see each other from time to time. They both live in New York. Well, Dad does. My mother's really a gypsy, flitting around the world, going wherever her work takes her."

"Do you have any brothers or sisters?" Bill inquired.

"No." Vanessa sat up straighter and looked from Bill to Frank, then began to laugh again. "What a lot of questions you both ask!"

"We're journalists. It's our job to ask questions," Frank replied.

They walked to the Calle Vallaresso, just off San Marco, where Harry's Bar was located.

It was a cold night. Frost hung in the air and ringed the moon, a clear silver sphere in an ink-dark sky. Cloudless and clear, it was littered with a thousand tiny pinpoints of brilliant light.

The streets were relatively deserted. Only a few people were about. As the three of them walked along, they could hear the clatter of their own shoes on the cobblestones.

"Hollywood couldn't have done it better," Bill remarked at one moment, glancing at the sky. "Hung that moon up there like that. What a fantastic film set Venice is, actually."

Vanessa exclaimed, "That's what my mother used to say when she came to visit me! She has always thought Venice to be the most theatrical of places in the whole world."

"She's right," Bill said, taking hold of Vanessa's arm, guiding her as they went down the narrower streets in the direction of the famous restaurant. He loved the closeness of her, the scent of her perfume. It was light, floral. Enticing. Just as she herself was enticing. He was very drawn to her, just as he had been yesterday, but tonight the feeling was more powerful.

They walked on in silence for a few seconds until Bill said, "I suppose you know all about Harry's Bar."

"Not really," she responded. "I went there with my parents, but only once. Didn't Ernest Hemingway make it his hangout?"

"He did, yes, along with a lot of other writers and journalists and celebrities. It was founded in the nineteen thirties, when an American, Harry Pickering, the now famous Harry, borrowed money from a hotel barman. The bartender was Giuseppe Cipriani, and when Harry paid him back he gave him additional money to open a bar. And *voila!* The restaurant was born."

"I love stories like that," Vanessa said, and then shivered slightly, drew further into her coat.

"Are you cold?" Bill asked solicitously.

"No, no, I'm fine."

Frank, who had been silent during the walk to the restaurant, announced, "There's Harry's Bar, straight ahead. We'll be inside in a minute."

They were given a royal welcome when they walked into Harry's Bar. Once they had shed their coats, they were escorted to one of the best tables at the back of the room. "Welcome, Signore Fitzgerald," Arrigo Cipriani said. "And 'appy Thanksgiving."

"Thanks, Arrigo. Now, how about some Bellinis to celebrate the holiday?"

"Good idea," Frank said.

"That'd be lovely," Vanessa agreed, and once they were alone she turned to Bill, and said, "I've forgotten what a Bellini is. I mean, I know it's champagne but what's in it besides that?"

"Fresh peach juice."

"Now I remember! They're fabulous."

A great deal of camaraderie had developed between them in the short time they had known each other. Vanessa had taken their probing questions at face value, had not been offended, and they in turn had been struck by her attitude, realizing what a good sport she was. And so the gaiety and banter continued at Harry's, only to be interrupted when a waiter arrived at their table, presenting the menus with a flourish.

"I ordered a special main course for us all last night," Bill explained.

"Si, Signore Fitzgerald, I know. But you didn't order a first course."

"True, I didn't. What do you suggest?"

"What about *risi e bisi*, I know you like it." Looking at Vanessa and then at Frank, the waiter continued, "It's a wonderful risotto. Mmm." He kissed his fingertips. "Rice with peas, ham, and Parmesan cheese. Delicious."

"Sounds good enough to eat," Frank joked.

Bill grinned at Vanessa. "It is good. I think I'll have it. How about you?"

"All right. Thank you."

"We'll all have it," Frank added. "And let's take a look at the wine list, please, Antonio."

"Si, Signore Peterson." The waiter nodded and departed.

Vanessa pushed back her chair and said, "Excuse me for a moment," and left the table, heading for the ladies' room.

Bill leaned over and said to Frank, "So, what do you think of her?"

"She's lovely, and you were right, she's not a bit flaky. In fact, I think she's a very nice young woman, one who's rather serious by nature."

Bill said, "I like her."

"It's more than *like*, Bill, that's too soft a word."

"What do you mean?"

"You're bowled over by her, and you're going to get involved with her. She with you."

"I'm not so sure."

"About yourself? Or her?"

"Both of us."

Frank smiled broadly, and a knowing glint entered his black Irish eyes. "Oh Bill, my boy, take my word for it, you are heading for the big one here. She's irresistible to you, has all the things you love in a woman. As for her, she can't take her eyes off you. She's intrigued, flattered by your interest in her, and she hangs onto every word you say."

"I think you exaggerate."

"Trust me, I don't. I've got eyes in my head, and I've been watching you both for almost two hours now. You're both trying to hide it, but you're falling for each other."

"I wonder who that Italian is? Giovanni?" Bill muttered.

"We can't very well ask her. Anyway, she's not wearing any rings, at least not a wedding ring, only that crested signet on her little finger."

"But that doesn't mean anything these days. And she does spend a lot of time here, she said so."

"That doesn't mean anything either, Billy. I'm telling you, that young woman —" Frank stopped as Vanessa glided up to the table.

The two men rose, and Bill helped Vanessa into her chair.

Once she was seated, she smiled across at him, and said, "You reminded the waiter you'd ordered a main course last night. Not a turkey?"

"Of course it's a turkey. I ordered a traditional Thanksgiving dinner for us, and fortunately they were able to oblige. After all, that was your condition, Vanessa."

She stared at him for a long moment, and shook her head slowly. Her eyes twinkled mischievously when she finally murmured, "But I was only teasing. I never thought for one moment that you'd find a turkey in Venice . . . "

Bill stared at her.

Vanessa's touch was featherlight as she rested her hand on his arm. "You see, I *wanted* to spend Thanksgiving with you . . . with or without a turkey."

5

What Francis Peterson had predicted finally came to be.

Bill and Vanessa fell in love.

As Bill said much later, they probably did so on Thanksgiving night at Harry's Bar, although it took them several days to acknowledge their feelings.

During the Thanksgiving weekend they got to know each other better. In fact, they were a threesome, since they spent Friday and Saturday with Frank.

For these two days Vanessa became their guide, showing them places in Venice that not even Bill, the Venice aficionado, knew about. These were small, unique art galleries, museums and churches off the beaten track, bars and cafés known only to the Venetians themselves, shops where the best bargains were to be had.

At Bill's insistence, she took them out to Murano, where she did much of her work. They went to the island by *vaporetto*, a water taxi that took only seven minutes to get there.

Bill and Frank both wanted to see her designs, and so they visited the ancient glass foundry where her glass pieces were handblown. Both men were impressed by her stunning designs, her talent and creativity, and they realized she was a true artist.

That evening, at her request, they escorted her to a cocktail party given by an old friend of hers from her student days, who owned a palazzo on the Grand Canal situated diagonally across from the Gritti Palace. They needed a gondola to get there.

The two newsmen found the slightly ramshackle palace an amazing place, and were fascinated by its many treasures. Carlo Metzanno, their host, was an interior designer, and he had given the massive, centuries-old palace a great deal of style and elegance. As he showed them around, he explained the provenance of many of the art objects, paintings, and antiques. Prominently displayed were several extraordinary pieces by Vanessa. These were fluid, sinuous, and impressive.

The three of them stayed at the cocktail party for an hour, mixing with a colorful group of people including a couple of local artists, a famous French movie star, a playwright from London, and an American architect.

When they left the palazzo, the same gondola that they had hired for the evening took them to the Giudecca, the narrow sliver of an island across the Canale della Giudecca. Vanessa had invited them to dinner, and she had booked a table at Harry's Dolci, the charming and intimate "little sister" of Harry's Bar. After their meal they strolled over to the Hotel Cipriani for espressos and stregas before going back to Venice in the gondola. "We've become the three musketeers," Frank said as they took their seats, settling back to enjoy the ride to the Gritti Palace. "We're now old pals." Bill and Vanessa laughed, and Bill said, "I think that's swell."

Bill had planned what he termed "an adventure" for Saturday night. Once again, a gondola was hired for the evening, and this carried them down the narrow winding backwaters of Venice until they arrived at an old house that looked like a hole in the wall. It turned out to be a marvelous family restaurant, one Bill knew well, which was a popular eating place favored by Venetians in the know.

It was a gay evening filled with bonhommie. They laughed and joked, exchanging a lot of amusing banter. A considerable amount of genuine affection flowed between them. The two men had grown quite close to Vanessa, and she to them.

"Here's a toast, then," Frank said as the dinner drew to a close. "To dear friends—old and *new*." He clinked his glass of red wine to Bill's glass and then Vanessa's. Smiling at her genially, he added, "You're a good sport, kid, the way you've put up with us. Especially *me*, with all my questions. I've enjoyed being with you for the last couple of days. You've been like . . . a breath of fresh air."

Vanessa colored slightly, the flush rising from her neck to touch her face. Frank had teased her a lot, and now she was touched by his compliments, his unexpected courtliness.

"What a nice thing to say, Frank, thanks, and I've enjoyed *your* company."

"I'm going to miss you both," Frank went on, looking from Vanessa to Bill. "Most especially you, William Patrick. Battlefields are not the same without you."

"I know," Bill replied, his eyes focused on his best friend. "I'll miss you, too, but who knows, we may well be covering the same story in the next few months."

"Could be," Frank said. "I hope so."

As they left the restaurant a short while later, Vanessa shivered and moved nearer to Bill, who put his arm around her protectively and drew her close against him.

Venice in winter, and especially in the evening, was mysterious, even frightening. The gondola glided down many dark waterways, heading for the Gritti Palace. Mist rose up from the murky canals, and there was no noise except for the slap of the oars as they hit the water. Everything was shadowy, eerie in the dim light.

On either side of the narrow waterways, buildings

loomed up like strange inchoate monsters under the threatening sky. At times the mist was more like fog, thick and almost impenetrable. The dampness clung to them, seemed to penetrate their clothes.

The three friends stayed huddled in the gondola, shivering, fighting the cold, talking quietly until they reached the hotel.

"I'm glad we're back," Vanessa said with another shiver as Bill helped her to alight at the small dock in front of the Gritti Palace. "There are times when Venice at night frightens me, fills me with foreboding—" She cut herself off, feeling suddenly foolish. After all, she had two men to protect her, not to mention the muscular gondolier who looked like a prizefighter.

Since they each had their rooms on different floors, they said good night in the lobby.

Frank, who was leaving the following morning for Milan and then a direct flight to New York, kissed Vanessa on both cheeks. He gave Bill one of their customary bear hugs.

"See you, William," he said nonchalantly, walking to the elevator. Suddenly, he paused, turned around, and looked at them both for a split second, the expression on his face unexpectedly serious.

"Take care of each other," he said and disappeared behind the sliding doors of the elevator.

*   *   *

Bill and Vanessa remained standing in the lobby, staring at each other.

Vanessa's eyes were full of questions as she murmured, "What an odd thing for him to say—" She stopped, her gaze still riveted on Bill.

"Not really," Bill answered quickly. Then, after the merest hesitation, he went on, "You see, he knows how I feel about you."

"How is that?"

"I'm very . . . *drawn* to you, Vanessa."

She was staring up at him; she nodded. "I guess he knows I feel the same way."

"You do?"

"Oh, yes, Bill."

Bill inclined his head slightly. "So, Frankie *was* right. He sensed it from the beginning. He was quite positive he knew exactly how we *both* were feeling."

"He's very astute." She spoke in the softest of voices.

"He is. Do you want a nightcap? Or something hot, maybe? Hot lemon tea?"

"Not here, though," Vanessa said.

"Your room or mine?"

"Oh yours, please," Vanessa answered with a small, shy smile. "You have a suite, mine is nothing so grand."

Putting an arm around her shoulder, Bill led her to the other elevator at the far end of the lobby. The minute the door closed, he did what he had been wanting to do for the past three days. He took her in his arms and kissed her.

Vanessa kissed him back, and with such intensity he was momentarily startled. When the elevator came to a halt, they quickly pulled apart. As they stepped out, he noticed her flushed face. She was usually so pale.

Drawing a finger down one side of her cheek, he leaned into her and whispered, "You're burning up. Hot to the touch."

She looked at him swiftly but said nothing.

With their arms wrapped around each other, they walked along the corridor to his suite. After letting them in, Bill closed the door with his foot. Shooting the bolt with one hand, he pulled her into his arms with the other. Once more they clung together, kissing with growing fervor.

Suddenly Bill held her away from him and said, "Let's take off our coats." So saying, he helped her out of hers, struggled to shrug off his trench coat, and threw both on a nearby chair.

Silently Bill took hold of her hand tightly, led her into the adjoining bedroom and over to the bed. Vanessa seated herself on the edge of it, all the time watching him as he bent down and took off her shoes, first one and then the other.

After kissing each foot, he slid his hand under her wide, flared skirt, stroking her leg, moving up until his fingers caressed her inner thigh.

"Bill?"

"Yes?"

"Let's get undressed."

A half smile touched his mouth. With swiftness he rose, took her hands in his and pulled her to her feet, so that they were facing each other. Vanessa moved closer, placed her arms around his neck, kissed him on the mouth passionately. As she did so, he reached behind her and unzipped her wool skirt.

The skirt fell to the floor, lay in a swirl of purple at her feet. She stepped away from it, then swung back to him, her eyes focused on him with intensity.

Bill looked at her closely. What he saw surprised and pleased him. Her face was flushed, full of desire, and her silvery eyes brimmed with longing. For him.

Roughly Bill pulled her to him, bent his face to hers, and kissed her deeply. He slid his tongue into her mouth, let it graze hers, and she did the same, exciting him more than ever with her fervor and unabashed desire. He felt the blood rush to his face; he was aroused as he had not been aroused for years. He wanted her so much, had wanted her for days, and now he felt as though he would explode. He had an enormous erection. He pressed himself against her; she bent to his will, letting her whole body flow against his.

Leaning away from her slightly, he looked down at her breast, touched it gently. How taut it was under the thin silk blouse. Fumbling, he undid the first few buttons, put his hand inside her blouse. He kissed her breast, then sucked on the hardening nipple.

"Please, let's lie down, Bill."

Clinging to each other they staggered to the bed. She began to take off her blouse, but he stopped her.

"Let me do it," he said in a low voice. "I want to undress you. Please, darling."

She nodded. Her eyes never left his face as he opened her blouse. After slipping it over her shoulders, he began to kiss her neck, her arms, and brought his mouth back to her breast. As his tongue tantalized the nipple, he undid her bra. At last both of her small, rounded breasts were free and he buried his head between them.

Bill could feel Vanessa's strong hands in his hair, smoothing and stroking, massaging his neck and shoulders. He heard her soft moans as he moved from one breast to the other, tenderly kissing and touching them, inflaming himself as well as her.

After a moment he sat up, looked down at her stretched out on the bed. How exciting she was to him, so vulnerable in her delicate beauty. She wore a lacy, black garter belt and sheer, black stockings. Carefully he undid the suspenders and rolled down each stocking, took off one, then the other. His eyes ravished her body, so trim and lean, yet shapely. Unfastening the garter belt, he slipped it off.

She stared up at him, her eyes wide and unblinking. "I want you," she said in a husky voice.

He nodded, stood up, threw off his clothes haphazardly, lay down next to her. Taking her in his arms, he kissed her eyes, her lips, her ears. "I want to kiss every part of you," he whispered against her hair.

"I'd like that," she murmured.

He slid down the bed, brought his mouth to the core of her. She responded wildly, crying his name. Her body suddenly convulsed in a spasm, and she grasped his shoulders hard, gasping as she did so.

Before he could stop himself, Bill was astride her, lying on top of her. Both his hands reached up into her dark curls, and he covered her mouth with his, touching his tongue to hers. He needed to take her to him. Now. Without further delay. Bracing his hands on either side of her he raised himself up, stared down into her eyes.

"Yes," she cried. "Oh, yes, Bill."

His hands left her hair, moved on to fondle those taut breasts with their erect nipples. He pushed his hands under her back, then her buttocks, lifting her closer to him, fitting her body to his. He was harder than ever and slid inside her easily.

And she welcomed him with her warm and pliant body, cleaving to him, thrusting up to him. She became welded to him. She moved her legs, threw them around his back, as high as they would go, so that he could shaft deeper and deeper into the warm, soft core of her. And they found their own rhythm, moving faster and faster until they were frenzied.

Bill thought his heart was going to burst. He sank deeper and deeper into her until he was entirely enveloped by her. "Vanessa," he gasped. "Vanessa."

"Yes, Bill!" she cried. "Don't stop."

He brought his mouth to hers again, and holding her tightly in his arms, they came to a climax together, sharing their ecstasy. And their joy in each other was unparalleled.

6

"That was all too quick," Bill said, encircling her with his arms, pulling her closer to him. "I'm afraid I was overanxious."

"No, you were wonderful."

"I've wanted us to be together like this since the other afternoon, when I almost knocked you over."

"So have I."

"Really and truly, Vanessa?"

"Yes, honestly."

He felt her smile against his chest. Before he could stop himself, Bill asked, "Who's Giovanni?"

She swiveled her eyes to look up at him. "How do you know his name?"

"I heard you greet him the other afternoon, just after I'd chased your hat."

"I see. He's an old friend . . . we met when I was doing my graduate course here. We became close, he helped me in lots of ways."

"Are you lovers?"

"No." Vanessa hesitated, then added, "Giovanni lives with someone, has for several years . . . another man."

"Oh." Bill cleared his throat, and after a moment he said, "We asked you lots of questions, Frankie and I, but we didn't ask your age, being the gentlemen that we are. But how old are you, actually?"

"Twenty-seven. Soon to be twenty-eight. And you're about thirty-five, aren't you?"

He laughed. "Thanks a lot! And no, I'm thirty-three," he replied and kissed the top of her head. "You said you were staying another four days. That means you're leaving on Wednesday. Correct?"

"Yes, I have to work at the glass foundry on Monday and Tuesday."

"Can I see you in the evenings? Can we be together until you leave?"

"Of course, I want that too, Bill."

"Listen, I'm coming to New York in December. For the Christmas holidays, in fact. Are you going to be around?"

"Yes." There was a small pause before she continued, "Bill, there's something I must tell you."

He heard an edge in her voice all of a sudden and he frowned. "Go ahead."

Vanessa took a deep breath and plunged. "I'm married."

For a moment Bill did not respond, and then he moved up on the pillows.

Vanessa struggled free of his embrace, turned to face him.

They stared at each other intently.

Vanessa saw surprise mingled with hurt on his face.

"Don't be angry with me. Don't look at me like that," she cried.

"How do you expect me to look, for God's sake? I'm disappointed, Vanessa. You lied to me."

"No I didn't, we never mentioned my marital status."

"You lied by omission."

"What about your private life, Bill? Is there a woman in *your* life? You don't need a piece of paper to make a commitment to someone. Making it legal doesn't necessarily make the bonds any stronger, the attachment greater. Do you live with a woman?"

"No."

She sighed.

He said, "Do you live with him?"

"Sort of . . ."

"What does that mean?"

"He's away a lot. And I go to my studio in the Hamptons a great deal of the time. I have a barn and a cottage in Southampton. So we're not together often."

"And when you are? Is it a proper marriage?"

She shrugged.

"Do you sleep with him?" he pressed.

Vanessa did not respond.

"Your silence is golden . . . it means that you do."

"It's not a good marriage—"

His hard laugh stopped her short. "Ah, the misunderstood married woman!" he exclaimed.

"No, it's not like that!" She leapt off the bed, ran into the bathroom, and came back a moment later wrapped in a terry cloth robe. Seating herself on the edge of the bed, she took hold of his hand.

Bill looked at her, his face taut. He was trying to come to grips with his emotions. After making such passionate love he had been euphoric, a feeling he had long forgotten existed. And he had felt at ease with this young woman who had come so unexpectedly into his life. He knew he wanted to get to know her better, to spend time with her. Her announcement that she was not free had been a bombshell.

Vanessa exclaimed, "Please, Bill, don't be angry. Let me explain."

"I'm not angry, and go ahead, be my guest. *Explain,*" he said and there was a sarcastic note in his voice.

Ignoring this, Vanessa said, "Peter's a lawyer, a show-business lawyer and very successful. He's away a lot, mostly in Hollywood. It wasn't like that at first, but his business has grown. And I'm traveling, too. I suppose, in a way, we've grown apart a bit. But he's a good man, and he's been very supportive of me, as I have of him. So we sort of . . . muddle through. It's not a great marriage, but it's not a bad one either."

"Have you never thought of leaving him?"

She shook her head. "He's a good man, as I just said. I wouldn't want to hurt him."

"What about you, Vanessa? Aren't you entitled to have a happy relationship with a man?"

"I don't think it's possible to build one's happiness on someone else's unhappiness."

"I know what you mean."

"In any case, Peter would fall apart if I left him. I just couldn't have his pain on my conscience."

"Do you have children?"

"No, sadly we don't."

"How long have you been married?"

"Four years."

"Do you still love him?"

"I care about him—" She came to a halt, looked thoughtful, finally confided, "Peter's been in my life for such a long time. We're good friends, and we have a lot in common. He's always encouraged me in my work, my career, never stood in my way. He's a nice person. I like him. I respect him, and I love him. But—"

"You're not in love with him, is that what you're try-ing to say?"

"Yes." Vanessa bit her lip and shook her head. "I mean, how could I be here with you like this if I were?"

Bill laid his head back against the pillows and closed his eyes. A small sigh escaped, and without opening his eyes, he said softly, "I just wish you'd told me you were married, that's all."

"I wanted to," Vanessa said. "I intended to, and then we started to have such a good time together. I liked you so much. I wanted to be with you, and I just thought you'd lose interest if you knew I had a husband."

He said slowly, "You should have been straightforward with me."

"Have *you* been with me?"

He sat up swiftly and stared at her. "Yes, I have. There isn't a woman in my life. You know I'm widowed. My God, the whole world knows I'm widowed. And I haven't had a really good relationship since Sylvie died. Oh, yes, there've been a few women, but I've never fallen in love, or had a meaningful relationship since my wife died six years ago. To tell you the truth, I thought that you and I might have something going for us, that this was the beginning of something special. I want a good relationship, Vanessa, I want to have another chance at happiness." He shrugged. "I guess I was wrong to think it might be with you."

Vanessa said nothing, looked down at her hands twisting nervously in her lap.

The awkward silence grew.

At last she said, "How do you *really* feel about me, Bill? Be scrupulously honest."

He gave her a hard penetrating stare. "We've just made passionate love, and you ask me that?" He gave a short laugh, pursed his lips. "Obviously I'm overwhelmingly attracted to you, turned on by you. I enjoyed making love with you. Let's face it, we've just had wonderful sex. I like being with you. I admire your talent. As I told you in the lobby a short while ago, I'm very taken with you, Vanessa."

"And I am with you, Bill. So much so I haven't really been able to think straight for the last couple of days. All I know is that I just want to be with you. Whenever we can. You're a foreign correspondent, you're obviously going to go back to Bosnia or somewhere else, and I have my own career . . ." She shook her head, and tears brimmed in her eyes. "I thought we would see each other whenever we could, be together as often as possible and . . . see what happens."

"Let things work themselves out in their own time, is that what you mean?"

"Yes. Whenever my mother was facing difficulties, she would always say to me, 'Vanny, life takes care of itself and a lot of other things as well. And usually it's for the best.' That's still her philosophy, I think."

Bill looked at her thoughtfully. "So, what you're saying is that you want to have an affair with me? A secret affair. Because you don't want your husband to be hurt. Am I correct?"

"It sounds terrible when you put it that way."

"But it *is* the truth. And as a newsman, I *am* a seeker of truth."

Vanessa shook her head, biting her lip again. Slowly, tears trickled down her cheeks.

"Oh, for God's sake, don't start crying!" he said, and reached for her, pulled her into his arms. He flicked her tears away with his fingertips, then tilted her face to his. Softly, he kissed her on the mouth.

When he stopped, she said, "Please tell me you're not angry with me, Bill."

"I'm not angry. Only selfish. I always want things my way, like most men. And listen, you haven't committed a crime. Anyway, why should you stick your neck out for me?" He laughed. "I'm always in harm's way . . . a bad risk."

"Don't say that!" she cried, her eyes flaring.

Tightening his grip on her, he brought his face closer to hers and whispered, "I *want* to be your lover. Now why don't you take off that robe so that I can start practicing."

7

It was an extraordinary day, clear, light-filled. A shimmering day. The sky dazzled. It was a perfect blue, unmarred by cloud, and the sun was brilliant above the rippling waters of the lagoon. The air was cool, but not as cold as it had been over the past few days, and the mist had dissipated.

On this bright Sunday afternoon, Bill and Vanessa walked through the streets and squares for several hours, holding hands, hardly speaking but comfortable in their mutual silence. Both were swept up in the beauty of Venice. They walked on past the Accademia, down the Calle Gambara into the Calle Contarini Corfù, until they came at last to the Fondamenta Priuli-Nani.

"Of course I remember this area now," Vanessa said, turning to Bill, smiling up at him as they headed down the street. "That's the old boatyard of San Trovaso, where gondolas are repaired," she continued, gesturing to the decrepit-looking buildings ahead of them. "I came here once with my father. He wanted to see the Church of San Trovaso. It's very old, if I remember correctly."

"Yes, it is," Bill replied. "It was built in the tenth century, and that's where I'm taking you now, actually. To the church. I want to show you one of my very favorite paintings. It's by Tintoretto. And incidentally, gondolas are also *made* at the San Trovaso boatyard, it's one of the last of the building yards left in Venice."

"They've all more or less disappeared. So many of the old crafts have become defunct," she murmured, sounding regretful. "But, thank goodness, glassblowing hasn't!" she finished with a light laugh, grinning at him.

They continued on past the boatyard, and walked up over the Ponte delle Meravegie, the bridge of marvels. Within seconds they were approaching the Church of San Trovaso, its cream-colored stone walls and slender bell tower rising up above the trees, a sentinel silhouetted against the cerulean sky.

After they had entered the church, Vanessa and Bill stood quietly for a moment, adjusting their eyes to the dim light and the overwhelming silence. They both genuflected, and Bill threw Vanessa a swift glance but made no comment, realizing that she also must be a Catholic. They slowly moved forward, walking down the nave toward the altar.

Immediately, Bill brought Vanessa's attention to the two paintings hanging on either side of the choir. "Both are by Tintoretto," he explained. "The last two pictures he ever painted. In 1594. Come on, let me show you the one I love the most." A moment later they were in front of *The Adoration of the Magi*, Tintoretto's great masterpiece.

"I've always liked this particular Tintoretto myself," Vanessa volunteered. "It's absolute perfection. The colors, the images, the incredible brushwork."

"Wasn't he marvelous," Bill said, "A towering genius." He fell silent, simply stood staring at the picture, rooted to the spot, unable to tear his eyes away.

At this moment it struck Vanessa that Bill was mesmerized by the painting. Several times she threw him a surreptitious look, but she made no comment, not wanting to break the spell for him; she understood how moved he was by this great work of art.

Finally dragging his eyes away from the painting, he said, "When I look at this Tintoretto, and the other treasures in Venice, and consider man's incredible talent, his ability to create incomparable beauty, I can't help wondering how man can also be the perpetrator of an evil so stupendous it boggles the mind. It's hard to reconcile the two."

"But the two have always coexisted," Vanessa answered, putting her hand on his arm. "Venice *is* the total personification of visual beauty. It's there for us to *see*, to take pleasure from, wherever we look. The art, the architecture, the many different treasures that have been accumulated here over the centuries, the very design and layout of Venice itself—" She paused for a split second before she added softly, "You have just come out of Bosnia, where you witnessed inhumanity and savagery, cruelty beyond belief. And those images must still be in your mind, Bill. How can you not make comparisons?"

"You're right, yes, I know that," he said, and turning away from the painting at last, he took hold of her arm and led her down the nave, back to the front door of the ancient church. "I suppose the beauty of paintings and music help to make the hard realities of life . . . bearable."

"I think so."

Once they were outside in the sunlight, Bill blinked and shook off the images of the Balkans war that had momentarily overtaken him. He exclaimed, "It's such a long time since I've taken a gondola up the Grand Canal. Shall we do it, Vanessa? It's still the most spectacular trip, isn't it?"

"Absolutely. And I'd love it. It's ages since I've done it myself, and I guess the Grand Canal personifies Venice, doesn't it? Besides, I find gondolas a very relaxing way to travel."

Bill felt a sudden rush of happiness surging up in

him. He knew it was because of Vanessa, her presence by his side. He put his arm around her, hugged her to him. "I'm glad we met, I'm glad we're here today in Venice. I'm glad we made love last night. I'm glad we have a few more days together." He stopped, tilted her face to his and looked at her, a faint smile briefly touching his mouth. "Whatever your circumstances are, Vanessa, you're the best thing that's happened to me in a long time." He kissed the tip of her nose. "Clandestine though it must be, I want our affair to continue." His eyes searched hers questioningly.

She nodded. "So do I. Whenever we can, wherever we can," she answered, and reached up, threw her arms around his neck, pulled his face to hers, and put her mouth on his. "There," she added, "sealed with a kiss."

He laughed, and so did she, and with their arms wrapped around each other they walked back the way they had come. Retracing their steps past the old boatyard, they went down the narrow streets until they came again to the Campo dell' Accademia, where Bill hired a gondola to take them back to the Gritti.

Immediately they were seated, Bill put his arm around Vanessa again and pulled her closer to him, realizing as he did that in only a few days this woman had come to mean so much to him. It didn't seem possible that he could care so deeply for someone other than Helena or his mother, but he did now. And it was all very sudden at that.

For her part, Vanessa was thinking similar things, and wondering how her life would ever be the same again. It wouldn't, she was positive. Not ever again. Because of Bill.

The two of them sat with their backs to the gondolier, who was in the prow. They were facing St. Mark's Basin, the vast expanse of water that rolled up to the quay.

Directly in front of them were the island of San Giorgio, the Church of the Salute, and the Dogana, the beautiful domed customs building. These buildings, known as the three pearls to the entrance of Venice, were turning golden in the late afternoon sunlight.

"The light of Turner," Bill said, leaning forward intently, looking at the sky. "Vanessa, do you see the changing light? It's gone a peculiar yellow, the yellow Turner captured so perfectly on canvas. I've always loved the paintings he did of Venice."

"So have I. And this view is the very best," she replied. "The entire city floating on water, the water changing with the light. The whole scene is . . . dream-like . . ." Vanessa paused, thinking how truly lovely it was. Magical, almost otherworldly. It moved her; she felt the unexpected prick of tears in her throat, touched as she was by the beauty of this city.

Sky and shifting water merged, golden, then irides-cent in the lowering light of the afternoon. All the col-ors of Venice were reflected now in the Grand Canal as they floated along it, heading for the hotel.

Fading sunlight caught the cupolas of the basilica, streaking them to silver, touching the pale colors of the palazzos, giving the pink, terra-cotta, ocher, and pow-dery yellow a dusky, golden cast. All these colors of La Serenissima blended in a delicate mix, with just the hint of green here and there. And everywhere the sense of blue . . . blues bleeding into watery grays.

The gondola slid slowly up the Grand Canal, past the ancient palazzos jammed close together, almost higgedly-piggedly, tall and narrow. The houses were built on stilts, just as Venice itself was built on pilings pounded into the sand, silt, and rock centuries ago.

Sinking, she thought, they say it's sinking. And it was, very slowly, even though some of the rot had been stopped.

Vanessa stared at the palazzos, all of them full of priceless treasures, works of art by the great masters, paintings, sculptures, silver and gold objects, tapestries, furniture. How terrible if it all sinks, she thought with a shudder. What a tragedy that would be.

Bill increased the pressure of his arms around her, and she leaned back against him. She was falling in love with him. She shouldn't, but she was, and she didn't know how to stop herself.

They sat in the bar of the Gritti Palace and had hot chocolate, tiny tea sandwiches, and small, delicious cakes. It was growing dark outside, the bright sunlight of earlier had dulled to leaden gray, and a wind had blown up, but it was warm inside, comfortable in the bar. They were enjoying being together, getting to know each other better.

At one moment Vanessa murmured, "You haven't really said where you're going from here, Bill. Is it Bosnia again?"

He was silent for a moment and then he nodded, his face suddenly grim. "But only to do a wrap-up. I won't be there longer than three or four days, thank God."

"The war must have been awfully hard to cover . . . I saw such horrors whenever I turned on the television. I can't imagine what it was like to actually be there."

"It was hell."

"It affected you . . . I know from the way you spoke with Frank."

"Yes, the war did affect me, change me. I've been a witness to genocide . . . the first war and genocide since the last war and genocide in Europe. That was in the thirties when the Nazis started persecuting the Jews, exterminating them, along with the gypsies and anyone else they thought needed killing off. I never imagined it could happen again, or if it did, that the world would permit it." He shook his head and shrugged. "But the world *has* permitted it, and the civilized world, at that. Excuse me, Vanessa, I shouldn't use that term. Nobody's civilized as far as I'm concerned. All any of us have is a thin veneer; scratch that in the right place and a monster will appear." He gave her a hard look, and went on, "As a newsman I have to be dispassionate, objective and balanced. Like a bystander, *watching*, in a sense."

Vanessa nodded. "Yes, I understand, but that must be very hard for you."

"It is now. At one time I could move around at will, from battlefield to battlefield, without being upset or disturbed. Bosnia has altered all that. The savagery, the butchering of innocent, unarmed civilians. My God, it was horrific at times . . . what we all witnessed. There are no words strong enough or *bad* enough to describe it."

Vanessa was silent.

After a moment she reached out and took hold of his hand, held it tightly in hers, knowing better than to say a word.

Bill was quiet for some time. He finally said, "I'm going to be doing a special on terrorism. I have two months to put it together. We'll start filming in January through February, so that we can air it in March."

"That's why you're not going to be based in Sarajevo?"

"Correct. I'll be traveling through the Middle East."

"Will . . ." She tightened her grip on his hand and leaned into him. "Will we be able to meet?"

"I hope so, darling. I'm counting on it."

"Shall we make Venice our place of rendezvous?"

He squeezed her hand. "I think that's a brilliant idea."

"When are you coming to New York in December?"

"About the fifteenth. I have two weeks' vacation due." He searched her face. "That won't present a problem will it, meeting in New York?"

"No, of course not. And I've a favor to ask," she said, smiling.

"Then ask it."

"Can I meet your daughter?"

"Do you want to *really*?"

"Yes, Bill, I do."

"Then you've got a date. I'll take you all to lunch. Helena, my mother, and you. It'll be great, having my three best girls out on the town with me."

8

Vanessa Stewart had always prided herself on her honesty. It was not only an honesty with those people who occupied her life, but with herself. For as long as she could remember, she had despised prevaricators and even those who merely half-fudged the truth.

But now on this icy December day she had to admit to herself that she had not been honest for a long time. At least, not as far as her private life was concerned.

There was no longer any question in her mind that she had lied to herself about the state of her marriage. And lied to Peter, too, by not forcing him to admit that their marriage was floundering, not working on so many different levels.

I've lied by omission, she thought, remembering the line Bill had used in Venice some ten days ago now. By not being open with Peter, I've only compounded our basic problem. I'm as much at fault as he is. And there was a problem. More than one, in fact.

Face the truth, Vanessa suddenly admonished herself. Be a big girl, accept things the way they are now. They're not the same as they once were; they haven't been for a long time.

A distracted look settled on her face as she focused on her marriage, the drawings spread out in front of her now forgotten. She and Peter no longer communicated very well, hardly at all, really. The shared confidences of their courtship and the early days of their marriage had long since been abandoned. Their sex life was practically nonexistent. And whenever they did make love these days it was usually because they had quarreled. Peter had always believed that this was the best way of making up. Certainly the easiest for him, she now thought.

But quite aside from this, they spent a great deal of their time apart. They were always in different places, or so it seemed to her.

And their interests were very different. They had grown apart . . . as they had grown in different ways.

It's no marriage at all, Vanessa thought. It's just a sham, truly it is. We stay together out of . . . *what*? Suddenly she did not know why they stayed together. Unless it was out of habit. Or loyalty. Or lack of a better place to go. Or someone else to go to. Or laziness. Which one of these reasons it was, she had no idea. Perhaps it was all of them in combination.

Placing the pencil on top of her drawing board, Vanessa leaned back in the tall chair where she sat and stared out of the huge window in front of her. Her mind was racing.

Her design studio was in a building downtown in Soho, on the corner of Mercer and Grand. It was a fifth-floor loft looking south, and she had fallen in love with it at first sight because of its spaciousness and extraordinary natural light.

The view from her window was familiar to her, but it never failed to please her. She had not grown tired of looking out at her own special corner of Manhattan. The splendid nineteenth century buildings were lined up before her eyes, while behind them the pristine twin towers of the World Trade Center, all black glass and steel, pierced the afternoon sky.

Two centuries juxtaposed, she thought, as she did every so often. The past. The present. The future.

The future. Those words danced in her head.

What was *her* future?

Was it to continue to live this lie with Peter? This lie that was their marriage . . . no, the remnants of their marriage.

Or was she going to leave him?

Is that what the future held? A life without Peter Smart, the only man she had ever known, except for Bill

Fitzgerald? Well, that wasn't quite the truth either, if she were scrupulously honest. There had been one other man in her life. Steven Ellis. Her college beau. Her first lover, her only lover until she had met Peter. And then married him.

And now Bill Fitzgerald was her lover. Her clandestine lover. Was it because of Bill that she was suddenly looking truth in the face? Had her relationship with him forced her to be honest for the first time in several years? More than likely. Yes, it's because of Bill and the way you feel about him, a small voice in her head whispered.

A deep sigh escaped her. She did not know what to do. Should she make Peter see their marriage for what it was, a sham? If she did, what would happen? And what did *she* want to happen? Peter might say they should start all over again, try to make a go of it. And where would she be then? Was that what she wanted? A future with Peter Smart?

What she had said about him to Bill was true. Peter was a good man, a decent human being. And he did love her in his own way. Furthermore, he looked after her well, and he had been extremely supportive about her work, had encouraged her career. Peter was a caring man in a variety of ways, and reliable, dependable, loyal.

And she was absolutely convinced he would be hurt and unhappy if she left him. He depended on *her* in so many ways.

Why would she leave Peter anyway?

Because of Bill?

Yes.

But Bill hasn't asked you to leave Peter. He hasn't made any kind of commitment to you, that insidious voice whispered. In fact, he rapidly agreed to an affair, a secret affair. He accepted the idea of being your clandestine lover. Actually, he suggested it, the voice added.

But Bill or no Bill, her life with Peter had grown . . . empty? *Yes.* Stale? *Yes.* Lonely? In many ways, *yes.* They didn't share anything anymore, at least that was the way she saw it, the way she felt. There was so much lacking in their relationship. For her, anyway. Maybe Peter felt differently. Maybe he expected less of marriage than she did.

And what did she want in a marriage?

Emotion. Love. Warmth. Companionship. True feelings shared. Sexual love. Understanding. Was that too much to ask of a man? Surely not. Certainly it was not too much for her to give.

Peter had not offered her many of these things lately, quite the contrary. And wasn't that one of the reasons she had ended up in bed with Bill in Venice?

Yes, the little voice answered. But it had also happened because she was overwhelmingly attracted to Bill. Falling in love with him? Yes, it was happening. Hadn't she known that days ago in Venice?

Falling in love, Vanessa thought. More like falling into madness.

It was dusk when Vanessa left her studio and got into the waiting radio cab that she had ordered earlier. As the driver headed uptown, her thoughts again turned to the problems in her life. Wrestling with them was not proving to be very fruitful; certainly she wasn't coming up with any answers for herself. The only thing she knew for sure was that her Venetian interlude with Bill, the feelings they had shared, had only served to point up the unsatisfactory relationship she had with Peter.

Comparisons, she thought, I hate comparisons. They're odious. But, of course, how could she not compare the emotional closeness she and Bill had enjoyed with the aridness of her life with Peter?

It suddenly struck her that Peter was denying her his love, himself, just as he had denied her a child. Instantly, she crushed that thought, not wanting to confront it, or deal with it now.

On the spur of the moment, she leaned forward and

said to the driver, "I need to make a stop on the way uptown. I'd like to go to Lord & Taylor, please."

"Okay, miss," the driver said, and turned left off Madison when they reached East Thirty-ninth Street. He headed west to Fifth Avenue, where the famous old store was located.

The driver parked the cab on the side street, but Vanessa walked around to Fifth Avenue and stood looking at the Christmas windows. They were always the best, she knew that from her childhood. The windows were full of wondrous mechanical toys, breathtaking scenes from famous fairy tales and the classics, magical to every child.

Pressing her nose against the window, as she had done when she was a child, she smiled inwardly, watching an exquisitely made toy ballerina, dressed in a pink tutu, pirouetting to the strains of "The Sugar Plum Fairy." The music was being piped out into the street, and it brought back such a rush of forgotten memories that Vanessa's throat tightened unexpectedly.

Her mother and father had always taken her to see *The Nutcracker* if they were in New York over Christmas, just as they had brought her here to see the store's windows before going inside to meet Santa Claus and confide her Christmas wish.

Sometimes they had not been in Manhattan at

Christmas, but in California or Paris or London, depending on her mother's current movie or play. Or what her father, Terence Stewart, was directing at the time. She was an only child, and they had always taken her with them on location or wherever they went. She had never suffered because of their theatrical careers; she had had a lovely, and very loving, childhood and had remained extremely close to her parents.

Eventually Vanessa turned away from the window, suddenly overcome by feelings of immense sadness and loneliness. An aching emptiness filled her, as it so often did. It was a feeling that threatened at times to overcome her. Somehow, she always managed to throw it off. She knew what it was—the longing for a child. But Peter did not want the responsibility of a child, and so she had buried the longing deep inside herself, sublimated the desire for a baby in her work. But, occasionally that terrible yearning gripped her, as it was doing now. She tried to still it, wishing it away.

Pushing through the swinging doors, Vanessa went into the store, her mind focusing on Helena, Bill's little girl. She was looking for something truly special. Helena was six, and there were so many things to buy for a child that age. Taking the escalator, she rode up to the children's department, spent ten minutes looking around and left empty-handed. Nothing had caught her eye.

As she hurried across the main floor, Vanessa stopped to buy tights and winter boot socks, then picked up eye makeup she needed before returning to the cab.

When she arrived at their apartment on East Fifty-seventh Street, Vanessa was surprised to find her husband at home. He usually never got in from his law office before seven in the evening at the earliest.

She shrugged out of her topcoat in the foyer and was hanging it up in the closet when he came out of their bedroom.

He was holding a couple of silk ties in his hand, and his face lit up at the sight of her. Smiling hugely, Peter said, "Hi, sweetie."

"You're home early," she answered, walking forward.

He nodded, kissed her on the cheek as she drew to a standstill. "I wanted to get my packing done before dinner."

"Packing?" A frown marred the smoothness of her wide brow. "Where are you going?"

"To London. Tomorrow morning. I have to see Alex Lawson. As you know, he's filming there at the moment. Anyway, his contract for his next two movies is finally ready, and I've got to go over it with him, walk him through it. It's a bit more complicated than usual."

"Oh, I see."

"Don't look so glum, Vanessa. I'll be back in ten days, certainly in time for Christmas."

"Does it take ten days to walk an actor through a contract? Or is he particularly dumb?"

"Vanessa! How can you talk like that about Hollywood's biggest heartthrob," he said and laughed a deep-throated laugh, amused by her comment. "You, of all people! Coming from a show business family as you do."

When she made no response and moved away, Peter took hold of her arm and gently turned her to face him. "I thought we'd go somewhere special for Christmas. Mexico . . . Bali . . . Thailand. Anywhere you want."

"But my mother will be in New York for Christmas . . ." Her voice trailed off. Suddenly she felt depressed.

"All right, then we'll stay here; it was just an idea. But no problem, no problem at all, sweetie." He went back into the bedroom.

Vanessa followed him, placed her Lord & Taylor shopping bag on the bed, and sat down next to it.

Peter spent a moment or two sorting ties, then he turned around and gave her a puzzled look when he saw the expression on her face. "What's the matter?" he asked, walking over to the bed, looming up in front of her.

She met his steady gaze with one equally as steady, but the expression on her face was thoughtful. Her husband was thirty-eight years old. Slim, attractive, a man in his prime. He had a genial personality, natural charm, and was popular both with his friends and clients. A brilliant lawyer, he had become highly successful in the past few years, and the success sat well on him. Peter Smart had everything going for him. And yet his personal life was abysmal. She ought to know; she shared it with him. It was empty, arid, pointless. As was hers. Didn't he notice this? Or didn't he care? Then it suddenly hit her like a ton of bricks: Was there another woman in his life? Is that why he had nothing to give *her* anymore?

"You're looking odd," Peter remarked in a quiet voice.

She cleared her throat. "I'm sorry you're going away; I'd hoped we could spend a quiet weekend together. I want to talk to you, Peter."

He frowned. "What about?"

"*Us.*"

"You sound serious."

"I feel serious. Look, you and I . . . things are just not right between us these days."

He gaped at her. "I don't know what you mean, Vanessa."

"What's our life about?" She gave him a penetrating stare. "We seem to be . . . drifting apart."

"Don't be so silly!" he exclaimed with one of his light, genial laughs. "Our life is very much on track. You're a doer and an achiever, and you have a career you love. You're doing extremely well, and you've accomplished so much with the design studio. I'm going great guns at the law firm. Things couldn't be better on that score. So why do you ask what our life is all about? I don't understand what you mean."

All of a sudden she knew that he didn't, that he was genuinely puzzled. She exclaimed, "But we're never together. We're always in different places, and when we are in the same city, you constantly work late. And when we're at home you haven't got a lot to say to me anymore, Peter; and there's another thing, we don't seem to be as close physically as we were." It was on the tip of her tongue to ask him if he was having an affair, and then she changed her mind. He might well ask her the same question, and then what would she say?

Peter was shaking his head, looking miserable, the laughter of earlier wiped out of his eyes. He threw the ties onto a chair and sat down on the bed next to her, took hold of her hand. "But, Vanessa, I love you, you know that. Nothing's changed. Well, I guess it has. I'm successful, very successful, and in a way I never dreamed I could be. This is the big one for me, the big chance, and I don't want to screw it up. I can't, because what I do now, how I handle everything now, is for our future. Yours and mine. Our old age, you might say."

"Old age!" she exploded. "But I don't care about that! I want to live now, while I'm still young."

"We are living, and living very well. And doing well. That's what counts, sweetie." He gazed into her eyes, and said more softly, "I guess I've been neglecting you lately. I'm sorry." He put his arms around her, tried to kiss her, but Vanessa drew away from him.

"You always think you can solve our problems, our disagreements, by making love to me," she said.

"But you know we always *do* solve what ails us when we're in bed together. We work it out that way."

"Just for once it would be nice to make love with you because we *want* to make love, not to get us over one of our quarrels."

"Then let's do it right now."

"I don't want to, Peter. I'm not in the mood. Sorry, but this little girl doesn't want to play tonight."

He recoiled slightly, startled by her sarcastic tone, and said slowly, "Is this about the baby? Is this what all this talk of drifting apart is about? Is that it, Vanessa?"

"No, it's not."

"I know I've been tough on you about having a baby—" he began and stopped abruptly.

"Yes, you have. You made it perfectly clear that you didn't want children."

"I don't. Well, what I mean is, I don't right now. But listen, sweetie, maybe later on, a few years down the line; maybe we can have a child then."

She shook her head and before she could stop herself she said, "Perhaps we ought to separate, Peter. Get a divorce."

His expression changed immediately and he sat up straighter on the bed. "Absolutely not! I don't want a divorce and neither do you. This is silly talk. You're just tired after all the work you did in Venice, and the schedule you've set for yourself with the new collection."

Vanessa was regarding him intently, and she realized that he was afraid of losing her. She could see the fear in his eyes.

When she remained totally silent, Peter went on swiftly, "I promise you things are going to be different, Vanessa. To be honest, I thought you were happy, excited about your design career. I hadn't realized . . . realized that things weren't right between *us*. You do believe me, don't you?"

"Yes," she murmured wearily. "I believe you, Peter." She got up off the bed, and walked toward the bedroom door. Dismay lodged in her chest. "There's not much for dinner. Shall I make pasta and a salad?"

"Certainly not. I'm going to take you out, sweetie. Shall we go next door to Mr. Chow's?"

Vanessa shook her head. "I don't feel like Chinese food."

"Then we'll go to Neary's pub. Jimmy always gives us such a great welcome, and I know you love it there."

9

SOUTHAMPTON, LONG ISLAND, DECEMBER 1995

Vanessa surveyed the living room of the cottage through newly objective and critical eyes. There were no two ways about it, the room looked shabby and decidedly neglected.

She did not care about the shabbiness; the faded wallpaper, the well-washed chintz and worn antique rug were all part of its intrinsic charm. It was the feeling of neglect that bothered her. She knew that the entire cottage was scrupulously clean, since it was maintained by a local woman. But the living room, in particular, had a lackluster air to it.

Bill would be arriving in a few hours to spend the day and part of the next with her, and she wanted the cottage to look nice. Since he spent so much of his time roughing it in battle zones and second-rate hotels, she felt the need to make it comfortable, warm and welcoming for him.

When her parents had divorced several years ago, they had not known what to do with Bedelia cottage. Neither of them had wanted it and yet they had been reluctant to sell it, oddly enough because of sentimental reasons. They both had a soft spot for it.

And so they had ended up giving it to their daughter. Vanessa had been thrilled.

It was located at the far end of Southampton and stood on three acres of land that ran all the way up to the sand dunes and the Atlantic Ocean.

The cottage was not in the chic part of town, nor was it very special, just a simple, stone-and-clapboard house, about forty years old. It had four bedrooms, a large kitchen, a living room, and a library. There was a long, covered veranda at the back of the cottage which fronted onto the sea.

Once the house was hers, she had turned the old red barn into a design studio and office and converted the stone stables into a small foundry with a kiln. It was here in the studio and foundry that she spent most of her time designing and executing the handblown glass prototypes she took to Venice to be copied and produced in Murano.

Being as preoccupied as she was with work, Vanessa did not give the cottage much attention. Piles of old newspapers and magazines, which she had saved for some reason, were stacked here and there; current books, which she hoped one day to read, were piled on a chest and the floor; and, several large vases of dried flowers, which had looked so spectacular in the summer, had lost their color and were falling apart.

Glancing at her watch, she saw that it was just eight o'clock. Bill was arriving at one. Mavis Glover, who had looked after the cottage for years, usually came at nine.

Suddenly deciding not to wait for her to appear, Vanessa made a beeline for the piles of books, carried them to the library next door and found a place for them all on the bookshelves. For the next hour she worked hard in the living room, discarding newspapers, magazines, and the bedraggled dried flowers.

Finally, standing in the middle of the room and glancing around appraisingly, Vanessa decided she had made a vast improvement. Because the room was no longer cluttered, the furniture was suddenly shown off to advantage. The French country antique pieces stood out. Their dark wood tones were mellow against the white walls and the blue chintz patterned with pink and red tulips, which hung at the windows and covered the sofas and chairs.

Not bad, not bad at all, Vanessa thought, and hurried out to the large family-style kitchen. Last night, when she had arrived, she had put the flowers she had brought from the city into vases; now she carried one of these back to the sitting room. The second one she took upstairs to her bedroom.

This had once been her parents' private sanctuary, and to Vanessa it was the nicest room in the cottage. Certainly it was the largest. It had many windows overlooking the sand dunes and the ocean beyond, and a big stone fireplace was set in one of the end walls.

Entirely decorated in yellow and blue, the room had a cheerful, sunny feeling even on the dullest of days. It was comfortable to the point of luxury.

Hurrying forward, Vanessa put the vase of yellow roses on the coffee table in front of the fire, and then went into the bathroom to take a shower. Once she was made up and dressed she would start on lunch while Mavis cleaned the rest of the cottage.

As she stood under the shower, letting the hot water sluice down over her, Vanessa luxuriated for a moment or two in thoughts of Bill. He had arrived in New York last Friday, December the fifteenth, as he had said he would. That was five days ago now. They had managed to snatch several quick drinks together on Sunday and Monday. He was busy with CNS most of the time; but when he was not, she did not want to intrude on hours he had set aside for his daughter.

"I'll drive out to the Hamptons on Wednesday morning," he had told her over their last drink at the Carlyle. "I can stay over until Thursday, if that's all right with you. How does it sound?"

It had sounded wonderful to her, and her beaming face had been her answer to him.

She could hardly wait to see him, have his arms around her, his mouth on hers. At the mere thought of making love with him, her body started to tingle. She snapped her eyes open and turned off the shower.

No time for fantasizing, she chastised herself, reaching for a towel. Anyway, within the space of a few hours she would have the real thing. They would be together.

Once she was dry, Vanessa dressed quickly, choosing a heavy red sweater to go with her well-washed blue jeans. Since it was a cold day, she put on thick white wool socks and brown penny loafers. Her only jewelry was a pair of gold earrings.

Once she had applied a little makeup and sprayed on perfume, she ran downstairs to prepare lunch for Bill.

He was late.

Vanessa sat in the small library, leafing through *Time* and *Newsweek*, wondering where he was, hoping he was not trapped in traffic.

Foolish idea that is, she thought. It was a Wednesday morning in the middle of December, and the traffic had to be light from Manhattan. It was only in the summer that it became a nightmare. She was quite certain Bill would find it straight sailing today; she had given him explicit driving instructions, and, anyway, the cottage was easy to find, just off the main road.

By one forty-five, when he had still not arrived, her anxiety was growing more acute by the minute. She was just deciding whether or not to call the network when she heard a car drawing up outside and she rushed to the front door.

When she saw Bill alighting, then taking his bag out of the trunk, she felt weak with relief. A moment later he was walking into the house, his face wreathed in smiles.

He took hold of her at once, pulled her into his arms. She clung to him tightly.

"Sorry, darling," he said against her hair. "I was delayed at the network and then it was tough getting out of New York this morning. A lot of traffic. Christmas shoppers, I guess."

"It's all right . . . I thought something had happened to you."

"Nothing's going to happen to me," he said, tilting her face to his in that special way he had.

"Let's go into the living room. It's warmer," Vanessa murmured, taking his arm. "I've got white wine on ice, or would you prefer scotch?"

"White wine's fine, thanks."

They stood together in front of the roaring fire, sipping their wine and staring at each other over the rims of their glasses.

"I've missed you, Vanessa."

"I've missed you too."

"You know something . . . I think about you all the time."

"So do I—I think of you, I mean."

"It's funny," he said softly, looking at her closely. "I feel as if you've been in my life always, as if I've known you always."

"Yes. It's the same for me, Bill."

He shook his head, smiled faintly. "I didn't dare touch you when we were in the bar of the Carlyle . . . you're very inflammatory to me."

She stared at him, saying nothing.

He stared back.

Putting his glass on the mantelpiece, he then did the same with hers, moved closer to her, and brought her into the circle of his arms. He kissed her hard, pressing her even closer to him, wanting her to know how much she excited him.

Vanessa tightened her embrace, responding to him with ardor, and this further inflamed him. Bill said in a low, hoarse voice, "I want you so much, want to be close to you."

Pulling away from him, she nodded, took hold of his hand, and led him upstairs to her bedroom.

There was tremendous tension between them. They undressed with great speed, sharing an urgent need to be intimate and closely joined. As they fell on the bed, his hands were all over her body. Loving hands that touched, stroked, explored, and brought her to a fever pitch of excitement.

They could not get enough of each other. He continued to kiss her, and she returned his kisses with the same intense passion she had felt in Venice. And Bill luxuriated in the nearness of her, in the knowledge that she longed for him, needed him so desperately. He felt the same need for her. It was a deep, insatiable need.

Stretching his body alongside hers, he took her suddenly, moving into her so swiftly he heard her gasp with surprise and pleasure. As she clasped him tightly in her arms, her legs wrapped around him, they shared a mounting joy.

Vanessa lay quietly in his arms.

The wintry afternoon sunshine cast its pale light across the yellow walls, turning them to bosky gold.

The only sound was the light rise and fall of Bill's breath as he drowsed and, far beyond the windows, the faint, distant roar of the Atlantic Ocean.

She found the stillness soothing.

Their lovemaking had been passionate, almost frantic, and even more feverish than in Venice. Their need for each other had been so overwhelming, it had stunned them both; afterward they had stared at each other in astonishment. Now this tranquillity was like a balm.

Stretching her body slightly, trying not to disturb him, Vanessa took pleasure from her sense of satisfaction and fulfillment. How different she was with Bill; she even surprised herself. Each time they made love, they seemed to soar higher and higher, reach a greater pitch of ecstasy. It always left her reeling.

In some ways, Vanessa no longer recognized herself. She knew she had undergone a vast change since meeting Bill Fitzgerald. He brought out something erotic and sensual in her, made her feel whole, very feminine, very much a woman.

Pushing herself up onto one elbow, Vanessa looked down at him. The tense, worried expression he invariably wore had disappeared. In repose, his face was smooth, free of pain and concern. He looked so young, very vulnerable. And he touched her deeply.

Vanessa was aware that they had an intimacy of heart and mind as well as body, and it pleased her. They genuinely understood each other, and this compatibility gave them a special kind of closeness that few people shared.

She knew she was in love with him. She knew she wanted to be with him. For always. But was that possible? How could it be? She was not free. She had a husband who loved her, who was terrified of losing her. And for her part, she owed him loyalty and consideration.

Troubling thoughts of Peter insinuated themselves into her mind. She pushed them to one side. Too soon to think of the future . . . Later. She would think about it later.

In the meantime, she was absolutely certain of one thing. With Bill Fitzgerald she was her true self, without pretense or artifice. She was the real Vanessa Stewart.

She brought a tray of food and a bottle of white wine upstairs to the bedroom, where they had a picnic in front of the fire. And after they had devoured smoked salmon sandwiches, Brie cheese and apples, and downed a glass of wine each, they dressed and went out.

The thin sun still shone in the pale azure sky and the Atlantic had the gleam of silver on it. It was a blustery day with a high wind whipping the waves to turbulence.

Bundled up in overcoats and scarves, their arms

wrapped around each other, they walked along the dunes, oblivious to the world, to everything except themselves and their intense feelings for each other.

At one moment Bill stopped and spun her to face him, looked down into her expressive gray eyes. "I'm so happy!" he exclaimed. "Happier than I've been for years."

"What did you say?" she shouted back, also competing with the roar of the ocean.

". . . happier than I've been for years," he repeated, grinning at her, catching her around her waist, pulling her to him. "I love you," he said, his mouth on her ear. "I love you, Vanessa Stewart."

"And I love you, Bill Fitzgerald."

"I didn't hear you," he teased.

"I LOVE YOU, BILL FITZGERALD!" she screamed at the top of her lungs.

His joyous laughter filled the air.

She joined in his laughter, hugging him to her.

And then, holding hands, they ran along the sand dunes, buffeted forward by the wind, euphoric in their love, happy to be alive, to be together.

Later that evening they sat in front of the fire in her bedroom, listening to Mozart's violin concertos.

Vanessa, suddenly looking across at Bill, saw how

preoccupied he was as he stared into the flames, noted how tensely set his shoulders were.

"Are you all right?" she asked in a soft voice. When he did not respond, she pressed, "Bill, is something wrong?"

He lifted his head, looking directly at her. But still he said nothing. Disturbed by the sadness on his face, she went on, "Darling, what is it? You look so . . . unhappy . . . even troubled."

He took a moment, averting his eyes, focusing again on the fire. Finally he said, "This is not a game for me."

Frowning, she gaped at him. "It isn't a game for me either."

Bill said, "This afternoon I told you I loved you. It's the truth."

There was such a questioning look on his face she couldn't help but exclaim, "And I love you. I *meant* what I said, Bill. I don't lie. Do you doubt me?"

He was silent.

"How could you possibly doubt me?" she cried, her voice rising. "It's not possible to simulate the kind of emotions you and I have been sharing since we met."

"I know that, and don't misunderstand my silence," he was quick to answer. "I know you have deep feelings for me." Leaning forward, he took hold of her hand, gripped it in his. "I just want you to know that I'm serious about you—" He paused, pinned his eyes on her. "I'm playing for keeps."

Vanessa nodded.

"Just so long as you know," he said.

"Yes, I do, Bill."

"I'll never let you go, Vanessa."

"You might change your mind," she began, but halted when she saw the stern expression on his face.

"I won't."

Vanessa sat back on the sofa, gazed abstractedly at the painting above the fireplace.

He asked in a low voice, "What are you going to do?"

"I'll tell Peter I want a divorce."

"Are you sure?"

"Yes, I'm sure."

"So am I. I've never been more sure of anything in my life." Moving closer to her on the sofa, he put his arms around her and held her against him. And he knew he had the world in his arms. She was the only woman for him, the only woman he wanted.

10

Bill had asked Vanessa to meet him at Tavern On The Green at twelve-thirty on Saturday, and as she walked into the famous restaurant in Central Park she realized what a good choice it had been.

Always festive at any time of year, it was spectacular during the Christmas season. Beautifully decorated Christmas trees were strategically placed, strings of tiny fairy lights were hung in festoons throughout while branches of holly berries in vases and pink and red poinsettias in wooden tubs added an extra fillip to the seasonal setting.

The magnificent Venetian glass chandeliers, which were permanent fixtures in the main dining room, seemed more appropriate than ever at this time of year.

Bill spotted her immediately. Rising, he left the table and hurried forward to meet her.

As he came toward her, she thought how handsome he looked, and he was extremely well-dressed today. He wore a navy blue blazer, blue shirt, navy tie, and gray pants. He was bandbox perfect, right down to his well-polished brown loafers.

Grabbing her hands, he leaned into her, murmured, "You look great, darling," and gave her a perfunctory kiss on the cheek. "Come and meet the other two women I love," he added as he led her to the table, the proud smile still in place.

Vanessa saw at once how attractive and elegant his mother was, and she seemed much younger than sixty-two. Dressed in a dark red wool suit that set off her beautifully coiffed auburn hair, she looked more like Bill's older sister than his mother.

Sitting next to his mother was undoubtedly the most exquisite child Vanessa had ever seen. She had delicate, perfectly sculpted features, wide-set cornflower blue eyes that mirrored Bill's, and glossy dark blonde hair that fell in waves and curls to her shoulders.

"I've never seen a child who looks like that," Vanessa exclaimed softly, turning to Bill. "Helena's . . . why she's positively breathtaking."

He squeezed her arm. "Thank you, and yes, she is lovely looking, even though I say so myself."

They came to a standstill at the table, and Bill said, "Mom, I'd like to introduce Vanessa Stewart. And Vanessa, this is my mother, Drucilla."

"I'm so glad to meet you, Mrs. Fitzgerald," Vanessa said, taking his mother's outstretched hand.

"Hello, Miss Stewart." Drucilla smiled at her warmly.

"Oh, Mrs. Fitzgerald, please call me Vanessa."

"Only if you call me Dru, everyone does."

"All right, I will. Thank you." Vanessa looked down at the little girl dressed in a blue wool dress, who was observing her with enormous curiosity. "And you must be Helena," she said, offering the six-year-old her hand.

"Yes, I am," Helena said solemnly, taking her hand.

"This is Vanessa," Bill said.

"I'm delighted to meet you, Helena," Vanessa murmured, and seated herself in the chair Bill had pulled out for her.

"Now, what shall we have to drink?" Bill asked, looking at all of them. "How about champagne?"

"That would be nice," Vanessa said.

"Yes, it would, Bill," his mother agreed.

"Is this a celebration?" Helena asked, gazing up at Bill, her head on one side.

"Why do you ask that, Pumpkin?"

"Gran says champagne is only for celebrations."

"Then it's a celebration," Bill responded, his love for his child spilling out of his eyes.

"And what's this celebration?" Helena probed.

Bill thought for a moment, looked at his mother, and answered, "Being here together, the four of us. Yes, that's what we're celebrating, and Christmas, too, of course."

"But I'm not allowed champagne," Helena remarked, staring at him, then swiveling her eyes to Dru. "Am I, Gran?"

"Certainly not," her grandmother responded firmly. "Not until you're grown up."

Bill said, "But you are allowed a Shirley Temple, and that's what I'm going to order for you right now." As he was speaking, Bill signaled to a hovering waiter, who promptly came over to the table and took the order.

Vanessa said to Dru, "It was a great idea of Bill's to suggest coming here for lunch; it's such a festive place."

Dru nodded. "You're right, it's fabulous. Bill tells me you met in Venice. When he was there with Frank Peterson."

"Yes . . ." Vanessa hesitated and then, noticing Bill's beaming face, she went on more confidently, "We spent Thanksgiving together."

"The only three Americans in Venice on that particular day," Bill interjected. "So we had no alternative but to celebrate together. And a good time was had by all."

"I'd like to go to Venice," Helena announced, looking from her father to her grandmother. "Can I?"

"One day, sweetheart," Bill said. "We'll take you when you're a bit older."

"Do you work with my daddy?" Helena asked, zeroing in on Vanessa.

"No, I don't," Vanessa answered. "I'm not in television, Helena. I'm a glass designer."

The child's smooth brow furrowed. "What's that?"

"I design objects, lovely things for the home, which are made in glass. In Venice."

"Oh."

Vanessa had been carrying a small shopping bag when she arrived, and this she had placed with her handbag on the floor. Now she reached for it, took out a gift tied with a large pink bow, and announced, "This is for you, Helena."

The child took it, held it in her hands, staring at the prettily wrapped present. "What is it?"

"Something I made for you."

"Can I open it now, Daddy?"

"Yes, but what do you say first?"

"Thank you, Vanessa." Helena untied the ribbon, took off the paper, and then lifted the lid off the box.

"It's quite fragile," Vanessa warned. "Lift it out of the tissue paper gently."

Helena did as she was bidden, held the glass object in her hands carefully, her eyes wide. It was a twisted, tubular prism that narrowed to a point. Its facets caught and held the light, reflecting the colors of the rainbow. "Oh, it's beautiful," the child gasped in delight.

"It's an icicle. An icicle of many colors, and I made it specially for you, Helena."

"Thank you," Helena repeated, continuing to hold the icicle, moving it so that the glass caught the light.

"It is very beautiful," Dru murmured, turning to Vanessa. "You're a very talented artist."

"Thank you."

Bill said, "May I look at it, Helena?"

"Yes, Dad. Be careful. Vanessa says it's fragile."

"I will," he murmured, his eyes smiling at Vanessa as he took the icicle. "This is quite wonderful," he said, and then nodded when the waiter brought the champagne in a bucket of ice. "You can open it now, please," he said.

After the glass icicle was returned to its box and put on the floor next to Helena's chair, and the wine had been poured, Bill lifted his flute. "Happy Christmas, everyone."

"Happy Christmas," they all responded.

Helena took a sip of her Shirley Temple and put it

down on the table. Turning, she stared hard at Vanessa, and, with undisguised inquisitiveness, she asked, "Are you Daddy's girlfriend?"

Taken aback by the child's candor, Vanessa was speechless for a moment.

Bill answered for her. "Yes, she is, Helena." He smiled at his little daughter, then looked over her head at his mother, raising a brow eloquently.

Drucilla Fitzgerald nodded her approval. And she did approve of this pretty young woman whom she had known for only twenty minutes. There was something about Vanessa that was special; she could tell that, being the good judge of character that she was. Vanessa was to be encouraged, Dru decided. Anyone who could bring this look of happiness to her son's face had her vote of confidence. He had been so lonely after Sylvie's death. And morose for years. She had not seen him so buoyant, spirited, and full of good cheer for the longest time. Suddenly, she felt as if a weight had been lifted off her shoulders.

"Let's order lunch," Bill said. "Do you know what you want, Pumpkin?"

"Yes, Daddy. I'd like to have eggs with the muffin, like we did last time."

"Eggs Benedict," Dru clarified. "I'd love it too, but I don't think I'd better. Not with my cholesterol. I suppose I'll have to settle for crab cakes."

Bill looked at Vanessa. "Do you know what you want?"

"I'll have the same as your mother, Bill, thank you."

"And I'll keep Helena company, go for the Eggs Benedict," he said.

Helena touched Vanessa's arm. "Are you going to marry Daddy?"

Vanessa was further startled by the child's outspoken question, and by her precocity. She glanced swiftly at Bill.

Dru sat back in her chair, observing the three of them.

Bill grinned at Helena and said, "You ask too many questions, Pumpkin, just like Uncle Frank does sometimes. And we don't know yet whether we're going to get married or not ... we need to spend more time together, get to know each other better."

Helena nodded.

Bill went on, "But you and Gran will be the first to know if we do. I promise you."

Later, as Bill helped Vanessa into a cab, he whispered, "Not a bad idea my kid had, eh?"

"Not a bad idea at all," Vanessa replied.

"Take this, darling," he said, pressing something into her hand.

"What is it?" she asked, looking down at it, realizing that it was a key. "What's this for?"

"The suite I booked at the Plaza. For us. Suite 902. Can we meet for a drink later tonight? Say around nine?"

"But of course," she said and slipped the key into her bag.

11

VENICE, JANUARY 1996

It had been raining all afternoon, hard, driving rain that was still coming down in an endless stream. The sky was the color of anthracite, pitted here and there with threatening black clouds, and below her the Grand Canal was swollen, looked as if it might overflow at any moment.

Vanessa turned away from the window and moved into the room, shivering slightly. Although Bill had turned up the heat earlier, when she had first arrived from the airport there had been a chill in the air. It was a dampness that seemed to permeate her bones. She tightened the belt on the bathrobe she was wearing and shrugged further into it as she huddled in a chair near the radiator.

Vanessa was glad to be back in Venice with Bill. It was the first time they had seen each other since Christmas. He had left New York at the end of December, to travel through the Middle East and Europe. Tel Aviv, Jerusalem, Amman, Beirut, Ankara, and Athens were some of the cities on his list. He was busy preparing his special on international terrorism for CNS; time was of the essence since it had been scheduled to air early in March.

Bill had arrived at the Gritti Palace a day earlier than Vanessa, flying in from Athens the night before just as she was leaving New York. They would have five days together in their favorite city. She had work to do out at the glass foundry on Murano. Bill was going to polish his script for the show, and they would be together in the afternoons and evenings.

A smile touched her mouth as she thought of Bill and her love for him. He meant more to her than she had ever imagined possible. He was the man of her life. For the rest of her life. They were meant to be together, and there was nothing that could keep them apart. She knew that now.

A small sigh escaped as she thought of the past few weeks. Apart from seeing Bill, meeting his mother and Helena, December had been a ghastly month for her. Peter had stayed in London longer than he had intended, and after his return to Manhattan he had left almost immediately for Los Angeles. He had been away so much she had barely had a chance to discuss their private life, and Christmas had been miserable for the most part.

Finally, early in January, she had cornered him one evening when he returned from the office earlier than usual. Endeavoring to be as gentle as possible, while displaying no weakness whatsoever, Vanessa had told him she wanted a divorce.

Peter had reacted badly, overreacted really, and had been adamant that they remain married. Even though he had agreed, in the end, that their relationship was no longer what it had once been, he nonetheless refused even to consider divorcing. Very simply, he balked at the idea and wouldn't listen to her. At least not that particular evening.

Vanessa had come to realize that there was only one thing to do, and that was to get on with her life, lead it as she saw fit, and be independent. Ten days before leaving on this trip to Venice, she had taken her courage in both hands and left Peter, moving all of her clothes and possessions into the loft in Soho.

The loft had once been an apartment before she had turned it into a studio-office, and it had a good-sized working kitchen, a full bathroom, plus a guest toilet. Once she had purchased a sofa bed and installed it in the back storage room, turning this into a bedroom, the loft had become a comfortable place to live. Most important, it had made Peter realize just how determined she was to end their marriage. Her departure had a tremendous impact on him; he at last understood how serious she was about a divorce.

As her mother had said to her, "Actions make more of a statement than words ever could, Vanny, and it's best to end this now, while you're both still young enough to start all over again, find new partners." Both of her parents had been very supportive of her decision to leave Peter. However, she had not told them about Bill, deeming it wiser to keep her own counsel at this moment.

Vanessa heard Bill's key in the lock and glanced at the door as he came in. Getting up, she went to him, her face full of smiles.

He had gone downstairs a few minutes earlier to pick up a fax which had arrived from New York. Now he waved it and said, "Neil Gooden and Jack Clayton *love* the footage so far. Neil says he can't wait to see the rest of it." Bill handed her the fax. "Here, read it yourself, darling."

She scanned the two pages, digested everything, and handed it back to him. "Congratulations, Bill. From what Neil says, you've worked miracles and in less than three weeks. Aren't you thrilled he thinks it's going to be a smash?"

"From his mouth to God's ears," Bill said with a huge grin, and putting his arm around her shoulders he walked her over to the sofa.

"I do think it's coming together, though. I just need

to cover two more cities and then it's a wrap, as far as the field reporting is concerned. When you go back to New York, I'll head for Paris, work there a couple of days with my crew and the producer. Then we'll all go on to Northern Ireland, make Belfast our last stop. Incidentally, I've finally come up with a good title."

"What is it?"

"I'm thinking of calling the special *Terrorism: The Face of Evil*. What's your feeling about it?"

"I think it sounds good. And it says exactly what you mean."

He nodded. "Yes, I guess it does. What I've managed to do is cover terrorism around the world. I've been filming interviews with experts, and some terrorists who are in jail in Israel. I'm backing up the new stuff with footage of past acts of terrorism, from the 1972 killing of the Olympic athletes and Lord Mountbatten's murder by the IRA to the Lockerbie crash, the World Trade Center bombing, and the Oklahoma City explosion. I've endeavored to make it very personal, very intimate. I want it to hit home, touch the average American. I'll be using some interviews I did with survivors of terrorism, and relatives of victims of terrorists. I'm quite gratified by the way it's come together." Bill got up, walked across to the mini bar, and took a bottle of mineral water from it. "Do you want anything, Vanessa?"

She shook her head.

Bill strode back to the sofa, sat down next to her. After taking a sip of water, he placed the bottle on the coffee table and placed his arm around her. "Moving into the loft was a very good idea, Vanessa. It's shown Peter how serious you are about a divorce."

"Yes, it has. He phoned me yesterday, just as I was leaving for Kennedy. And while he didn't actually *agree* to a divorce, he did sound more amenable, if a little crushed. I have the feeling he's beginning to accept the idea."

"That's a relief." Bill looked at her intently. "Did you tell him about me? About us?"

"No, I didn't, Bill. I didn't think it was necessary. And anyway, it would be like a red flag to a bull. Very inflammatory."

"I don't care if he knows, you know. I'm a big boy. I can look after myself."

"Yes, but why rub salt in the wound? Anyway, Peter really has come to accept how bad our relationship has been for the last few years . . . I prefer to leave it at that."

"Whatever you say, sweetheart, you're the boss."

She gave him the benefit of a loving smile.

He leaned closer, kissed her on the mouth. "The concierge just told me Venice will be flooded by seven o'clock. No Harry's Bar tonight, I'm afraid. We'll have to eat here."

"That's fine, Bill. The restaurant downstairs is good."

"Oh, but I thought we would have room service, eat here in the suite."

"Yes, if you want, I think it's more comfortable anyway, and I don't have to get dressed."

He nodded and reached for her. "My thought precisely."

"You once suggested that we make Venice our point of rendezvous," Bill said to her much later that evening, after they had made love, eaten dinner, and made love again. "And I think that's a great idea. It's going to be very convenient for me."

They were in bed and Vanessa lay within the circle of his arms. She swiveled her eyes to meet his. "What do you mean?"

"When I've finished the special on terrorism, I'm being assigned to the Middle East. I'll be based either in Israel or Lebanon, that's up to me. But whichever it is, I can fly straight up to Venice. It's an easy trip. I'll try to be here whenever you're working at the foundry in Murano, if only for a couple of days, or a long weekend."

Her face lit up. "Oh, Bill, that'll be wonderful, being able to see you every month. Well, more or less. Why the Middle East, though?"

"I didn't want to go back to Bosnia, as you know, even though there's trouble there again. There always will be, too, if you ask me. And the peace accords are very fragile, not likely to last, especially if the UN troops leave. Still, I wanted out, and Jack Clayton was aware of that ages ago. So he asked me if I'd like to go back to the Middle East to cover the whole area. I know it well, and Frankie's in Lebanon. So it'll be like old home week." He grinned at her. "As I'm telling you this, I'm beginning to realize that I will base myself in Beirut, set up camp with Frankie at the Commodore Hotel."

"When will that be, darling?"

"In March sometime. I'll be cutting and editing at CNS in New York in the middle of February, preparing the special. And then I'll go."

"I thought everything was quiet in the Middle East right now."

"As quiet as that area will ever be. There are always rumblings of some kind, somewhere, be it Iran, Libya, Saudi Arabia, Syria, Israel, or Iraq. You name it. Flare-ups happen all the time," Bill explained.

"If your assignment starts in March, when do you think we can meet here again?"

Bill held her closer, smiling at her, his blue eyes crinkling at the corners. "In March, of course. The end of March."

12

"Are you sure there are no messages for me?" Vanessa said, her eyes focused intently on the concierge standing behind the desk at the Gritti Palace.

"No, Signora Stewart, no messages." His faint smile seemed almost apologetic as he added, "No, nothing at all. No faxes, nothing, signora."

"Thank you." Vanessa turned away from the desk and walked rapidly toward the elevator.

Once she was back in her room, she sat down at the writing table in front of the window and gazed absently out at the Grand Canal.

It was a cool, breezy Saturday in late March, but the sun had come out and given a certain radiance to the afternoon. Yet she was hardly aware of the weather; her thoughts were focused on Bill. She opened her appointment book and stared at the date. It was March the thirtieth, and she had been in Venice for four days, working at the foundry on Murano. Bill was supposed to have arrived on Thursday afternoon, the twenty-eighth, to join her for a long weekend.

But he was forty-eight hours late, and she did not understand why. After all, it was not as if he were in a war zone and in any danger. Beirut was quiet at the moment; he had told her that himself. She dismissed the idea that something might have happened to him.

It struck her then that he could have gone some-where else in the Middle East to cover a story. He had talked about Egypt and the Sudan to her when he had been in New York in February. They had been able to meet only once at that time because he had been busy editing his special on terrorism, and then he had had to leave for Beirut.

Yes, that was most likely the reason he was late. Right now he was probably on a plane, flying to Venice from some distant spot. This thought cheered her, but an instant later she was worrying again. If he had been delayed because he was caught up on a story, why hadn't he phoned her?

Frowning to herself, Vanessa reached for her address book and quickly found the number of the Commodore Hotel in Beirut. Glancing at the hotel's chart for direct dialing to foreign cities, she picked up the phone and punched in the numbers for Beirut and the hotel.

It was only a second or two before she heard the hotel operator saying, "Hotel Commodore."

"Mr. Bill Fitzgerald, please."

"Just a moment, please."

She heard the ringing tone. It seemed to her to be interminable. He did not pick up. He was not in his room.

"There's no answer," the operator said. "Do you wish to leave a message?"

"Yes. Please say Vanessa Stewart called. He can reach me at the Gritti Palace in Venice." She then gave the operator the number and hung up, sat staring at the phone.

After a few moments, she rose and walked over to the coffee table. Picking up the remote control, she turned up the volume on the television set. The CNS weatherman was giving the weekend forecast for the States. She sat down on the bed and watched CNS for the next couple of hours.

World news. American news. Business news. Sports news. But no news of Bill Fitzgerald, chief foreign correspondent for CNS.

Later in the evening, for the umpteenth time that day, Vanessa checked her answering machines at the Manhattan loft and the cottage in Southampton. There was no message from Bill.

At one point she ordered sandwiches, fruit, and a pot of hot tea. She had not eaten anything since breakfast, and suddenly she was feeling hungry. After her light supper she watched CNS until the early hours, although she did so with only half an eye. It was mostly repeats of everything she had seen earlier, and her mind was elsewhere anyway.

On Sunday morning, after she had drunk a quick cup of coffee, Vanessa dialed the Commodore Hotel in Beirut and asked for Bill Fitzgerald.

Once again, there was no answer in his room.

This time, Vanessa asked to be put through to Frank Peterson. She clutched the phone tightly, listening to the ring, hoping that at least Frank would pick up. He did not.

After a split second the hotel operator was back on the line. "I'm sorry, both of them seem to be out, miss. Would you like to leave a message?"

"Yes, for Mr. Fitzgerald. Please ask him to call Vanessa Stewart at the Gritti Palace in Venice."

Vanessa spent a miserable Sunday, waiting for the phone to ring and watching CNS and CNN on television, alternating between the two cable networks. At one point she checked her answering machines in the States, but there were no messages. Not a whisper from anyone. She even phoned the international news desk at CNS headquarters in New York. But they wouldn't give her any information about Bill's whereabouts.

By late afternoon she had given up hope of Bill arriving. In any case, she was due to leave for New York on Monday morning, and so she got out her suitcase and began to pack. She did so in a flurry of emotions —frustration, anger, disappointment, worry, and dismay.

That night, when she went to bed, Vanessa was unable to sleep. She turned restlessly for hours, praying for morning to come.

Eventually she must have dozed off because she awakened with a start as dawn was breaking. As she lay there in the dim, gray light Vanessa finally acknowledged what she had been denying all weekend: The real reason Bill had not shown up was because he was no longer interested in her. Their affair was over for him. Finished. Dead.

No, she thought, he cared too much. I'm wrong.

And yet deep down she knew she was right. There was no other possible reason for his absence.

She closed her eyes, remembering all the things he had said to her ... that he loved her ... that he was playing for keeps ... that he was serious about her ... that this wasn't a game for him. He'd even encouraged her to divorce Peter. Why did he do that, if he hadn't meant what he said?

Well, of course he meant those things when he said them, that niggling voice at the back of her head muttered. He was glib, slick, smooth. A wordsmith. Clever with all those wonderful words that tripped off his tongue so lightly. Wasn't that all part of his talent? Hadn't he told her that his grandmother had always said, when he was growing up, that he'd kissed the Blarney Stone?

There was another thing, too. He was back in the close company of Frank Peterson, his best friend, his alter ego. Frank was a man Bill had characterized as a womanizer with a terminal Don Juan complex. Those had been his exact words. Maybe they were off somewhere together for the weekend. Bill was very close to Frank, and impressed by him. And perhaps some of Frank's habits were contagious.

Suddenly she felt like a fool. She had been sitting here waiting for Bill for four days and there hadn't been the slightest word from him. As chief foreign correspondent for CNS he had access to phones wherever he was. He could have called her from anywhere.

But he had not, and that was a fact she could not ignore.

Dismay lodged in the pit of her stomach and she found herself trembling. Tears sprang into her eyes and she sat up, brushing them aside as she turned on the light, looked at her travel clock. It was five o'clock. She sat on the side of the bed for a moment, endeavoring to pull herself together. As painful as it was, she had to admit that she had been dumped. Why, she would never know. She began to cry again, and she discovered that she could not stop.

13

"Over the years, I've discovered that the more you love a person, the more they're bound to disappoint you in the end," her mother had once said to her, adding: "And, in my opinion, men understand this better than we do. That's why they rather cleverly spread their bets. Always remember that, Vanny. Don't give all for love. And don't be duped."

But she had given all for love. And she had been duped. And she had remembered her mother's wise words far too late for them to matter.

Was it true? Did men spread their bets when it came to women? Was that what Bill had done?

Certainly she had loved him a lot, put all of her trust in him. And in the end he *had* bitterly disappointed her. But no, wait, it was so much more than disappointment, wasn't it? He had humiliated her, made her feel foolish, even ridiculous, and he had hurt her so badly she thought she would never recover from that hurt. It cut deep . . . deep into her very soul.

She had been so open with him, so honest, baring her soul, her innermost secret self. She had given him everything she had to give, far more than she had given any other man, even her husband.

Seemingly, her gifts of love and adoration had meant nothing to him. He had discarded her as easily as he had picked her up in the bar of the Hotel Gritti Palace.

Unexpectedly, and quite suddenly, she remembered something he had said to her about Frank, something about Frank hedging his bets as far as women were concerned. Perhaps all men did that.

Vanessa let out a long sigh and walked on across the sand dunes, her heart heavy, her mind still fogged by the pain of Bill's defection.

It was a fine, clear day in the middle of April—cold, with a pale sun in a pale sky. The Atlantic Ocean was calmer than it had been for days despite the wind that was blowing up.

She lifted her eyes and stared up into the sky when she heard the *cawk-cawk* of seagulls. She watched them as they wheeled and turned against the clouds.

The wind buffeted her, driving her toward the beach. She hunched down farther into her heavy duffle coat and stuck her gloved hands into her pockets. She felt dispirited to the point of depression.

She was well aware that her depressed emotional state was because of Bill Fitzgerald and what he had done to her. She found it hard to believe that he had disappeared from her life in the way that he had, but it was true. At times she even tried to tell herself she didn't care. But of course she did.

Their love affair had been so intense, so sexual, so passionate in every way and so . . . *fierce.* He had swept her off her feet and into his bed and then out of his life when he had grown tired of her. Just like that. *Puff!* She was gone. Had their affair been too hot? Had it burned out too fast for him? She was not sure. How could she be sure . . . of anything . . . ever again?

Vanessa felt the splatter of raindrops on her face and immediately looked up. Thunderheads were darkening that etiolated sky, turning it to leaden gray, and there was the sudden bright flourish of lightning, then the crack of thunder.

Turning swiftly, she walked back to the cottage at the edge of the dunes. She made it just in time. It was a cloudburst. The heavens opened and the rain poured down.

She locked the door behind her, took off her duffle, and went into the library. Here she turned on lamps, struck a match, and brought the flame to the paper and logs Mavis had stacked in the grate.

Since she had returned, Mavis Glover had taken to coming almost every day, fussing over her, bringing her fruit and vegetables and other groceries. Once Mavis had even offered to pick up newspapers and magazines, but Vanessa had told her not to bother. She was not interested in the outside world; she had cut herself off from it.

She had returned from Venice and moved out to Southampton permanently. She had turned herself into a virtual hermit. She had unplugged her telephone and pulled the plugs on the radio and the television. In fact, she vowed she would never look at television again as long as she lived.

She was out of contact with everyone. Out of action. The only person she saw or spoke to was Mavis.

Licking my wounds, she thought now as she sank onto the sofa in front of the fire. Licking my wounds like a sick animal.

The truth was, she did not want to see anyone, not even her mother. The world was well lost for her.

Peter had sent the divorce papers; they had arrived yesterday by special delivery. She had laughed loudly and hollowly when she had seen them. As if they mattered now. She had pushed for the divorce when Bill was a part of her life, and now seemingly he had discarded her.

The anger flared again in her and with it came the hot, endless tears. Pushing her face down into the cushions, she cried until she thought there were no tears left in her.

She sat up with a start. The fire had almost gone out. Glancing at the mantelpiece, she focused on the clock. It was just five. Time to go to work.

Pushing herself up off the sofa, Vanessa looked out of the window and saw that the rain had ceased. The late afternoon sky, washed clean of the dark clouds, was clear again.

After putting on her duffle coat, she walked slowly across the lawn to the red barn, then stopped for a brief moment as she passed the small copse of trees to the left of the house. Years ago her mother had planted hundreds of daffodils, and she had added to them since she had owned the cottage.

Many of them were pushing their golden heads upward, fluttering in the breeze, pale yellow beacons in the soft light. How fresh and springlike they looked. So pretty under the trees. Her eyes filled. She brushed her damp cheeks with her fingertips and walked on.

Once she was inside her studio, Vanessa focused on her work. Going to the drawing board, she switched on the light above it and was soon sketching rapidly, drawing spheres and globes, until she found her way through the many shapes springing into her mind. She settled, at last, on kidney and oval shapes.

Her work had become her salvation. She found it hard to sleep at night, and so she had reversed her routine. From five o'clock until eleven she created her designs in the barn. She had a drink and ate dinner at midnight, and then read half the night, until fatigue finally overcame her.

And once the designs on paper were finished, she worked in the foundry, hand-blowing the glass pieces. As she did she would ask herself how she would ever be able to go to Venice again. She would have to because of her work. But she knew she must find another hotel. She would never again set foot in the Gritti Palace.

14

"You were *there*, Joe! What really happened?" Frank Peterson exclaimed, his voice rising slightly. His face was pale, and he looked strained and anxious.

Leaning over the table, he pinned his eyes on Joe Alonzo. "What the hell happened to Bill?" he demanded again.

Joe shook his head. He looked as if he were about to burst into tears. "I'm telling you, Frank, it was over before I could blink. We were in West Beirut, not too far from here, near the mosque. We all got out of the car, Mike, Bill, and me. Bill started to walk toward the mosque; Mike and I went to the trunk, to take out our equipment. Suddenly this big Mercedes slid to a stop. Three young men jumped out, grabbed Bill, and hustled him into the car. Then the Mercedes sped off."

"And you didn't follow it!" Frank said in a hard, tight voice, staring at the CNS soundman. "Jesus, Joe!"

"I know, I know, Frank, I can guess what you're

147

thinking. But the point is, Mike and I were stunned for a second. We couldn't believe it."

"And so you didn't react."

"We did, but not fast enough! Within a few seconds we ran to our car, raced after the Mercedes, but we couldn't find it. The damned thing had just disappeared. Literally, into thin air."

"These local terrorists know all the side streets and back alleys," Frank said, and eyed Joe thoughtfully. "And if you and Mike hadn't been taking your equipment out of the trunk, you would've probably been grabbed as well," he asserted in a quieter tone.

"Damn right we would!" Mike Williams said, coming to a halt at the table where Frank and Joe were sitting in the bar of the Marriott in the Hamra district of Beirut.

Frank jumped up at the sight of Mike, grabbed his hand and shook it. "Join us, Mike, I've just been talking to Joe about Bill's kidnapping."

"It's a hell of a thing . . . we're at our wits' end . . ." Mike sat down heavily. He looked tired and worried. "When did you get back to Beirut, Frank?"

"Last night. From Egypt. I was covering a story there when the new trouble between the Israelis and Hezbollah erupted. The civil war is over, everything's on the mend, and then they start skirmishing again. But did they ever *really* stop?"

"I doubt it," Mike replied. "Still, it's the first time the Israelis have attacked Beirut directly in fourteen years. And with laser-homing Hellfire missiles, no less, shot from four helicopter gunships off the coast. My jaw practically dropped when it happened two days ago."

"Yeah, but the Israelis were actually responding to Hezbollah's bombing of Israel," Joe pointed out quickly.

Frank nodded. "And after Israel's attack on Beirut, Hezbollah retaliated yesterday by sending another forty rockets into Israel. The war of attrition continues."

"Nothing changes much," Mike murmured and motioned to a waiter, ordered scotch on the rocks.

Frank said, "I couldn't believe it when I saw the story on CNS about Bill's kidnapping. My God, I'd just left him when he was taken. I flew out of Beirut on March twenty-seventh and he was grabbed the next day. And for most of the time I was away I thought he was having a good time in Venice."

"He never made it to Venice," Mike responded. "I'm sure you realize the network sat on the story for a few days, hoping he would be released quickly. When he wasn't, they got it on the air at once."

"Who's behind it? Have you heard anything?" Frank probed.

"No, we haven't," Joe answered.

"I was just on the phone to Jack Clayton," Mike

explained. "The network still doesn't have any information. Nobody's claiming this, the way the bastards usually do. It's a bit of a mystery. Total silence from all terrorist groups, according to New York."

"It's got to be Hezbollah," Frank said in a knowing tone. He turned from Mike to Joe, raising a brow. "Who else but them?"

"You're right," Joe agreed. "That's what Mike and I think, too. At least, we believe that the Islamic Jihad is behind it. You know better than anybody, Frank, that the terrorist arm of Hezbollah is full of wackos. They're the ones who took Terry Anderson and William Buckley, and they're not known for fast releases."

"Terry Anderson was a hostage for seven years," Frank muttered.

"Don't remind me," Mike said dourly. "By the way, we've been in touch with Bill's mother."

"I spoke with her myself from Egypt," Frank answered. "As soon as I knew what had happened. It's remarkable the way she's holding up."

Joe volunteered, "We try to call her every few days. Unfortunately, there's not much we can tell her."

"Hearing from you helps her a great deal, I'm sure of that." Frank lifted his glass, downed the last of his scotch. Leaning back in his chair, he thought for a moment about Vanessa. He had tried to reach her for days, but there was no answer at her left or the cottage in the Hamptons. "What's the network doing about trying to find Bill?" he asked.

"There's not a lot they can do," Mike said. "Bill's picture has been circulated throughout Beirut, the whole of Lebanon, in fact. And a great deal of pressure has been put on the Lebanese and Syrian governments, and right from the beginning. Even though the story wasn't released immediately, the CNS top brass were on top of the situation at once, the same day Bill was snatched.

"And pressure was put on the White House as well. Let's face it, Frank, there's nothing anyone can do until an organization claims the kidnapping as theirs. Only then can the U.S. Government and the network start pushing for Bill's release."

"I always kidded him, said he was bulletproof," Frank began and stopped when Allan Brent, the Middle East correspondent for CNN, stopped at their table.

"We've just had a news flash," he said. "Hezbollah is claiming they have Bill Fitzgerald."

"Oh, Jesus!" Frank cried.

"How long ago was the flash?" Joe asked.

Allan Brent glanced at his watch. "It's now seven, about six-thirty, thereabouts."

Mark Lawrence, who was covering Bill's kidnapping

for CNS, appeared in the doorway of the bar. When he spotted the CNS crew with Frank and Allan Brent, he hurried over. He said to Mike, "I guess you've heard that the Islamic Jihad has Bill."

"Yes," Mike said. "Allan just told us."

"I hope to God Bill's all right," Frank cried. "I *pray* to God he's all right. That group is fanatical, unstable, and unpredictable."

It was always dark in the cramped, airless room.

They had nailed old wood boards over the windows and only thin slivers of light crept in through the cracks.

Bill Fitzgerald turned awkwardly on the narrow cot; his movements were restricted by handcuffs and leg chains. Managing at last to get onto his back, he lay staring up at the ceiling, trying to assess what day it was.

All along he had attempted to keep track of time; he figured he had been a hostage for almost two weeks. When he asked his various guards, they wouldn't tell him. All they ever said was, "Shut up, American pig!"

He felt dirty, and wished they would allow him to have another shower. He had only been permitted two since his capture. His clothes had become so filthy he had begged them to give him something clean, which one of his guards had done yesterday. *Finally.* Cotton undershorts, a T-shirt, and a pair of cotton pants had been thrown at him, and he had been unchained in order to change into them. The clothes were cheap, but it was a relief to have them.

He had no idea where he was, whether he was still somewhere in Beirut or in the Bekaa Valley, that hotbed of Hezbollah activities where the Iran-backed militia was in control. So many hostages had been held there.

Bill didn't even know why he had been taken, except that he was an American and a journalist. But he *was* certain of one thing—the identity of his kidnappers. They were young men of the Islamic Jihad, the terrorist arm of Hezbollah, and dangerous. Some of them were slightly crazed, on the edge, capable of anything.

They kept him chained up, shouted abuse at him, beat him every day, and gave him little food or water. And what food they did provide was stale, almost inedible. Yet despite their continuing mistreatment of him, he was not going to let them break his spirit.

Bill kept his mind fully occupied as best he could.

He thought mostly of his child, his mother, and of Vanessa, the woman he loved. He worried about them, worried about how they were reacting to his kidnapping, how they were handling it. He had faith in them, knew they would be strong; even his child would be strong.

As he lay staring at the dirty ceiling, he envisioned Vanessa's face in his mind's eye, projected her image onto the ceiling.

How lovely she was, so special, and so very dear to him. And how lucky he was to have found her. He knew they would have a wonderful life together. The first thing he was going to do when he was free was make a child with her. She wanted one so badly; she had confided that to him the last time they had been together.

He had worried about her for the first few days he was in captivity, knowing she was alone in Venice, waiting for him. And with no idea why he had not shown up.

Bill heard the key turning in the lock. He focused his eyes on the door and steeled himself for his daily beating. In the dim light he saw one of his captors entering the cell.

"Put on blindfold," the young man said, walking across the room, showing the grimy rag to Bill.

"Why?" Bill asked, endeavoring to sit up.

"No speak, American pig! American spy!" the young man shouted and tied the blindfold around Bill's eyes roughly, pulled him to his feet, and led him across the cell.

"Where are you taking me?" Bill demanded.

"No speak!" the terrorist yelled, pushing Bill out of the room.

15

Vanessa sat up with a jerk, feeling disoriented, blinking as she looked around the library. Dimly, in the distance, the thudding noise that had awakened her continued.

She pushed herself to her feet, hurried across the room and out into the hall. Instantly the thudding sounded louder, and she realized that someone was hammering on the front door of the cottage.

She ran across the hall, shouting, "I'm coming," and flung open the door. Much to her surprise and consternation she found herself staring into the face of Bill's mother.

"Dru!" she exclaimed, completely taken aback. "Hello! Have you been knocking long?"

When his mother did not answer, but simply stared at her blankly, Vanessa went on, "Why have you come to see me? What are you doing here?" Her brows knitted together in a frown when suddenly she became aware of Dru Fitzgerald's troubled face and bloodshot eyes. She also noticed that she looked painfully thin. "Dru, what's the matter?" she asked, urgency echoing in her voice.

Dru leaned against the door jamb, unexpectedly breathing hard, as if she was experiencing some sort of difficulty. She managed to say, "May I come inside, Vanessa?"

"How rude of me to keep you standing here. Of course, please come in. Can I get you anything?"

"A glass of water, please. I must take a pill."

Vanessa took hold of Drucilla's arm and escorted her into the cottage. After leading her to the sitting room, and settling her in a chair, she went to the kitchen for the water.

A moment later Vanessa returned. She handed the glass to Dru, waited for her to take the pill, then said, "I can tell you're distressed about something. What's the matter?"

Drucilla Fitzgerald, staring intently at her, realized with a small jolt that Vanessa did not know what had happened to Bill. How that was possible she wasn't sure, but, nonetheless, she was quite certain it was true. Dru wondered how to tell her. Tears flooded her eyes, and she clasped her hands together to stop them from trembling.

Vanessa was about to ask her again what was causing her upset when Dru cleared her throat, reached out and took hold of Vanessa's hand.

Dru said slowly, almost in a whisper, "I've been trying to reach you on the phone for days." No longer able to control herself, she began to weep. She groped in her wool jacket for her handkerchief.

"I've had my phone turned off," Vanessa explained, and as she said these words she had a terrible sense of foreboding. "It's Bill! Something's happened to Bill, hasn't it?"

Dru continued to cry, her sobs almost uncontrollable, her pain even more apparent now.

Vanessa went and sat next to her on the sofa, put her arm around Dru's shoulders. "I'm totally in the dark, Dru. I've had not only the phone turned off but the television as well. I've cut myself off from the world for the past two weeks."

Dru turned to look at her, the tears streaming down her pale face. Her mouth began to tremble. "He's dead," she said in a voice that was barely audible. "My son is dead. My only child has been taken from me in the most cruel way. Oh Vanessa ... Vanessa ... Why did they kill him? They shot him. He's never coming back. He's gone. Oh, whatever shall we do without him?" She continued to weep, gasping, holding her arms around her body. Her sorrow was unendurable.

Vanessa was gaping at Dru. She had gone cold all over, and she was stunned, reeling from shock, unable to respond for a moment. Her eyes welled, and she began to shake. At last, she said, "I don't understand . . . *who* killed Bill?" Choking on these words, she was unable to continue, just held onto Dru tightly. The two women clung together, sobbing.

Eventually, through her tears, Dru said, "It was Hezbollah. The Islamic Jihad. They kidnapped Bill, Vanessa. I realize now that you didn't know, otherwise you would have come to Helena and me, to be with us."

"When?" Vanessa gasped. "When was he taken?" Her voice shook and fresh tears flowed; she knew the answer even before Dru spoke.

"March the twenty-eighth," Dru answered. "It was a Thursday. They took him that morning in Beirut. He was out with the crew, Joe and Mike—"

"Oh, my God! My God!" Vanessa cried out, pressing both of her hands to her face, trying to stem the tears. They slid through her fingers, fell down onto her cotton shirt, leaving damp splotches. "I was waiting for him in Venice, and he didn't come! I thought he'd lost interest in me, that it was over between us. But he couldn't come, could he? Oh, Dru, Dru . . ."

"No, he couldn't. He loved you, Vanessa, he wanted to marry you. He told me that. He also told me that you were married, that you were getting a divorce."

Vanessa swallowed hard. "Bill was mine and I was

his and that was the way it was. How could I have forgotten that?"

Drucilla sighed and looked into Vanessa's face sadly. "When we're in love, things are always very extreme, intense . . . "

"I love him with all my heart. I shouldn't ever have doubted him in Venice. I should have known something terrible had happened, something beyond his control."

Dru was silent for a second, and then she said softly, "You were feeling hurt."

Vanessa suddenly lost control again and started to weep bitterly. "When was he shot?" she asked through her tears.

"We're not sure." Dru found it hard to continue. She brought her hand to her trembling mouth, and took a few moments to regain her composure.

Slowly, she went on, "Andrew Bryce, the president of CNS, and Jack Clayton, Bill's news editor, came to see me yesterday." Pausing, she took a deep breath before saying, "To tell me themselves that the Islamic Jihad had just announced they had executed Bill. They left his body at the French Embassy in Beirut, who have given it to the American Hospital to send home."

"But why did they kill him?" Vanessa cried. "*Why,* Dru?"

"Andrew and Jack don't know. No one knows. The Islamic Jihad haven't said anything. They've given no explanation."

The two women who loved Bill Fitzgerald sat together on the sofa, not speaking, lost in their own troubled thoughts, silently sharing their heartbreak and sorrow.

After a while, Vanessa spoke. Looking at Dru, she said, "Where is Helena?"

Dru covered her mouth with her hand once more, the tears starting afresh. After a moment she said, "I brought her with me. I hadn't the heart to leave her. She's walking the dunes with Alice, the nanny. The child's heartbroken, she worshiped him so."

Vanessa nodded. Rising, she walked across the room to the window, stood looking out at the dunes, her mind full of Bill and the love they had shared. She thought of his child. And she came to a sudden decision.

Turning to look at Bill's mother, Vanessa said, "I think you and Helena should stay here with me for a few days, Dru. Bill would want us to be together."

Much later that night, when she was alone in her bedroom, Vanessa wept for Bill once more. She wept for the loss of the man she loved, the life they would never share, and the children they would never have.

It was a long night of tears and anguish. There was a moment when guilt reared up, but she crushed it before it took hold. It was a ridiculous waste of time to feel guilty because she had doubted him briefly. He would be the first to say that, just as his mother had.

As dawn broke over the dunes, Vanessa came to understand that her grief would last for a long time, and that she must let it run its course. Bill Fitzgerald had been the love of her life, and she had lost him in the blink of an eye. Lost him because of some insanity on the other side of the world. It was wrong, all wrong. He had been far too young a man to die.

It should not have happened, but it had, and she was alone. Just as his child and his mother were alone, bereft and lost without him. They were her main concern now. She would do what Bill would want her to do . . . console and comfort them.

They needed her. And she needed them.

16

"I'm glad Alice listened to you, Dru, and took her vacation," Vanessa said, stirring the chicken soup she was making, peering into the pot on the stove. "It would have been foolish of her to cancel it, when she had it all planned. But you know, she never did say where she was going."

Dru did not respond.

Vanessa said, "Where has she gone, actually?"

Still Dru did not answer and Vanessa swung around, exclaimed, "My God, what's wrong," threw down the wooden spoon, and rushed across the kitchen.

Drucilla was leaning back in the chair, her face drained of all color, starkly white against her red hair. She was clutching herself and wincing.

Vanessa bent over her. "Dru, what is it?"

"Pain. In my chest. My left arm hurts. I think I'm having a heart attack."

"Don't move! I'll get the car. Southampton Hospital's not far away. On Meeting House Lane. I'll have us there in a few minutes. Just don't move, Dru. Okay?"

Dru nodded.

Vanessa ran to the garage, backed the car out, parked it near the cottage, and leapt across the lawn to her studio. She had left Helena drawing there earlier. Pulling open the door, she called, "Helena, come on, we have to go!"

"Where?"

"To the hospital. Your grandmother's not well."

"I'm coming," the child shouted fiercely, jumped off the stool, and flew across the floor. "Is it her heart?"

"She thinks so, yes," Vanessa said, took hold of Helena's hand, and ran with her to the cottage. "Get in the car, honey, and I'll be out in a minute with Gran." As she spoke, Vanessa helped Helena into the backseat and fastened the safety belt.

Inside the house, Vanessa grabbed her handbag from the hall closet, and dashed back to the kitchen; Dru was slumped in the chair with her arms still wrapped around herself.

Bending toward her, Vanessa asked, "Dru, do you feel any worse?"

"No. Just the same."

"Can you make it to the car?"

"Yes, Vanessa. If you help me," Dru murmured in a weak voice.

Together the two women walked slowly across the

kitchen and outside to the car. "Try not to worry. You're going to be all right," Vanessa said as she fastened the seat belt around Dru, praying that she would be.

And she kept on praying all the way to the hospital.

"Mrs Fitzgerald *has* had a heart attack, fortunately not too severe," Dr. Paula Matthews said, drawing Vanessa to one side of the waiting room. "She's going to be all right, but she will have to watch herself, take care of herself."

"Yes, I understand, Dr. Matthews, I'll see that she does. In the meantime, how long does she have to be in the hospital?"

"A few days. Five at the most. She's in our cardiac care unit, more for observation and a rest than anything else." The doctor smiled at Vanessa, then glanced at Helena, who was sitting on a chair near the window. "I've never seen such a beautiful child," she said. "You're very lucky."

"Yes," Vanessa murmured, not knowing what else to say.

"Anyway, I know Mrs. Fitzgerald's anxious to see you both, so let me take you to her room."

A moment or two later Vanessa and Helena were sitting by the bed where Drucilla lay looking pale and weak. "I'm so sorry, Vanessa, to put you to all this trouble," Dru said in a low voice. "What a nuisance I am."

"Don't be so silly," Vanessa exclaimed. "You're not any trouble to me at all. And Helena and I are going to come and see you every day."

Helena said, "And Vanessa says we'll bring you things. Like books and magazines." She smiled at her grandmother. "And flowers, Gran."

"Thank you, darling," Dru murmured.

"Please don't worry about Helena," Vanessa went on, taking hold of Drucilla's hand, squeezing it. "She's no trouble, we'll be fine together."

"But your work . . ." Dru began, looking worried.

"I can do my work and take care of Helena," Vanessa reassured her. "Just think about yourself and getting better."

"I don't know how to thank you."

"Thanks are not necessary, Dru, you know that. And I'm here for you, whenever you need me."

"Bill told me you were a loving woman, and he was right," Dru said. She averted her face for a moment, blinking back tears. Then, turning to look at them both again, she forced a smile. "A hospital's no place for you two. Go and have lunch, and I'll see you tomorrow."

"'Half a pound of tuppeny rice, half a pound of treacle. Mix it up and make it nice. Pop goes the weasel!'"

Vanessa sang, leading the child around the room in a circle, holding both her hands.

Helena laughed, much to Vanessa's relief. She had been in floods of tears all morning, suddenly reacting to her grandmother's departure for the hospital the day before. Drucilla's heart attack, coming so quickly after Bill's death, had been too much for the little girl to handle.

Vanessa understood Helena's concern for her grandmother, but she had not been able to stem her tears, or comfort her. At least not until now. The little game they were playing seemed to have helped. It had brought a sparkle to the child's eyes.

"What a funny song," Helena said. "What's a weasel?"

"A little furry animal with a bushy tail that lives in the woods."

"How do you know this song?"

"When *I* was six, I was living in London for a while with my parents. I had a nanny who was English. She taught me the song."

"Can you teach me?"

"Of course. Sing along with me, Helena. Here we go. 'Half a pound of tuppeny rice, half a pound of treacle. Mix it up and make it nice. Pop goes the weasel.'"

Helena sang with her, and they went round and

round in circles, holding hands. After half a dozen times Helena knew the words, had committed them to memory.

She laughed merrily and clapped her hands. "I'll sing it for Gran when we go to the hospital this afternoon."

"What a good idea, Pumpkin."

The smile slid off Helena's face and she recoiled, gaping at Vanessa.

"What is it? What's wrong?"

"Don't call me Pumpkin. Only Daddy calls me that. It's his name," she cried fiercely, and burst into tears.

Vanessa went to her, put her arms around her, held her close. "I'm sorry, Helena, I didn't know. Don't cry, honey. Please."

But Helena could not stop sobbing, and she clutched Vanessa as if never to let her go.

Vanessa smoothed her hand down the child's back, endeavoring to comfort her, to soothe her, making hushing noises.

After a while the sobs lessened, and Helena grew calmer. Vanessa led her across the studio to the sofa, lifted her up onto it, and sat down next to her. Taking a tissue from the box on the coffee table, she wiped Helena's eyes, then drew her into the circle of her arms. "In a little while we'll go into town and have a hamburger for lunch. How does that sound?"

"Can I have french fries?"

"Of course."

"And an ice cream?"

Vanessa smiled at her. "Yes, if you want."

Helena nodded; then she bit her lip, suddenly looking tearful again.

"What's wrong, honey?"

"Is Gran . . ." Her bottom lip trembled and tears shimmered on her long lashes. "Is Gran going to die?"

"No, of course not! Don't be silly!"

"People die of heart attacks, Vanessa. Jennifer's grandmother did."

"Who's Jennifer?"

"My friend."

"Well, *your* gran isn't going to die, I promise you that."

"But she's in the hospital."

"I know, and she's getting better. I explained to you yesterday, the reason Gran is in the hospital until Friday is because she needs a rest. That's all. Her heart attack wasn't a bad one, honey. Trust me, she'll be all right."

"They're mending her heart at the hospital."

"Yes," Vanessa murmured, giving the child a reassuring smile.

"Gran's heart is broken. It broke the other day. When the men came."

"Men?" Vanessa repeated, momentarily puzzled.

"Daddy's men. From the network."

"Oh, yes, of course."

"They told her my daddy is dead and it broke her heart."

"Yes, darling . . . "

Helena gave Vanessa a piercing look. "Is Daddy in Heaven?"

Vanessa swallowed. "Yes," was all she could manage.

The child continued to look at her closely. "With my mommy?"

"That's right. They're together now," Vanessa said, striving hard for control.

"When is he coming back, Vanessa?"

"Well . . . well . . . you see . . . he won't be able to come back, Helena. He's going to stay with your mother . . . he's going to look after her." Vanessa averted her face, brushed away the tears.

Helena seemed confused. She frowned hard. "I want him to look after me."

"I know, I know, but he can't, honey, not right now. Gran's going to look after you."

"But what if she dies too?"

"She won't."

"How do you know?"

"I just do, Helena."

"Why did the men kill my daddy?"

"Because they're bad men, darling."

Helena stared at Vanessa and started to weep again. "I want my daddy to come back. Make him come back, Vanessa."

"Hush, hush, honey, don't cry like this," Vanessa murmured, endeavoring to soothe her. "I'm here. I'll look after you."

Helena pulled away, looked up into Vanessa's face. "Can we live with you?"

For a moment Vanessa was taken aback, and then she replied, "We'll have to talk to Gran about that."

Helena nodded.

"By the way, where has Alice gone on vacation?" Vanessa continued, wanting to change the subject, distract Helena.

"To Minnesota. To see her mom and her brothers and sisters. Alice has a great-grandmother and she comes from Sweden."

"Tell me some more about Alice."

"Well, she takes me to school and picks me up from school, and she takes me to Central Park and she plays with me."

Vanessa leaned back against the sofa, relieved that the six-year-old was now chattering normally, that she had managed to divert her.

17

On Friday morning Drucilla Fitzgerald was released from Southampton Hospital.

Vanessa and Helena were there to pick her up and take her back to Bedelia Cottage on the dunes. After the three of them had lunch together, Vanessa sent Helena to draw and paint in the studio. She needed to be alone with Dru for a short while in order to talk to her.

"Helena's a lovely little girl, she's a real credit to you," Vanessa said as she and Drucilla relaxed over a cup of herb tea in the sitting room. "We've become very good friends."

Dru smiled and nodded. "I know. She told me, and she sang 'Pop Goes the weasel' for me. She enjoyed herself with you, Vanessa, and I'm so glad she wasn't a problem."

"No, not at all, Dru," Vanessa began, and paused, then said, "But I think . . ." She shook her head. "I was going to say I think there's a problem, but I don't mean that at all."

Dru was frowning, looking perplexed. "What are you getting at, Vanessa dear?"

"I remember that when I was little I worried about a lot of things. All children worry; Helena worries."

"About my health, is that what you mean?"

"Yes. Children can easily feel insecure, and threatened, when a parent is sick or in the hospital. And I believe Helena feels very vulnerable."

"Yes, I'm sure she does, but she'll be all right, now that I'm out of the hospital. However, it'll take her a long time to . . . get over her father's death." Drucilla choked up. It was a moment before she finished softly, "It'll take us all a long time."

"Yes, it will . . ." Vanessa's voice trailed off as she stood, walked to the window, and gazed out at the sea. It was a deep blue on this mild afternoon in early May, streaked with sunlight and no longer bleak and uninviting. In her mind's eye she saw Bill's face; he was never out of her thoughts. She focused on his little daughter, and she knew exactly what she must say to Drucilla.

Turning swiftly, Vanessa came back to the sofa and sat down next to Bill's mother. She gave her a thoughtful look, and said, "Before your heart attack, you told me you had no relatives, and I was wondering if you had ever appointed a legal guardian for Helena?"

Drucilla did not seem at all startled by this question, and she answered evenly, "No, I never have. We never have. It didn't seem necessary. But I know what you're getting at, Vanessa. You're wondering what would become of Helena if I were to die. Isn't that so?"

"Yes, it is. You're a young woman, Dru, and this heart attack has been a . . . well, a sort of warning, I think. I know you'll look after yourself from now on, and you're not likely to die until she's grown. But—"

"You're only voicing what I was thinking as I lay in that hospital bed this week," Dru cut in. "I've worried a lot about Helena, worried about her future. I'm sixty-two, as you know, and I aim to live for a long time. Still, you never know what might happen. Life is full of surprises and shocks . . . "

"Would you consider me? Could I become Helena's legal guardian, Dru?"

"Oh, Vanessa, that's lovely of you to volunteer, but would you want that kind of responsibility? I mean, what if I did die while she's still little? Would you want to care for a child . . . you're young, only twenty-seven, and one day you're bound to meet someone else. To be the guardian of another man's child could be a burden . . . a stumbling block to a relationship."

"I don't see it that way, Dru, I really don't. If I were Helena's legal guardian I would fulfill my obligations to her, no matter what the circumstances of my life. I realize you don't know me very well, but I am sincere and very trustworthy."

"Oh, darling, I know that. Bill loved you so very much, and certainly I trust *his* judgment. Besides, I'm a good judge of character myself, and the day I met you, at Christmas at Tavern On The Green, I knew the sort of person you are. I felt then that a weight had been lifted from my shoulders because I could see how changed Bill was because of you. He was so happy. And I suddenly feel as if a weight has been lifted from me again." Dru took hold of Vanessa's hand and held it tightly; suddenly her eyes welled. She said, "I can think of no one I would like more to be Helena's legal guardian. I know that with you she would always be safe."

Vanessa's eyes were also moist. "Thank you, Dru. As soon as you're up to going to New York, I'd like to make an appointment with my lawyer. Or yours, whichever you prefer. We will set all this in motion. Is that all right with you?"

Dru nodded. "I hope to live to a ripe old age, but it's good to know you're there in the background."

"I'd like us to be together, Dru; I'd like to get to know Helena better, and you too. I was wondering, would you consider spending the summers here with me?"

If Drucilla was startled she did not show it. Without hesitation, she said, "I'd like that, Vanessa, I really would. And I know Helena will be happy. She loves it here."

"Then it's settled." Vanessa leaned closer, kissing Dru on the cheek. "There's something else I have to tell you."

"Yes, what is that?"

"Frank called very early this morning. He's come to New York . . . with Bill's things . . . from his hotel room in Beirut. He wants to come and see us tomorrow. Is that all right?"

Drucilla found it hard to speak. She simply nodded her head and held Vanessa's hand all that much tighter.

"He was my best friend, I loved him," Frank said quietly, looking at Bill's mother. "Everybody loved Bill. He was such a special man."

"He's dead and our lives will never be the same," Dru murmured, her face ringed with sorrow. "But we must go on, and bravely so. That's what he would want."

"Only that," Frank agreed. "He was the bravest man I ever knew. He saved my life. Did you know that, Dru?"

"No, I didn't," she replied. "He never told me that, Frank."

"He wouldn't, he was very modest in his own way—"

"Uncle Frankie!" Helena cried as she appeared in the doorway with Vanessa and rushed forward into his arms.

Frank held her tightly. She was part of Bill, and she looked so much like him, he thought. His throat tightened and for a moment he couldn't speak, so choked up was he.

Frank looked over Helena's head, his eyes meeting Vanessa's, and he nodded slightly. Then, releasing his godchild, he went to greet Vanessa, embracing her. "I'm so sorry, so very sorry," he said.

"So am I," she whispered. "I loved him, Frank."

"I know. He loved you . . . I have something for you." Drawing away from her, Frank reached inside his jacket, took out an envelope. "I found this in Bill's room at the Commodore in Beirut." He handed her the envelope.

She stared down at it. *Vanessa* Bill had written across the front. She bit her inner lip, pushing back the tears when she saw his handwriting. She stared at it for a long moment, afraid to open it.

Dru, watching her carefully, said softly, "Perhaps you'd like to be alone when you read it, Vanessa. We'll leave you."

"No," Vanessa said. "It's all right . . . I'll go . . . outside." She left them in the sitting room and went across the back lawn and down to the dunes, clutching the letter tightly in her hand.

There was a sheltered spot where she often read,

and she sat down there for a while, staring out at the sea, thinking of Bill, her heart aching.

Finally she opened the envelope and took out the letter.

Beirut
Monday, March 25th, 1996

My very dearest Vanessa:

I know I'll be seeing you in a few days, holding you in my arms, but I have such a need to talk to you, to reach out to you tonight, I decided to write to you. Of course you'll be reading this letter when I'm there with you in Venice, since I'll be bringing it with me.

The next few lines blurred as her eyes filled with tears, but after a few moments she managed to recover, and went on reading.

I don't think I've ever really told you how much I love you, Vanessa—with all my heart and soul and mind. You're rarely out of my thoughts and all I want is to make you happy. You've brought me back to life, given new meaning to my life. And now I want to share that life with you. You will, won't you, darling? You will be my wife and as soon as that's possible?

In my heart I can hear you say yes, yes, yes in that excited way you have. And I promise you I'll love and cherish you always. You know what, let's make a baby in Venice. I know how much you want a child. And I want it to be mine. I want to know that part of me is growing inside you. So let's do it this weekend, let's make a baby.

I've never told you this before, but in the last six years my life has been hellish. Three people I loved very much died on me. First Sylvie, then my father, and finally my grandmother. Their deaths broke my heart.

But over the past few months I've come to understand that the heart broken is the strongest heart.

Bill.

Vanessa sat there for a long time, holding the letter. And then she folded it carefully, put it back in the envelope, and rising, she walked slowly across the dunes and into the cottage.

BARBARA TAYLOR BRADFORD

POWER OF A WOMAN

As always, for Bob,
who makes my world go round,
with all my love

CONTENTS

PART ONE

Thanksgiving

1

A FINE MIST FLOATED LIKE PALE WATER OVER THE MEADOWS, DRIFT-
ing, eddying, blurring the trees, turning them into illusory
shapes that loomed against the somber sky.

Beyond these meadows, the distant Litchfield hills were pur-
plish in the dimming light, their bases obscured by the rising
mist so that only their peaks were visible now.

And all about this wintry landscape lay an unremitting
silence, as if the world had stopped; everything was washed in a
vast unconsciousness. The stillness was all-pervasive; nothing
moved or stirred.

In the summertime these low meadows were verdant and
lush with billowing grass, and every kind of wildflower grew
among the grasses. But on this cold Wednesday afternoon in
November they appeared bleak and uninviting.

Stevie Jardine normally did not mind this kind of misty
weather, for inevitably it brought the past back to her, and happily
so, reminding her as it did of the Yorkshire moors and the lovely
old farmhouse she owned. Yet now the vaporous air was chilling
her through and through; it seemed to permeate her bones.

Unexpectedly, she experienced a rush of apprehension, and this startled her. Pulling her woolen cape closer to her body, she hurried faster, trying to shake off the strange feeling of foreboding that had just enveloped her. Involuntarily, Stevie shivered. Somebody walked over my grave, she thought, and she shivered again. She looked up.

The sky was remote and cold, turning color, curdling to a peculiar faded green. A bitter sky, eerie; she increased her pace, running, eager now to get home. She no longer liked it outside, regretted her decision to take a long walk. The fog had closed in, but earlier the weather had been beautiful, almost an Indian summer's afternoon, until the dankness had scuttled the day.

Her feet knew well the path across the fields, and her step was sure, did not falter as it suddenly dipped, curved down into the dell. The fog was dense on this lower ground. Shivering once more, she drew herself farther into her cape.

Soon the narrow path was rising upward as the landscape changed, became hilly; the mist was evaporating up there, where the land was higher. When she reached the crest of the hill the air grew colder, but it was much clearer.

From this vantage point Stevie could make out her house nestling cozily in the valley below, and she felt a surge of relief. Smoke curled up from its chimneys, lights glimmered brightly in the windows. It was a welcoming sight, warm and inviting in the dusk.

She was glad she was home.

The house was two hundred years old, built in 1796, and stood in a long, green valley under the shadow of Connecticut's Litchfield hills. It had been something of an eyesore when she had first seen it five years before, an unsightly hodgepodge of additions that had been built onto it over the decades. After some skillful remodeling and restoration, its former graciousness and charm were recaptured.

Stevie moved rapidly across the wet lawn and up the steps onto the covered porch, entering the house through the side door, which led directly into the cloakroom.

Once she had hung up her damp cape she went into the great hall. This was vast, with a wide staircase at one end and a dark wood floor so highly polished it gleamed like glass. A beamed ceiling, heavy oak doors, and mullioned windows bespoke the age of the house.

Stevie always thought of the great hall as the core of the house, since all the other rooms flowed around it. From the moment she moved in, the hall had been used as a family living room, where everyone congregated. Several pink-silk–shaded lamps had been turned on, and they glowed rosily, adding to the inviting atmosphere. It was a comfortable, welcoming room, with an old, faded Savonnerie rug in front of the fireplace, antique Jacobean tables and chests made of dark carved wood. Big sofas, covered in a fir-green tapestry, were grouped with several chairs around the fire.

Stevie's face instantly brightened as she crossed the hall. It was cheerful, safe, reassuring. A log fire roared in the big stone hearth and the air was redolent with the spicy scent of pine, a hint of wood smoke and ripe apples. From the kitchen there floated the fragrant aroma of bread baking.

Coming to a standstill at the fireplace, Stevie stood with her hands outstretched to the flames, warming them. Unexpectedly, laughter bubbled in her throat and she began to laugh out loud. At herself. How foolish she had been a short while ago when she was crossing the meadows. There was no reason for her to feel apprehensive. Her sense of foreboding had been irrational. She laughed again, chastising herself for her uneasiness earlier.

After a few seconds she turned away from the fireplace and crossed to the staircase, heading upstairs. She loved every corner of this lovely old house, in particular the small study that opened off her bedroom. As she pushed open the door and walked in, she could not help admiring the room. It was beautifully proportioned, with a cathedral ceiling, tall windows at one end, and a grand fireplace flanked on either side by soaring bookshelves.

Stevie had had the study decoratively painted by an artist, who had layered innumerable coats of amber-colored paint on the walls, then given them a glazed finish. This Venetian stucco treatment created a soft golden sheen, as if sunshine had been perpetually trapped within the confines of the room.

Lovely paintings, selectively chosen over the years, family photographs in silver frames, a variety of treasured mementos, and well-loved books were the things that made this room hers, and very special to her.

The fire was laid and she went and knelt in front of it. Striking a match, she brought the flame to the paper and within seconds a roaring fire was blazing up the chimney.

Rising, she walked across the floor and seated herself at the oval-shaped Georgian desk in the window area. Papers from her briefcase were neatly stacked on it, but after a quick, cursory glance at these she turned away from them, sat back in the chair. Her mind was suddenly far, far away.

She found herself gazing at various objects on her desk, an absentminded expression etched on her delicate face . . . the Art Nouveau lamp she had picked up for next to nothing in the flea market in Paris, a Georgian silver inkwell her mother had given her years before, a plethora of photographs of those she loved, her grandmother's Meissen cream jug in the Red Dragon pattern filled with small pencils, and a copy of an ancient Hindu saying displayed in a mother-of-pearl frame.

Staring intently at this, she read it again, perhaps for the thousandth time in her life: "He who buys a diamond purchases a bit of eternity."

This old saying had been written out by Ralph in handwriting so beautiful it was like calligraphy, and he had given it to her not long after they were married. As he would so often tell her, the saying summed up what he felt about diamonds. They were his business, he loved them; and it was from him that she had learned so much about them herself.

Stevie's light gray-green eyes strayed to the photograph of Ralph and her, taken on their wedding day in November 1966. Thirty years ago to this very day. Ever since early this morning, Ralph had been in and out of her thoughts, and once again she fell down into herself, for a moment contemplating him and their early years together.

He had been such a good man, the best person she had ever known, so very loving, adoring even, and devoted to her from the first moment they met. And certainly he had taken a strong stand against his parents when they had fiercely objected, and vociferously so, to the idea of their marrying.

Bruce and Alfreda Jardine had disapproved of her right from the start, because, they said, she was far too young. And also an American, not to mention a girl with no background or fortune, although her nationality and the word *money* had never crossed their lips.

Stevie had always somehow known deep within herself, had actually *understood* without ever being told, that had she been born an heiress with a great fortune to bring to the marriage, her age and her nationality would have been of little or no importance to the Jardines.

To her, Ralph's parents were as transparent as glass. They were snobs who had long harbored grand ideas for their son, formulated grand plans for him, at least where matrimony was concerned. But Ralph was not having any of that. Always his own man, he had been unshakable in his determination to make her his wife. He had openly defied them, and in so doing had ruined their elaborate schemes, thwarted their ambitions for him.

From a very long distance she heard a faint echo reverberating in her head. It was Bruce Jardine's aristocratic English voice raised harshly in a shout of rage, as he uttered the most ugly words she had ever heard, words she had never forgotten.

"For God's sake, man, you're twenty-seven! Surely by now you know enough about sex to take care of matters properly! Why didn't you have your way with her without getting her pregnant? You'd better make arrangements for her to get rid of it. Talk to Harry Axworth. He's a bit of a bounder, I'm the first to acknowledge, certainly not someone I would normally wish you to associate with. However, because of his nefarious indiscretions, he's the best chap for this purpose. He'll be able to point you in the right direction. He's bound to know a doctor down on his luck who'll no doubt do the job for fifty pounds."

She had been waiting for Ralph in the grandiose front entrance hall, sitting on the edge of a chair, a nervous wreck, her hands trembling, her heart in her mouth as Bruce Jardine's voice had echoed through the closed mahogany door.

Ralph had chosen not to dignify his father's words with a response. He had walked out of the library and straight into her arms. After holding her close for a moment, calming her, he had then led her out into the street and away from the Jardine mansion in Wilton Crescent. His face had been white with fury, and he had not said a word to her until they were safely inside his bachelor flat in Mayfair. Once there, he had told her how much he loved her, and that he wanted to spend the rest of his life with her.

They were married two weeks later in the register office in Marylebone. She had been sixteen years old, younger than Ralph by eleven years, and four months pregnant by then.

The elder Jardines, always contentious, had shown their disdain and anger by boycotting the marriage of their only son. So had Alicia, Ralph's sister.

But her mother had been present, her beautiful mother, Blair Connors, once the most famous model in the world, a supermodel before the term had even been invented.

Accompanying her mother that morning had been *her* new husband, Derek Rayner, the great English stage actor who everyone said was the heir apparent to Larry Olivier's crown.

After the wedding ceremony, Derek had taken them all to lunch at The Ivy, London's famous theatrical restaurant, which the elite of stage, film, and cafe society favored. And then they had gone to Paris for their honeymoon.

Ostracized by Ralph's parents, Stevie and Ralph had lived for each other, and the world had been well lost to them.

A wistful sigh escaped her. For a long time now she had recognized that the weekends and holidays she had spent on the Yorkshire moors had been the most happy of times for her, perhaps the happiest in her entire life. It saddened her that they could never be recaptured, that this particular kind of happiness would never be hers again.

So young, she thought, I was so young then. But already the mother of three: Nigel, born when I was just seventeen, and the twins, Gideon and Miles, when I was nineteen.

A smile animated her face as images of her children leapt into her mind unbidden. Three tow-headed little boys, each with eyes as blue as speedwells. Grown men now. And she was still young herself, only forty-six, but a grandmother for the past two years, thanks to Nigel.

Stevie laughed inwardly. How often she was mistaken for her sons' sister, much to Nigel's chagrin. He did not like it; the twins, on the other hand, gleefully encouraged this deception whenever they could. They were incorrigible, loved to pass her off as their sibling to those who were unsuspecting of the truth, and they were usually successful at their mischievous little game.

Gideon and Miles were proud of her youthful looks, slender figure, energy, and vitality. Nigel felt just the opposite. It seemed to her that everything about her was an irritant to him. A small frown furrowed her smooth brow as Nigel's presence nudged itself into her mind. Swiftly, she pushed aside the flicker of dismay that flew to the surface.

She loved her eldest son, but she had always known he had a lot of his grandfather in him. And Bruce Jardine had never been one of her favorites, although as the years had passed, he had behaved decently toward her. Most especially after Alfreda's death. But as long as her mother-in-law had been alive, that awful contention had persisted, at least as far as Alfreda was concerned.

A small sigh escaped her and she turned her head, looked toward the fire, her mind sliding back in time as she remembered Alfreda and Bruce as they were then . . .

Four years after she and Ralph had been married, his sister, Alicia, had died of leukemia. The elder Jardines had been forced to reconsider the situation and effect a compromise, in order to come to terms with them. Ralph and she were the parents of their only grandchildren, their heirs, three boys who one day would follow in their grandfather's and father's footsteps, running Jardine and Company of London, the Crown Jewellers.

Eventually she and Ralph had succumbed to his parents' conciliatory overtures, albeit somewhat reluctantly, and certainly with a great deal of trepidation. They had accepted the proffered olive branch. As it turned out, they were forever fighting off interference from the senior Jardines, who tried, without success, to take over the rearing of the boys.

Their great escape had been the trips to Yorkshire to stay at Aysgarth End, the farmhouse on the moors above the Dales, where they had fled with the children whenever they had been able to get away. Large, rambling, in constant need of repairs, it was, nevertheless, their blessed haven, a little bit of heaven on earth, the place they really called home.

They liked their apartment in Kensington; it was spacious and comfortable, ideal for rearing a growing young family. For some reason Aysgarth End meant so much more to them emotionally. Stevie had never really been able to fathom what it was *exactly* that made the farm so special, except that it was full of love and laughter. And a special kind of joy.

She still believed, as she had all those years ago, that this joy sprang from Ralph's natural goodness, his genuine spirituality. He was truly a pure man, the only one she had ever known, filled with kindness and compassion, and he had had such an understanding heart.

That absolute joy in each other and their children had flourished at Aysgarth End until the day Ralph had died. He had been only thirty-four. Too young, by far.

She had become a widow at twenty-three.

And it was then that her troubles had begun.

Of course it was her parents-in-law who were the troublemakers. Endeavoring to brush her aside, ignoring her terrible grief and the enormous sense of loss she was experiencing, they had tried to wrest the children away from her. Foolishly so. They did not have a leg to stand on. She was the perfect mother, exemplary, without blemish, and untouched by any kind of scandal or wrongdoing.

Ralph's best friend, James Allerton, had also been his solicitor, and with Ralph's death he had become Stevie's legal representative. It was to James that she had turned when her in-laws had started to make their moves.

At a meeting with the Jardines, James had almost, but not quite, laughed in their faces, and had told them to go to hell, in more polite terms, of course. Not only was the law of the land on her side, there was the matter of Ralph's will. In it he had made his feelings for her abundantly clear. He had reiterated his love and admiration of her, not to mention his confidence in her ability to rear their sons. He had left her everything he owned, and in so doing had ensured her financial security. He had also made her entirely independent of his parents.

The trusts he had inherited from his grandparents he had passed on to his three sons; he had named his wife as the administrator of the trusts and executrix of his will.

As James so succinctly pointed out to the Jardines, Stevie was holding all the cards and she had a winning hand. They slunk away, defeated; for once they had been outmaneuvered.

It was her resentment of the Jardines, and her anger at them, that had served her so well in 1973. Especially the anger. She had turned it around, made it work to her advantage; it had also fueled her determination to keep her sons close at all times.

Although she did not know it at that moment, the anger had kindled her ambition as well, and eventually it would spur her on to do things she had never dreamed possible. At the back of her mind a plan was developing, a plan that would make her indispensable to Bruce Jardine, and ensure her control of her children until they were old enough to fend for themselves. That year, beset as she was with problems and crushed by grief, the plan did not come to flower. But the seed had been sown.

Stevie was a pragmatist at heart. She never forgot that one day her sons would inherit the family business, and that they must be properly educated and prepared for this. Founded in 1787 by one Alistair Jardine, a Scottish silversmith who had made his way to London and opened a shop there, Jardine's had always been run by a Jardine.

And so in 1974, as she began to recover from Ralph's death and regain her equilibrium, she had contacted his parents. Her main purpose was to affect a rapprochement, which she eventually was able to do with the help of James Allerton; but it was an uneasy truce at best. Alfreda seemed determined to upset her, or cause trouble, and whenever her mother-in-law could make her life difficult, she did.

Nonetheless, Stevie realized that her sons must come to know their grandparents, most especially their grandfather, who was the key to their future. It would be Bruce who would train them, lead them through the labyrinths of the family business, so that when he retired they could take over.

Jardine's had been the Crown Jewellers since Queen Victoria's day. It was important that her sons understood their inheritance, the great jewelry company that would be theirs one day, and the family dynasty into which they had been born.

The ringing of the telephone made her start, and, as she reached for it, Stevie was pulled back into the present.

"Hello?"

"I'd like to speak to Mrs. Jardine, please."

"This is she."

"Hello, Stevie, it's Matt Wilson."

Taken by surprise, she exclaimed, "Hello, Matt! And where are you calling from?" She glanced at her watch; it was five-thirty. "Not Paris, surely? It's very late at night there."

He laughed, and said, "No, I'm in Los Angeles. With *Monsieur*. We arrived yesterday to see a client. He would like to speak with you. I'll put him on."

"Thank you, Matt."

A moment later André Birron was at the other end of the wire. "Stephanie, my Stephanie, *comment vas-tu?*"

"I'm wonderful, André," Stevie said, smiling with pleasure on hearing his voice. At seventy-five, André Birron was considered to be one of the greatest jewelers, perhaps even *the* greatest jeweler, in the world. Known as the *grand seigneur* of the jewelry business, he had been her lifelong friend. He had always been there for her whenever she had needed him.

"It is a pleasure to hear your voice, Stephanie," he went on, "and it will be an even greater pleasure to see you. I am coming to New York in about ten days. For the Sotheby's auction. You plan to be there, I am certain of that."

"I do. And I hope you'll have time for dinner, André. Or lunch."

"Whichever, or both, *ma chérie.*" There was a small pause before the Frenchman asked, "You are going to bid on the White Empress, are you not?"

"Yes."

"I thought you would. You have always wanted to own it." He chuckled. "You have dreamed about it, Stephanie."

"Salivated, actually," she responded, laughing with him. "And how well you know me, André. But listen, who wouldn't want to own it? I consider the White Empress to be one of the most beautiful diamonds in the world."

"You are correct; however, *I* shall not bid on it, Stephanie. Out of deference to you, really. If I bid, I would only escalate the price exorbitantly, and there will be enough people doing that. And, of course, I do not have the love for this diamond that you do, although I can admire its beauty. Yes, it is a diamond you and only you should own."

"Thank you for letting me know you're not going to participate. I expect the bidding to go sky high. Don't you agree?"

"Yes, I do. The stone has not been on the market since the fifties, and so obviously there is a great deal of interest in it. That is the reason I telephoned you, Stephanie, *ma petite*, to inform you we shall not be bidding against each other, competing. But it will be my great honor to escort you to the auction, if you will permit me to do so."

"I'd love it, André, thank you."

"And after the auction we shall dine together, and it will be a grand celebration."

She laughed a soft, light laugh. "We'll be celebrating only if I get the White Empress, my dear old friend."

"There is no doubt in my mind that you will, Stephanie."

2

ALTHOUGH SHE KNEW EVERYTHING THERE WAS TO KNOW ABOUT HER favorite diamond, Stevie could not resist taking the Sotheby's catalogue out of her briefcase after she had said good-bye to André Birron and hung up.

Flipping open the catalogue, she quickly found the page where the White Empress was featured, and gazed for a moment or two at the photograph of the gem. The picture was excellent, but even so it did not do justice to the magnificent stone.

The White Empress. Stevie repeated the name to herself. It certainly deserved to be called that. It was so named because it was graded D-flawless and was therefore perfect. And as such it was colorless—pure white, brilliantly, blindingly white—hence the first portion of its name. Because it was extremely rare and very beautiful, and also categorized as a *grand* stone, the title of Empress had been chosen to complete its name.

Automatically, Stevie's eyes shifted to the left-hand page of the catalogue, and she scanned the text. Yet again she was reminded that the White Empress had started out as a 427-carat diamond of exceptionally fine color, and that it had been found in 1954 at the Premier Mines in South Africa.

This piece of rough was subsequently sold in 1956 to Harry Winston, the renowned American jeweler, as part of an eight-million-four-hundred-thousand-dollar parcel.

The largest stone Winston cut from this piece was a 128.25-carat D-flawless pear-shaped diamond, and it was this stone that retained the original name of White Empress. Harry Winston had the stone set as a pendant on an exquisite diamond necklace, designed specially, and then he had sold it that same year to a European industrialist.

Now, after forty years in the hands of one family, it was finally back on the market. Sotheby's would put it on the auction block at their auction rooms on York Avenue in New York at the beginning of December.

Stevie's eyes lingered on the photograph for a short while longer before she finally closed the catalogue and returned it to her briefcase. Her thoughts settled on André. Though he was not bidding on the stone, there were many others who *would* be bidding, and automatically the price would be driven up, as it usually was at these big auctions for important items.

It could skyrocket, she thought, sitting back in the chair, frowning. No, it *would* skyrocket. There was no doubt in her mind about that; she made the decision to stay in the bidding no matter what, since she was determined to acquire the stone whatever it cost.

Seven-figure numbers jumped around in her head. Six million dollars, seven million dollars . . . no, too low. Eight million, she speculated, her eyes narrowed in concentration. Still too low, she decided. Suddenly she was convinced the stone would be sold in the eight-figure category. Ten million, she said under her breath. Could it go as high as that?

At this moment Stevie knew that if she had to, she would pay that amount for the stone. She craved it, not for herself, of course, but for Jardine's in New York, which she had founded.

Once she owned the stone, she would hold on to it for a year or two, displaying it at exhibitions, making it the centerpiece of the store's permanent collection. She had no intention of cleaving it—cutting it—into several stones, or disposing of it immediately. It was quite obvious to her that the White Empress was a great investment, and in a variety of ways, not the least of which was the publicity the diamond would engender for Jardine's.

Certainly it would never decrease in value; it could only increase, in fact; and she knew she would have no problem selling it whenever she wished to do so. There were many rich men and women in the world who coveted the grand stones, some of whom were already her clients, and there would always be buyers for this most spectacular of diamonds. After all, in the business it was now considered to be a *historic* stone.

Owning the White Empress would be the crowning glory of Jardine's. This thought pleased her. She had started the American company eight years earlier, and although she had done so with Bruce Jardine's consent, his accord had been grudgingly given. Even today he barely acknowledged its existence.

The store on Fifth Avenue was an enormous success and had been from the very first day it opened. And so Stevie always felt justified in pushing for it, vindicated, in a sense, because the annual earnings were enormous, the profits burgeoning on a yearly basis.

When she had told her father-in-law that she wanted to take Jardine's, the Crown Jewellers of London, to New York's Fifth Avenue, he had blanched, gaping at her in astonishment. Naturally, he had balked at the idea. Right from the beginning he had predicted nothing but failure. She had had to use a great deal of charm and persuasiveness to get him finally to agree.

Stevie had realized immediately that he fought the idea of her moving to New York because he wanted to keep her by his side at the London store. Later, he had admitted that this was indeed the case. Put simply, he could no longer do without her. As he grew older, he was becoming more and more dependent on her at work.

When he had stopped ranting at her and calmed down, Stevie had pointed out that he had a grandson who was almost twenty-two, and very capable of taking her place at his side. A young man who couldn't wait to step into her shoes, in point of fact.

"Under your supervision, Nigel will do a fine job," she had reassured her father-in-law. Bruce knew as well as she that this was the truth, but he would not admit it, and once more he scotched the idea of opening a store in New York. Stevie had bided her time, worked on him in a gentle but persistent manner, and never lost a chance to point out to him how profitable the American branch could be.

"But I'll miss you, Stephanie," Bruce had murmured one afternoon, weeks after she had first presented her plans for Jardine's of New York. Those few muttered words had told her that however reluctant he was to do it, he was, nonetheless, going to give her his support. This he did, although he never ceased to remind her that it was against his better judgment.

That had happened in 1987; one year later, in 1988, the Fifth Avenue store had opened its doors. And for the first time in more than twenty years she had found herself living in the city where she had been born. She had moved to London at the age of fourteen, after her mother had married Derek Rayner. Even though she had visited New York, it was a foreign city to her. Within the short space of a few weeks, Manhattan was under her skin, and she felt comfortable, at home.

Stevie rose and walked over to the hearth, where she threw another log onto the fire, and then sat in a chair, leaned back, and closed her eyes. It seemed to her that her mind was full of the past today, perhaps because it was November the twenty-seventh. A very special date in her memory. Her wedding day. If Ralph Jardine had lived, this would have been their thirtieth anniversary.

She had never remarried. Some of her friends thought this was odd, but she didn't, no, not at all. It was really very simple. She had never met anyone she cared about enough to marry. No, that was not strictly true, she corrected herself. After Ralph's death she *had* loved another man once, for a brief time, long ago. Marriage had never come into play, at least not from his standpoint, but it had from hers. She knew she would have married him in a flash if he had asked her. He never had. It wasn't meant to be, she told herself, as she had done over and over again for years. Some things just weren't meant to happen; and, anyway, you couldn't have everything in life.

But we believe we can when we're young, she suddenly thought. When we're young we're so certain of our invincibility, our immortality. We're full of *ourselves*, blown up with ourselves, our power, our strength. We're just so *sure* of it all, so *sure* we can mold life to our will, make it bend whichever way we want. But we can't, that's not the way it is. Life gets at us all in one way or another. It mangles us, brings us down, causes us so much pain. It's the great leveler, the ultimate equalizer.

Still, my life's not been so bad, she reminded herself, looking at the positives, as she always did. Her children had turned out relatively well; at least, none of them was drug addicted or soaked in alcohol. And she had built herself a career out of nothing. After all, she had not been gifted with some sort of creative talent to use as a springboard into success. All she had was a practical nature, a steady, levelheaded temperament, and a good head for figures and business, as it had turned out.

She had once said this to André. "But you also know the diamonds, *chérie*. Ralph taught you almost everything he knew about the stones," the French jeweler had exclaimed, looking at her in surprise. Vaguely, she heard André's voice coming to her from a long distance, from the past. "You have a good idea, Stephanie. Go to Bruce. You will see; he will listen to you. The argument you have is a strong one. *Valid*. Indeed, it is a necessity."

Her thoughts leapt backward in time, back to the year 1976, and in her mind's eye she could see Bruce Jardine as he had been then. Tall, dark, good-looking in a saturnine way. But as stubborn and rigid as always. An unbending man.

How well she remembered his scornful expression, his mirthless laugh when she had told him she wanted to work. And at Jardine's, at that.

Before he could answer her, she added in a quiet voice that she wanted him to train her to run the company.

He had stared at her speechlessly, disbelievingly, all those years ago, and then he had asked her if she had taken leave of her senses.

Twenty years ago. Yet sometimes it seemed like only yesterday. She had been a young widow of twenty-six that summer; it was exactly three years after Ralph's bungled operation for an appendicitis. Her rage about this shocking tragedy had dissipated with the passing of time, and yet, when she least expected it, she would feel a spurt of anger and dismay about her husband's unnecessary death.

As it turned out, Ralph had not had appendicitis at all, but a perforated peptic ulcer. The surgeon had not recognized the trouble on the operating table. He had performed the appendectomy, but had not made a second incision to reach and repair the perforation. Peritonitis had advanced to cause the sepsis that had killed Ralph. Everyone knew it was a death that should never have happened.

With his son Ralph gone so unexpectedly, Bruce was now the only Jardine in the family business. His older brother, Malcolm, had retired several years earlier because of ill health, and Bruce was suddenly carrying the burden of Jardine's entirely alone.

And then, without any warning, he was struck down with a heart attack in February 1976; when he finally recovered, he was debilitated, and panicked.

Stevie had instantly recognized the latter, and had understood the reason for his nervousness. Young though she was at the time, she had a great deal of insight into people, knew what made them tick, what motivated them to do the things they did. In a sudden flash, and with genuine clarity of vision, she realized what she must do, what the solution to Bruce's problem was.

She was the solution.

And so she had taken André's advice and gone to see her father-in-law on a warm Thursday afternoon in July, arriving at his office in the Bond Street store unannounced. He had been startled and put out by her unprecedented visit, but being a gentleman of the old school, and courteous, he had invited her into his inner sanctum.

"Teach me the business, train me," she had said earnestly. "I'm the only Jardine you have right now. Nigel and the twins are still little boys. What will happen to the company if you have another heart attack? Or get sick? Or die?"

Startled by the bluntness of her words, he had looked affronted. And he had stared at her askance, for a moment at a loss for words in the face of her breathtaking directness.

Swiftly she had gone on to explain. "Look, nobody wants to

think of his own mortality, or think about dying, I know that. But *you* have to, you *must*. Ralph always said you were the most intelligent man he knew. He told me you were extremely clever, a genius really, and clearheaded. So think clearly now. Think *unemotionally*. You need someone you can trust, a person who could run the company if ever you were incapacitated. And it must be someone who has your grandsons' interests at heart. Since I'm their mother, that's me. Obviously. You need *me*. Anyway, face up to it, I'm the only Jardine available."

Bruce Jardine had seen the rightness of her words. She *was* the only adult Jardine he could turn to, and therefore she was the only solution to his very real dilemma. Also, her sincerity, eagerness, and enthusiasm had convinced him that she really did want to work for him and learn the business. And so he had taken her on as his junior assistant, hoping she would not disappoint him.

"You've got to love this business if you're going to be a success at it," he would tell her repeatedly during the first years she worked at Jardine's, and Stevie quickly discovered she did love it, every facet of it.

She loved the diamonds particularly, and the other gems and the creative side of the jewelry business. Yet it was the intricacies of the financial and corporate side that fascinated her. Within the first six months of working at Jardine's, she displayed a talent for figures plus business acumen as well. Bruce had been pleasantly surprised.

It was only natural that she became indispensable to her father-in-law. Bruce Jardine, once her deadly enemy, eventually came around to making his peace with her. He recognized her considerable attributes, her talent, her genuine ability, and her willingness to work hard for long hours. As the months passed, he came to respect her. And he depended on her more and more.

One day, after she had been at Jardine's for five years, the animosity and contentiousness she had come to expect simply ceased to exist.

Alfreda never became one of her admirers. On the other hand, Bruce's wife had apparently realized the validity of her husband's moves; she well understood that Stevie was the one person they could trust as the mother of their grandchildren, their heirs. And so she had kept a civil tongue in her head and stayed out of her daughter-in-law's way. Alfreda had died in 1982, almost fifteen years ago, but right up to the day of her death she had disliked Stevie, had never shown her any affection or made even the smallest friendly gesture.

Rising, walking back to the desk, Stevie bent forward, picked up her wedding photograph, and peered at it intently for a moment or two. How young she and Ralph had looked. But then, they had been young, she most especially. *I was just a little girl, only sixteen,* she thought. *A child. Why, I was younger than Chloe is now.*

Oh, Ralph, who would have believed it? Believed that your father would take me into the business? Or that one day I would be head of Jardine's on both sides of the Atlantic? She could not help thinking that life, the great leveler, was also so very unpredictable. *I couldn't have accomplished all that I have without friends, good friends, and most especially André Birron.* She knew that André had taught her as much as Bruce ever had about the jewelry business. He had been her mentor in certain ways, and a genuine friend, almost like a father.

André had always given her the best advice, the soundest. When she was twenty-seven, she fell in love again, after four years of widowhood. She discovered she was pregnant a year later, and it was to André she had turned. She had flown to Paris to see him, to confide in him, although, being wary by nature, she had done so only to a degree. She had merely alluded to the identity of her lover, the father of her unborn child. Even before she had finished her sentence, André had held up his hand as if in warning.

"Do not tell me who he is. I do not want to know. Remember this, my Stephanie. Confide a secret to one person and it is a secret no longer," the sage old Frenchman had cautioned.

And so she had kept her own counsel always, for this was her natural inclination. No one had ever known who her lover had been, or even tried to guess the man's real identity. Not even Chloe knew who her father was.

Chloe. Stevie's expression changed, became softer as she thought of her eighteen-year-old daughter. Now *she* was a D-flawless diamond. Quite perfect.

Stevie suddenly broke into a chuckle. Well, not really. Her daughter was only almost perfect, thank goodness. No one wanted a paragon of virtue. They were no fun, and usually too good to be true.

Chloe would be arriving later that afternoon, hopefully in time for dinner, and they would enjoy a cozy evening together. Tomorrow her mother and stepfather would be driving up from Manhattan to spend Thanksgiving Day with them, and the rest of the holiday weekend. She was looking forward to it, just as she knew Chloe was.

Derek Rayner had been knighted by the queen some years before, and he and her mother were now Sir Derek and Lady Rayner. As had been predicted long ago, he was now the greatest classical actor on the English stage, and at sixty-eight a living legend. He had been good to her mother and to her and her children.

Derek and her mother were childless, and so he played the role of father and grandfather to the hilt. But his love for them all was very genuine, and he adored Chloe.

Her son Miles was driving to Connecticut with the Rayners. He was her favorite son, if the truth be known, although she always tried to hide this fact from the others. She loathed playing favorites amongst her children.

Miles was a talented artist and a brilliant set designer. Currently he was living in New York, where he was designing the stage sets for a Broadway play. Unlike his brother Nigel and his twin, Gideon, he had never shown any desire to go into Jardine's, although with his artist's eye he had always appreciated the beauty of the jewels and the other objects of art Jardine's made.

Despite his lack of interest in working in the family business, his grandfather had insisted he become a director since he was a major shareholder in the company. He had done so immediately. Jardine's was his inheritance, and it had always been an important part of his life; his mother had seen to that.

It was Gideon who was the true jeweler in the family; Stevie had recognized that when he was a child. He was a talented, indeed gifted, lapidary, and he had inherited his father's love of stones, most especially diamonds. Like Ralph, he was an expert when it came to cutting stones, and as one of the chief lapidaries at Jardine's, he was involved in the creation of the exquisite jewels that the Crown Jewellers had been renowned for over the centuries.

Nigel, ever the businessman, and the spitting image of Bruce in so many different ways, ran the business end of the company, under her direction.

But Nigel wanted it all for himself.

Stevie was well aware of this these days. There were even moments when she thought her eldest son was plotting her departure from the company, planning her fall from grace.

Now she expelled a long sigh as she strolled back to the fireplace. She stood leaning against the mantelpiece, her thoughts focused on Nigel.

She had no real evidence to go on, it was just plain old gut instinct that told her that her son was against her. For a long time now she had seen Nigel for what he was . . . very much the way Bruce had been when he was a younger man—cold, calculating, controlling, and very ambitious.

There was nothing wrong with ambition as long as it was focused in the right direction. She was the first to admit this. But it was somewhat ridiculous of her son to be ambitious at her expense. After all, the business would be his one day. He would share it with his brothers equally, of course, but he would be running it as the eldest of the three and the undoubted business brain.

She wished she could shake off the worrying suspicion that Nigel wanted her to trip up in order for him to justify taking over from her in London. And indeed, New York as well.

Fat chance of that, she muttered. Bruce would never permit it. Her father-in-law was eighty-two now, and semiretired after some terrible attacks of gout, which had plagued him for years. But he was as alert as ever, not a bit senile, and very spry when he was free of his crippling ailment. She was very well aware that he cared about her, even though he did not show it very often.

Furthermore, and perhaps more to the point, he trusted her implicitly when it came to running the company. She had earned that trust, had proved to him time and again that she not only knew what she was doing but that she was brilliant at it. No, Bruce would not tolerate Nigel's machinations, what he would term "youthful insubordination." And he would be on her side.

Rousing herself from her thoughts about her eldest son, Stevie hurried out of the study and headed along the second floor landing. Of medium height and slim, Stephanie Jardine was an attractive woman, with a head of dark curls, light gray-green eyes, and a well-articulated face. High cheekbones and a slender nose gave her a look of distinction; she was elegant in an understated way, dressed in a loden-green wool pants suit and sweater that brought out the green lights in her eyes.

Stevie took the stairs at a rapid pace, realizing that she had wasted a great deal of time dwelling on the past and Ralph, living through her memories both good and bad. She had guests arriving the next day, and even though they were family, everything had to be well prepared for them nonetheless. Her mother, in particular, had very high standards and was accustomed to a great deal of luxury as the wife of a famous star of stage and screen.

As she reached the great hall, the grandfather clock standing in the corner began to strike. It was exactly six o'clock. Chloe was due to arrive in an hour, and a smile touched Stevie's eyes at this thought. She could not wait to see her daughter.

Somewhere nearby a door was banging, and she felt a rush of cold air blowing down the great hall. It seemed to be coming from the direction of the sun room, and she went through the archway that led to this area of the house.

The solarium, as it was usually called, was long with many windows; two sets of French doors led out to the covered porch that stretched the length of the back facade of the house. One of the doors had sprung open and it was swinging back and forth on its hinges, banging against a wooden chair.

She went to close it, then paused at the door and peered out. It was a dark night, with a black sky empty of stars. A corridor of bright lamplight streamed out from the solarium, illuminating the porch and its stone balustrade beyond. It diminished the darkness.

Stevie went outside, as she often did at this hour, loving the tranquility, the silence of the countryside. It was so pleasing to her after the din of New York, and especially so at nighttime.

Her eyes scanned the sky and the landscape surrounding her. She noticed then that the mist of earlier had settled in the well of the garden. It was heavier now, and it hugged the grass, swirled in thick patches, obscuring the stone benches, the fountain, and the flagged rose garden. How eerie everything looked tonight, she thought. Stevie swung around and made a swift retreat back to the house.

As she stepped inside, a strange feeling swept over her. It was a premonition really . . . and it made her catch her breath. The feeling was similar to the one she had experienced that afternoon, but this time it was much stronger, more forceful.

She threw it off. And then Stevie Jardine laughed at herself again, as she had earlier, and shook her head. She, who had never believed in portents or omens and was totally unsuperstitious, was actually having presentiments of trouble. Ridiculous. She laughed again.

Some months later Stevie was to remember these strange feelings, and wonder.

3

Everyone said she was special.

Chloe herself, when she was old enough to understand such things, did not agree, although she did know she was different. She was different because she was illegitimate.

She bore the name Jardine because that was her mother's name, but she had long understood that she was not actually *of* the Jardine family.

Her mother had never hidden her illegitimacy from her, and when she was eight years old she had carefully explained the details of her birth to her. It was for this reason that Chloe had always accepted the facts in the most natural way. So did her three brothers. Even Old Bruce, as she and Miles called him, seemed to tolerate her, and obviously he did not object to her using his name. Nor did he seem to mind that she called him Grandfather; as far as they both were concerned he was exactly that, and he had always treated her the same way he did his biological grandsons.

When she was a small girl she hadn't wanted to be different or special. This only confused her, made her feel self-conscious. She just wanted to be like everyone else—ordinary.

Once, when she was about ten years old, she had asked Miles why people said she was special. He had looked at her closely through his piercing blue eyes, and smiled his warm, gentle smile. "Because you're such a happy little sprite, Pumpkin, all airiness and golden light. You remind everyone of the summer and sunshine . . . even in winter, and you're brimming with laughter, full of gaiety. That's the first reason—your effervescent personality. Secondly, you're a very pretty girl, who's beautiful inside as well as out. And finally, you're . . . well, you're an old soul, Pumpkin."

She had frowned at him, instantly picked up on this last thing. "What does that mean, Miles? What's an old soul?"

"Someone who's been here before, who seems to have a knowledge beyond her years, who is wise . . . "

"Oh." She had pondered this for a second or two and then asked, "Is that good?"

Miles had burst out laughing, his eyes crinkling at the corners, and he had rumpled her hair affectionately. "Yes, I think so, and be glad you're all the things you are, little sister. There are too few of you in this ugly world we live in."

Miles was her favorite brother. He had always been easier to be around than his twin, Gideon, and their elder brother, Nigel. Miles was never too busy for her, even though he was nine years older than she.

Despite the fact that Miles had explained why she was special, to the best of his ability anyway, she never thought of herself in that way. She was merely different, that was all, and then only because of the circumstances of her birth. There was nothing more to it than that.

Chloe had never felt embarrassed or awkward about her illegitimacy, nor had she given much thought to it when she was growing up, other than occasionally to wonder about her father. On her birth certificate his name was given as John Lane. She wasn't even sure if this was his real name, since her mother was so secretive about him.

Recently, thoughts of her father had insinuated themselves into her mind, and she had been besieged by questions, things she wanted to ask her mother but didn't dare.

Whenever she had broached the subject of her paternity in the last couple of years, her mother had simply repeated what she had always said: John Lane, her father, had been killed in a car crash.

Because her mother had always looked extremely upset, even on the verge of tears, when they had these discussions, Chloe never did probe further. Of late, she had needed to know more about her father, wanted her mother to describe him to her, tell her other things about him, give her an inkling of his personality and character. And so, on the drive up to Connecticut, she had wondered if she could question her mother at some point during the Thanksgiving weekend.

Now Chloe stood in front of the mirror on the dressing table in her bedroom, staring at herself but not really focusing. Instead, she was thinking of her mother, whom she had always adored. Chloe was absolutely certain there was no one quite like Stevie Jardine. Her mother was a true original, loving, generous spirited, and kind. She usually gave everyone the benefit of the doubt and tried always to see the best in people. Even in Old Bruce, who was such an ogre.

Her mother had brought her up well, given her all the right standards; Old Bruce had once told her that. Her mother and she were very close, pals really, and so many of her classmates at Brearley envied her. "Your mother's so cool," her best friend, Justine Seawell, was always telling her, and Justine was correct. Stevie was more like an older sister in so many ways, and yet she was a tough disciplinarian. Chloe had to abide by the rules at all times.

Chloe suddenly knew she wouldn't be able to summon up the nerve to talk to her mother during the family weekend; it would upset her if she brought up John Lane, dead more than eighteen years. It occurred to her that she could talk to her grandfather, Derek Rayner. She was close to him, and he had always treated her as an adult, even when she was a small child. Derek could enlighten her, if anyone could.

With this decision made she felt more cheerful, and the acute worry she had been feeling miraculously abated. Leaning forward, Chloe picked up a silver hairbrush and smoothed it over her shoulder-length dark hair, then adjusted the cowl neckline of her burgundy cable-knit tunic.

Stepping away from the mirror, she was able to get a better view of herself, a full-length view. She decided she liked the way she looked in the tunic with its matching leggings; she was five feet seven inches tall, and the outfit made her appear taller and more willowy than she already was. This pleased her. After spraying on a light floral scent, she put on a pair of gold-coin earrings, left her bedroom, and ran downstairs.

When she had arrived at the house half an hour earlier, her mother had been making a beeline for the kitchen, and so Chloe headed in that direction.

She found Stevie sitting at the big oak refectory table talking to Cappi Mondrell, their housekeeper and cook. Both women stopped chatting and glanced across at her as she came in.

"Hi, Chloe!" Cappi exclaimed, smiling broadly, obviously glad to see her.

"Hello, Cap!" Chloe responded, and rushed over, gave the housekeeper an affectionate hug. Cappi had been with them for eight years, and was like a member of the family; Chloe was devoted to her, and it was very clear the older woman loved the eighteen-year-old.

Wrinkling her nose, Chloe said, "Do I smell my favorite dish cooking?"

"You do indeed. Chicken in the pot for my favorite girl."

"You spoil me, Cappi."

"I know, but it gives me such pleasure," the housekeeper shot back, laughter echoing in her voice.

"You look lovely in that outfit," Stevie said with a glowing smile. She couldn't help thinking that her daughter was beginning to look so very grown-up all of a sudden. And she really was a beautiful girl with her shining dark eyes, luxuriant hair, and creamy skin.

"Thanks, Mom. You don't look bad yourself. Positively blooming, as I said when I first got here."

"Thank you, darling."

"When are the others arriving?" Chloe asked.

"Tomorrow morning, around noon."

"Is Miles bringing his girlfriend?"

Stevie was so startled, she sat back, surprised. "I don't think so," she answered. "He would have mentioned it. Anyway, I didn't know there was a girlfriend. At least, not anyone special." She stared at Chloe intently, and when her daughter didn't answer, she pressed, "Well, is there?"

Chloe shrugged, leaned against the table, and said hesitantly, "Not sure, Mom." She pursed her lips. "Maybe. He's been seeing a lot of Allison Grainger, but he's been really closemouthed about it."

"Who's Allison Grainger?" Stevie asked, a dark brow lifting quizzically.

"The costume designer who's working on the play with him. You've met her, Mom. She's got red hair and lots of freckles."

"Oh, yes, I remember her now. She's rather pretty." Stevie's eyebrows drew together in a frown. "Is it serious, do you think?"

"I doubt it," Chloe responded, and began to laugh. "I guess it will be for about another week or two. And then it'll probably be over. You know Miles and Gideon, Mom, they're very alike when it comes to women."

"What do you mean?"

"When they fall for a woman they get very intense for a few weeks, it's finally the great love at long last. But it quickly peters out. And they always like to surround themselves with extra girls, just in case. And anyway, Miles says there's safety in numbers."

Stevie smiled; how well her daughter knew her brothers. "He's coming alone apparently, so it may well be over already."

"I wouldn't be surprised," Chloe murmured, and then looked from her mother to Cappi. "Did I interrupt anything? You were very deeply engrossed."

"No, we were just planning the menus, going over a few things for the weekend. And actually we were just about finished when you came into the kitchen."

Cappi said, "I'd better set the table for —"

"Oh, don't bother," Stevie cut in. "Let's eat in the little sitting room tonight. It's much cozier. Two trays in front of the fire will do us fine, thanks, Cappi."

Later that evening they were halfway through dessert when Chloe put down her fork, looked at her mother, and said, "There's something I want to talk to you about, Mom."

"Yes, darling," Stevie said, swiftly glancing at her daughter, noting the sudden tenseness of her voice. "Tell me."

"It's about next year, Mom. I mean about going to college after I graduate from Brearley. And, you see . . ." Chloe's voice trailed off, and she gazed at her mother, biting her lip.

"What is it, Chloe?"

"I really don't want to go . . . I mean go to college."

Stevie sat up a little straighter and stared at her daughter. "Do you mean you don't want to go to college here in America? Or college anywhere?"

"Correct, Mom! I don't want to go to college."

"Not even to Oxford? You talked about that so much, and you always sounded very excited. Why, only a few months ago you said you couldn't wait to go there."

"I know. But I've changed my mind. I'd prefer to go into the jewelry business, Mom. I want to work at Jardine's."

Stevie was genuinely surprised by this announcement, even though she had always known her daughter liked the store in New York. She said cautiously, "I like the idea of you working with me at Jardine's, but I still want you to attend university. You can come into the business with me when you're twenty-one or twenty-two."

Chloe shook her head vehemently. "Honestly, Mom, I really don't want to go to college. What's the point, when I want to go to work. Surely you of all people understand that. You work like a dog and enjoy every minute of it."

"That's true, I do. And I understand everything you're saying, but nevertheless, I would like you to finish your education. It's important, Chloe."

"You didn't go to college."

"I wish I had."

"What could you have learned at college? About the jewelry business, I mean. Nothing. And look how successful you've been. You're a terrific businesswoman, you know all about diamonds and other precious stones. You're . . . well . . . Gideon says you're a legend in the business. Not going to college didn't hurt you, or stop you from becoming what you are."

"True. But then again, I learned a lot from Ralph in the early years of our marriage. And later I had Bruce to teach me. Working with him was like going to several universities. He was the greatest professor there was, and so was Uncle André. I learned a lot from him as well."

"And I can learn a lot from Gideon in London. That's where I want to go, Mom, I want to go to London and work with Gideon at the Bond Street store."

Stevie was taken aback by this statement, and for a moment she made no response. Then she said slowly, a little hesitantly, "But why wouldn't you want to work with me in New York? I don't understand . . ." She did not finish her sentence, just sat staring at her daughter through baffled eyes.

Chloe said quickly, "Oh, Mom, I'd love to work with you in New York. Eventually. But I want to start out in London because Gideon is such a great lapidary and he could teach me so much. And besides, the London workshops are much bigger than the one in New York. I just think I'd get better training there, and Old Bruce is there. I mean, I know he's semiretired and all that, but he does go to the store twice a week, and, well, I mean, he could teach me a lot, just like he taught you."

"I see."

"Are you angry, Mom?"

Stevie shook her head.

"Yes, you are, I can tell. Please don't be cross with me, Mom. Please."

"I'm not angry; really, I'm not, Chloe."

"Then what?"

"Disappointed, I suppose."

"Because I don't want to go to college?"

"Yes, there's that. But I'm also disappointed that you don't want to work with me in New York. Of course, the workshops *are* much larger in London, that's true. But ours is not so bad, you know. And we do have Marc Sylvester and several wonderful lapidaries at the Fifth Avenue store. They could teach you just as much as you'd learn in London."

"But I want to learn from Gideon."

"I know you've always been close to him."

"I'm closer to Miles actually, Mom, but I love Gideon and he's a good teacher. He's taught me a few things about jewelry already when I've gone to see him at the workshops during vacations."

"He's certainly patient and painstaking, and a bit of a perfectionist, so I have to believe you when you say he's a good teacher. Yes, I can see that aspect of him." Stevie gave her daughter a long, speculative look, and then asked quietly, "Have you discussed this with Gideon already?"

Chloe shook her head. "Oh, no, Mommy, I haven't! I wouldn't do that, not before talking to you." Chloe leaned forward, her young face expectant and eager. "Can I go, then?"

"I don't know. I'll have to think about this. It's a big step for you, going to live in London. Alone."

"But Mother, I wouldn't be alone. I've got two brothers and a sister-in-law there, plus Old Bruce. And my grandparents. Blair and Derek would keep an eye on me for you."

"*If* I agreed, and it is an *if*, I'd want someone to do much more than keep an eye on you, Chloe. You'd have to live with a member of the family."

Chloe was immediately crestfallen on hearing this, and it showed on her face. "You mean I can't live in your flat in Eaton Square?"

"Certainly not. There's no one there to look after you."

"There's Gladys."

"Gladys comes in only a few times a week to clean. No, no,

that would be out of the question, *if* I agreed to this plan of yours."

"I could live with Gideon. He'd love it."

"Nonsense. He'd hate it. A single man of twenty-seven who has legions of women friends, according to you, wouldn't want his baby sister for a roommate. It would cramp his style no end."

"Nigel would have me. He's *married,* and Tamara likes me a lot."

"Yes, I know she does. But once again, it wouldn't be suitable. They're practically newlyweds, they wouldn't want you around."

"Oh, Mom, they have two kids!"

Stevie bit back a smile, amused by Chloe's logic, then she said, "Even so, a young couple like Nigel and Tamara don't need the responsibility of looking after you. They have their hands full as it is."

"I wouldn't want to live at Old Bruce's house in Wilton Crescent, if that's what you're thinking. That place is so gloomy, it would be like being in prison. You wouldn't do that to me, would you, Mom?"

"I haven't agreed that you can go, Chloe."

"Grandma would let me live with her and Derek, and you know they love me . . . a lot," Chloe volunteered.

"Yes, they do. But you're putting the cart before the horse. I have to think about this matter, and at great length. I'm certainly not going to make any hasty decisions."

"When will you decide?"

"I don't know."

"But, Mommy —"

"No buts, darling," Stevie interrupted. "You've told me what *you'd* prefer to do, and now *I* must give it some thought. I want you to think about it as well, Chloe. Think about what you'd be missing by not going to university. Think about those three years at Oxford and all that they would mean. Not just the education you'd get, but the fun you'd have, and the people you'd meet. Friends you make at university are your friends for the rest of your life. And I must admit, Chloe, I'm a bit baffled, you were always so keen about studying at Oxford. What happened?"

"I've changed my mind, Mom."

"Promise me you'll think about this."

"Oh, all right," Chloe muttered, looking suddenly put out.

Stevie glanced at her quickly and said in a sharp tone of voice, "Don't sound so grudging about it, Chloe. It doesn't become you one little bit."

Chloe flushed at this chastisement, mild as it was, and bit her lip. Then, pushing the tray table away, she jumped up and sat next to Stevie on the sofa.

Taking hold of her mother's hand, she squeezed it, then reached up and kissed her on the cheek. "Don't be angry with me, Mommy."

Observing her daughter's worried expression and detecting the concern in her eyes, Stevie murmured softly, "I'm not angry, Chloe, but I do want to do what's best for you, and you must try to understand that. After all, *you've* obviously been thinking about this for some time, whilst *I've* just heard about it . . . so please, give me a few days to get used to the idea. And let me talk to Gideon. And my mother and Derek."

Chloe nodded and her face brightened considerably as she exclaimed, "So you're definitely not saying no?"

"No, of course not . . ." A faint smile surfaced on Stevie's face. "I'm saying . . . *maybe*."

Stevie had learned long before that when she couldn't sleep it was far better to get up and keep busy, especially if she had a problem on her mind. To her way of thinking, it was much easier to worry when she was upright and moving around than when she was lying down.

She and Chloe had both gone upstairs to bed at eleven. Stevie had fallen asleep at once, lulled into a deep slumber by the two glasses of red wine she had drunk at dinner.

Then she had awakened suddenly several hours later, at three in the morning. Sleep had proved elusive thereafter; at four o'clock she had slipped out of bed, taken a shower, dressed in a pair of blue jeans and a sweater, and gone downstairs.

After making a cup of coffee and a slice of toast, Stevie had walked around the house, collecting her many orchid plants. These she had taken to the plant room next to the laundry; carefully, methodically, she had watered them individually in the big sink, letting the water run through each one, then slowly drain away.

Everyone knew she loved orchids, and so she frequently received them as gifts. In consequence, her collection was quite large; two or three dozen were scattered throughout this house, and there were more in her New York apartment.

Mostly they were various species of the Phalaenopsis, with white or yellow blooms, plus pale, blush-pink cymbidiums. She also collected the miniature slipper orchid with pale green or dark brown blooms, and the dark brownish-wine–colored Sharry Baby with its tiny flowers and delicious chocolate scent.

But of them all her real favorites were the white and yellow Phalaenopsis, and she did very well with them, making them last for months. The house was an ideal spot for them to grow, cool, and full of soft, muted light most of the time.

Now Stevie lifted a pot containing a yellow-blooming Phalaenopsis and carried it through into the sun room, where she returned it to its place.

Stepping back, her head on one side, she admired it for a

moment, thinking how beautiful it looked, so elegant against the white walls and standing on the dark wood surface of the antique chest. This was positioned in a corner between two windows, and the orchid had the most perfect light there.

Stevie moved around the house for almost another hour, carrying the plants back to their given spots in different rooms, and then she poured herself a mug of coffee and went back to the solarium.

She stood in front of the French windows, warming her hands on the hot mug, sipping the coffee occasionally. Her eyes scanned the sky. It was cold and leaden, and she could tell already that it would be a gray day, bleak, overcast, sunless. Even the landscape had a bleak look to it, the trees bereft of leaves, the lawn covered with a sprinkling of white frost. Thanksgiving Day 1996 had not dawned very brightly.

Stevie turned away from the window. Seating herself on one of the large overstuffed sofas, she put the mug on the table in front of her and leaned back, resting her head against the soft cushion covered in a faded antique chintz.

What to do? What to do about Chloe? She was not sure. In fact, she was very uncertain, really. Her daughter had surprised and disappointed her when she had abruptly announced she did not want to go to university, most especially since she had been so gung-ho about attending Oxford. Stevie had always wanted Chloe to have a good education, to graduate with a college degree. The last thing she had expected was to hear her daughter express the desire to work at Jardine's. There had never been any real indication on Chloe's part that she was keen on the jewelry business, other than a passing interest in the New York store.

Admit it, she's hurt you badly, wanting to work in London, a small voice at the back of her head whispered. And yes, that was the truth. Chloe's words had been like a slap in the face.

Stevie knew that Chloe could learn everything in New York. There was no need for her to go to London. Jardine's was the one store left on Fifth Avenue that had its own workshop on the second floor, and it was excellent. Marc Sylvester, her top lapidary, was brilliant, and Chloe could learn as much from him as she could from her brother Gideon, or Gilbert Drexel, the chief lapidary at the London shop.

Am I being selfish, wanting to keep her with me? Stevie asked herself. Possessive? Overprotective? If she was honest with herself, she had to admit it was a little bit of all three.

But then again, what mother didn't want to keep her daughter by her side, and for as long as possible? And if not by her side, then at least in the same country. What Chloe wanted was not only to leave the nest, but fly away to distant shores.

Stevie let out a long sigh, thinking of her daughter. Chloe was only just eighteen, and she was so much younger in many different ways, more like fifteen, in fact. For one thing, she had led a very sheltered life, particularly when they had resided in London. She had been surrounded by family . . . her three brothers, and her grandparents, and had attended Lady Eden's exclusive private school for young ladies as a day girl. The harsh everyday world had hardly penetrated her consciousness.

Even in the eight years they had lived in New York, Chloe's life had been somewhat cloistered. She'll never make it on her own, Stevie thought. She'll be overwhelmed. She's too sensitive, too delicate, and just far too young to be away from home, away from me. I'm going to say no. I must. I'm not going to let her go to England. She can go a year from now only if she is enrolled at Oxford.

It seemed to Stevie at that precise moment that a load had been lifted from her shoulders. Just making the decision was a blessed relief. The tight pain in her chest, which had been like a steel band since four o'clock that morning, was beginning to ease at last.

4

No matter how busy she was, Stevie always found time at some point each day to write in her daily journal. And so that morning, while she waited for her mother, Derek, and Miles to arrive, she opened her current diary and wrote: *Thanksgiving Day 1996: Connecticut,* then sat staring at the page, lost in her thoughts.

She had kept a journal for years, most of her life, and there were volumes of them locked away in a cupboard at the other side of the upstairs study, where she now sat at the desk.

Thirty-four years had been recorded in them since her mother had presented her with her first diary when she was twelve. That had been in 1962. It seemed very far away now; so much had happened to her in the intervening years. She had lived a lifetime and then some, or so it seemed to her.

Her first diary had had its own little lock and key and it had withstood the test of time very well; she had looked at it recently and been amazed that it had weathered the years so well. The paper was a bit yellowed at the edges, the ink faded on some pages, but that was the only damage, if you could even call it that.

On the whole, a miracle of preservation, Stevie thought, and put down her pen, sat back in the chair, her thoughts turning to her mother, who had also kept a diary most of her life. They had always been close, had had a symbiotic relationship when she was a child. Her father, Jerome Anderson, had not been the right husband for Blair, nor had he been a very good father, and this had brought her and her mother even closer together.

Newspaperman, ladies' man, bon vivant, and man-about-town, Jerry had not been cut out for family life, and that was exactly what her mother had craved. Beautiful, glamorous, international supermodel Blair Connors had wanted only to be a wife and mother. She was the success she was because of her face and figure, the way she dominated the catwalk and made love to the camera. It was certainly not because of drive or ambition. Even at the height of her career she had wanted to stay at home and cook, raise children, be a housewife, a mother, and a good wife to the right man. Domesticity was her idea of bliss.

Derek Rayner, English classical actor par excellence, handsome matinee idol and movie star, had seemed such an unlikely candidate for the role Blair had cast him in all those years ago. The wrong man, as far as Blair's friends were concerned.

But as it happened, he *had* been the right man, the perfect choice, the perfect mate. Blair and Derek had been married for over thirty years and still adored each other. Their only disappointment was that they had not had any children of their own. Perhaps that was one of the reasons they were inseparable, and Derek never went anywhere without his beautiful and accomplished wife.

Stevie was relieved they were coming to spend Thanksgiving with her. On the phone yesterday her mother had sounded worn out, which was unusual for her. She had mentioned that Derek was exhausted after twelve weeks on location making a movie in

Arizona, then looping at the studio in Los Angeles. The film assignment had come right on top of his long run in the Broadway revival of *Becket*. According to her mother, it was now essential that he get a good rest.

"No more work for a while," Blair had said. "He's really looking forward to the long weekend with you, Stevie, before we fly back to London next week," her mother had added, and Stevie was determined to make it a wonderful few days. She wanted her mother and Derek to have the great luxury of peace and quiet in comfortable surroundings, with lots of good food and rest. And certainly no pressure.

She thought suddenly of Chloe. She would have to have a talk with her later, warn her not to take all of her little problems to Derek. She had a tendency to pester him at times. Stevie supposed that was understandable, in that Derek was the closest thing to a father Chloe had ever had.

Certainly Bruce Jardine had been more like a grandfather. He was much older than Derek, less active, and decidedly crotchety a good part of the time. No wonder Miles and Chloe called him Old Bruce. He *was* such an old man in many ways; he had not aged well at all.

Stevie was aware that Chloe loved him, despite her protestations to the contrary and desire to cast him in the role of ogre or tyrant. As for Bruce, there was no doubt in Stevie's mind that Bruce Jardine loved the girl in return. He had shown her daughter too much favor, displayed too much kindness to her for it to be otherwise. Whilst this baffled Stevie occasionally, it nonetheless pleased her. Bruce had treated Chloe as a Jardine all of her young life, and Stevie would always be grateful to him for that.

Bruce was not an easy man to care about or even like, but she had grown quite attached to him over the years. They had worked well together in a very temperate climate for twenty years, and there had rarely been any display of temperament or outbursts of anger on his part. Most of the years had rolled by on a very even keel, it seemed to her now.

It struck Stevie that it might be a good idea to talk to Bruce about Nigel. She and Chloe were going to spend Christmas in London, and that would be the ideal time to unburden herself. *Unburden myself*, she thought in amazement. Do I really feel that strongly about Nigel's attitude? She sighed, thinking that perhaps she did.

Not only did she love her eldest son, she admired him no end, and there *was* a lot to admire. He was a clever, indeed brilliant young man with a great deal of talent and a good head on his shoulders. But he had a flaw, and it was a flaw that was fatal. He believed he knew better than anyone else, was convinced of the rightness of his ideas and beliefs, and he never took no for an answer, would brook no argument. He was far too stubborn and opinionated for his own good. His attitude verged on arrogance. It dismayed her that he could not compromise, that he was so rigid.

He was just like his grandfather. No, he's worse, she thought, and laughed a hollow little laugh. He *was* Bruce's clone. As Bruce had been when he was a younger man. Perhaps more so.

It would be hard to speak critically to Bruce about his clone. This brought a smile to Stevie's face. She wasn't going to talk to Bruce about her son's character, rather about her suspicion that he wanted to oust her from the company. If this were the case, Bruce would surely put a stop to his manipulations.

But then, she could do that herself. She could fire Nigel.

He was, after all, her *employee*.

He worked for *her*.

She was the managing director of Jardine's of London and president of Jardine's of New York, just as Bruce was chairman of the board. Nigel was a director of the company, as were his two brothers, and they would always be directors. That was their right, their inheritance.

But she could take Nigel's job away from him at any time if she so wished. It was as easy as that, just like snapping her fingers together.

No, not so easy, she reminded herself. He's my son, my first-born, I wouldn't want to hurt him, to humiliate him, or to destroy him. Besides, he's good at his job. The very best.

I simply have to make him toe the line, curb his ambition for the moment. He has to bide his time until I retire.

Stevie laughed out loud. Easier said than done when she was on the other side of the Atlantic . . . thousands of miles away.

Her mind swung to Gideon. Now, there was a son who was not one bit ambitious, at least not when it came to possessing the company and amassing power. All he wanted was to create flaw-less diamonds from the rough . . . make beautiful things. Gideon did worry her on a personal level, and she had been worried about him for some time now. He had not looked well, had seemed distracted, fretful, and impatient when she had seen him at the London showroom in late September. She remembered how pale and gloomy he had looked. In her opinion, he hadn't been himself since he had broken up with Margot Saunders. Had he cared for that young woman more than he'd let on? She would talk to Miles about his twin during the weekend.

Her face instantly changed, took on a warm glow, and her eyes brightened. Miles was her pride and joy, she admitted it freely . . . in the privacy of her thoughts.

And Miles would help to take Chloe in hand too; she could rely on him to do that. Chloe and Miles had always had an affin-ity for each other and he was good with his little sister. Unlike Gideon, who had considered her to be a bit of a nuisance. And now Chloe wanted to learn from her brother Gideon. Stevie shook her head. People were so very strange.

She had often thought how odd it was that although Miles and Gideon were identical twins and looked alike, when it came to their personalities and characters, they were as different as chalk and cheese.

Miles was so much lighter, more carefree, gentle, well balanced, and a genuine charmer. Conversely, his twin was introverted, stubborn—more like Nigel in that way—and a perfectionist who at times seemed ridiculously persnickety, almost old-maidish. And yet he could be generous to a fault, and he truly did have the soul of an artist. He loved anything and everything that was beautiful, be it a woman, a painting, a sculpture, a tree, a seascape, a garden, a priceless gemstone, or a piece of jewelry. And he had an extraordinary eye, refined and exquisite taste.

Picking up her pen, Stevie looked down at the page and realized she had put nothing on paper so far other than the day and where she was.

Slowly she began to write, and when she had filled two pages, she screwed on the top of her fountain pen, took the diary in her hands, leaned back in the chair, and read it.

Thanksgiving Day, 1996
Connecticut

When I think of my children and the things they do, it seems to me they are like strangers. Except for Miles. But then, he is the child of my heart, so like me in so many ways. Of course, I love them all, but he has always been special to me since he was small. I wonder, are all mothers like I am? Do they favor one child more than the others? I'm sure that it is so, but it's hard to ask anyone that kind of . . . leading question. And do the children know? Do they detect it, sense it, feel it? Do they know there is one who is the real favorite of the mother?

Each of my children is different. Yet I can see traits in them that are mine. And some are Ralph's. There are traits in them that come from Bruce. Fortunately, none of them have inherited anything of their grandmother, Alfreda, and for that I can honestly say I'm thankful. She was not a nice woman; she was cold, repressed, and bitter. She never had a kind word for me or anyone she considered to be her inferior. It is their other grandmother who shows up in them. My mother. Chloe has inherited her beauty, her willowy figure, her pleasing personality, and her desire to please; Miles has inherited her sense of humor and geniality.

I love them. I love all of my children. It's the truth, I do. Maybe too much. And yet somewhere along the way I suppose I hurt them, damaged them without meaning to do so. But then we're all damaged goods, aren't we? Life damages us, people damage us, we even damage ourselves. I must have caused them pain and heartache. And hurt their feelings. We do that so often to those we love the most without even realizing it or meaning to. And perhaps I did neglect them at times when I was caught up with work and travel. But I never stopped loving them.

I think of them as my children. But, of course, they're not children, not anymore. They're adults. Grown-ups. People. Other people, not my children. They're so different in so many ways. Strangers. Sometimes, anyway. Even Chloe is grown-up all of a sudden, knowing her own mind, hell-bent on getting her own way.

Soon I'm going to stop being a mother, stop thinking of myself as such. Instead I'll be . . . ? I'll be . . . just there for them. If they need me. Is that possible? How do you stop being a mother? How do you stop worrying about them? Caring about them? Perhaps you don't. How DO you stop being a mother? Can anyone tell me that?

Will I fare better with my grandchildren? I asked myself that question in the middle of the night, when I woke up with such suddenness. I will be a good grandmother to Natalie and Arnaud. Grandmothers are better than mothers, I've been told. Less possessive. My grandchildren are so precious and Nigel is lucky to have them, to have Tamara. She's a good wife, a wonderful mother. A good young woman.

I think I'm beginning to resent the fact that Gideon teases her, calls her "the foreigner." Her father is French, her mother Russian, and Gideon wants to make an issue about it. Why, I'll never know. But it's unkind. He says it's in jest; yet I sense that's how he really perceives her. I'd hate to think he was bigoted in some way. But I am very aware that my son Gideon thinks that anything not English is inferior. I wonder why he's not learned otherwise yet? I did years ago.

Chloe. I can't let her go to London. Chloe alone there at the age of eighteen! No, never. I feel it's unwise. She's too young. And she must go to university. She can't just drop out.

Soon my family will be with me. Well, some of them, and that makes me happy. And each one of us has a lot to be thankful for this November of 1996. And I, in particular, am such a lucky woman. I have so much.

Stevie closed her diary, put it in the desk, and locked the drawer. As she pushed back her chair and rose, she heard the sound of the car on the gravel driveway outside.

Moving to the window, she pulled back the lace curtain and looked out. Her heart lifted when she saw Miles alighting.

He glanced up at the window, saw his mother, and waved.

She waved back, dropped the curtain, and hurried out, almost running down the stairs to the great hall.

5

Miles Jardine couldn't help thinking that as he and his twin brother grew older, their mother appeared to be getting younger.

That morning she looked like a woman in her mid-thirties, and quite wonderful, as she came down the front steps to greet him and his grandparents. She was wearing a chalk-stripe gray-wool pants suit and a white silk shirt, and she was her usual elegant self.

It struck him that Gideon was correct when he said they were rapidly catching up with her, and that when they were forty-six she herself would still be forty-six, at least in her appearance anyway.

But then, she *had* been a mere nineteen-year-old when they were born, and she was blessed with youthful looks, thanks to her genes. His grandmother, who would soon be sixty-seven, didn't look her age either, nor did she seem it. Blair was as youthful as anyone he knew, had great vitality, energy, and an enormous sense of fun.

"Hello, Ma," Miles said as his mother drew to a standstill in front of him. "You look fabulous." He smiled at her hugely, dropped the two bags he was carrying, and hugged her to him.

"I'm so glad you're here, Miles darling," she responded, smiling back. "And thanks for the compliment." She drew away and went on down the steps. His eyes followed her as she embraced her mother and then Derek, who had been helping the driver unload the trunk of the car.

Suddenly Cappi and the two local young women who worked with her on weekends were greeting him. One of them grabbed his suitcases despite his protestations that he could manage perfectly well; she paid no attention, simply departed with the luggage.

Miles shrugged to himself and went on down the last few remaining steps, close on the heels of Cappi and her other helper.

But when he heard Chloe calling his name, he paused, swung around, and a second later his sister was hurtling into his arms.

"Hi, Pumpkin," he exclaimed, and gave her a big bear hug.

"I've been waiting all morning for you, Miles, you're late."

He grinned at her. "I think I'm *early* actually, kid. We weren't due until noon, and it was just eleven thirty as we turned into the gates. Anyway, how're things at Romany Hall?"

"Okay," she answered laconically. There was a slight pause, then she added softly, "But I want to—" She broke off abruptly, as if she had changed her mind.

"Come on, Pumpkin, what were you going to tell me?"

"Oh, nothing . . . it was nothing important, honestly."

Miles thought otherwise, but he made no comment, as always discreet. "Come on, then, let's help Cappi and Lola with all that stuff. When the Rayners travel, it's like old-style royalty on the move. And God only knows what they bring with them."

"The kitchen sink," Chloe chortled. "That's what Mom says

anyway. She told me earlier that they'd arrive with two dozen suitcases plus the kitchen sink."

"Not quite, but almost," Miles agreed, laughing with his sister.

They went down to the driveway holding hands. Chloe glanced at him out of the corner of her eye. "So you didn't bring Allison."

Miles threw her an odd look. "Now, why would I bring *her?*"

"Bring who?" Derek asked as he braced himself for Chloe's enthusiastic hugs and kisses.

Stevie stared at her son, waiting to hear his response to her stepfather's question.

Glancing at Derek, Miles said, "Nobody. Nobody important, that is."

Well, at least that's to the point, Stevie thought. And leaves nothing to our imagination.

"Hello, darling," Blair murmured, accepting Chloe's kisses, which were, to her relief, more restrained than those just bestowed on Derek. "And who is Allison?" she asked, casting her glance on them all.

"Don't look at me, I've no idea, my darling," Derek intoned in his mellifluous actor's voice and, hoisting two of the valises, went up the steps. Stevie and Blair followed, carrying some of the smaller bags.

After Miles had thanked the driver and tipped him, he too made his way to the front door with Chloe in tow. He said in a pointed voice, "Little pigs not only have big ears, but apparently loose tongues as well."

Chloe giggled.

"Why did you mention Allison of all people, and in front of our mother? You know she's longing for me to get married and have kids, so she can have more grandchildren. It was wrong of you, Chloe."

"Well, you have been seeing a lot of Allison, and I thought it was . . ." Her voice trailed off lamely; she looked chagrined. And she felt suddenly uncomfortable under his fixed scrutiny.

"That's my business, kid, not yours."

"I thought it was getting serious between you two."

"No. And even if I did have serious intentions, that has nothing to do with you or Mother or anyone else. It's a private matter and it's certainly not open for discussion within the family."

"Oh." There was a momentary pause, and she looked at him through worried eyes. "Are you mad at me?"

"No, but let's not discuss my personal business in front of the rest of the family. Okay?"

"Yes, Miles, and I'm sorry."

"That's all right. Just remember what I said though. You've got to learn some discretion. You're not a little kid anymore, you're eighteen, and you must start growing up, behaving like an adult."

Chloe nodded, her face suitably serious for once.

After coffee and hot buttered scones in front of the fire in the great hall, everybody dispersed in different directions. Stevie sent Cappi, Lola, and Chloe to help Blair and Derek unpack their voluminous luggage; Shana, the other young woman who worked with Cappi, took Miles's bags up to his room. And his mother hurried off to the kitchen, explaining that she had to baste the turkey that was roasting in the oven.

Left alone, Miles wandered down the great hall into the dining room, and then slowly strolled through into the living room which adjoined it. He couldn't help admiring the ambiance his mother had created in the house. It was immensely seductive, just as it was in her other homes. But he especially liked Romany Hall because it was an airy, spacious house filled with clear, crystalline light that poured in through the many windows upstairs and down, a great number of which were unencumbered by draperies.

Everything was sparkling and fresh throughout. The white paintwork was pristine; the windows shone; the wood floors gleamed, and there was not a speck of dust anywhere. No shabby corners, worn fabrics, or frayed rugs here. His mother was something of a perfectionist, and she maintained the house at the highest level. Every piece of furniture, each object and painting, was well cared for and in its proper place.

Although it was beautifully decorated, Romany Hall was not overdone and there was no unnecessary clutter or ostentation. The air was fragrant with potpourri, perfumed candles, and the unusual chocolate smell of the Sharry Baby orchids, their curvaceous stems laden with exotic dark blooms.

Miles did not linger very long in the living room, but continued on to the solarium, a room he generally gravitated to at least once every day when he was staying with his mother.

He had always been taken with its simple yet effective beauty—white walls, warm terra-cotta–tiled floor, and the eye-catching Pierre Frey fabrics patterned in reds, yellows, and blues that his mother had used on the sofas and chairs. The solarium had a French feeling to it, with its high-flung cathedral ceiling and beams, stone fireplace and the French Provençal furniture his mother had picked up at sales in the Loire Valley and the Maritime Alps.

The many windows and French doors made the solarium seem part of the outside, and the clarity of light was particularly noticeable here. Although it was a sunless day, and somewhat bleak, the cloudless sky was a soft bluish-white, almost etiolated, and it was incandescent.

A good light for painting, he thought, and made up his mind

to bring his easel and paintbox down there tomorrow. He was suddenly in the mood to do a few watercolors.

Orchids abounded throughout the house, but there was a greater profusion of them in the solarium. His mother had always been addicted to orchids; and, even as a child, he too had been fascinated by them, by the intricacy of the flowers, the fantastical shapes of the petals, and the truly exotic colors.

He had grown up with orchids; there had always been a plethora of them in their farmhouse on the Yorkshire moors. Once a week he had helped his mother to water them, then put them in large metal bowls to drain.

"*Sissy, sissy, sissy!*" From a long way off, in the far reaches of his memory, he heard Nigel's voice echoing down through the years. His elder brother had always teased him about watering the orchids with their mother. He hadn't really cared; he had been independent even then. But his mother had cared when Nigel's taunting had become a tiresome pattern, and his older sibling had been suitably punished.

Their mother had made Nigel clean all the lavatories at Aysgarth End, six in all, and he had had the last laugh, although he hadn't dared to crack a smile. If he had, there would have been retribution of some kind. Nigel had been born a tough little bugger.

And nothing's changed, he thought coldly.

Opening the door, Miles stepped out onto the covered porch, walked over to the balustrade, and stood looking out toward the distant hills. Kent was such a beautiful part of the world, his kind of country with its rolling wooded hills and crystal lakes. It reminded him of Yorkshire and of his childhood, a good part of which was spent there.

These days it was mostly Nigel who used Aysgarth End as a weekend home when he could get away from London, and for all the national holidays when they didn't go to France to see

Tamara's parents. Certainly it was a marvelous spot to raise a family. When he went back to England he would go up there for a few days. He had long been planning to do an oil painting of Nigel's two children, and he wanted to paint them against a moorland background.

Now the view of the distant Litchfield hills reinforced this idea, was quite inspirational in a way. His fingers suddenly itched to hold a brush; he would start tomorrow, do a few sketches of Natalie and Arnaud from memory. It would be the beginning of the portrait. The prospect pleased him.

Miles shifted his stance slightly and glanced down into the garden below. It looked dank and foggy, and the mere sight of the sunken rose garden stripped of all its summer radiance and color made him conscious of the cold weather. He turned away and went inside.

Drifting back to the great hall, he sat for a few moments in front of the fire, staring into the flames, thinking unexpectedly about Allison Grainger.

He had been startled, not to mention miffed, when Chloe had brought her name up in front of the others. He was loath to give his family anything to speculate about, even his mother, whom he adored. Nonetheless, like all mothers, she wanted to see him settled for life.

He liked Allison, liked her a lot in fact. She was a really great human being and a lovely young woman, and they had had a lot of fun together these past few months. But he did not want to spend the rest of his life with her—for a very simple reason. He was not in love with her.

In any event, he had learned his lesson today, and learned it well. Young Chloe wasn't to be trusted. It was patently obvious that she was a little blabbermouth, and this disturbed him. She was always poking her nose into his business, and he was going to have to put a stop to that. He loved her, and he didn't want to hurt her feelings, but she didn't know how to edit herself. Wasn't it his fault though? He had let her into his life since he had been in New York. Oh, what the hell, he thought, no harm done, and I'd better keep my own mouth shut from now on. At least around baby sister.

Later, upstairs in his bedroom, Miles glanced around with satisfaction, noting the blazing fire, the bowl of fresh fruit, the bottled water, and the collection of magazines and newest books on a long library table behind the sofa.

His mother had always paid great attention to detail, and provided great comfort in her homes, thinking of everything. The perfect reading lamp stood close to the overstuffed armchair next to the fireside; a cashmere blanket was thrown over the back of the sofa; a plump duvet skimmed across the top of the big double bed; and naturally, orchids bloomed on tables in various corners.

She cossets, he suddenly thought, that's exactly the right word. She did the same when we were children. She's always done it, pampered us, and everyone else. "Smothers us, more like," he heard Nigel's voice say. He frowned, thinking of his brother once again. Nigel had developed a very acerbic tongue of late and could be quite vituperative. It's as if he's bitter, Miles muttered under his breath, walking over to the fireplace, standing with his back to the blazing logs. He had no clue what was wrong with Nigel; Gideon deemed him the man with everything, and this was true. He had a beautiful, intelligent wife, two marvelous kids, a successful career with a guaranteed future. And one day he would be the big cheese at Jardine and Company, the Crown Jewellers of London. But seemingly this wasn't enough. What a fool his brother was.

Miles sighed, dragged his thoughts away from Nigel, and walked into the bathroom. After washing his hands, he ran a comb through his hair and then peered at himself. He saw a reflection of his parents gazing back at him. He had his mother's dark, wavy hair, the same finely etched face, but he had inherited his father's long, straight nose and vivid blue eyes. And, of course, he was a replica of his identical twin.

Gideon. He had been very much on his mind of late. He couldn't understand what was ailing him. His brother was morose, moody, and depressed. Last week, when he was in London, he had attempted to talk to Gideon; but all he had got for his trouble was a flea in his ear. And several warning glances from his brother had finally made him back off completely. But there *was* something wrong with Gideon. As Derek, who was always quoting Shakespeare, would say: *Something is rotten in the state of Denmark.*

6

"The actor playing the heavy became suddenly ill, and there we were, in the middle of the picture and in a mess, looking for a replacement, and, of course, everyone was mentally casting," Derek explained to them, his marvelous voice echoing around the great hall.

"And," he went on, "I happened to remark to the assistant producer that who we needed was Sydney Greenstreet. I told her that he'd be great as Redner, the villain. And she asked me who his agent was so that she could be in touch and try to hire him at once."

Derek began to laugh. It was infectious. The others laughed with him, as always enjoying his anecdotes about the movies he had worked on. "Anyway, she was appallingly dense, the poor girl, and I'm afraid none of us could resist taking the mickey out of her. Most of the time too. Very young, of course. Too young for the job, as a matter of fact. Didn't know that old Sydney had gone to meet his maker long ago. Doubt if she'd ever heard of him. Or seen *The Maltese Falcon*."

"Or *Casablanca*," Chloe volunteered. "I loved him in that."

"So did I, darling girl," Derek agreed, beaming at her.

Chloe beamed back. "*Casablanca* is my all-time-favorite movie. It's *awesome.*"

"My favorite too," Miles said, and then, glancing at Derek, he remarked, "I had a similar sort of conversation the other day with one of the young women working in Wardrobe. I said that Deborah Kerr had been the greatest Anna ever, that she'd been brilliant in the part, and the girl just gaped at me, looking totally blank."

Derek nodded, moved forward in the chair slightly, sounding serious. "Look here, I'm all for youth and a great booster of this generation, but some of these kids in their late teens and early twenties who are working in the theater and movies today seem awfully uninformed to me. Not a bit knowledgeable about the past, even the recent past."

"Only too true," Miles agreed. "It's like they've landed from another planet."

"Deborah was divine in *The King and I,*" Blair murmured.

"And so was Yul Brynner. They don't make stars like that anymore," Derek said quietly.

"Well, I wouldn't go as far as that!" Blair exclaimed a trifle heatedly. "What about you, my love?"

Derek merely inclined his head and smiled at his wife.

Stevie said, "Mother's right, of course, but I do know what you mean. So many of the great stars I love have retired or died."

"Very gloomy thought indeed, my dear," Derek answered. "And I must admit, I miss quite a number of them. Larry Olivier, Jack Hawkins, Duke Wayne, Bill Holden, but most especially Rich. God, we had some splendid times together. He was such an extraordinary man, an extraordinary talent. I remember when he was in *Hamlet* in the fifties. I think it was 1953, when he was with the Old Vic. Claire was in it with him, played Ophelia to his

Hamlet. They were fabulous together. I went up to Edinburgh to see it, to see them. Rich was bloody marvelous. *Miraculous.*" There was a moment's pause, and then Derek added softly, "I always envied him his voice, you know."

"You did!" Miles sounded surprised, and he threw Derek a curious look. "But *your* voice is wonderful. Everybody remarks about it, Derek."

"Thank you, Miles, however, it's not as great as Burton's was. Rich had ... well, probably the greatest voice that's ever been heard on the English stage. It was a *thrilling* voice, and it was much more sonorous and emotional than Larry's, in my opinion anyway. It was the Celt in him, the Welsh in him, we love words so, us Welsh do. And as they always say in our native valleys of Wales, he had a bell in every tooth. Usually they say that about a singing voice, but it can be applied to a speaking voice as well, you know. As far as Rich was concerned, that is. His voice liter-ally *rang* with feeling, and I for one could listen to him for hours."

"As we all could, and did," Blair reminded him.

"I think I'd better check with Cappi about lunch," Stevie exclaimed, and rose, began to walk across the great hall. "I should find out how things are progressing. And anyway, they probably need a bit of help in the kitchen."

"I'll come with you, darling," Blair murmured, and followed her daughter.

Chloe called, "Do you need me, Mom?"

"No, darling, we can manage, I'm sure," Stevie answered over her shoulder before disappearing into the kitchen.

Derek strolled across to the tray of drinks on a large Jacobean chest, picked up the bottle of white wine, and swung to face Miles, showing him the bottle. "Need yours topped up?"

"No thanks, Gramps, I'm fine."

Derek poured himself another glass of the wine and then walked back to the fireside. He sat down on the sofa next to Chloe and, glancing across at Miles, he asked, "How're the sets coming along for *The King and I*?"

"Pretty good, actually. It's a fabulous play to work on, and I can really give my imagination free rein with this one. Temple bells and Buddhas, carved elephants, exotic fabrics, lots of gold and silver. And jewels. And vivid colors. All of those things that help to recreate the palace in Siam are really very visual, and have tremendous impact from the stage. And, I have to say, the costumes are sensational, especially Anna's . . . all those lovely floating crinolines."

"As a musical, it does take a lot of beating because it is such a fabulous play to look at, quite aside from listen to." One of Derek's brows lifted eloquently as he now asked, "How's Martine Mason faring? *How* is she as Anna?"

"She's good, Gramps, and so is Ben Tresner as the king. He may not be Yul Brynner, and Martine's certainly no Deborah Kerr, but I think we've got a winning package."

"And therefore a hit, presumably."

"From your mouth to God's ears, Gramps!" Chloe exclaimed.

The two men exchanged amused looks and laughed.

Cappi appeared suddenly in the great hall and beckoned to Chloe. "Your mother wants you to come and help us, nothing too complicated. We just need another pair of hands for a few minutes."

"I don't care if it *is* complicated, you know I'm very good at complicated things," Chloe shot back, and ran across the room, exclaiming to her brother and grandfather, "Excuse me, I won't be long, and please don't talk about me while I'm gone."

Again they laughed in amusement. Derek said, "You should be so lucky."

Once they were alone, Miles rose, took a chair closer to Derek, and began. "I want to ask you something before Ma comes back from the kitchen."

Derek looked at him with alertness, wondering what this was all about. "Go ahead, Miles old chap. I'm all ears. What's troubling you? And I guess you *are* troubled, if the look on your face is anything to go by."

"Yes, I am troubled. I'm worried about Gideon."

"Oh." Derek sat up straighter, giving Miles his full attention.

"I know you saw Gideon when he came to Los Angeles on business three weeks ago, and I just wondered what you thought. I mean—" Miles paused, cleared his throat, and went on. "What I mean is . . . well, what did you think about Gideon? His demeanor? His behavior?"

Without even having to think about this, Derek answered immediately. "He seemed relatively normal to me. But what are you driving at?"

"I saw him last week, when I was in London for a few days, and . . . well . . . frankly, I thought he seemed a bit under the weather, not himself at all."

"I see. However, Miles, I can honestly say I didn't notice anything different about him. No, not quite true, actually. He *was* a bit vague the second night we saw him for dinner. I'd even go so far as to say he was remote, and now that I think about it more carefully, he was somewhat distracted."

"He was depressed when I was with him, *and* morose," Miles said.

"He's always been a bit gloomy, Miles, even as a child," Derek pointed out. "You might look alike, but your personalities are very different."

"I know. But listen, his moroseness has been more pronounced than usual. And you didn't notice it then?" Miles stared at his grandfather.

Derek shook his head. "No, and neither did your grandmother, or she would have mentioned it to me. As I just said, he appeared to be distracted, as if he were preoccupied about something, and he was a bit distant. Looking back now, I remember I thought his mind must be on business. But that's all." Derek's eyebrows furrowed. "Tell me something, why didn't you want your mother to hear this conversation?"

"You know how she worries. And about everything."

"Yes, but she's always coped, no matter what's been flung at her. And brilliantly so, I might add."

"That's true. But I didn't want to bring Gideon up today, not on Thanksgiving. You know, it's her most favorite holiday of all. I didn't want to spoil it for her, voicing my concern about my twin."

Derek was chuckling. "Oh, I know it's her favorite holiday, and none of us has escaped it. Ever. I've eaten more of your mother's turkey over the years than I care to remember, and it's not even my favorite bird. I prefer duck, pheasant, or partridge any day. But she hasn't ever listened to me, at least not about turkeys anyway."

Miles half smiled, and wondered whether to bring up his elder brother. After a moment's thought he decided he would do so, since Derek had always been his confidant, and like a father to him all his life. He said slowly, "Has Ma mentioned Nigel to you?"

"No, she hasn't, but then, Blair and I haven't seen her in New York. We've been back from Los Angeles only a few days, and she seems to have been awfully busy at Jardine's. Is there something wrong with Nigel too, in your considered opinion, Miles?"

"No, not that I know of. However, Ma's indicated to me a few times that she thinks he's . . . sort of—" Cutting himself off, Miles hesitated, and then, dropping his voice an octave, he finished in a stage whisper, "Plotting against her."

"Ah, I see." There was a dramatic pause. Then, holding Miles with his eyes, Derek intoned, "Uneasy lies the head that wears a crown."

"I suppose there's truth in that. Shakespeare always got it right, didn't he? And you should know, you've been in enough of his dramas."

A thoughtful look crossed the actor's expressive face, and he was silent for a moment or two, and then he asked quietly, "Do you believe he's plotting, Miles?"

"I . . . I just don't know."

"I *know* your mother. She doesn't imagine things, she's far too pragmatic for that. Therefore, if she thinks he is, then he is. Although, to be truthful, I'm damned if I know the reason he would do such a thing. After all, the business will be his one day."

"Maybe he's in a hurry."

"I can't imagine the reason."

"Neither can I, Gramps."

Derek sighed. "Ambition. Greed. The lust for power. It's toppled many a throne, caused murder and mayhem on a grand scale. We've only got to look at the Plantagenets and the Tudors to understand that." He shook his head, and a sad, rather regretful expression settled on his handsome face. "Nigel always was something of a mystery to me, Miles, I must admit. I never really understood him when he was a child. Nor did I understand his actions when he was a teenager. But then, that's another story altogether, isn't it?"

"Yes, it is. I didn't understand all that mess either."

Derek stared off into space for a moment, lost in memories of the past, before saying eventually, "How is Nigel's marriage? Is that all right? No problems with Tamara?"

"None as far as I know, and she's a smashing girl. He's bloody lucky to have her and those two great kids."

"Ah, but does *he* know it, Miles?"

Miles shrugged, lifted his hands in a helpless gesture.

Derek averted his head, looked into the fire, lost in thought again.

After a moment Miles said, "Getting back to Gideon, I've been wondering if he's upset about Margot. But then, why would he be, when *he* broke it off with her?"

"Could he possibly have regrets?" Derek suggested, turning to face Miles, looking directly at him.

"Maybe. But it wasn't very good between them in the end. I think she was getting on his nerves. Margot always was something of a social butterfly, and you know Gideon's not very keen on partying. He's too serious, too dedicated to work." Miles exhaled heavily. "Oh, God, I don't know . . . and who knows what Gideon really thinks or feels? It beats me."

"Have you tried talking to him?"

Miles threw back his head and guffawed. "Oh, come on, Gramps, of course I have! And he bit my head off the last time I did."

"Perhaps he's just going through one of those phases all young men go through—at some time or other," Derek said, thinking out loud. "Trying to find himself, et cetera, et cetera, et cetera. But more than likely, it's woman trouble." A brow lifted knowingly. "That's usually what's ailing men when they appear troubled and despairing but without any real reason to be so afflicted."

"I suppose you're right, Derek."

A split second later, Chloe appeared in the archway of the great hall. "Coo-ee, coo-ee," she called, waving frantically, trying to gain their attention. "It's almost three-thirty and lunch is ready! Mom would like you to come to the dining room. *Now,* she says."

"Her wish is our command, my darling." Derek put down his glass and rose.

So did Miles.

Together the two men went to join her, and the three of them slowly made their way to the dining room.

1

It was a festive lunch.

Everyone talked a lot and laughed and exclaimed about the good things offered to them, since by now they were all extremely hungry.

Cappi and her two helpers had prepared a truly memorable Thanksgiving lunch. There were all manner of delicious and succulent things to eat with the large, plump turkey—sweet potatoes with a marshmallow topping, mashed potatoes as well as potatoes roasted in the oven, and parsnips, red cabbage, cranberries, a thick, fragrant-smelling gravy, and, of course, Stevie's famous, mouthwatering sage-and-onion bread stuffing.

Along with the turkey, Cappi had baked a Virginia ham and roasted a batch of quail, much to Derek's amusement. He knew that these had been made in order to tempt him; after years of complaining to Stevie about her Thanksgiving turkeys, she had apparently taken the hint. And yet hadn't he always explained to her that English turkeys were not as good as those to be found in America, an important point, since over the years most of her Thanksgiving meals had been served in London.

He had been partially teasing her; she had taken his words to heart.

"A little of everything," he told Cappi, who was hovering around the sideboard, where the turkey, ham, and quail were arrayed on large platters, alongside all the accompanying vegetables. "And only dark meat, please, if you're giving me turkey."

"And what about vegetables, Sir Derek?"

"Mashed potatoes would be lovely, and stuffing and gravy, but that's it, thanks, Cappi. Must watch the waistline, you know."

Miles moved slowly around the table, pouring the red Bordeaux, a Château Gruaud-Larose, his favorite Saint-Julien. It had been bottled in 1989, a good year, and he commented on this to Miles, who nodded and smiled. "Chosen specially for you," Miles told him with a conspiratorial wink.

Chloe followed on her brother's heels, filling their water glasses; Blair passed around the basket of homemade breads and Stevie offered cranberry sauce. Then at last they were all served, and they settled down to eat.

Derek ate slowly, savoring his food, saying a word or two occasionally. Mostly he listened, and observed everyone.

He was very content to be here today, enjoying this respite from his work, enjoying being with his family. Part of his family, at any rate. He could not help wishing Gideon were here, and Nigel and Tamara with their two children, and then they would have been complete. A true family all together under one roof for once.

This was his second family; long ago there had been his daddy and his mam, his brothers, Owen and David, and sister, Gwyneth. The family of his blood, whom he had loved so much when he was growing up in Ystradyfodwg, that little parish that was the Rhondda. *The Rhondda* . . . how he loved the sound of it, loved rolling the name around on his tongue. The place of his heart ... where all his hopes and dreams had been born ... another of the great industrial valleys of South Wales, where coal mining was the main industry.

The pit. The dreaded pit. The giver of wealth, the taker of life.

His daddy had worked in the pit all his life, from being a young boy until the day he died. Claimed by the pit. It was an explosion in the belly of the earth that took so many of their men and ravaged the town. His daddy had died with the others when the walls of the mine had collapsed and water had flooded the shafts.

His brother Owen had not been on the same shift as their daddy that day, and so, thankfully, he had been spared. Spared to become the breadwinner for them all.

It was because of his elder brother that *he* had been spared. Owen, and Gwyneth too, had seen something special in him when he was a boy. Eventually they had come to calling it "the gift," and as it turned out, it was just that, something deep within himself that he could draw on and that would eventually take him to great heights as an actor, although he had not known it then. Nor had he or they known at that time exactly what this gift was, not really. They could not define it. But, very simply, his brother and sister had discerned something in him that made him different, lifted him high above the mediocrity of the crowd.

In a sense, it was a mixture of things: his talent for acting, his genius for mimicry, his boy's soprano voice that everyone said was so beautiful—this would go, they all knew that—but they recognized these attributes in him and rejoiced. Owen, in particular, appreciated his aptitude for learning and was convinced that this alone was his great chance. That rare chance to escape the fate of most boys of his age in South Wales in the 1940s: Working in the mines underground.

"He's not going down the pit, I won't let him," Owen was for-ever announcing to Gwyneth; his sister, mother, and brother, David, would agree that he was too good to be wasted "down there."

Owen was awed by his renditions of poetry; he had a natural talent for reciting reams of it, all learned by heart and committed to memory; equally, Owen was awed by his overwhelming ambi-tion, his consuming desire to act. To be an actor, that was his goal.

He wanted to walk out on a stage and become someone else. Yes, *to act*, of all things, and he a poor boy from the Welsh val-leys. Yet they had a rare respect for the language in those once-glorious valleys where the bright hillsides had been spoiled, seamed as they were with mine shafts, the tops of the lovely green hills scarred by pit heads.

They had immense respect for the written word, and the spoken, those Celts did. That strangely alien tribe, which, some said, was the lost tribe of Israel. This love of words was inherited from their ancestors, his ancestors, and he too loved the lan-guage, perhaps more than anything else. As a boy he had loved the music and the singing in the chapel on Sundays and the eisteddfods, those wonderful musical festivals where he had excelled whilst his voice had lasted.

His first language, as a boy, had been Welsh, and he still spoke it, loved speaking it. But he had learned that foreign tongue, *English*, when young, had conquered it, made it his own in a most singular way.

Owen and Gwyneth had saved him from going down the pit. He had been forever grateful to them for that, and he had shown his gratitude whenever he could. He was fiercely loyal to them; his brothers and sister meant the world to him. They had, after all, given him this life. Or at least given him the chance to grab

· this life, make it his own, just as he made a stage his own whenever he stepped onto it.

His Welsh family, his blood family. They were fortunately still intact, except for his mamgu, his mam, who had died twenty years ago. She had lived to witness his success, his triumphs, had seen him play Henry IV and Henry V. She had been thrilled by his Hamlet and had applauded his Richard III, had sat there in the theater and watched him mesmerize an audience, hold them spellbound for two and three hours at a stretch. His beloved Welsh family, to which he forever returned, as always reveling in his roots, his heritage, dragging this with him wherever he went, like a banner in the wind.

Wait. He was wrong. Surely he was wrong. Not two families in his life, but three. There had been another one long ago, a family of actors, a few young men who had gravitated to each other in the early fifties.

Rich, of course, and Stanley Baker, and himself. And a handful of other Welshmen who had eventually fallen by the wayside. But all of them of common background, come out of those great green valleys of rugby football and singing, poetry, poverty, and the pits. Working-class boys who became working-class heroes. Especially to each other.

He and Rich and Stanley had been real boyos in those days, treading the boards and boozing it up in the pubs, and wenching hard when they were lucky enough to get the chance. Boasting more than doing, as he recalled it now. And the three of them had shared a love of rugby football, playing it, watching it, and cheering on the Welsh team.

Oh, how young they had been and full of power and pride and piss and vinegar. And each of them growing more famous. Heady stuff it had been then, in the London of the fifties.

It was their Welshness, their talent, and their acting that had bonded them together, bound them as a family, and Richard Burton, his beloved Rich, had been their leader. The Welsh chieftain out of the valleys, and ready to lead them on to triumphs beyond their wildest dreams. And he had done so. Their wonderful Welsh warrior, all fire and brilliance, with his brightly burning genius, immensely powerful as a man, charismatic and compelling, and one of the greatest classical actors of his time. Of all time, in fact, with a voice one critic described as "memorably beautiful." And that voice was, in his opinion, the source of Rich's genius as an actor.

And then Rich had gone and died at the age of fifty-eight, in 1984, and how he had wept for him, just as he and Rich had wept for that other fallen friend, Stanley, when he had died so absurdly young in 1976. *Sir* Stanley Baker by then, honored by all. And he and Rich had mourned him, and they had shared their rage, their anger that he had died so young and left them so bereaved.

And it was only a short eight years later that Rich was gone himself, felled by a massive brain hemorrhage at his home in Switzerland. And that little family of actors was no more. There was only him left.

But he had *this* family. It was they who concerned him now as they all sat around Stevie's circular table in her dining room at Romany Hall in Kent, Connecticut, so far away from the valleys of South Wales and his youth.

He glanced at Miles, who caught his eye and smiled. Derek smiled back, but immediately he fell inward, thinking about *this* family, these people who had become, over the years, the mainspring of his life.

Miles. More like a son than a grandson. He had tried to help Stevie raise him after Ralph died so young, at least as much as she would allow. Fiercely independent, she had not wanted any interference with the boys, not from anyone.

He had also tried to help her bring up Gideon and Nigel, but her attitude had been the same. "I'll manage," she would say, and yes, she had always managed, there was no denying that.

Gideon had been such a moody boy, but *good* like Miles, who had been everybody's favorite because of his sweetness of disposition, easygoing nature, and steady reliability. He hadn't changed much, simply grown better, if the truth be known. Miles was the most lovely human being and certainly the peacemaker in the family.

Nigel had been too much of a Jardine to listen to anyone, not even his mother. But she had a strong will and had won the day in the end. But Nigel would not listen to *him;* after all, what did a mere actor know, and one who was his grandmother's husband to boot and not a blood relative. Nigel had gravitated to Bruce Jardine automatically, almost without having to think about it. He had allied himself with the Jardines, even standing with them against Stevie at one moment in time.

Derek had never really been able to forgive Nigel for that desertion. He had tried, even convinced himself at times that he *had* forgiven Nigel for his treachery. But he hadn't really; he had merely elected to *forget,* in order to get on with the business of fraternizing with Nigel, since he was Stevie's eldest son and an integral part of the family. Temporary amnesia, Blair called it.

Blair. The woman he adored and had from the first day he met her. When he had first set eyes on her he had forgotten everyone and everything, and in an instant he had known that he had been looking for her his whole life.

His marriage to Nina, his first wife, was already beginning to break apart, to crumble. And his falling for Blair, head over heels falling, had been like someone throwing a stick of dynamite into the marriage. All had come tumbling down in a heap around him. What's more, he hadn't really cared. Nothing mattered but her. He wanted Blair. He was going to have her. He and Nina had no children to be concerned about, and Nina was already dissatisfied with him, so *anti* him at that point in their life she had described him to an acquaintance as a drunken actor, which he wasn't, far from it. An actor, yes, but not a drunk. Many things, but not that.

And so he and Blair had eventually married and, contrary to what everyone had predicted, they lived happily ever after. She was his true love, his muse, his devoted partner, his greatest critic, and his greatest fan.

She was the one who was always there for him, cheering at the ringside; always there to bandage his wounds; to mop up the mess; assuage his pain; ease the terrible hurts of his daily life. She was everything to him. Like his mother and sister before her, she was a woman he idolized as he had idolized them, and as he still idolized his sister, Gwyneth.

He and Blair had not had children, but this did not really matter to him. After all, there was Stevie and her children, and Nigel's children. He loved them all, even Nigel, who was so difficult and hard to understand at times. But he was part of Stevie and part of Blair, and therefore he deserved to be loved despite his transgressions.

He glanced at Chloe, who was sitting next to Blair. How amazing it was . . . she looked as Blair must have looked when she was a young girl. There was no mistaking *her* genes. Chloe will be a heartbreaker one day, he decided, observing her surreptitiously. If he and Blair had had a daughter, he felt sure she would have looked like Chloe.

Chloe. So young, almost too young for eighteen in this day and age, or so it seemed to him. Children were so very grown-up now. He loved Chloe; she was his adored grandchild. And he was terribly guilty of spoiling her, but he just couldn't help himself.

She was very precious to him, this young girl, and he decided that he must talk to Stevie about Chloe going to college. To Oxford University. That was what she had always wanted. This summer, after she graduated, she must come to England and live with them and do the Oxford extrance exams. Chloe was an intelligent girl, and artistic like her twin brothers, and sharp in the way that Stevie was sharp. He was sure she would do well, go as far as her mother had gone.

Stevie. His dearest Stevie. He had always thought of her as his daughter, and she was exactly that, blood or no blood. She had been fourteen when he and Blair married, and rebellious. He had known immediately that she would be a handful, but he simply hadn't cared or worried about that. He had been ready and willing to take her on and bring her up as his own when he had married her mother. Those two came as a package, but it was a lovely, and loving, package, one he had been more than happy to accept.

As it turned out, he hadn't had much bringing up to do in the end. Just two years. And then Stevie had met Ralph Jardine and married him within the short span of a year.

He had not been sure about Ralph in the beginning, asking himself what kind of a man it was that seduced a girl of sixteen, an innocent, inexperienced girl who was eleven years his junior.

But their marriage had worked, and he knew that Ralph had truly loved Stevie. He had grown to like Ralph as time went on, and it was with sorrow that he had mourned Ralph's passing.

Derek shifted in his chair and looked across at Stevie, his eyes suddenly appraising. He was very proud of her. She had become an extraordinary woman. Powerful in so many ways. Powerful in her own business, powerful in the international world of jewelry, and yet it was the power she had within herself that impressed him the most. Her inner strength constantly amazed him. The power of a woman could be formidable.

She was the one who had held everything together after Ralph's sudden death, once her grief had begun to abate. Bruce Jardine had been hugely affected by his son's death. After his own heart attack, the man had been half useless, as far as he could ascertain at the time. As for Alfreda, she had been one of the most stupid women he had ever met, a numbskull if ever there was one. An ignorant woman totally crippled by her own ridiculous, and laughable, snobbery.

He knew that it was Stevie who had pulled the company around, kept everything running smoothly, and she a mere girl with no experience of business whatsoever then. She had inherited her mother's guts, and she had immense intelligence, not to mention an uncommon kind of bravery. For indeed it had taken a great deal of courage to go in there at the age of twenty-six and start helping Bruce to run the business. Bruce could deny her tremendous efforts and contributions as much as he wanted, until the day he died, but Derek knew what had really gone on, how much she had done. It was because of Stevie that Jardine and Company, the Crown Jewellers, still existed in London today.

Now his eyes rested on her lovingly. It saddened Derek that she had never remarried. He felt sorry that she was alone, and he frequently worried that she would be lonely in her old age without a partner by her side. For the moment she was a busy woman, of course, caught up in the daily running of Jardine's. But one day she would retire, step down, hand over to Nigel.

Nigel. His mind settled on Stevie's eldest son. There was no question that Nigel must be plotting against her, if she believed this. But why? It didn't really make sense.

8

"Grandpa! Grandpa! Wait for me. *Wait for me!*"

Derek swung around and saw Chloe racing after him across the lawn, and so he paused, stood waiting for her.

"What is it, Chloe? Is there something the matter?" he asked when she finally drew to a standstill next to him.

"No, Grandpa," she panted, endeavoring to catch her breath. "I just wanted you to wait for me so that I could come with you on your walk."

"And I thought there was a major disaster, the way you were screaming like a banshee."

She threw him a swift glance, saw at once that he had a teasing look in his light blue eyes. She relaxed, laughed lightly, then she said, "I *can* come with you, can't I?"

"Of course, but come along, let's not stand here. It's not that warm today. I was making for the summerhouse down by the river. It's a pleasant walk there and back."

Chloe nodded, tucked her arm through Derek's, and fell in step with him.

He said, "You mustn't shout like that, Chloe, screaming so hard, you could very easily damage your voice."

"But I'm not going to be an actress, Gramps."

"Nevertheless, you could hurt yourself, strain your larynx. I once did, and it was very painful, let me tell you."

"When did you do that?"

"Oh, a long time ago, when I was a young actor just starting out. I was shouting very loudly instead of throwing my voice. You see, I wanted it to reach the back of the theater, and I really did hurt myself in the process, quite badly too. It taught me a good lesson. I went out of my way to learn how to project my voice after that. I could pitch it quite high, but that wasn't really what was needed to reach the last row. So I worked with a voice coach, who told me that if I spoke very distinctly, I would make everyone in the theater hear me. I soon learned that volume didn't matter. It was distinctness that did. I also learned to enunciate my words very carefully, without making it seem labored."

"It must have been exciting when you first became an actor."

"It was, and it still is, Chloe. There's nothing quite like walking onto a stage for me, or saying those first lines. It's truly thrilling, if a little frightening sometimes."

"Frightening?"

"Oh, yes. Like many actors, I often suffer from stage fright. Not as much as I used to, but it still attacks me now and then."

"You?" Chloe swung her eyes, looked at him, and shook her head in wonder. "Gramps, I can't believe it! Not *you*, Sir Derek Rayner, the greatest classical actor on the English stage today."

He smiled slightly. "As I just said, many actors do have attacks of stage fright. My friend Rich did, he used to tremble excessively at times. Other actors I know experience nausea, and poor old Larry Olivier had a curious nervous laugh when he first walked onto a stage. At the beginning of his career, that is. He managed to get that laugh under control eventually, at least most of the time."

"And you, Grandpa? What happens to you?"

"I shake a bit, feel sick, think I'm going to vomit, worry that I'm going to forget my lines and make a fool of myself. I suppose that's what stage fright is about actually, the terrible *fear* that one is going to make a mess of it all and look ridiculous in front of an audience."

"I understand. It must be awful."

"It is. Fortunately, it doesn't last long for me. Once I've said my first few lines, I'm off and away, and I forget everything because I've become the character I'm playing. The drama of it sweeps me along."

"Sometimes I've thought that I would like to be an actress, and I once even talked to Grandma about it, but she sort of . . . put me off."

"Did she now." Derek's eyes twinkled. He continued. "But you should follow your star, my dear, and never listen to anyone."

"You'd better not let Mom hear you say that, she'll be mad at you," Chloe cautioned.

"You're right, she would indeed be angry. However, she's bright enough to know that I speak the truth. Shakespeare said it best when he wrote, 'To thine own self be true.' You must always remember that. If you live by this yardstick, you won't go too far wrong."

"What Shakespeare meant was that we should be true to our own beliefs. Isn't that so?"

"Indeed it is. You're eighteen now, Chloe, and growing up fast. It'll be time for university soon."

"Yes," she said quietly, and held her breath for a moment, wondering whether to confide in him.

"That's a very small yes, and not at all like you. Why, you sound like a scared little church mouse."

Chloe had to laugh. "No, I don't."

"Well, what about it? I thought it was always Oxford for you."

When she did not respond, Derek came to a sudden stop, took hold of her shoulders and turned her to face him. "Chloe, Oxford is magical . . . a city of colleges and quads, domes and shining spires, the Bodleian Library, All Souls, and the Union. This glorious place does exist, if you want it, darling."

"I don't know anymore, Gramps," she answered, as always being scrupulously honest with him because of his immense integrity and his love for her.

"I see." There was a moment's pause before he murmured, "But you were so very positive about going up to Oxford when you were old enough." He stared at her keenly, his eyes penetrating. "What's happened to make you change your mind?"

Chloe hesitated fractionally, then answered quietly, "Nothing, not really." She shrugged her shoulders lightly. "I think . . . well, to be honest, I don't want to go to college at all, Gramps. I'd like to . . . work at Jardine's."

"Good God! You can't be serious!" Not waiting for her to say anything, he rushed on. "I can see that you are *very* serious from the look on your face. Why the change of heart, darling?"

"I don't know, I can't really explain it."

"Have you told your mother this?"

Chloe nodded. "Yes, on Wednesday night, when I first got here."

"Mmmm. Is she pleased that you want to go and work with her at the store?"

Chloe bit her lip. "Mom wants me to finish my education, go to college. More specifically, she wants me to go to Oxford."

"That's perfectly understandable."

Before she could stop herself, she blurted out, "I'd like to work with Gideon at the London store."

Derek was flabbergasted when he heard this, although his expression was unreadable when he said, "I sincerely hope you didn't tell your mother that."

"Yes, I did."

"Oh, dear . . . she must have been terribly upset."

Chloe bit her lip and nodded again.

Derek took hold of her hand, tucked her arm through his, and started to walk on toward the river. A silence fell between them.

Eventually, Derek broke the silence when he murmured, "I am quite certain that it hurt her very much, Chloe, hearing this from you."

"I suppose so," she mumbled.

"I don't understand you!" he exclaimed, sudden irritation rushing to the surface. "Why London? You could learn as much in New York. And there's no one smarter than your mother. Being at the Fifth Avenue store with her would please her no end, I know that for a fact. It wouldn't do you any harm either."

"I think I would learn a lot more about stones and designing jewelry in London. The showrooms are bigger, so are the work-shops, and there are many other kinds of craftsmen there, as well as lapidaries—silversmiths, goldsmiths. Anyway, Gideon would teach me better than anyone. He's one of the greatest lapidaries there is, and he's the Crown Jeweller, the only person allowed to handle the Crown Jewels of England."

"Yes, yes, I know all that," Derek exclaimed irritably. "But look here, Chloe, you could work at Jardine's, be it in London or New York, *after* you've graduated. I'm the last person to stop you from chasing your dream, didn't I just say that to you? Nevertheless, won't you consider going to university? For yourself, for your mother, and for me too, but mostly for yourself. It's so important for your future, whatever career you choose ultimately."

There was only the slightest hesitation before she said, "I'll think about it, Grandpa."

The two of them walked on quietly, without speaking, lost in their own thoughts, still heading in the direction of the river that flowed past the house at the bottom of the gardens.

Derek was truly dismayed about his conversation with Chloe, and genuinely upset for Stevie. Knowing her as well as he did, he realized how terrible she must be feeling, hurting inside. Oh, the young, how carelessly cruel they could be with their rash words, usually uttered without a single thought. And no hurt ever intended, of course. *Selfish youth.* But then, hadn't he been selfish when he was young? When he thought he knew it all, believed he had all the answers?

He was sixty-eight years old now, and in so many ways he felt as though he knew nothing, had learned nothing, in spite of the multitudinous experiences in his life. The longer he lived, the less he knew, or so it seemed to him. He was always telling Blair that nothing surprised him anymore, because he always expected the worst. Yet he was constantly being surprised. Chloe had just done that.

They arrived at the summerhouse, which stood under the willows close to the river's bank. Derek marched purposefully up the steps, saying over his shoulder, "Let's sit in here for a few minutes, it's nice to watch the wildlife on the river from here, and we're protected from the wind. Anyway, I need a rest, that was quite a long walk."

Dutifully Chloe tramped after him up the short flight of steps and joined him on the wooden bench where he had seated himself.

Slowly she unwound her scarf, pulled off her knit cap, and sighed as she ran her hands through her hair, pushing it away from her face.

"All the troubles of the world on your shoulders, eh, Chloe?"

She shook her head.

He looked at her intently and realized that she was on the verge of tears. Reaching out, Derek put his hand on her arm and murmured gently, "Now, now, what's all this?"

"Nothing, nothing, Grandpa," she said, shaking her head, and then she flicked her fingers across her eyes, swallowed hard, and tried to smile without success. Her bottom lip quivered slightly.

"There's nothing to cry about, Chloe. Was I too harsh with you, darling? I didn't mean to be."

"No, no, you weren't. Honestly, you weren't. It's just me. I'm being silly, I suppose."

"In what way?"

"I've upset my mother about not going to college, and you too, Grandpa. And I guess I've really hurt her feelings, telling her I prefer to work in London. I didn't want to cause trouble. I really didn't, and I didn't want to hurt anyone either, especially Mom."

"I know that, Chloe, and I'm quite certain that she does too. Anyway, you did say you would consider going to Oxford first, before embarking on a career, be it at Jardine's or not. If you tell her this, you will please her, make her feel so much better, I promise you."

Chloe was silent. After a split second she nodded and then, swiveling her head to Derek, she stared at him, biting her lip nervously. Quite unexpectedly, and much to her mortification, tears welled in her eyes, slowly slid down her cheeks.

"Chloe, Chloe, whatever's the matter?" Derek asked, staring at her in concern, reaching out once more, taking hold of her hand this time.

When she remained silent, he asked, "Is there something you want to tell me? Do you have some sort of problem?"

Taking a deep breath, Chloe replied, "One of the reasons I wanted to come for a walk with you was to ask you something—" She cut herself off and simply stared at him as blankly as before.

Derek nodded. "Go on, then, ask me. I'm not going to bite your head off, you silly goose."

"It's . . . it's about . . . about my father."

"What about him?" Derek asked, although he knew at once what she was going to say.

"Who was he *really*?"

Derek sighed heavily. "I don't know, truly I don't, Chloe."

"Would you tell me if you *did* know?"

"I most certainly would."

"I don't think my mother is being fair to me. I'm grown up now. Anyway, I've known about being illegitimate for years. I think I should know about my father, know about his background, who he was, what he was like."

"I agree, Chloe," Derek replied, and he meant this.

"Then help me, Gramps, please."

"How, darling?"

"Talk to Mom. She listens to you. Tell her she should tell me everything about my father."

"She won't tell you."

"Why not?"

"I've no idea." He shook his head. "She's always been very secretive about him."

"You never met him? Never knew him?"

"No, I didn't, Chloe."

"And Grandma?"

"She didn't meet him either. He was always . . . the mystery man."

"I don't even know what my father looked like," Chloe whispered, her eyes filling.

"Don't cry, sweetheart."

"Grandpa, please talk to her."

"First, let's go and talk to your grandmother."

9

Blair STOOD IN THE MIDDLE OF THE SMALL SITTING ROOM THAT adjoined their bedroom, staring first at Derek and then at Chloe. She exclaimed, "You're both looking very conspiratorial! What is it?"

Derek said, "Ask Chloe, my dear," and walked across the room, where he positioned himself in front of the fire, stood warming his back against the flames.

"Is something wrong, Chloe?" Blair asked, searching her granddaughter's face intently, frowning as she did so.

"I want to know about my father, everything about him. Mom has never told me a thing. Please, Grandma, you tell me," Chloe said, getting straight to the heart of the matter. "*Please?*"

Blair was somewhat taken aback and showed it. Then she sat down heavily in a chair and said, "But I can't tell you anything, Chloe. For the simple reason I never knew your father. I never met him, never even spoke to him on the phone."

"But Mom must have said something about him, mentioned him to you."

"She didn't."

"But how . . . how did she tell you about *me*, Gran?"

"She came to me one day and said she was pregnant. I was very happy for her, enthusiastic, because naturally I thought there was going to be a wedding."

"But there wasn't because—" Chloe stopped with abruptness. She went and flung herself on the sofa, looking disconsolate.

Derek and Blair exchanged pointed looks, and Derek said, "Because *what*, darling?"

"Because he was *dead*. She told me my father was killed in a car crash before they could get married."

"Oh," Blair said.

"Didn't she tell you that, Grandma?"

Blair shook her head.

"Then *what* did she say?" Chloe demanded quietly.

"Nothing much, actually, Chloe," Blair told her, and explained, "When I said something about her getting married, how happy I was for her, she said, 'I'm not getting married. There won't be a wedding.' I've always remembered her words, remembered that particular day very clearly. It was a rainy day in London, and I recall walking over to the window, looking out at our garden. We lived in Hampstead in those days. Near the Heath. I just stood there, feeling numb, looking out at the sodden trees, watching the rivulets of water running down the panes. And I thought, it's like my tears, the rain is like my tears."

"So you were upset then, Gran?"

"Of course I was upset! For your mother. After all, she wasn't getting any younger, she was almost twenty-eight. I wanted her to find happiness with someone, have a second chance at life, a chance with another husband."

"Instead of another husband, she got me. The bastard."

"Chloe! Don't speak in that way! You've never been made to

feel unwanted or unloved, and certainly you've never been made to feel like a bastard. That's most *unfair* of you," Blair chastised, her voice reproving, her face stern. "We've all loved you very much, Bruce Jardine included. And you're a Jardine, don't you ever forget that. Why, nobody's given a thought to your father, or asked questions about his identity, for the past eighteen years. There's another thing you should remember—" She paused, and her voice softened as she finished. "You've given us all a great deal of joy, and you've made a difference in all of our lives. As I just said, we love you, Chloe, cherish you."

"Indeed we do!" Derek exclaimed. "And we want only the best for you. Your mother most of all wants that."

Chloe said, "On my birth certificate it says my father was John Lane. *Who* was John Lane?"

"I don't know. Your grandpa doesn't know." Blair leaned forward, an earnest look washing across her face. "Until the day your mother told me she was expecting a child, I didn't even know she had a boyfriend. She worked extremely hard, and she was bringing up your brothers, and it seemed to me she didn't have very much time left to conduct an affair, have any kind of personal life."

"She had John Lane, Gran. Ask her. Ask her about *him*. Make her tell you. *Everything*. I've a right to know."

"I understand how you feel, I really do. And I'll gladly speak to your mother. However, I can't promise I'll be successful. She's my daughter, don't forget, and I know her better than anyone. Once she's made up her mind about something, she rarely, if ever, changes it."

Chloe sighed. "If she'll tell anyone, it'll be you, Gran."

"Well, I don't know about that," Blair responded carefully, shaking her beautifully coiffed blonde head. "She's kept him a secret since before you were born, so why should she divulge anything now? Not even André Birron knows about your father, and if she'd been going to confide in anyone, it would have been André. They've always been very close."

"You've discussed this with Uncle André?"

"A long time ago, yes."

"And he had no clue?"

"No, he didn't, and he actually told me to leave it alone. He told me my prying would do no good, only antagonize Stevie, possibly even cause an estrangement if I wasn't careful, if I persisted. Since I didn't want that to happen, I took André's advice."

Derek said, "I feel for you, Chloe, and I know your grandmother does too. It's only natural for you to want to know a little more about your father. If your grandmother is in agreement with me on this, *I'll* speak to your mother this weekend. But you must leave it to me, Chloe, you mustn't pester me. I'll do it when the right opportunity presents itself."

"Oh, thank you, thank you, Gramps!" Chloe cried, and jumped up, ran across the room, hugged him tightly.

Derek held her close to him, loving her. She was so young, so vulnerable. He met Blair's eyes across the room, smiled faintly, and raised a brow. He had recognized the look on his wife's face instantly. It mirrored what he himself was thinking: Stevie would tell him nothing.

Later that afternoon, Derek put down the script he had been reading and, looking over at his wife, he said, "Do you think all families are like ours?"

"What do you mean?"

"Dysfunctional."

"How can you say that, Derek! We're not dysfunctional!"

"We're trotting along in that direction."

"I don't believe we're having this conversation."

"Believe it, darling." Derek laughed hollowly. "There's nothing new about dysfunctional families. They've been around since the Stone Age." He glanced at the script on the ottoman next to his chair. "Take the Plantagenets, for example."

Blair simply gaped at him.

Derek grinned, amused by her expression of mingled disbelief and denial. "Seriously, Blair, look at Henry Plantagenet and Eleanor of Aquitaine, their three sons, Richard, Geoffrey, and John, and Alais Capet, their French ward who was also Henry's mistress. Now, that was a dysfunctional family if ever there was one. Things haven't changed much since 1183, when Henry II was king of England and half of France."

"Are you going to do the revival of *The Lion in Winter*?" Blair asked, her eyes swinging to the script he had been reading.

"I might. It's an awfully good play and it hasn't been seen on Broadway since 1966. The dialogue is fabulous. And James Goldman really got it right, had Henry and Eleanor down pat. There's such wit, comedy, and drama in it. A lot to get my teeth in here."

"But will a revival work? Don't you think people remember the movie with Katharine Hepburn and Peter O'Toole?"

"I sincerely hope they do, and with pleasure, so that they'll want to see it again. As a play." Derek paused for a moment, and then added quietly, "But leaving the year 1183 behind, and getting back to 1996, and *our* dysfunctional family rather than the royal Plantagenets, what are we going to do about Chloe?"

"You're going to talk to Stevie."

"If you think I should."

"I do," Blair murmured. "She'll accept that kind of discussion from you more than she would from me, Derek. She'd just be very dismissive if I mentioned any of this to her. Anyway, she's always listened to you, paid attention to your words."

"She's awfully angry."

"Chloe?"

"Who else?" Derek replied, shifting slightly in the chair. "And I can understand why. Stevie should have told her all about John Lane years ago. God knows, she told the girl she was illegitimate."

Blair shook her head sadly. "Stevie had to tell her that, once she was old enough to understand. After all, there was no man around, and Stevie was a widow."

"Why all the secrecy about this John Lane?" Derek asked.

"Years ago you said that wasn't his real name. Have you changed your mind? Are you now saying that it *is* the man's name?"

"No, I'm not, Blair. I've always thought it was phony, that Stevie invented it for convenience's sake."

"In order to protect someone's identity?" Blair said softly.

Derek nodded.

"But who?" she asked, her voice full of puzzlement.

Derek raised a brow eloquently. "Who indeed? I've often thought it might be somebody we know. I've said that to you in the past, but you always pooh-poohed the idea, told me I was on the wrong track."

"I don't believe that. Not anymore, Derek. It could easily have been one of our friends, or someone she met through us. If you look back, really think about it, we were the only diversion she had in those days, working the way she did and stuck with the boys. Any social life Stevie had was with us. Perhaps she got involved with one of your actor chums. And it would have had to have been somebody famous. Otherwise, why bother to protect him?"

"Correct," Derek said, and rose. He walked across the room and stood looking out of the window for a few moments.

Blair's eyes followed him, rested on him, and admiringly so. To her he was the most extraordinary man she had ever known. Great actor, glamorous star, a man whose singular talent had won him accolades around the world.

And yet to her, perhaps the most amazing thing about him was his beginning. She had always found it incredible that at a very early age he had plucked himself up out of the Rhondda Valley and flung himself into the center of London's theatrical world, making a name for himself very quickly when he was so young, only nineteen.

What was even more astounding was that with only a ridiculously meager amount of training he had turned himself into a great classical actor, literally by an act of will. His first rendition of Hamlet in the West End was still talked about with awe.

Aside from his spectacular talent, Derek was a lovely man, very down to earth and real; he had humility, was honorable, and honest, not to mention a kind and loving human being. And he truly had an understanding heart. All were characteristics she valued, and she was certain she would have been hard pressed to find them *all* in anyone else.

Derek had loved her, and loved her well, for all those years, and she had loved him in return. They had been a good team, were still a good team. Looking back, she realized how much his astonishingly beautiful voice had cast a spell over her when she met him all those years ago. It still thrilled her, and when she sat listening to him in a theater, she was spellbound. Naturally, she had also fallen for his dark good looks, as most women did, had found herself mesmerized by those expressive, liquid eyes of a blue so light they were almost transparent.

He's sixty-eight but he doesn't look it. He's still straight as a ramrod, broad of chest, tall, and unbowed. And yet he seems tired today, Blair thought. His face was relatively unlined and youthful, except for tiny, finely etched lines around his eyes, but there were white wings at his temples now.

Suddenly Blair hoped he would not do the play. He was exhausted from his long Broadway run in *Becket* and the movie he had just finished in Arizona. She had hoped he would take a well-earned rest once they returned to London, but perhaps this wasn't possible for him.

Did he really want to play Henry II? Strut around a stage as that roaring Plantagenet king of England whom he had just portrayed in *Becket?* Probably. Henry II seemed to hold some sort of fascination for him, and anyway, Derek could be a glutton for punishment.

Derek interrupted his wife's thoughts when he swung away from the window and said, "She's eighteen, and naturally she is fascinated by her father . . . who he was, what he was like as a man. She wants to know all about him in order to know herself, understand herself better. However, Blair, I'm afraid Chloe has other problems, quite aside from the true identity of Papa."

"She does?"

"She did rather a lot of confiding on our little walk after lunch today."

"Apparently. What other bricks did she drop on you?"

Derek sighed and rubbed his hand over his face. "Chloe doesn't want to go to college."

"Now, *that* does surprise me!" Blair exclaimed. "In fact, it almost takes my breath away. Chloe has been so enthusiastic about going to Oxford, and for as long as I care to remember. In fact, she got me to drive her there last summer, then dragged me around the university and the city, if you recall. And she was excited about the whole idea of it. Look here, although she says she doesn't want to go to college now, she could easily change her mind later. The young only realize how tough it is when they get out there on their own."

"I hope Chloe will change her mind, but I have my doubts," Derek murmured, sounding regretful. "It's sad really that she intends to forgo Oxford. Those would be wonderful years for her, years she'd draw on and remember for the rest of her life. And it's upsetting for Stevie, who has wanted her to go there so badly."

"She's told her mother?"

"Yes. She's also informed Stevie that she wants to work at Jardine's."

Startled to hear this, Blair was silent for a moment. Then she said quickly, "Not my choice for her. On the other hand, perhaps it will please Stevie."

"Jardine's of London."

"*Oh, dear.* And I suppose she's announced that to her mother?" Blair looked at him questioningly.

"Yes, she did. When do the young ever hold anything back? They love to let it all hang out."

"No wonder you're talking *dysfunctional.*"

"There's more, my darling."

"No, Derek, don't say that. What else could possibly be troubling Chloe?" Blair's face filled with sudden apprehension.

"Oh, it's not Chloe I'm speaking about, but Miles."

"Miles is the sanest of us all."

"Very true. However, he's worried about Gideon. He thinks his twin has problems. Miles described him to me as being gloomy and depressed. He asked me how we thought Gideon seemed when we saw him in Los Angeles."

"Self-involved," Blair shot back.

Derek threw her a rapid glance and continued. "I told Miles that I thought Gideon appeared to be preoccupied. With business."

"Self-involved," Blair repeated in a knowing, confident voice.

Derek said, "There's more."

"Do tell. Get it over with, Derek." She sat back, waiting.

"Miles says that his mother believes Nigel is plotting against her, and that he wants to oust her from the company."

"Whatever will she think of next?"

Derek frowned. "Don't you believe it's true?"

"All joking apart, I'm afraid I do. I trust Stevie's judgment absolutely. I've never known it to be flawed. Apparently Nigel's is though." Blair's face grew thoughtful, and she sat staring into space for a second or two before continuing. "If Stevie says Nigel is working against her, then undoubtedly he is. And no wonder you bring up the Plantagenets. Shades of that bloodied family indeed, what with their plotting and double-dealing, secrets and scheming . . . their constant quarreling and hidden agendas."

He laughed. "Are *we* as bad as that, do you think?"

Blair leaned against the needlepoint cushions on the sofa and stared at him without making a comment. Suddenly she said, "Aren't all families?"

"I'm not sure. It depends on what's at stake. Let me ask you something else, Blair. Why would Nigel plot against his own mother? Especially when he will be taking over the company from her one day anyway."

"That's what is so baffling, Derek." Blair lifted her shoulders in a shrug. "I haven't got a clue. But Nigel has always been devious, that we both know." She threw him a pointed look. "Even as a child, remember? Anyway, darling, what are we going to do?"

"Do what all families do . . . work it out the best way we can, I suppose." Derek moved closer to the fire and sat down in the chair he had vacated a moment before. He picked up the script of *The Lion in Winter*, which dealt with a small segment of royal Plantagenet family life, and began to read again. After only a few minutes he closed the script, leaned back in the chair, and studied his wife.

Blair sat relaxed on the sofa, lost in thought; there was a faraway look in her eyes, and he knew she was worrying about the family, as she had been prone to do for years.

Blair was a remarkable woman—stoic, stalwart, dependable, and diplomatic. She had been blessed with an understanding of people, had enormous insight into them. He knew that being married to an actor, and a famous one at that, was no easy ride on a merry-go-round for a woman. Quite the opposite. You had to be strong, tenacious yet flexible, and willing to compromise. It struck him that she looked more beautiful than ever today. When he had first met her, he had thought of her as the epitome of the all-American beauty, tall, long-legged, with a clear, shining skin, glossy blonde hair, passionate dark eyes, and gleaming white teeth. Blair had a truly lovely face, and Chloe, in particular, resembled her greatly.

He nodded to himself. Blair had aged well, like a really good wine, and she was as slim and elegant as ever. But it was her integrity, the joyousness of her spirit, her wit, humor, and warmth that he loved the most.

Blair said, "When should we talk to Stevie about Chloe, Derek?"

He shrugged. "I'm not sure, when we find the right moment, I suppose. Today's Saturday, and we're leaving tomorrow afternoon. I think it will have to be tonight sometime. After dinner might be best." He shook his head and exhaled. "I have a feeling she's not going to like it. You know how she hates interference."

"Maybe you should see Steve alone. She has always respected you and taken your advice into account."

"I've never discussed John Lane with her before."

"There's always a first time for everything, Derek."

10

"I wish you could tell Chloe something about him, Stevie," Derek said quietly. "Believe me, anything at all would help to assuage her rampant curiosity, my darling."

Stevie returned her stepfather's steady gaze with one that was equally as steady, then walked across the study and draped herself against the mantel. She answered in a low voice, "I can't, Derek. You see, I don't know anything about him myself . . ." She let her sentence dangle, at a sudden loss for words.

Derek appeared surprised, and he gave her an odd look, his brows furrowing. "I'm not sure I'm following you."

Clearing her throat, Stevie murmured, "I hardly knew him. I think the best way to explain it is to say that it was a . . . a . . . brief encounter. We met at a cocktail party, discovered we were incredibly attracted to each other, and went off to dinner. Later that same week we met again. At a hotel. I slept with him. And that's when I got pregnant."

"And what did the gentleman in question have to say about

that? I presume you told him you were pregnant when you found out?" Derek replied carefully.

"Yes, I did tell him. Actually, he couldn't handle it, Derek."

"He didn't want to marry you?"

Stevie shook her head. "We hardly knew each other."

"So he threw you onto your own resources?"

"If you want to put it that way, yes."

"Charming."

Stevie was silent.

Derek said slowly, "He didn't really die in a car crash before Chloe was born, did he, darling?"

"No, he didn't. I told Chloe that story because it seemed to be the best explanation there was, the only thing I could come up with anyway. She had started to ask so many questions about him. I was embarrassed, to tell you the truth." Stevie cleared her throat. "But he is dead."

"Isn't there anything you could give her, Stevie?"

"Such as what?"

"A letter, a photograph, something tangible of that sort."

"Don't be silly, I hardly knew him."

"When *did* he die?" Derek asked.

"About a year after Chloe was born."

"How did he die? What of?"

"Natural causes."

"And presumably you found out about his death."

"Correct."

"How did you find out?"

Stevie gave Derek a hard stare and began to laugh. "What's this, the Spanish Inquisition? You sound like Torquemada."

"I'm sorry," Derek apologized swiftly, looking chagrined. "I'm afraid I'm a bit guilty of being curious myself. After all, we've never ever discussed this before."

"I know that and I cut off any discussion with Mom years ago. And you never asked me. Good thing you didn't too!" she exclaimed, and laughed again.

"If you didn't know this man, had no contact with him, how on earth did you know that he had died?"

"It was in the papers," she improvised.

"Ah, so he was well known, then," he asserted.

"Sort of."

"And was John Lane his real name?"

"Only partially."

"You changed the surname for convenience?"

"I thought it better, wiser to keep him totally anonymous."

"Would I recognize the name? Did I know him?"

Stevie stood staring at Derek, who had now seated himself in a chair near the fireplace.

"Was he an actor?" he asked when she did not respond.

"Listen, Derek, I don't really want to continue this conversation. It happened years ago. It's not very important who he was."

"Chloe seems to think it is," he reminded her.

Stevie let out a long, weary sigh. "I don't know why she's got a bee in her bonnet about her father all of a sudden. She's not mentioned him to me for years, now she's bothering you and God knows who else. As if it mattered in the scheme of things. Here's a girl who's had everything handed to her on a plate. Now she wants to know about her father. A man who has done nothing for her, played no role in her life. Come on, Derek, let's be fair."

"You're absolutely right, unfortunately the young are just that: *young*. She seems to think you're being unfair. And please don't kill the messenger, I'm only relating what she said."

"Derek, surely I've made it clear. It was a one-night stand! I'm embarrassed. I told you that before. The grieving widow of three years had a fling one night and got caught. It's an old, old story, and it's happened to countless women since the beginning of the world . . . sleeping with a man for the first time and getting pregnant."

"I understand."

"Unfortunately, Derek, there's nothing I can tell you or Mom or Chloe about him . . . because of the circumstances."

"I know. But listen to me for a moment. You said you met him at a cocktail party. So it was most probably at our house, wasn't it? And no doubt he was an actor. In which case, I would have known him. Tell me his real name, and I'll think of something suitable to say to Chloe."

"I didn't meet him at your house, Derek! Mother and you did not know him!" Stevie exclaimed, her voice full of exasperation, her face taut.

Derek looked at her keenly. He knew without a shadow of a doubt that she was lying.

After Derek had left, Stevie changed into her nightgown and then went back into the study adjoining her bedroom. Seating herself at her desk, she opened her daily journal and reached for the pen.

But she did not write, merely gazed blankly at the empty page, her mind awash with so many different and troubling thoughts.

A sudden knock on the door startled her, made her jump, and she sat up in the chair. "Who is it?"

"It's only me," her mother said from the doorway.

"Another nocturnal visitor, I see."

Ignoring her sarcasm, Blair glided into the room, came to a stop at the desk, and put a hand on Stevie's shoulder. "Derek thinks he's upset you."

"He hasn't. He never upsets me, and he should know that after over thirty years. Look, Mom, I know he means well, but—"

"But the road to hell is paved with good intentions."

"I didn't say that, Mother."

"That's what you meant. Come, sit with me on the sofa."

Stevie got up, followed her mother, seated herself next to her, and said, "I hope you haven't come here to rehash everything Derek and I discussed."

"Certainly not. Nor do I want to start asking questions about something that happened so very long ago. The details of your relationship with John Lane, or whatever his name was, are your business. You didn't want to tell me anything at the time. Now it's eighteen years too late."

"An intelligent comment at last."

"Derek feels the same way I do, you know, Stevie. He's rather sorry he started this tonight, but we were both concerned about Chloe. She seemed so troubled this afternoon. Full of questions about her father."

"God knows why! I've been mother and father both to her, and frankly, I thought I'd done a good job. I've nurtured her, loved her, given her understanding and guidance. Furthermore, the whole family loves her, supports her, caters to her, and actually spoils her terribly. She has everything a girl could ever possibly want. An education, money, a future. And now, suddenly, she's running around asking, 'Who's my father? Why won't she tell me about him?' That's her new cry." Stevie shook her head and gave her mother a hard stare. "I can't tell her anything because I didn't have a relationship with him. It was a one-night stand. He was a total stranger."

"Derek told me all that," Blair replied, and sighed. "I know you sacrificed a great deal for Chloe, so I'm not one bit surprised that you're feeling impatient with her now."

"I never thought of it as a sacrifice, Mother," Stevie muttered with a frown.

"Yet it was, in my opinion. You were so devoted to her, you never gave yourself a chance to meet anyone, to have a life of your own, get married again. And you could have, Stephanie. By then the boys were all away at boarding school and you had Nanny for Chloe."

Stevie made no comment; she knew that everything her mother had just said was true. But she had felt so guilty about the circumstances of Chloe's birth, she had overcompensated in so many different ways. She had denied herself the possibility of personal happiness with a man, had chosen instead her children and her work.

"The young are very selfish, Stevie dear," Blair remarked. "Well, we're all selfish, I suppose, that's the human condition. But the young are more selfish. I remember I was, and so were you when you were a girl. And then there's that awful, all-consuming self-centeredness of the young. When we're in our teens and twenties we think we're the only thing that matters in the entire world. And that's what Chloe is going through now, Stevie. She has the pressing need to know about her biological father because of her need to know about herself. In a way, it has nothing to do with you, it's not against you. I hope you realize that."

"Yes, I guess I do, Mom. I'm just a bit annoyed she dumped all of this on Derek this weekend. I wanted you both to have a rest, enjoy yourselves."

"Oh, but we did, and we've loved being here. It's been wonderful, very cozy and relaxing. You've spoiled us." Blair shifted slightly on the sofa and looked at Stevie closely. "Do you think Derek looks tired?"

Stevie shook her head. "Not at all. He seems marvelous to me. Full of vim and vigor."

Blair smiled. "I do worry about him, you know. A long run in a play is always very taxing. Are you coming to London for Christmas?"

"Don't we always? I wouldn't miss it for the world."

After the merest hesitation, Blair asked, "Is she serious about not going to college?"

"I honestly don't know, Mom. I've decided to play the waiting game . . . let's see what she says after she's graduated from Brearley next summer."

"And what about her working at Jardine's?"

"That could be a whim. She seems to be somewhat focused on Gideon at the moment. And I don't know why. She and Miles are closer."

"What *about* Gideon, Stevie? Miles seems to think his brother is depressed. He told Derek he's very gloomy."

"Gideon has always been rather gloomy . . . perhaps morose is a better word. It's funny, they're so different in temperament. Miles is positive, his cup is always half full, while Gideon is just the opposite. Anyway, as far as Gideon's present mood is concerned, I personally think he's suffering from women trouble. More precisely, Margot trouble. I've noticed this odd mood of his in the past few months whenever I've been in London, and I think he's perturbed because he broke up with her."

"Is that all! Goodness, we'll soon fix that!"

Stevie laughed. "Oh, Mom, there's no one like you. You're always so positive you can cure what ails us."

After her mother had left, Stevie went back to the desk and once more picked up her pen. Again she did not write anything in her journal. Instead, she sat back, her thoughts centering on Chloe. I mustn't be too hard on her. My mother's right. This is not about me. It's about her. If only I could tell her something about her father, but I can't.

Stevie thought about him for a brief moment. She closed her eyes, and his image danced around in her head, as it had so often in the past. Thinking about him was futile, she knew that, but there were moments when she couldn't help herself. Like now. How different her life, their lives, would have been if only she had had more courage . . . the courage to tell him the truth. It was all too late now. No use dwelling on the past. As her mother had said earlier, it was eighteen years too late.

Almost against her own volition, Stevie rose and went to her briefcase, where she found her keys. Crossing the floor, she unlocked the large cupboard, bent down to the safe, and punched in the code on the keypad, then turned the handle. All of her diaries were stacked in neat piles inside the safe; it took her only a split second to find the one dated 1977. She took it out and went and sat on the sofa in front of the fire.

Stevie sat staring at the diary for a while without opening it, smoothing her hands over the gold-embossed numbers on the leather front: *1977*. What a year that had been. All kinds of memories flooded her, and *he* jostled for prominence in her mind. But she shook off thoughts of him, swiftly began to flip the pages until she came to the first week of December. Here it was, that fateful day, the day she had made all of her decisions. She began to read.

December 5th, 1977
London

I've been thinking a lot about the predicament I'm in. In fact, I've thought of nothing else really for days. And tonight I made my decisions. I'm going to have the baby.

Last week, when Jennifer Easton took me to see her doctor, I was thrilled when he confirmed that I was about eight weeks pregnant, as I suspected. And then on the drive home reality took over. I began to panic. Jennifer told me about a doctor in Mayfair. A well-known doctor who was associated with a clinic. Jennifer said that all I had to do was go and see him for an examination and explain my circumstances. He would then check me into the clinic and perform a D & C. When I came out I would no longer be pregnant. But I don't want to have an abortion. I want the baby. His baby. I never thought I would love another man after Ralph, but I do. I love him. We cannot be. But I can have his child. Some people are not so lucky.

Jennifer asked me what I'm going to tell people if I go ahead and have the baby. I've decided I'm not going to tell them anything. They can't force me to, and nobody's going to put me up against a wall and shoot me because I'm silent. My mother and Derek won't be a problem. Alfreda might make trouble, but I don't care about her. And anyway, I'm holding all the cards as far as the Jardines are concerned. My three sons. Sons who are in my custody. They are Jardines. Heirs to the Jardines. As for Bruce, whatever he really thinks he'll be diplomatic, careful with me. He needs me at Jardine's. He's not a well man; sometimes he seems much older than his years. Daily he grows more dependent on me. No, I won't explain myself. Not to anyone. I cannot tell him either. What to do? I'll have to break off with him. It will be difficult because I care about him.

There was more on the page, and the page after that, but Stevie had read enough. And so she closed the diary without finishing that particular entry to the end, just sat there, absently gazing at the dying embers in the grate.

Rightly or wrongly, those had been her decisions and she had abided by them. She filled with sadness. It was an old familiar, that ache inside. She had learned to live with it long ago.

11

WHENEVER SHE WAS WITH ANDRÉ BIRRON, STEVIE FOUND HERSELF
smiling. There was something about him, about his demeanor
and his personality that made her feel at ease, even happy, and it
seemed to her that he brought out the best in her.

André was a small, stocky, energetic man with silver hair, a
round, cherubic face, and shrewd eyes that looked like shiny
black buttons. He had been a friend of her husband who had
described André to her as "a little leprechaun of a man," and that
first description had stayed in her mind ever since.

She had met André just before Nigel was born, when she had
been heavy with child and slow on her feet. André, the father of
two himself, had been very solicitous of her, and caring. This
kindness aside, they had taken to each other at once. Despite the
difference in their ages they had become fast friends over the
years.

After Ralph's unexpected, very sudden death, André had
gone out of his way to stay in touch with Stevie. "I must keep a
fatherly eye on you," he would say whenever he came to London.
And for many years now he had been her mentor; she listened to

him, took his advice, and had never regretted doing so, since he always brought to her problems an unprejudiced point of view. And he was wise in the ways of the world.

It was from André that she had learned about the international side of the jewelry business, and about such great designers as Belperron, Boivin, and the Duke of Verdura, to name only a few.

André was an expert on these renowned designers of the thirties, forties, and fifties, as well as on Jean-Baptiste Tavernier, the intrepid merchant-traveler who had moved between Paris and the Golconda mines of India in the seventeenth century, and who had first brought diamonds back to Europe from the subcontinent. Tavernier had supplied diamonds to Louis XIV, the Sun King, and those members of the French court who could afford them. One of the first big "name" diamonds was called the Grand Mazarin, named after Cardinal Mazarin, who bequeathed it to the Sun King on his death.

Ralph had already taught her a great deal about diamonds by the time she met André; the latter had been impressed that a woman so young and inexperienced had acquired so much knowledge in so short a time. As she explained to him, she was a quick study, had a photographic memory, and had always harbored a genuine desire to learn about precious stones and Ralph's business, which fascinated her.

Ralph had told her once that he had two great passions in his life. "You, my love, and diamonds. So let me share my second passion with you, my first."

And that was really how she had been given such a well-rounded education about diamonds and other gems. Ralph had impressed two things on her when teaching her about diamonds: that the rarity and value of a diamond was determined by the four Cs: carat—the weight and size—plus the clarity, color, and cut of a stone, and that only the largest, rarest, and most dazzling stone is given a name.

And tonight, for the first time in her twenty-one-year career as a jeweler, she herself was going to bid on a big "name" diamond, the famous White Empress, which would go on the auction block at Sotheby's at seven o'clock exactly.

Only a few hours away. She did not feel nervous or apprehensive. Quite to the contrary. She was relaxed, self-confident and calm. And her mood, she was quite sure, was due to some extent to André's reassuring presence.

Stevie sat with him now in the sitting room of his suite at the Carlyle Hotel, sipping a glass of carbonated water, her attention riveted on him.

"And so, *ma chérie*, it was a decision I made . . . to show you the pieces first, before disposing of them elsewhere if you are not interested."

"I'm sure I will be, André," Stevie responded, smiling at him. "As you know, I'm always looking for lovely old things for the antique jewelry department at the London store. Some of my clients are interested only in the very old pieces these days."

"They are in vogue, yes," he answered, and got up, hurried off to another room in the capacious suite. Within a few seconds he returned, explaining, "Matt is bringing them so that you can view them, Stephanie."

Once again he sat down opposite her and then instantly jumped up, as sprightly as ever at seventy-five. He exclaimed, "Let us sit over there. At the table near the window. It is the better light, I think, no?"

"Yes, it is," Stephanie agreed, adding, "And there's also a good lamp on the table." She followed him across the room, eager to see what he had brought with him from Paris.

André Birron owned one of the most elegant and prestigious jewelry shops in the world, located on the Place Vendôme near the Ritz Hotel. The business had been founded in the nineteenth century by his great-grandfather, Pierre Birron, who had made a name for himself when he had outbid other jewelers for some of the royal jewels. At an auction in Paris in 1887, the diamonds of the Crown of France had been put on the block by the Third Republic. All the great jewelers were present, including Frédéric Boucheron of Paris, Tiffany & Company of New York, and Bonynge of London. It was Pierre Birron who had won some of the more magnificent spoils by going for broke. He never looked back. Like Jardine's, Birron et Cie was family owned and run. André's two sons worked with him at the Place Vendôme shop.

Matt Wilson, André's assistant, came in carrying a briefcase, which he brought over to André.

"*Bien, bien, ouvrez-le!*" André exclaimed.

Matt opened the briefcase, took out various gray suede pouches and jewelry wallets. Opening one of the large wallets, he pushed it toward Stevie without comment, but his expression said more than any words could.

Stevie stared at the necklace Matt had revealed. It was made of two strands of stained blue chalcedony beads. She felt a little shiver run through her as she gazed at the blue-gray beads that glistened as they caught and held the light. Then she exclaimed, "It's Belperron, isn't it?" Her voice held a note of excitement as she glanced at André.

"Yes, it is most probably Belperron." He let out a small sigh and shook his head, looking regretful. "It is unfortunate that Suzanne never signed her pieces. She believed her designs were so absolutely unique and unconventional that they were easily recognizable as being hers, and no one else's. 'My signature is redundant, André,' she used to tell me."

"More's the pity she never signed her creations. May I look at this more closely?"

"*Mais naturellement.*" The Frenchman lifted the necklace out of the suede wallet and handed it to her.

Stevie held it under the lamp on the table, examined the chalcedony beads and the flowerhead clasp. This was composed of larger, carved chalcedony stones that formed the petals; the center was set with a cluster of eight cabochon sapphires and bands of brilliant-cut diamonds.

André sat back in his chair, observing her, thinking what a stylish woman she was. Tonight she wore a well-cut tailored suit of black wool with black satin lapels and cuffs, and to his seasoned eye it was obviously couture. Her only pieces of jewelry were mabe pearl earrings, a single strand of large South Sea pearls, and a platinum watch. Simple, understated, very chic. She had a refined and elegant taste in all things, and especially so in jewelry; not unnaturally, her perfect taste was reflected in her own personal style of dressing.

André Birron was very proud of Stephanie Jardine and of what she had become. He had watched her grow and change and develop; he had also watched over her for some twenty-odd years. She was like the daughter he and his wife Elise had never had, and his wife was just as fond of her as he was.

Stephanie had turned herself into a formidable business-woman, and a jeweler par excellence. This gave him great pleasure and satisfaction, since she was his protégé in a sense.

But beyond her professionalism, there was something else, a uniqueness about her that made him feel all that much better for knowing her. Frequently, he had tried to define this particular quality in her, and had eventually come to the conclusion that it was the mixture of her integrity, decency, and genuine compassion that lifted her so high above others, made her so different.

There was something fine in her that was very rare, and admirable.

André felt that at the core of her there was a repose, a calmness, and a certain kind of aloofness that had more to do with reserve than snobbery, and it was also this that set her apart.

There were times when he wondered about the lover Stephanie had taken when she was a young widow, the father of Chloe, wondered why the relationship had never flourished, gone forward, led to a permanent situation such as matrimony. He had constantly discouraged her from confiding the intimate details of her life in him or anyone else, and apparently she had always followed those guidelines he had given her so long ago.

No one knew a single thing about Stephanie Jardine's private life other than what was obvious, which was there for all to see; not even her family had an inkling about what she did. If anything at all.

He assumed there must have been other boyfriends over the years, maybe even lovers, and yet he had never seen her with a man other than a business associate. In consequence, there was not one shred of gossip about her. That in itself was an accomplishment, he believed.

It suddenly struck him, and quite forcibly, that perhaps there was no gossip because there was nothing to gossip about. There was the strong possibility that her children, Jardine's, and her career had been, and were, enough for her. Yet only part of him believed this. He was a Frenchman and a romantic, and therefore he could not envision life without love. And what a barren life that would be, and so very lonely. To be alone was not enviable. He shrank from the thought that Stephanie lived such a cold and isolated private life. Surely that could not be so? he asked himself, and discovered he had no answer. And he did not have the courage to ask her.

It took Stevie only a moment longer to examine the necklace before she glanced up at André and said in a confident voice, "It's Belperron. No question in my mind about that. She made it anywhere between 1935 and 1938, I'd say. Yes, André, only Belperron herself could have designed this—" Very abruptly Stevie cut herself off, looked at him intently, and exclaimed, "You know, we've seen something very similar, you and I. In 1987, at the Sotheby's sale of the Duchess of Windsor's jewels in Geneva. Don't you remember, there was a necklace of hers that was rather like this one? One could say it was the sister to this. I certainly raved enough about it at the time, so I'm sure you couldn't possibly have forgotten."

"I do recall the occasion. And your enthusiasm." He smiled at her warmly. "That is one of the special things about you, *ma chérie*. You are not jaded. And when I saw this necklace a few weeks ago, I realized that you would be the one to truly appreciate its beauty. Do you not recall that when we were in Geneva for the Windsor sale, I told you that the duchess had been a frequent visitor to the Herz-Belperron shop in the rue de Châteaudun in Paris in the thirties?"

"Yes, I do remember."

"It was apparent to me in Geneva that the necklace at the auction was a Belperron piece, even though it was listed as 'probably Belperron.' Unfortunately, that is the problem with an unsigned item, it can only ever be listed as *probably*. But it was real. It had to be. The duchess wore a great many of Suzanne's creations. The one you are now holding is of the same style, quality, and period, do you not think so?"

She nodded. "Where did you find it?"

"The owner is a very well-known Frenchwoman, from *le gratin*, the upper crust, in Paris. She inherited it from her mother, who inherited it from *her* mother. She insists it is Belperron, not a fake, not a copy from the thirties."

"We are all in agreement," Stevie murmured. "But surely Belperron would have made earrings to match."

"*Voila!* My clever one! You know your designers well." He laughed.

"Thanks to you," she said, smiling back at him.

"These are the ear clips that complete the set." He took them out of a pouch and placed them on a table in front of her.

Reaching for the earrings, Stevie held them in the palm of her hand and examined them carefully. They were made of the same stained blue chalcedony, each one designed as a small leaf and set with a tapered band of diamonds and surmounted by a cluster of cabochon sapphires and diamonds.

"They're exquisite, and the set is perfect. I have just the right client, an elegant woman who collects thirties jewelry. I am sure she will be interested. She's in London though, not New York."

"That does not present any problem, as you are well aware. When I return to Paris this weekend, I will have the jewelry sent to London by the usual courier, the way I have done in the past."

"How much is the set?" she asked.

"Forty-five thousand dollars."

"Expensive."

"No, I do not think so, Stephanie, not for Belperron. The Duchess of Windsor's necklace and earrings went for more than that in 1987. Nine years ago."

"But that was a glamour auction and all the world came to it, don't forget. The prices were driven sky high because of the great interest in the Windsors—to be more precise, in the Duchess of Windsor."

André chuckled admiringly. "You never forget a thing, and what you say is true. However, let me please explain this particular situation. *I* am not selling the jewels, they are *not* the property of Birron et Cie. I am merely acting as a—how do you say?—a go-between, for a client. I am doing her a favor. She had the necklace and ear clips appraised and was informed they were worth about forty thousand dollars approximately. She asked me if I could get my own appraisal, which I did, and, *mon Dieu!* My appraiser came in with an even higher figure—fifty thousand. So we decided, she and I, to set a price somewhere in the middle. I will explain everything to you later if you decide to buy the pieces. Let you know how you will pay for them."

"All right."

"You do not doubt that the jewels are by Belperron, do you?"

"Oh, no, of course I don't. They bear her inimitable stamp, signature or not. The price is not a problem. What else did you bring from Paris?" she asked, now eyeing the other gray suede pouches on the table, her curiosity getting the better of her.

"Ah, yes, I will show you. There is a diamond pin by Jeanne Boivin. *Signed.* A lovely example of her individualistic work. Perfection, I think. Here it is." He took it out, gave it to Stevie. "It is owned by the same woman in Paris, and again it is a family heirloom. *Très jolie, oui?*"

"It is indeed." Stevie held the pin out in front of her, gazing at it, and admiringly so. It was a spray of flowers, Queen Anne's lace, she thought, and beautifully executed. It was typical of Jeanne Boivin's nature-theme designs of the mid-thirties, when the renowned designer copied her favorite plants and simple flowers in diamonds and platinum.

"I like this very much, and it's perfect for another client of mine," Stevie explained, instantly thinking of Derek. Her stepfather had asked her to look for something unusual he could give her mother for Christmas. Certainly this pin would suit Blair. It was stylish without being overwhelming.

"This is extremely rare," André announced as he presented a dramatic orange-shell brooch to her next.

"It's Verdura!"

André smiled with pleasure. "It seems I taught you well, *ma chérie*. Yes, it is the duke's famous lion's paw shell pin. As you know, he made several of them in the thirties, until the shells became extinct, difficult to find anymore. It has become a much-sought-after piece of jewelry, not only because of its individuality but because it is by Verdura. When my client showed it to me, and hesitated about putting it up for sale, I convinced her to do so. She will never wear it and she is in need of money. But look, Stephanie, at this workmanship . . . at the encrustation of diamonds set in gold strips which run up the front of the paw. The work is superb, *incroyable*, do you not agree?"

"I certainly do, and it's a very unusual pin. Ideal for a brunette with a strong personality." She placed the shell pin on the table and leaned back against the chair, smiling at her old friend. She had not had to think twice about buying the antique jewelry, and so she said, "I shall take this, as well as the Boivin and the Belperron pieces. It's not very often that something by Verdura comes on the market, and the duke's jewelry has become very popular in the last few years."

"I am happy you are taking them. Each item is unique. Because they are so rare they are extremely valuable. You can almost put any price on them you want, *chérie*."

Stevie laughed. "You'd better get out your calculator and tot this up. And then I think we must leave for the auction. I want to get there early."

"*Mais oui*, the auction! I am looking forward to it. And even more than that, I am looking forward to being your escort. What a triumph it is going to be for you, Stephanie, when you win the White Empress."

Stevie stared at him but said nothing. Quite unexpectedly she felt apprehensive and at a loss for words.

André said, "Before we leave I have something for you. Excuse me." He almost ran out of the room, calling for Matt as he disappeared into the small foyer of the suite. In a moment he was back, holding a black leather box in his hands. Giving it to Stevie, he said, "This is for you, Stephanie, and it comes to you with our love."

Stevie was so completely taken aback, she gaped at him, and then she opened the box. She caught her breath when she saw the delicate diamond pin on the black velvet; it was a long, curling feather and it was extraordinary. "Oh, André, it's beautiful! But I can't accept this . . . it's far too valuable."

"No, no, you cannot refuse! You must not refuse. It is special . . . a *cadeau, ma chérie,* for your birthday."

"My birthday's not until next week."

"I will not be in America next week."

Realizing how ungracious it would be to argue with him any further, she said, "Thank you, André, it was so lovely of you and Elise to remember. I shall call her tomorrow to thank her."

"My wife adores you . . . to her you are like a daughter."

"I know. And I love her too." Stevie now began to laugh, shaking her head. "I can't believe I am going to be forty-seven next week. It doesn't seem possible."

"I cannot believe it either. What has happened to the time? It seems to me it was only the other day I met you with Ralph. You were not quite seventeen and very pregnant. Thirty years ago."

"*Please!*" she exclaimed. "Don't remind me!"

"I am proud of you, proud of what you've become. And if he were alive, Ralph would be also proud. You are only forty-seven and at the apex of your career . . . considered to be one of the world's great jewelers. And you are revered."

"Thank you for your lovely words, André," she replied, touched by what he had just said. "But it is *you* who is *revered,* not I." Rising, she walked across to the mirror hanging on a side wall and fastened the diamond feather on the lapel of her jacket. Then she turned around, her expression one of great affection. "How does it look, your beautiful feather?"

"*Superbe, ma chérie.*"

She walked across to him, bent down, and kissed him on each cheek. "Thank you again, André. I shall treasure it always."

He nodded, and patted her hand resting on his shoulder, his dark eyes twinkling. He was pleased their gift had been so well accepted, and said, "I will tell Matt we must leave for the auction at once," and got up, strode off.

Stevie sat down at the table, began to put the jewelry back in the pouches and wallet. Then she placed them in the briefcase.

Together, André and Matt came into the sitting room; they were both wearing their overcoats and Matt carried Stevie's Trigère cape of black wool lined with red silk. He helped her into it, then locked the briefcase and picked it up.

André's assistant said, "I'll take the briefcase down with us, leave it in the hotel safe."

"*Bien, bien,* but let us hurry now, Matt, we must not be late."

As the three of them went down in the elevator, Matt turned to Stevie. "The brooch is gorgeous on you. And you know what, you could wear it on that black velvet beret you favor . . . then you'll have"—he grinned at her, and finished—"a feather in your cap."

"Oh, Matt . . ." She smiled up at him, shaking her head.

André also smiled, then asked, "And how are you feeling, *chérie?* Excited, I am quite certain."

"No, nervous," Stevie answered, and gave a funny little laugh.

"No, no, you must not be nervous! You must be your usual cool self. Cool and contained. I am here. Matt is here. All will be well. You will see. And it is going to be your evening, my Stephanie."

12

Stevie felt the buzz in the air the moment they arrived at Sotheby's on York Avenue. A sense of anticipation and excitement permeated the auction rooms, and to her they seemed like palpable things. People milled around, greeting each other, talking, laughing, and commenting about the auction due to take place within the next half hour.

As Stevie glanced around, she spotted a bevy of well-known New Yorkers, some of them her clients, and also recognized any number of renowned jewelers from London, Paris, Rome, and Geneva as well as from New York.

It was a smartly dressed crowd. The men wore expensive, well-tailored suits; the women were mostly in black, as they usually were in New York at night. She had lived there long enough now to know that black with diamonds or pearls was the compulsory, and very chic, uniform. She had enough black suits, dresses, and silk pumps in her wardrobe to attest to that.

"Let's not waste time out here," Stevie said, glancing from André to Matt, and headed toward the room where the auction was to be held.

As they entered, they were given catalogues and numbered paddles to use for the bidding, and then moved on into the room. Matt found three good seats in the center, where they all sat down, with Stevie positioned between the two men. After settling in her seat, she glanced around, eyeing her immediate neighbors.

"*Quelle scène*," André said, his eyes sweeping around. "*Mon Dieu!* Everyone is here!"

"Sure they are—the world and his mother," Matt remarked.

"Such quaint expressions you have, Matt," André murmured, then exclaimed, "Ah, there is my old friend, Gilberto Guantano from Brazil. It is a long time since I have seen him. I must go to him, embrace him. Excuse me, Stephanie, Matt." So saying, he slipped out of his seat and hurried down the aisle to speak to his friend.

After a moment, Matt rose, stood looking around, wondering who was there that *he* knew. He saw two notable jewelers from Paris, lifted his hand in greeting, and remained standing next to Stevie, his eyes continuing to scan the room, his curiosity running high. "André is correct, this is some turnout," he said, looking down at Stephanie. "Everyone is here, or they've sent representatives . . . I see people from Harry Winston, Cartier, and Boucheron. I've just spotted one of the directors of Van Cleef, the Garrard group, and David Morris is over there with his wife, Suzette. Quite a lot of people from London have flown in."

"Yes, I know. And I saw a couple of familiar faces from Geneva as well."

Matt finally took his seat, then went on. "But I wonder how many are actually serious bidders?"

"I'm not sure," Stevie responded, "but I have a feeling I'm going to get a run for my money."

"And my money's on you," Matt said with a wide grin.

Stevie shook her head. "I don't know, Matt . . . well, we'll see."

"Nervous?"

"A bit," she admitted, and gave him a rueful smile.

"Try not to worry," Matt advised. "You'll see, it'll be all right."

"That's what André keeps telling me. I hope he's right."

"He is. We both feel it in our bones, you're going to get the White Empress."

"By the looks of this crowd, I'm going to have to pay for it . . . *really pay.*"

"Have you set a limit on it?"

"I don't really want to go beyond ten million," she said sotto voce, not wanting anyone to overhear. "But I will if I have to. I'd go up to twelve million."

Matt nodded but made no further comment. Then he stood up again, glancing around, wondering somewhat worriedly who her *real* competitors were going to be.

Stevie shifted slightly in her chair, endeavoring to relax, but it was hard for her to do so. She was taut with nerves, strung tight like a violin string, and growing anxious all of a sudden. She wanted the auction to begin so that she could get it over with, be done with it now. The noise level was rising as more and more people flooded in; she felt far too warm, and the smell of mingled perfumes was overwhelming.

The White Empress. One of the most fabulous diamonds in the world. Her mind settled on it for a moment or two. She wanted it. She was determined to get it, but there was the real possibility that she might not. Somebody might easily outbid her. She was accustomed to being in control—of herself, her business, her life, and she was not happy when she was not. It was certainly not possible to be in control of a public auction. Only the auctioneer had that kind of control, since it was he who determined everything, at least to a certain extent.

An unexpected thought popped into her head, and she had to bite back a smile. Of course she could be in control of this auction. But only if she was prepared to pay *anything* for the White Empress, top any bid. I will, she said under her breath, I'll outbid everybody here. Somehow this idea was liberating, and she felt the tension easing out of her. If she was prepared to pay any price, then she was not only in control already, she already owned the diamond. So invigorating and exciting was this possibility, Stevie clamped her mouth shut and looked at the catalogue. She was afraid that she might blurt out her thoughts to Matt. *A still tongue and a wise head,* she heard Ralph's voice saying in the far recesses of her mind.

Focusing in on the White Empress again, Stevie asked herself what she might conceivably have to pay for it, given her decision to outbid everyone present? Twelve, thirteen even fourteen million? Possibly. Maybe more. She wasn't sure. The auction could go any which way; she knew this only too well. The reserve price, the presale price, was six million. In a way this did not mean very much. As Matt had just pointed out to her, the auction was jammed with many prominent international jewelers as well as a number of multimillionaires and billionaires whom she had recognized instantly. If they *all* bid, the price would be pushed so high, it would be ludicrous.

André came back to his seat and squeezed her hand. "Gilberto thinks a lot of people are merely here for the excitement, for the fun of it. Do not worry."

"Oh, I'm not worried, André darling," she said, and she sounded positively nonchalant. So much so that both André and Matt looked at her alertly, then glanced at each other.

Suddenly the auctioneer was stepping up to the podium.

Instantly the room fell silent.

And so it began. The auction for the White Empress.

The lights dimmed and the color slides of the diamond suspended on its superb Harry Winston necklace flashed onto the screen that stood on the left of the podium. The auctioneer made his statement, giving all the details of the great diamond and its origins. The slide show finished, the lights went up, and the auctioneer started the bids rolling.

Looking out into the crowded room, he said with undisguised enthusiasm, "I'll take the opening bid to my right. Two million dollars." His eyes swiveled to the other side of the room. "Two million two hundred and fifty thousand from the center left. Two million five hundred thousand from the back of the room."

After the opening bid of two million, the price was rising in increments of two hundred fifty thousand dollars. After years of attending auctions all over the world, Stevie was aware that the amount could change at the will of the auctioneer. It was he who made the decisions.

Finally she raised her paddle. The auctioneer acknowledged this with the merest flicker of an eyelash. "Three million from the center. Three million two hundred fifty thousand to my left. Three million five hundred thousand to the left front. Three million seven hundred fifty thousand at the back. Do I hear four million?"

Once more Stevie raised her paddle, bringing the price up to the desired four. It went on climbing after this, as others raised their paddles and made their bids. The pace was rapid, the excitement mounting.

André and Matt were on the edges of their seats, as was she. Her adrenaline was pumping hard when she plunged in once more and made her bid for five million. Yet again it did not end there, as she had known it wouldn't; the reserve price had to be met. The person who had outbid her was outbid several times by others wanting to claim the White Empress as their own.

The auction was moving at a fast and furious pace. The tension in the room was a most viable thing, and Stevie felt as though she could reach out, touch it, take it in her hand. Just as she was determined to take the diamond in her hand—for Jardine's.

Another bid came in, and another, and then another, and another after that, until the price had escalated even higher, had gone well over the presale figure of six million.

Stevie was relaxed, sat staring straight ahead, holding her paddle in her lap, making no moves at all. I must wait now, she told herself. Drop back so that the auctioneer will wonder about me, wonder if I'm dropping out altogether. She kept a poker face, but inside she was smiling.

André, watching her closely, knew what she was doing. She was biding her time, not wanting to contribute to the acceleration of the price.

Twenty minutes later Stevie sat up straighter, her attention fully directed on the auctioneer, all of her senses alerted. The bidding had reached eight million five hundred thousand even without her participation. And then it had slowed. Several people had resisted, had not bid, and to all intents and purposes they had now dropped out. Stevie waited for the auctioneer to change the amount of the increments, which he did almost immediately. He lowered them to one hundred thousand dollars.

Now that this had happened, the bidding started to move again, although not quite as rapidly or as intensely as before. The price rose accordingly as ten bids came in, bringing the price up to nine million eight hundred thousand dollars. And then once more it slowed, and, somewhat unexpectedly, came finally to a halt.

"Nine million eight hundred thousand," the auctioneer repeated, his voice rising slightly. "Do I hear nine million nine?"

Stephanie raised her paddle.

"*Nine million nine hundred thousand in the center!* I want to hear ten million. Ten million dollars for the White Empress."

A bid came from somewhere in the room, and she heard the auctioneer cry, "Ten million from the front. *Ten million!* Ten-million-one, am I getting an offer of ten million one hundred thousand for this magnificent diamond?"

To Stevie the silence in the room seemed to magnify. It became so hushed, a pin dropping would have sounded like a crash. Every person sat on the edge of his or her seat, their attention focused on the auctioneer.

Stevie held her breath.

The auctioneer repeated himself. "Do I hear ten million one? Surely I do." There was a brief pause; not one paddle was raised.

"Ten million one hundred thousand. Do I have that offer?" The auctioneer cleared his throat. "Ten million, then, to the bidder at the front, unless I hear ten million one hundred thousand."

André touched her arm.

Stevie brought her paddle up.

"*Ten million one hundred thousand!*" cried the auctioneer, sounding triumphant, full of jubilance.

Stevie's heart was pounding against her rib cage and her mouth was dry like sandpaper. She sat as though turned to stone, again hardly daring to breath, waiting for the next bid, for someone to top her. But no one did. The stone was hers. For a moment it didn't seem possible.

"Ten million one hundred thousand dollars it is. Sold to the lady in the center."

Everyone in the room brought their eyes to her. Someone

began to applaud. Others joined in. The applause became louder. A woman cried, "Bravo! Bravo!"

André hugged her to him and kissed her cheek. And so did Matt, who exclaimed, "You're as cold as ice."

Stevie shook her head. "No, I'm fine, really I am, Matt."

"I would say you are indeed fine," André murmured against her ear, smiling broadly. "As fine as you'll ever be, Stephanie. And when you are ready to leave, I shall take you to dinner at La Grenouille."

They came to speak to her then, streaming across the room, people she knew, clients and friends, and colleagues from the jewelry business. And they brought their congratulations and they wished her well.

13

STEVIE SAT IN HER OFFICE ON THE TOP FLOOR OF THE JARDINE BUILD-
ing on Fifth Avenue in the fifties.

It was Tuesday morning, a few days after the auction at
Sotheby's the week before, and the White Empress had just been
delivered a short while ago. The previous Friday the paperwork
had been completed and the money had been wired bank to
bank.

And so here it was at last, one of the most important stones
in the world, and it belonged to her, or, rather, to Jardine's.

Stevie now lifted the necklace out of the dark blue leather
Harry Winston jewelry case and held it up in front of her. The
huge pear-shaped diamond was 128.25 carats with fifty-eight
facets on the crown and pavilion and eighty-five additional
facets around the girdle. The diamond threw off a myriad of
prisms as it blazed in the sunlight pouring in through the window. The stone was D-flawless and therefore perfect, and it was
so blindingly white, so pure, it was breathtaking.

It is magnificent, heartstopping in its beauty, she thought,
examining it very closely, appreciating its perfection. The stone

hung on a single-strand necklace composed of sixty-eight round and pear-shaped diamonds, and the whole thing was a spectacular piece of jewelry.

On the spur of the moment, Stevie rose and went across to the antique French gilt mirror hanging on the wall of her office and held the necklace against her black dress. It was stunning. And she could not help wondering, in an abstract way, who would end up wearing it one day, when she finally came to sell it.

Walking back to the antique Louis XV *bureau plat* near the window, she sat down and held the necklace up toward the light again, admiring the way its facets threw off a brilliant rainbow sparkle. Then she glanced up with a start as the door burst open unexpectedly, and her son Nigel marched in. Stevie was taken aback, so startled she almost dropped the necklace. It took all of her self-possession to keep her face completely neutral.

"Nigel! This is a surprise!" she exclaimed, and placed the necklace in the jewelry case. Rising, she took a tentative step toward him, intending to greet him, as always full of warmth and love for her firstborn, despite her growing suspicion of his duplicity.

"Hello, Mother," he said coldly, and immediately sat down in a chair, making it perfectly obvious that he wanted no displays of affection from her.

This gave Stevie no alternative but to sit down herself, which she did.

Glancing at the necklace on her desk, Nigel said in a scathing voice, "Drooling, I see."

Annoyed though she was with his tone and superior manner, she ignored both. "I didn't know you were coming to New York. When did you get in?"

"Last night."

"Oh." There was a slight pause on her part, and then she said,

"I wish you'd let me know beforehand. I could have planned something . . . for us all to get together."

A brow lifted sardonically, but he said nothing.

She said, "You could have seen Chloe and Miles."

He draped himself in the chair, looking immensely bored, and she felt compelled to add, "Wouldn't you like to see your brother and sister?"

"Not particularly."

Stevie leaned back, gazing at him, filling with dismay at his manner and at his attitude. He had behaved somewhat in the same rude and churlish way when she had last been in London, and it puzzled her. After a moment, she said, "What are you doing in New York?"

Nigel hesitated, but only fractionally. "The Sultan of Kandrea wants to see me. About some stones. And since he cannot come to London at the moment, I came here."

"Is he in New York or Los Angeles?"

"New York."

"We could easily have handled it ourselves if you'd informed us. In fact, I would have been quite happy to see the sultan myself. There was really no need for you to fly all this way, Nigel."

"But he doesn't want to deal with you, Mother. He prefers to do business with me."

"That's something of a departure, since he and I have been doing business for years. Perhaps it isn't so surprising, now that I think about it. The sultan does have a reputation for being unpredictable. And fickle. Be alerted to those traits, Nigel."

"I can make my own judgments, Mother. I'm no longer a snot-nosed boy in short pants."

Biting back the sharp retort on the tip of her tongue, she said, "Quite," gave him a slight smile and asked, "What kind of stones is the sultan looking for?"

"I don't know yet. I have an appointment to see him later."

"And how long are you staying in New York?"

"I'm either leaving tonight on the evening flight or on tomorrow's Concorde."

"We have some really spectacular stones available, and some magnificent —"

"The sultan certainly wouldn't be interested in *that*," he interrupted peremptorily, nodding his head at the White Empress, his expression disdainful.

"*That's* not for sale!" she shot back, and closed the lid of the jewelry case with a small thud. "But certainly it's *big* enough for him. He has always favored big diamonds, and I'm positive he still does."

"You paid far too much for that stone, Mother. A bad buy."

"No, it wasn't, Nigel. If and when I do decide to sell it, I will make a very good profit. I've already had two offers for it since the auction, and I took delivery of it myself only half an hour ago. If I'm not careful, it'll be whisked out of here before I can even blink. Quite aside from those offers, my purchasing the White Empress has generated enormous publicity. Jardine's acquisition of the stone has been reported in every newspaper in the world."

"I wouldn't boast about that kind of vulgar publicity if I were you, Mother."

"Not vulgar publicity, Nigel. *Good publicity.*"

"Jardine's doesn't need publicity of any kind," he snapped in his most superior voice, "at least, the London branch doesn't."

"*Touché*. But you're quite wrong, Nigel. We need good publicity on both sides of the Atlantic. We've a lot of competition these days, and we've got to sell ourselves as aggressively as any other jewelry company. That's the way it is in the nineties. Ask any spin doctor."

"Really, Mother, you begin to sound more American every day."

"I *am* an American, Nigel, and you are half American. Or had you forgotten that?"

"You go too far, Mother."

She wasn't quite sure what he meant by this, but choosing not to be goaded into taking the bait, she ignored his derisive comment, continuing evenly. "As for the White Empress, it was not only a good buy, but a bargain at the price."

"Grandfather doesn't think so. He also says you paid too much."

"Bruce said that?" she exclaimed incredulously, and then started to laugh. "Did he *really* say that?"

"Yes, he did," Nigel answered. "He says you have always paid too much for stones, especially diamonds."

"And when did I start doing this? Did he tell you that?"

Nigel inclined his head and gave her a defiant stare. "When you opened the Fifth Avenue store."

"What a curious thing for him to say when Jardine's in New York is actually making a huge profit. Do you think that Bruce has gone a bit senile?"

"Certainly not, Mother."

"And when did you last see him?"

"Yesterday. Before I left. He came into the London store. He's been coming in quite a lot lately."

"How interesting." Stevie rose, stood leaning against the *bureau plat,* her shrewd eyes leveled steadily on her son. "We have a new turn of events, so it seems. When I was in London a few weeks ago, your grandfather said he did not propose to come to the store anymore."

"Perhaps he changed his mind."

"Whether he did or not is quite beside the point. *I* run

Jardine's in London, as well as here, and Bruce's opinion about what I pay for stones doesn't particularly interest me. Nor does anyone else's opinion, for that matter. But getting back to your grandfather, he has no power. He retired long ago. And his title of chairman is simply a courtesy—" She paused to let her words sink in before adding, "A courtesy on my part."

Nigel stared at her, his expression hostile, but he knew better than to make any kind of adverse remark.

Returning his stare with one equally as cold, Stevie couldn't help thinking what a good-looking young man he was at twenty-nine, with his bright blue eyes set wide apart, aquiline features, and dark blond hair. And he was tall, well dressed, elegant. What a pity it was his personality did not match his pleasant and most appealing looks.

Nigel was the first to grow uncomfortable, to blink and look away from her icy gray-green eyes, her appraising gaze. He jumped up from the chair, edged toward the door. "I'd better be going," he muttered, and strode across the room, then paused in the doorway. "Good-bye, Mother."

"Will I see you again before you go back to London, Nigel?" she asked quickly, and cursed herself under her breath for her weakness, for suddenly being his mother rather than his boss.

"I don't think so. I want to catch the night flight if I can."

"I understand. Anyway, I'll be in London in about ten days."

"You're coming for Christmas?"

"Yes. Chloe and I are leaving on the twentieth."

He nodded, opened the door.

"Give my love to Tamara, and kiss the children."

"Yes," he said, and was gone, slipping out of her office without a backward glance, closing the door softly behind him.

Stevie remained standing, staring at the door, a look of total bafflement on her face. She understood him less and less. It sud-

denly struck her that he had not told her why he had visited
Jardine's that morning on his extremely quick trip to New York.
Perhaps he didn't have a reason, had just stopped by out of habit.
Or maybe he was curious to see what was going on in the store.
He might even have wanted to get a glimpse of the White
Empress despite his disparaging attitude about it. Or had he
come in intentionally to taunt her, to pick a fight? She did not
know.

Certainly he had not come in to wish her happy birthday,
which is what she originally had thought when he had first burst
in on her, but he had soon disabused her of that idea with his
contentious manner and obvious desire to be combative. He
hadn't even mentioned her birthday, in fact.

Later that same day, Tuesday, the tenth of December, Jardine and
Company closed earlier than the usual time of six o'clock.

Once the main doors, which opened onto Fifth Avenue, were
locked, the White Empress was put on display in an illuminated
showcase in the center of the main salon. This was a medium-
sized room with a high ceiling from which dropped several
antique crystal chandeliers; showcases in which jewels were displayed were built in on several walls, and were cleverly and effectively illuminated. Underfoot, a luxuriously thick silver-gray
wool carpet stretched the length of the floor; an antique Louis
XV *bureau plat* and two antique French desks were strategically
placed in different areas of the room. Normally used by the sales
executives, tonight they were decorated with beautiful arrangements of flowers.

At six-thirty promptly, members of the staff gathered
together in the salon to toast Stevie on her birthday, as well as
celebrate her acquisition of the great diamond. Champagne and
hors d'oeuvres were served to her employees and the few guests

she had invited. Miles and Chloe were present, along with Matt Wilson and André Birron. André, delayed in his return to Paris, was giving a small dinner for her birthday later that evening.

The four of them surrounded her like a phalanx, wishing her a happy birthday, singing her praises. And all were impressed by the pear-shaped diamond, stood there staring at it mesmerized, bedazzled by its beauty, unable to tear their eyes away from the display case.

André finally turned to Stevie and said, "I am glad I was delayed here on business, and that I could be present tonight, *ma chérie*. To see this incomparable diamond again and to celebrate your birthday, Stephanie, that is wonderful."

"I am happy you're here, André, and I want to thank you again for being so supportive the other evening at the auction. I really was full of anxiety."

"It was nothing at all. And as for your nervousness, you did not show it."

Moving forward, Chloe clutched her mother's arm, exclaimed, "Mom, it's just awesome! *Awesome.* And it was so neat, the way you beat everybody out at the auction. *Cool.* You're the greatest, Mom."

"Thank you, Chloe," Stevie murmured, pleased that her daughter was so enthusiastic and filled with her usual natural warmth. For the first few days after Thanksgiving she had been sulky and mute, acting up in the way teenagers could, making everyone else feel uncomfortable and miserable. This recalcitrant mood had slowly diminished, and completely vanished tonight.

André said, "It is indeed awesome, Chloe. And so is your mother, *ma petite*."

"There's nobody like her, Uncle André."

"I am glad to hear that you appreciate her. She deserves it. Shall we go over to the far side of the salon and look at the other jewels? Your mother just told me that she is showing the latest collection of new designs for the first time tonight."

"Okay," she agreed, and tucked her arm through his.

"I'll join you," Matt said, following André and Chloe across the salon.

Stevie now stood alone with Miles in front of the glass show-case where the White Empress reposed, and she was intrigued by the look on her son's face. "It does knock the breath out of you, doesn't it, Miles?"

"It sure does. I'm blown away by it, actually, Ma." Miles turned to his mother and went on. "I've never seen a stone like this one. But I guess you have."

"Yes, I've seen some which were just as big, and others which were even bigger. There is something about this particular stone that is . . . *unique.* Actually, all stones are unique because no two are ever *exactly* alike. There is just something so extraordinary about this one, something that is hard to describe."

Miles nodded, turned to the display case again. "What fire and beauty there is under its icy exterior."

"It's the cut. Harry Winston had this one cleaved from a large piece of rough, but he studied it for months and months on end first before he let a lapidary get anywhere near it. He had an unerring instinct about stones, Miles, and he could look at a piece of rough and see what others couldn't see."

"I'm glad you got it, Mother, you wanted it so much. Congratulations again. And happy birthday again. By the way, your present is being delivered to the apartment later. I hope you like it."

"I'm sure I will, darling."

"André's diamond feather is beautiful, Ma."

"Isn't it just? He's so pleased he can be here tonight after all, and so am I."

"Chloe seems on top of the world," Miles remarked, then grinned. "I wouldn't want to be a teenager again. It's a bumpy ride."

Stevie agreed, and then, turning away from the showcase, she took hold of Miles's arm, led him to a corner of the salon. "Nigel came into the store today."

"Nigel! What the hell's he doing in New York?" Miles stared at his mother, flabbergasted.

"He flew in to see the Sultan of Kandrea, who is apparently looking for some stones."

"I thought the sultan was your client?"

"So did I until this morning. Apparently he prefers to deal with Nigel now."

"Who says?"

"Nigel."

"I don't believe *that*!"

"Nigel made a great point of it in our brief conversation."

"He's lying. He was always full of it. I bet he's trying to worm his way into the sultan's good graces. Maybe he told Kandrea it was your idea, that you don't want to handle his business anymore. I wouldn't put it past Nigel."

"I don't know . . ." She shook her head, took a sip of champagne.

"If you phoned the sultan I bet he'd tell you exactly that, Mother. Tell you what's what."

"I really couldn't do that, it would seem a little . . . strange. And I certainly wouldn't want the sultan to think there was something —"

"Rotten in the state of Denmark?" he cut in, giving her a pointed look and raising a dark brow.

"That's one way of putting it, I suppose. But we must show a united front, I've always told you that. Anything else is bad for business."

"Nigel's definitely up to something, Ma."

She nodded. "He baffles me, Miles."

"I get the feeling he wants to be top dog at Jardine's. But is he capable of running the company by himself?"

"He will be eventually. He has a lot to learn yet, of course. Still, to give the devil his due, he's a good businessman. Not at all creative though, not in the way that Gideon is creative. And he doesn't know a lot about stones. On the other hand, there are a lot of experts on stones at Jardine's, both here and in London, so that's not so important. Not at the moment anyway." Stevie paused, her expression regretful. "And I tend to agree with you, he'd like me to disappear."

"You're too young to retire. What on earth would you do if you didn't work?"

"God knows, Miles. I'd be at a loss. Totally bored out of my mind. However, I'm not planning to retire, not for a long time, I can assure you of that. Whatever Nigel wants, Nigel *won't* get."

Miles laughed, then gave her an intent look. "You're forty-seven today."

"Don't remind me."

"Can I ask you something?"

"Anything, darling."

"You're a young woman, and yet you've ... you've never married again. Why?"

"For a perfectly good reason."

"Us, Ma?"

"Partially. But I've never met anyone I wanted to marry." She threw him an amused smile. "It takes two to tango, you know. Now that all my children are grown up, perhaps I'll start looking around for a husband." She chuckled, then, wishing to change the subject, she said, "Nigel was very churlish today, he didn't even wish me a happy birthday."

"Rotten sod," Miles muttered. "But then, he hasn't changed much. He was always a bit of a bugger even when he was a kid."

Stevie stared at her son, startled by the animosity in his voice. "I didn't know you so actively disliked your brother," she murmured, her eyes searching his face. "You never told me this before."

"Oh, Ma, why *would* I mention it? Anyway, I don't dislike him all the time. Only part of it. Nigel's a chameleon. One minute he's the basilisk, totally inscrutable and hard to read, the next he's turned into a romping puppy dog, licking your hand and bowling you over with his winsome personality and adorable charm."

"That's an apt way of putting it. But I must admit, I haven't seen much of Nigel's charm of late."

"He couldn't possibly have forgotten your birthday, Mother. He always made such a fuss about it when we were kids. He actually got to be a bit of a bore—" Miles cut himself off and his expression was chagrined as he added swiftly, "I didn't mean that the way it sounded."

"I know you didn't."

"I'm certainly glad you didn't invite Nigel to Uncle André's dinner for you tonight."

"I wouldn't do a thing like that!"

"Yes, you would, Ma! You've always been a bit of a softie when it comes to your family," he contradicted Stevie.

"It never crossed my mind to invite him, Miles. He was too unpleasant. Besides, he seemed hell-bent on catching the evening flight to London."

"I wonder how Tamara puts up with him?"

"Nigel can be very winning. You just said so. And Tamara is an exceptional young woman. She understands Nigel, has his number. Not only that, she's wise for her age, and she really knows how to handle him."

"I suppose she does. Is Uncle André taking us to La Grenouille?"

"Of course, it's his favorite restaurant in New York, and I like it too. But now we'd better circulate, don't you think, mingle with the other people here, otherwise they'll think we're being rude."

"Lead the way, Mother," he said, taking her arm affectionately, his pride in her much in evidence on his glowing face and in his wide smile.

PART TWO

Christmas

14

Stevie had lived in London half her life, and she was always happy when she returned.

It was not that she did not like New York, because she did. That city meant entirely different things to her, commanded another place in her heart. New York was the city of her birth, her early childhood, and teen years until she was fourteen, when her mother had married Derek and they had moved to London. New York also signified the last eight years of her life, of raising Chloe, buying and remodeling Romany Hall, starting and operating Jardine's on Fifth Avenue. She constantly thought of it as a city of new challenges and, in a certain way, of rebirth.

London represented the years of her marriage to Ralph, the birth and upbringing of her children, his untimely death, and, finally, her emergence as a businesswoman. It was the place she had spent her most formative years and where she had become a woman. And so, in a sense, London was a city of old challenges.

It was also a city rich in a multitude of memories and talismans of the past for her. Whenever she thought of it, she did so with enormous affection and nostalgia. Her mind would focus on those places that were special to her, meaningful because of their past associations, and she would be carried back in time.

As she sat at her desk in her office above the Jardine show-rooms in Bond Street, she found herself suddenly thinking of those earlier days in London and her favorite spots ... Whitestone Pond in Hampstead on a spring day bright with sun-light, where she and Ralph had so often taken the boys to sail their toy boats and then taken them to tea at Briar Lodge.

This was the big old stone house on Hampstead Heath where her mother and Derek had spent half their married life, and where she had lived for two years until she had married Ralph at age sixteen.

Stevie sat gazing into the distance for a moment, remember-ing Briar Lodge. It had been an oasis of love overflowing with welcoming warmth and hospitality, and she had been very attached to it, loved every nook and cranny of it.

Her mother had decorated the house with charming fabrics and antiques, old faded carpets and lovely paintings. Derek's books—thousands of them—reigned supreme, filling endless shelves in the library. His acting awards and the carefully col-lected, much-cherished theatrical memorabilia were given pride of place in his study. Stevie always thought of Briar Lodge as a house that had known only laughter and happiness.

The boys had loved to play hide-and-seek in the attics when they were young. Just by closing her eyes she was instantly trans-ported back to those days. She saw them as they had been then, her three sons, and their rambunctious shrieks and bloodcur-dling yells reverberated in her head, carrying her back into her memories even more deeply.

The garden of the house on the Heath had been another oasis for her, particularly in the spring and summer months. In spring it was a bower of leafy trees, green and restful; in summer the herbaceous borders and many rosebushes were riotous rafts of bright color against the smooth green lawn, and they filled the air with fragrance.

Several old apple trees created a canopy of shade on sunny days, and it was there that they had so frequently picnicked. Recalling those picnics now, her mouth suddenly began to water at the thought of the delicious tiny tea sandwiches filled with smoked salmon, egg salad, sliced cucumber, and watercress and cheddar. And there were always homemade scones lathered with Devonshire cream and strawberry jam, all washed down with scalding hot tea laced with lemon and poured from the big brown teapot Derek swore by.

It had been a rather sad day for her when Derek and her mother had sold Briar Lodge seventeen years ago and moved to the apartment overlooking Regent's Park, where they still lived. She had understood the move. Even though the flat was very large with many large rooms, it was, nevertheless, easier to run than the big old house.

There were other corners of London that she treasured in her heart. Cavendish Square was one, because it was there that she had first stumbled, and quite by accident, on Jacob Epstein's extraordinary sculpture, *Madonna and Child*. She hadn't known its name then, nor had she known the name of the sculptor, but she had made a point of finding out later, and she had become a devotee of his.

She had first noticed the sculpture one spring afternoon not long after Ralph's death, when she had been walking through the square, heading in the direction of Oxford Street. It had suddenly started to rain, and pausing, she had groped around in her handbag for her scarf. As she had tied it over her head she had happened to half turn around, and it was then that she had seen the sculpture; she had caught her breath, stunned by its beauty.

It was set on the wall above an archway in Deans Mews, which opened off the square. Mounted in such a way that it stood slightly away from the wall, it appeared to be levitating, actually floating upward of its own accord.

The sculpture was life-sized and towered toward the sky, and she had walked over to it fascinated, gazing up at it in the pale spring light.

Because of the manner in which it was sited on the wall of the arch, and its slight tilt forward, the rain struck the eyes of the sculpture. It seemed to her that the Madonna was crying real tears. They were trickling down her cheeks, dripping onto the head of the child Jesus, who stood immediately in front of the Virgin, also levitating.

Now Stevie saw the sculpture in her mind's eye, the image of it crystal clear. She recalled how she had been quite oblivious to the rain that afternoon, had been awed by the sculpture, had stood transfixed in front of it for ages. Only her dripping head scarf and soaking wet coat had forced her finally to hurry away, looking for a taxi. Its poignancy had touched her deeply, and she had made a point of going back to Deans Mews for many years afterward, in order to look at Sir Jacob's remarkable sculpture.

I'll go and see it this trip, she thought, before I go back to New York in January. And then she suddenly wondered why it was that she was so deeply engrossed in the past that morning.

Perhaps it was because she did not want to deal with the present. With Nigel, to be precise. After all, it was Monday, December the twenty-third, just two days before Christmas, and the last thing she wanted was to cause family discord at this time.

In any case, he was noticeably absent from the Bond Street showrooms that day; his secretary Angela had told her he had gone to Amsterdam with Gilbert Drexel, who was one of the diamond experts at Jardine's. She could not help wondering if they were off hunting stones for the Sultan of Kandrea.

After Christmas, Stevie thought, I'll tackle Nigel after the holidays.

The antique French striking clock by Le Roy et Fils of Paris, which stood on the William and Mary inlaid chest at the other side of the room, suddenly struck the hour. Stevie glanced up, peered at it, saw that it was noon. She had a luncheon appointment with Derek in half an hour. Rising, she crossed the floor to her small bathroom to freshen up before leaving to meet him at Harry's Bar.

When she first went downstairs, Stevie stood on the doorstep of Jardine's for a moment or two, debating whether to walk or take a taxi. It was a very cold day, but the sky was blue and the sun was shining, so she decided, in the end, to brave the cold wind and walk to South Audley Street where Harry's Bar, a private club, was located.

Wrapping her heavy red-wool cape closer around her, she set off at a brisk pace down Bond Street. Within minutes she was turning onto Grosvenor Street; she continued at the same rapid speed, heading up toward Grosvenor Square which would lead her into South Audley.

Stevie enjoyed walking in cities she liked, and because of the length of time she had lived in London, she knew it well, better than any other place. In particular, she enjoyed walking through Mayfair with its grand old mansions and stately hotels, cobbled mews with quaint little houses and tree-lined squares.

When she pushed open the door of Harry's Bar some ten minutes later and went inside, she saw Derek leaning against the bar, drinking a glass of water. Instantly he put it down, came forward to greet her, and helped her off with her cape.

"And don't you look smashing today, Stevie," he exclaimed, staring across at her and smiling, once they were seated at a corner table. "Positively blooming. Very bonny indeed."

She laughed and thanked him. "You don't look so bad either, Derek."

"I'm feeling pretty terrific." Leaning closer, her stepfather confided, "I've decided to do the play—*The Lion in Winter*. It's not going on until next autumn, and we won't start rehearsals until late spring, so I'll be well rested and ready to plunge into a new project by then."

"I'm delighted, I know how easily you get bored. What does my mother think about it?"

"She wants me to do it. She's been worried that I was over-tired and run-down after *Becket* and the film, but I'm feeling great and she knows it." Derek paused as the waiter came to the table to take their drinks order. "What would you like, Stevie? A Bellini perhaps?" Derek suggested.

"Thanks, that's fine."

Once the waiter had disappeared, Derek continued. "If it's a success in the West End, I think the producers will take it to Broadway eventually."

"I'm glad it's opening here, that you're going to be in London for a while. I think my mother really misses it when she's away."

"I agree with you, and speaking of your mother, tell me about the brooch you mentioned on the phone."

"It's a lovely old piece and it was designed by Jeanne Boivin, probably in the 1930s, thereabouts anyway. I thought it would suit my mother because it's stylish without being overpowering. It's made of clusters of small diamonds set in platinum, and it's two stems of Queen Anne's lace, and it *is* very *lacy*, rather delicate-looking. Of course, it's a signed piece and quite valuable. André found it by chance."

"So you said. Is that the feather pin André gave you for your birthday?" There was an admiring look on Derek's face as he eyed the lapel of her tulip-red wool suit.

"Yes, and I've never stopped wearing it since he gave it to me. It's the kind of pin that seems to go with everything. Night or day. The Boivin brooch is the same, actually, Derek, in that it can be worn at any time and with almost everything."

"I'd like to see it. From what you say, I think it'll make a wonderful Christmas gift for Blair. Actually, I was going to walk back to Jardine's with you later. After lunch."

"Great minds think alike. The same thing crossed my mind on my way here to meet you."

He nodded and asked, "Did you like your birthday present from Miles?"

Stevie glanced at her stepfather alertly. "Oh, so you knew about it, did you?"

Derek grinned. "We did indeed, but Miles swore us to secrecy."

"It's a beautiful portrait of Chloe. And apparently he painted it rather quickly. Just dashed it off, he said. He's a really good painter, isn't he? I sometimes wonder why he settled for designing stage sets, even though he is brilliant at it."

"His painting of Chloe is spectacular in my opinion, Stevie, and why he prefers to design sets I will never know either. The main thing, though, is that he's happy doing what he's doing. And happy with his life, it seems to me." Derek peered at her closely. "Have you seen Gideon since you arrived on Friday?"

"Ah, the other side of the coin, so to speak. Yes, we had—" She cut herself off.

The waiter had arrived with their Bellinis.

After toasting each other, Stevie went on. "Chloe and I had lunch with Gideon yesterday. I'm afraid he was morose, down in the dumps. Just as Miles said he was when he last saw him."

"Did Gideon mention anything? Confide in you? Tell you what's ailing him?"

"Oh, no, Derek, and with Chloe present I didn't want to question him. After all, he *is* twenty-seven. A grown man capable of taking care of himself. And whatever it is that's troubling him, he'll snap out of it, I'm sure. The young are very resilient."

"True," Derek agreed, and deeming it wise to move on, he changed the subject, said, "I think we'd better look at the menu, order lunch, darling."

"I know what I'm having ... the same thing I always have when I lunch here. A mixed salad, then risotto primavera."

"And I'm going to have fish and a small portion of pasta. One can't come to Harry's Bar without having a bit of pasta, now, can one?" Derek flashed her a smile and then turned his attention to the menu, concentrating on it.

When he finally looked up, Stevie said, "It's not Gideon I'm worried about, but Bruce."

"*Bruce?*" Derek threw her a questioning look, and he was unable to conceal his surprise. "What's wrong with Bruce?"

"I'm not really sure, to be honest. I spent some time with Gilbert Drexel at the showroom on Saturday, we'd quite a lot of business to go over. And he made a point of telling me that he was very worried about Bruce, and he did stress *very*. Gilbert thought he seemed frail, not agile anymore, although that could be his gout acting up again. He said Bruce kept going into the showroom, more than ever lately, which has surprised Gilbert, since Bruce had said he wouldn't be making many appearances."

"Interesting," Derek murmured. He wondered if Bruce Jardine harbored any suspicions about Nigel, but he did not say this. He asked, "Did Gilbert tell you anything else, Stevie?"

"Just that Bruce seemed very *preoccupied*." Stevie shook her head. "He was rather emphatic about that, mentioned it several times. I asked him if he meant that Bruce was senile, and Gilbert said no, not at all. He actually added that Bruce had all his marbles, and that was his exact expression."

"Mmmm." Derek looked thoughtful as he murmured, "He is in his eighties, of course. I don't suppose you've had a chance to see him yet, have you?"

"No, but I'm lunching with him tomorrow, as I have for years on Christmas Eve. It's a tradition with us."

"Bruce has always seemed so . . . *indestructible,* I think that's the best word," Derek mused out loud. "It just goes to show, none of us is that. Nor are we immortal, as we're often prone to think, as much as we'd like to be."

He sounded so rueful when he said this, Stevie couldn't help smiling, and she said, "If anybody's going to be immortal, it's you, Derek. After all, you're the one who's captured on film. You'll live forever, in a sense."

Derek smiled back at her but made no comment.

Stevie went on. "When I said I was worried about Bruce, I really wasn't referring to his health, but rather to his demeanor. I can't imagine why he continues to trail into Jardine's, there seems to be no purpose to it."

"I'm sure he'll tell you when you see him tomorrow."

"Yes, I suppose so."

"I think perhaps we ought to order lunch, don't you?" Derek said, picked up his Bellini, and took a sip. He couldn't help wondering about Bruce's behavior himself. Did that wily old bird know something no one else did?

15

"I KNOW YOU'RE GOING TO TELL ME TO MIND MY OWN BUSINESS, BUT I'm going to say this anyway." Miles paused, gave Gideon a hard stare, and added, "So please hear me out."

Gideon returned his brother's stare but made no response. Instead, he studied him for a moment. What he saw was a reflection of himself; dark brown hair, bright blue eyes, pleasant, well-defined face. A good-looking chap, Miles was. And very personable. Women went for him. Didn't he just know it. They shared the same problem. After all, he and Miles were identical twins. As their mother used to say to them, they were like two peas in a pod.

"Come on, Gideon, say something!" Miles exclaimed, leaning across the table. They were at Mark's Club in Charles Street, where they were having lunch, their first in a long time. It was obvious they were happy to be together.

Gideon permitted a small smile to slide briefly across his mouth, then he said, "I'm waiting for you to tell me what's bothering *you*. Spit it out. I won't bite your head off. Nor will I tell you to mind your own business."

"Right! It's *you*, Gideon, *you're* bothering me. Or, rather, your behavior is, and it has for the past few months. You're either morose or melancholic. Or worse, depressed and unapproachable. It's obvious you're disturbed about something. Ma's noticed it, Gid, and once she really gets on your case she's not going to give you a moment's peace. You know she can be like a dog with a bone when she gets her teeth into something."

"Thanks for the warning, Miles, but I can handle Ma. It's true, I have been a bit down for some time now. But I'm coming out of it, I promise."

"What's been wrong with you, for God's sake? I've been worried to death."

"Women. Bloody women. That's all."

"What women?"

"Not really women, but *woman*. Margot Saunders, to be precise. She's tried to create problems for me since we broke off— since I broke off with her, I should say."

"Do you mean she's been pursuing you?"

Gideon was silent for a second, then he explained in a low voice, "*Fatal Attraction* kind of pestering. You did see that film, didn't you?"

"Yes. But look here, you don't have a wife, and—"

"I know," Gideon cut in. "But she hasn't stopped harassing me, and she's been quite—" There was a pause before he finished in a mutter. "Quite pernicious, in a way."

"Odd word to use, but I know what you mean. Anyway, brother of mine, one must never forget that hell hath no fury like a woman scorned."

Miles looked at Gideon closely, his eyes narrowing, as he continued. "So, she's giving you a hard time. What can I do to help?"

"Nothing, but thanks for offering. Actually, she's going to go away like a good girl and not give me any further trouble."

"What makes you say that?"

"She promised."

"And you believe her?"

"Oh, yes." Observing the doubtful look on his brother's face, Gideon added, "Take my word for it, she won't create any more problems."

"I believe you. Mind telling me how you accomplished this feat?" Miles raised a brow, his eyes suddenly quizzical.

"I said I'd tell Jack Bellanger all about it, about her behavior . . . her following me, harassing me, virtually stalking me. And it put the fear of God into her. I mean, what socially prominent young deb wants to see her name splattered all over the *Daily Mail* and in such a way? And in the most widely read gossip column?"

"She really believed you'd do it?"

"Oh, yes, she's met Jack with me, knows we all went to Eton together, and that we're very close friends. You know Margot's pretty frightened of the Fleet Street boys, ever since that awful scandal involving her brother. She's never recovered from the press coverage. She thought it was diabolical, and her mother had a nervous breakdown."

"Very clever of you, Gid. And when did you accomplish all this?"

"Don't look so suspicious." Gideon laughed. "I've told you the truth. And I accomplished it about a week ago."

"Then why did you look so down in the dumps yesterday, when you had lunch with Ma and Chloe?"

"She told you that? Ma, I mean."

"Yep, she did."

Gideon sighed, decided not to answer his brother's question. Instead, he asked, "I wonder when the bangers and mash are coming? I'm famished."

"So am I, and any minute now, I'm sure. Bruno did say they were very busy today when I called to make the reservation. And you've only got to look around to see that the place is jammed. He did us a favor, pulled a table out of thin air for us, actually."

"I know." Gideon stared off into space for a split second, thinking of his dilemma. Then, brushing it aside, he attempted to reassure his brother. "Listen, Miles, I'm all right now, really I am. It's been a bad couple of months, I admit that. But Margot is well and truly disposed of, and I know my life's going to be easier."

"I'm glad to hear it." Miles took a swallow of his red wine, and there was a slight hesitation as he murmured, "Mind if I ask you something?"

"No, go ahead."

"Why *did* you break off with Margot? I for one thought it was the real thing at last."

"So did I. In the beginning. And for quite a while. And that's why I broke it off. Because it wasn't."

"I see." Miles leaned back against the banquette, toyed with the bread roll.

"And what about you and Allison Grainger? You haven't mentioned her lately."

"Same as you, old chap. Not the real thing. She's a lovely girl, and I still see her occasionally, but on a much more casual basis than before. I'm easing my way out of the relationship, in fact."

"Not to change the subject, Miles, but I was a bit surprised when Ma told me at lunch yesterday that Nigel showed up in New York just after the auction at Sotheby's."

"I was too. What do you make of it, Gid?"

Gideon shrugged, stared at his brother.

They exchanged long, pointed looks.

Finally Gideon said, "I don't know *what* to make of it. He

never told me he was going to New York. But on the other hand, why would he? He's a bit of a funny bugger these days. Bad tempered, more impatient than ever." Gideon shook his head and finished, "And very secretive."

"Ma thinks he's plotting against her," Miles volunteered.

"She told me."

"Were you able to confirm Ma's suspicions?"

"How could I? I don't know a damn thing, and I hardly ever see him at Jardine's. Listen, I'm sure nobody else knows anything. And in any case, Nigel's always played everything close to the vest. If he is plotting, then only Nigel knows he is."

"You're right," Miles agreed. "I wish I'd had a chance to see him, I might have been able to make a judgment, even found something out just chatting with him, drawing him out. But since I've been back in London I haven't had time to come over to Jardine's."

"Don't worry, you'll see him on Christmas Day with Tamara and the kids."

Miles did not hide his surprise. "He usually takes Tamara and the kids to see her parents in Paris for Christmas. Why the change of plans, do you know?"

"Her father has been ill. Very ill. He had a heart attack. Anyway, her parents decided to go to Martinique or St. Barts, somewhere like that, for the Christmas holidays, part of his recuperation, I suppose."

"So we're stuck with Nigel."

"Only too true. But there's Tamara, our beautiful little Russian."

"Oh, here's our sausage and mash," Miles said.

"About bloody time too," Gideon muttered.

Miles had to laugh. "We haven't been waiting all that long, Gid. You should have ordered something first if you were so hungry, potted shrimps or smoked salmon."

"Leave me alone," Gideon grumbled, and made a sour face. Then he winked at his twin. "I'm only kidding, you know how I like to grouse."

"Only too well."

They ate in silence for a while, but at one moment Miles glanced at his brother, his face serious. "All joking aside, Gideon, do you really think you're finished with this Margot business? Has she really gone away? And for good?"

"I'm certain of it. And it's a weight off my mind, I can tell you. It's been depressing me for ages. She really did behave in the most impossible way. Made my life miserable."

"I wish you'd told me, maybe I could have helped."

"Perhaps I should have."

"What's a twin for, if not to stand by your side and do battle with you? I'd expect it of you, you know."

Gideon smiled. "And I'd be right there for you, count on that."

Miles studied him for a moment, then said, "You don't know how happy it makes me to see you smile, Gid, to hear the lightness in your voice again."

Gideon nodded. "She really was rather a nuisance, Miles."

"It's rotten luck that you had to go through all that."

"Let's not talk about it anymore. It's over." As these words left his mouth, Gideon prayed that this was true.

Miles said, "What about Chloe? Is she going to be a nuisance to you at the store?"

"Oh, no, not at all. She's okay, you know, a good kid, and she's going to come in for only a few hours a day, until she goes back to New York with Ma in January."

"I'm glad Ma decided to let her hang around Jardine's. It was a very smart move on our mother's part, and it might make Chloe change her mind about working there after she graduates."

"I hope so, for Ma's sake. She really doesn't want this at all. In fact, she's dead set against it."

"I know, and she's being a very good sport. Do you realize how lucky we are to have a mother like Stevie Jardine?"

"I most certainly do!" Gideon exclaimed. "There's no one like Ma. She's the best there is."

Miles nodded, and, changing the subject, he said in a quiet voice, "I just want to add this to our previous conversation. Promise you'll confide in me, let me help you, if ever you're in trouble in the future."

Gideon only nodded, not trusting himself to speak. He wondered if this was the right time to unburden himself further to Miles. Don't do it, a small voice at the back of his mind warned. It's too dangerous. And so Gideon remained silent, concentrated on his food. For the next few minutes he was afraid even to look at his brother in case he gave himself away or blurted out what must be left unsaid.

Gideon Jardine sat in the study of his flat in Cadogan Square, his mind awash with troubling thoughts. It had turned seven, and he knew he ought to be dressing for the dinner he had been invited to by close friends; he was already running late. Suddenly his energy had ebbed away, and he felt an odd kind of lassitude settling over him.

Only one table lamp was turned on, and the light in the room was dim, but even this was too bright for him. Rising, he went and turned off the lamp, then lay down on the sofa under the window, stretching out his long legs, easing his back into the cushions.

The darkness soothed him. Everything was quiet in the flat. The only sounds came from the ticking of the carriage clock on the mantelpiece, the faint buzz of the traffic outside, the hiss of wheels traveling on wet roads on this damp night.

He was glad he had seen Miles for lunch today, and also relieved that he had confided in his brother. He had told Miles the truth . . . for the most part anyway.

Margot had not wanted their relationship to end, and she had striven hard to hold on to him, her demeanor growing uglier in the process. But there was no way for him to stay with a woman he did not love.

It was also true that she had begun to harass him, stalk him, phone him endlessly at work and here at home. She had made his life hell for weeks, until, as a last resort—when reasoning with her had proved to be fruitless—he had threatened her with Jack Bellanger.

Of course, it had worked. She loathed the tabloid press, the entire press corps in actuality, because, she said, they had crucified her brother and destroyed her mother. In all likelihood they probably had, but who could blame them really? They were only doing their jobs, and Julian Saunders had left himself wide open to become their target because of his extraordinary financial chicanery in the City. He felt sorry for the mother, though, an innocent victim.

Gideon knew he would never forget the expression of mingled disbelief and horror on Margot's face, and the way she had recoiled when he had said he planned to tell his good old chum Jack about the problems he was having with her.

When he had first thought of this as a means of combating her intrusive and frightening behavior, Gideon had instantly dismissed it from his mind, had backed away from it, loath to do that to her. In the end, though, he had come to realize that he had no choice. Threatening her with the press was his only weapon; he had to think of himself, defend himself.

Margot had become so obnoxious, she was verging on the deranged, and it had crossed his mind several times that she might do him bodily harm. He was only twenty-seven, and he did not want to die needlessly at the hands of a crazed young woman.

There was another thing, something Margot had seen, and which he could hardly bear to think about, because it made him vulnerable to her. On the other hand, he felt reasonably sure that with Jack Bellanger hanging over her head like the sword of Damocles, he was safe.

Gideon was unable to keep his eyes open; he felt his lids dropping, and he began to doze. Images of Margot danced in his head, and a remembrance of their last evening together seemed suddenly trapped under his lids.

Instantly, he snapped his eyes open, not wanting to think about it. Still, the memory insinuated itself into his consciousness once again, as it frequently did.

That night . . . more than three months ago now . . . they had gone out to dinner and then later in the privacy of her flat, he had realized he could not stay. He wanted to leave at once, go home to his own bed. He was not only exhausted, but worried about an old, old friendship that had spiraled out of hand and out of control in the past few weeks.

Margot had forced the issue, and, of course, it hadn't worked. Put simply, he had been unable to perform.

At first, Margot had been sweet, loving, and very understanding. And then unexpectedly, as he was dressing, she had turned on him with a vengeance, angry and vehement in her condemnation of him, which had been venomous.

"You're impotent with me because of *her!*" she had cried. "I knew you'd be unfaithful to me because of your reputation as a womanizer. But I hadn't realized that it would be quite so soon!"

Stunned by her words, by the seed of truth in them, he had stood gaping at her, cringing inside at the use of the word *impo-*

tent. And he had continued to stand there speechlessly, suddenly afraid to say a single word, knowing that somehow she would use it to her advantage and against him.

When she repeated her accusation about there being another woman in his life, he had swiftly denied that there was anyone else.

"But I saw you with her," she had shot back, dropping her bomb on him.

Aghast though he had been, he had managed to keep a poker face, and he had kept his mouth well and truly shut as well. It was as if he had known then that she was going to be trouble; he hadn't realized just how much trouble.

His silence had served only to goad her into saying more. She told him where she had seen him, and described the woman with him as "blonde, beautiful, but that goes without saying when you're concerned. She looked older than you though. That *was* surprising." Glaring at him, Margot had added, "Her face was so familiar. If only I could remember her name."

He hoped to God she wouldn't, because if she did, it would spell disaster. For himself. And others. He remembered now how he had finished dressing without saying another word to her, and he had left silently, without so much as a good-bye. But good-bye it had been for him. The next day, not wanting to waste any time, he had told her it was over, finished, kaput. She simply hadn't wanted to accept this decision on his part and that same week her harassment of him had begun.

The shrill ringing of the phone brought him upright with a start. Swinging his legs onto the floor, Gideon reached for it, glad that it had stopped the flow of his thoughts.

"Hello, darling," she said before he even spoke.

"Lenore?" Gideon gripped the phone a little tighter, knowing it was her. He knew that voice so well.

"Of course. Are you all right?"

"Sort of . . . where are you?"

"In the country. It's cold and gloomy up here in Yorkshire."

"Should you be calling me? Is it safe?"

"Oh, yes. I'm alone."

"Where are the chi ldren?"

"Here with me. What I meant was that—"

"I know what you meant," he said, cutting her off. "God I miss you, and it's been only two days."

"It's the same for me."

"I can't bear to think that he'll be there with you and—"

"Don't, Gid. Don't do this to yourself. It has to be like this . . . for the time being anyway."

"I wish you were here," he said in a low voice, picturing her in his mind's eye, seeing her sweet face, the blonde halo of hair, the misty gray eyes.

"So do I. All I want is to be in your arms, close to you, kissing you. I love it when you kiss me, darling. I always did when we were little. You were a good kisser then, but much better now that you're grown up." She laughed softly, it was a low, sexy laugh, and then she whispered, "I can feel your lips on mine, your tongue sliding into my mouth. Oh, Gideon, tell me what you want to do, how you want to make love to me."

"I can't," he answered, his voice rasping with emotion.

"Why not?" she murmured, breathing softly into the phone.

"You're exciting me too much."

"I'm excited too, Gideon. Oh, God, I do so want to be with you, darling. In the biblical sense. And with you for always for the rest of my life."

"Get a divorce, Lenore! Tell him about us. *Leave him.*"

"You're not the marrying kind, Gideon. You know it, I know. The world knows it."

"To hell with the world and what it knows. It knows nothing!" he exclaimed, and taking a deep breath, he said earnestly, "I love you. I've always loved you since we were children. I know. that now."

"And so have I. And I'll love you till the day I die."

"Don't talk about dying. Let's talk about living, about you living with me. Come and live with me in the New Year. Let's start it right."

"Gideon, I have children . . . one of them is your godchild, for heaven's sake. How *could* I live with you under the circumstances?"

"Get a divorce," he said again in a voice suddenly harsh.

"Gideon, I—"

"I want to marry you, for God's sake, don't you understand that?" he interrupted in a softer tone, and then he laughed quietly. "This is a hell of a way to propose to the woman you love, I think. Over the telephone. But here goes. Eleanor Elizabeth Jane Armstrong, will you marry me? Please."

"As soon as possible, Gideon." There was a tiny pause before she went on, "If only I were there now, darling, the lovely things I would do to you. Mmmmm. Yummy. Do you know, you do taste very yummy indeed."

"Don't do this, darling, it's too much for me to bear."

"Sorry. Did you really mean it, Gid? About getting married?"

For a moment he did not respond, and then he said steadily, firmly, "Yes. I meant it, and for what it's worth, this is the first time I've ever proposed."

"That's not true."

"But it is."

"No, you've proposed before. *To me.* When I was ten and you were nine. At the back of the stables at Aysgarth End. And I said yes."

"And you're saying yes again?"

"I just did. I said as soon as possible, didn't I?"

"Will Malcolm divorce you?"

She was silent.

"Well, will he?"

"I hope so, Gideon. You know what he's like, so stubborn and uncompromising. He knows our marriage has been over for a long time, but he won't see that or accept it. And even though he doesn't really care about me anymore, he doesn't want anyone else to have me."

"I'll talk to him."

"No, no! That'd be like a red rag to a bull. He's always grumbled about you, Gid, said you had a thing about me."

"I do."

"Thank God for that, since I have one about you. Where are you going tonight?"

"The Mallinghams have asked me to their Christmas party."

"Who're you going with?"

"No one. I'm strictly stag from now on, Lenore. Until I have you on my arm, my love."

"Christmas is going to be foul without you." She sighed heavily. "Never mind, it's a time for children, and they'll make it reasonably bearable. I wish I weren't so far away, I'd drive over to see you every day, Gideon darling."

"I know you would, and Christmas is going to be lousy for me without you. When are you coming back to town?"

"Not until Sunday . . . the twenty-ninth."

"Then I'll see you the next day, won't I?"

"Absolutely. Listen, I have an idea." She lowered her tone and said in that sexy voice of hers that he loved, "Can you take the morning off?"

"Yes. But why?"

"I could come over at ten, and we could have breakfast together. An intimate little breakfast for two."

"In bed," he asserted.

She was suddenly laughing, and so was he, and they had another five minutes of conversation before they hung up, after repeating their undying love for each other umpteen times.

Gideon lay on the sofa, staring up at the ceiling in the darkened room, thinking of the things they had just said. He had asked her, no, told her, to leave her husband and get a divorce. And he had promised to marry her. And yet he did not feel nervous or panic stricken that he had made the demand and the commitment. He wanted to marry her, and what he felt now at this moment was absolute certainty . . . certainty about his emotions and about her. He had known Lenore Philips all his life; they had grown up together, and he had loved her ever since those days.

That was the reason he had been a bit of a womanizer all these years . . . because *she* was the one for him. She had married another man, had married Malcolm Armstrong when his back had been turned, and before he himself had understood how much he loved her.

Margot Saunders had gotten one thing right, he decided. He was impotent with her *because* of Lenore. She was the only woman he wanted to make love to ever again.

So, he had proposed. She had accepted. And oh, the blessed relief of it . . . of knowing at last what his life was all about. *Lenore.*

16

"I AM PERFECTLY WELL, STEVIE, VERY MUCH IMPROVED, AND THANK you for asking," Bruce Jardine said, looking across at her and smiling.

Stevie smiled back, and there was both warmth and affection in her voice when she asked, "Was it gout again? Has it been bothering you lately, Bruce?"

He nodded. "But fortunately my doctor put me on a new medication a few weeks ago, and miracle of miracles, it seems to have done the trick."

She was about to ask him about the medicine, when there was a tap on the library door, and the butler entered carrying two glasses of sherry on a small tray. He offered one to Stevie.

"Thank you, Alan," Stevie said, and once Bruce had taken his glass, she raised hers and said, "Merry Christmas, and here's to your good health."

"And yours, Stevie, and I wish *you* a very Merry Christmas, my dear."

"Thank you." Taking another sip, Stevie glanced at him sur-reptitiously over the rim of her glass, thinking how well he *did* look. She had been pleasantly surprised when she had arrived at the house in Wilton Crescent a few minutes before. After her conversation with Gilbert Drexel the other day, she had expected to be greeted by a wraith on the verge of expiring. Instead, Bruce looked extremely fit and healthy, and not in the least debilitated. Nor was he showing his eighty-two years. To her this was most unusual, since she had always thought he had not aged well, but perhaps she had been wrong after all.

A tall, slender man with severe,m almost ascetic features, and silver hair, Bruce looked every inch the English gentleman and a member of the establishment.

That morning he was elegantly dressed in a navy blue pin-striped suit, a pristine white shirt, and a dark blue silk tie patterned with white dots. As she continued to study him, she couldn't help thinking that he seemed to have acquired a whole new lease on life. The last time she had seen him, only a scant few weeks earlier, he had appeared to be as transparent and brittle as glass.

As if he had just managed to read her thoughts, Bruce said, "I've been going to a new physician, Stevie, and he's worked wonders for me, especially with the new medications he has prescribed for my various ailments. He also sent me to see a nutritionist, an American, and she has created a special diet for me, and put me on all kinds of vitamins and supplements." He chuckled. "I take so many tablets these days, I'm surprised I don't rattle when I walk." Again he let out a deep-throated laugh before adding, "But her methods have shown excellent results, wouldn't you say?"

"They have indeed, and I'm delighted to see you looking so much better. You seem so fit, Bruce."

The phone suddenly rang and Bruce rose, excused himself, walked over to the desk, and lifted the receiver. "Yes, Alan?"

There was a pause as he listened to the butler, then he said, "Oh, all right, put her through."

As he stood there, speaking quietly to someone on the other end of the telephone, Stevie's eyes rested on him briefly before she turned her head away and stared at the fire, thinking of all the years they had known each other. Thirty-one years, to be exact, since she was sixteen; she had grown up and matured with him and Alfreda.

It had not always been as tranquil between them as it was now. Warfare had been the order of the day for a number of years. But they had settled their differences, made their peace long ago, and she had forgiven the little cruelties and slights, the heartache he had caused her in the past. Although in her innermost self she had not forgotten every one of them; indeed, some were deeply embedded in her soul, and would be for always.

The early years of battling, being at loggerheads with each other, were but a memory now, and she was glad of that. As it had turned out, in the end Bruce had become a good friend, and she had come to trust him because, finally, she had understood that he was on her side. For her part, she had proved herself to be a Jardine through and through, and this had pleased him greatly. He trusted her, confided in her, relied on her.

Glancing around, Stevie decided that her redecoration of the library had vastly improved it, as she had known it would when she had undertaken the job for Bruce in the summer. Although she had retained the paneling that lined the walls and the bookshelves, she had had the wood stripped and refinished to a lighter tone, and this had made the room look larger. She had also disposed of the old, very worn Oriental carpet and heavy blue velvet draperies; in their place she had used an antique Aubusson rug, blue-and-yellow-striped silk draperies, and she had reupholstered the sofas and chairs in a lovely rose-colored cotton brocade. The finished effect pleased her; the library had lost its Victorian heaviness that smacked of the late Alfreda's ponderous, uncompromising taste and the gloomy aspects created by the dark colors and outdated fabrics.

As her glance swung around the room approvingly, she noticed that one of the orchids in the big planter on the console table had two wilted flowers. She made a mental note to have the planter put somewhere in the room where the light was better.

Bruce finished his phone conversation, hung up, and walked back to the fireplace. Seating himself opposite her, he said, "It's very remiss of me not to congratulate you, Stevie, on the acquisition of the White Empress. An undoubted coup on your part, and I'm very proud of you, very proud indeed, as we all are at Jardine's, in fact. I thought it was quite a feather in our cap to get it, and the interest it has created in Jardine's is most extraordinary. It's brought many new customers into the showroom. By the way, you handled the media in a most masterful way, I thought, and the press coverage has been very positive."

Startled by his words, Stevie exclaimed, "But you thought I paid too much for the diamond."

"No, of course I didn't," he said with a laugh, looking at her oddly. "Actually, I believed the White Empress would fetch much more than it did. But whoever it was in the final bidding did us a great favor when they suddenly dropped out. That was a rather nice surprise, since the price immediately stabilized . . . for you. I read the report of the auction in *The Times* with a great deal of satisfaction, I can tell you." There was a small pause, and he looked at her keenly, as he finished. "However, even if you had paid twelve million dollars for it, I would have approved."

"I see," she said in a clipped voice.

"What is it, Stevie?" Bruce leaned forward slightly, peering at her intently and in sudden puzzlement. He had noticed the way she had stiffened; he could not miss the tone of her voice. "You have a most peculiar look on your face. What's wrong?" he probed again.

"Nigel told me that you thought I'd paid too much for the White Empress, and that—"

"Absolute nonsense!" he exclaimed, interrupting her. "I don't know where he got such an idea."

"He said *you* told him that."

"But it's not true!" Bruce's eyes narrowed, and there was sudden annoyance in his voice as he added, "The young whipper-snapper's lying! I'll have him on the carpet for this."

"He also told me you said I had *always* paid too much for stones."

Bruce sat up ramrod straight in the chair, and there was a faint tinge of white around his mouth, as if the skin were bleached. Stevie knew this was a sign of his anger; it was an odd physical trait she had grown accustomed to over the years. It happened whenever he was enraged, and it was something he could not fake.

After a moment, he said in a controlled voice, "I simply don't *understand.* Why would he tell you these ridiculous lies? Invent things I've never said? It's preposterous." His brows drew together, knitted in a frown. He shook his head. "I was very laudatory about your acquisition of the stone. I told Nigel that you'd done well, and I praised you."

"Perhaps that's why he concocted his lies."

Her father-in-law drew back slightly and stared at her, perplexed. "If that is so, then Nigel is not as clever as I have always believed him to be. Surely he must have realized he would be found out at some point, that his lies would catch up with him?" His eyes fastened on hers.

Stevie saw the truth in this comment, but she had no answer

for him. She simply shrugged her shoulders, shook her head in bafflement, and then leaned back against the cushions. She was quite resigned to the fact that her son was duplicitous, just as she had suspected he might be.

Bruce shifted in his chair, his expression thoughtful as he sipped the sherry.

It became very quiet in the library. There was only the tick-tick-ticking of the antique clock on the mantel and the crackle of the logs in the fireplace.

Eventually, Stevie broke the silence when she said, "I don't know whether you know this, but Nigel came to New York at the beginning of this month. He came to Jardine's on the Monday after the Sotheby's auction. It was December the ninth, actually. He didn't stay very long, and he didn't seem to have any business at the store. No one to see, as far as I've been able to ascertain. He came up to my office, chatted a few minutes, made some scathing comments about the White Empress, and then left. Apparently he was on his way to see the Sultan of Kandrea, who, he told me that morning, prefers to do business with him now, rather than with me."

"Balderdash! The sultan's always wanted to deal with you, Stevie, and no one else. We both know he dotes on you. He's made no secret of the fact that when you've gone to see him in Kandrea he'd like nothing better than for you to stay. Indefinitely."

Stevie had to laugh, despite the seriousness of the conversation about Nigel. "I'm not so sure of that, Bruce, he is a bit of a flatterer, you know. However, I am sure about one thing."

"And what is that?"

"Nigel came into the Fifth Avenue store to pick a fight with me. It was my birthday, and he knew it was, yet he didn't even mention it. And he did that on purpose. There's another thing

. . . I have the distinct feeling he's working against me. Plotting, actually."

"But with whom is he plotting, Stevie?" Bruce asked in a curious voice. His eyes did not leave her face.

"I don't know." She gazed at her father-in-law helplessly. Then she grimaced. "It's a silly thing to say, isn't it? After all, with whom *could* he plot? *No one.* What I think is this, Bruce . . . he's plotting with himself. Plotting in his head, plotting to oust me. He wants to run the whole show, you see."

Bruce grew disturbed, and this instantly showed in his face. He pushed himself up out of the chair, went and stood near the fireplace, resting one hand on the mantelshelf. For a moment he was silent, his worry showing in his eyes. Then he said slowly, "I can't believe he would be so foolish." He looked down at her sadly, and added in the quietest of voices, "He knows he's your successor, that he'll be taking over from you one day. He's the heir apparent, for God's sake. And that's something he's known all his life. He doesn't have to . . . *plot.*"

Stevie nodded her understanding, looking at him steadily. A long sigh escaped her, and she felt, for a moment, that Bruce doubted her words. Then all of a sudden it struck her that his demeanor had changed, was slightly different. His anger had abated and a resigned expression was registering on his face. As she went on staring at him silently, she noticed a knowing look enter his eyes.

And then it hit her. She nodded, as if to confirm something in her own mind, and said in a low, steady voice, "You've suspected him yourself. You just didn't want to say anything to me . . . unless I confided in you. And that's one of the reasons you've been going into the showroom more than usual. To keep an eye on him . . . and to snoop around."

When he made no response, Stevie continued. "I know I'm right, Bruce."

"Yes," he admitted at last, and sighed. "I have suspected Nigel, although to tell you the truth, I'm not sure what I've suspected him of really, Stevie."

She watched him closely as he moved away from the fireplace, came over, and sat down next to her on the big sofa. Taking hold of her hand, looking deeply into her face, he continued. "I had recently begun to realize that Nigel was courting a lot of your personal clients. I asked Gilbert Drexel about this, and he confirmed that Nigel was handling their business with us, or rather, endeavoring to do so, even though they wanted to deal with you. Gilbert didn't seem to think there was anything wrong with Nigel's taking over, since you were in New York a great deal. I sort of . . . well, actually, I took his word for this, when perhaps I shouldn't have, and therefore I never said anything to Nigel. At least, not initially."

"But you found it strange?"

"Yes, I did," he told her. "After all, when a client is going to spend five, ten, even fifteen million pounds with us, and often much, much more, I know you would take the Concorde in, which you have always done in the past. After I'd thought about this for a few days, I felt uncomfortable, so I did finally speak to Nigel. He told me he was merely trying to help, that he wished to alleviate your burdens, and that you were extremely grateful to him for doing so. I accepted this, why wouldn't I?" He emitted another long, slow sigh. "I had no reason to doubt him. I see now how wrong I was. I trusted my grandson. I believed him. I realize now that I should have spoken to you right away."

"Perhaps you should have." She averted her head, thinking that ten years ago, no even five years ago, Bruce would have been on the phone to her at once. His age *was* showing after all; he wasn't so fast on the draw anymore.

"Then again," he continued to explain, "Gilbert was totally

unconcerned. However, I began to notice a grave change in Nigel the past few weeks, and this has troubled me greatly."

"What do you mean exactly?"

"He's become extremely impatient and irritable. And he is temperamental. It's struck me numerous times he's rather sarcastic and acerbic with people when speaking to them. That's not the way to behave around the staff, nor is it the way to handle them. Or to run a business."

"I agree. But Nigel's always been a bit of a know-it-all, and he's—" she began to say, then stopped abruptly. She'd been about to say, like you were once, but had cut herself off just in time. Clearing her throat, Stevie went on quickly. "And he can be arrogant."

"Yes, that's true. And argumentative. He's had several run-ins with Gideon recently, and when Gideon was not in the least at fault."

"Run-ins about what?"

"Minor things apparently, of no real consequence. Nigel's exaggerated their importance, blown them out of all proportion."

He drew away from her, watched her quietly, waited for her to speak. He was troubled by this conversation, and he felt great empathy for her. She had grown up to be a brilliant woman; he had watched her grow, seen her become what she was today. She was steadfast, loyal, dedicated, hardworking, and a decent person. If Nigel *was* trying to oust her, then her son had made a terrible mistake. And there was no question in his mind whom he would back. If it came to that, of course.

The silence between them lengthened.

Bruce, glancing at her covertly, realized she seemed tired, and there was a stricken expression in her eyes. His heart went out to her. Stevie, aware of her father-in-law's scrutiny, drew herself up

on the sofa and half smiled at him. "So, you suspected him yourself . . . "

Bruce nodded. "But of *what* I wasn't at all certain." He
cleared his throat, said in a low, concerned voice, "I never
thought for one moment that he wanted—" He paused, looked
at her askance, and finished, "That he wanted your job, Stevie."

"I've realized that he did, does, and has for some time." Her
laugh was hollow as she added, "Ah, well, uneasy lies the head
that wears a crown."

"Quite so."

"It's funny, Bruce. At Thanksgiving I made up my mind to
unburden myself to you. Then on the plane coming over I
changed my mind. I decided all this could wait until after
Christmas. I didn't want to spoil the festivities with problems.
Now it's all come out in such a rush of words."

"Perhaps that's just as well, my dear. And we must talk to
Nigel, don't you think?"

Stevie bit her lip. "Yes, but I believe I should be the one to do
that. Not you."

"We should talk to him together, Stevie."

She shook her head vehemently. "I don't think so. It would
be much better if I saw him alone. Please, Bruce, let me handle
it."

"Very well," he replied in a somewhat resigned voice, having
learned long ago not to argue with her when she had already
made up her mind about something.

"After Christmas?" A dark brow lifted questioningly.

He nodded.

Stevie took a deep breath and continued. "He's not the only
one I have problems with."

"Oh." Bruce threw her a swift glance. "Who else?"

"Chloe."

"Not Chloe! That couldn't possibly be. She's such a sweet girl," Bruce murmured, staring at Stevie aghast.

She saw his love for the girl reflected in his eyes, and so very carefully she explained. "Chloe announced at Thanksgiving that she doesn't want to go to college."

"Not even Oxford?" he asked, sounding surprised.

"Correct. She wants to drop out."

"But she must at least graduate from Brearley," Bruce murmured with a worried frown. "She must not forgo that."

"Yes, you're right, and she won't."

"And then what?"

"She wants to work at Jardine's. *In London.* Chloe would like to go into the family business, Bruce."

Bruce Jardine could not help smiling. Try though he did to keep a sober face, knowing this was a serious matter, the smile forced its way through and settled on his mouth. It wouldn't budge.

Stevie, watching him, said, "Well, I might have known *you'd* be pleased."

"I shan't deny that I am, Stevie, my dear. You know I have an extremely soft spot for Chloe, and she's such a smart, intelligent girl. There's a place for her at Jardine's whenever she wants it as far as I'm concerned. However, you're her mother, and, of course, you're the managing director at Jardine's here. You run the company. Whether you want to give her a job or not is up to you." Reaching forward, he patted her hand, and there was an air of genuine friendship and affection in his manner. "She's so young, only eighteen. Don't be too harsh on her."

"I'm not being harsh. I just want to do what's best for her."

"Naturally, and so do I. Why don't you let her come to London next summer? She can live here with me at Wilton Crescent, and go to Jardine's every day. Gideon can take her under his wing. She can get her feet wet, so to speak, and she will soon know whether she likes the family business or not."

"That had also crossed my mind. Well, we'll see." She let out a long sigh.

Bruce eyed her keenly. "What is it?"

"She's a teenager. Not an enviable age. They're full of excitement one moment, depressed the next. They go through terrible mood swings, temperamental outbursts, and are at the mercy of raging hormones." She forced a smile. "By next summer she may have changed her mind yet again."

A smile touched his dark eyes. "I hope not. I'd like to think she'll be part of Jardine's eventually. The whole idea pleases me. . . . "

Stevie was silent for a moment and then she rose, walked across the room, stood at the window looking out. After a few seconds she swung around and said, "If I do let her come next year, she'll be living with my mother, Bruce. I think that would be the best thing for her."

She saw the disappointment flash across his face and settle in his eyes. "That's understandable," he murmured, sounding sad, and looked away.

Quietly, Stevie went on. "My mother's expecting you for Christmas lunch tomorrow. You are coming, aren't you?"

"I wouldn't miss it for the world."

"Nigel's going to be there."

"He told me he wasn't taking the family to Paris this year, so I assumed they would be with us."

"Why do you think he wants me out of the company? Because he does, you know," she asked unexpectedly.

Bruce seemed to be weighing her words. "I trust your judgment implicitly. If you say he does, then he does. And to answer your question, I can't imagine why. And it would be ridiculous to speculate."

"That's true."

There was a knock on the door and the butler reappeared. "Lunch is ready, Mr. Jardine. Cook would like you to come to the table. She's afraid the cheese soufflé might fall."

"Right away, Alan, right away," Bruce replied, and stood up.

Stevie said, "I just realized how hungry I am. And I love Elsie's cheese soufflé. It's going to hit the right spot."

Bruce merely nodded, and together they left the library.

As they walked across the grand entrance foyer to the dining room, Stevie remembered the night she had sat in this vast cavernous hall and listened to Bruce's voice raised in anger. He had told Ralph she should get rid of her baby. If she had, Nigel would never have been born.

17

"I'M CERTAINLY GLAD TO SEE EVERYONE'S BEHAVING WELL TODAY," Stevie said, turning to Derek, and then once more glancing around the room. "I can't believe it."

"Neither can I," he answered, following the direction of her gaze, observing the other family members, who were sitting or standing in different parts of the room, chatting to each other. "They actually seem rather chummy, which is something of a relief. There's usually some sort of contention going on, or an undercurrent. Mmmmm." He nodded to himself, added, "And these are noticeably absent, Stevie." Grinning at her, he said sotto voce, "As far as I'm concerned, they can all go off and murder one another later, so long as they don't upset the applecart this afternoon. Blair's been working for days to make this Christmas Day a very special one."

"Yes, I know she has," Stevie murmured, settling back on the sofa, "and everything will be fine, don't worry. Why even Nigel's smiling for once."

"So I noticed. And he'd better keep on smiling. If he doesn't, or if he starts any kind of trouble, I'll have his guts for garters."

Stevie began to laugh. "I haven't heard that expression for years. Oh, Derek, look how sweet the little ones are being with Bruce ... and he's so proud, tickled to death to have great-grandchildren. I ought to take a picture, don't you think? Three generations of Jardines."

"It's a great idea. Do it after lunch, when we're opening the presents. And perhaps you'll take one of your mother and me with the babies and Tamara. That would be a nice shot to have for our family album."

"Yes, I will, and doesn't Tamara look beautiful? I don't think I've ever seen her looking lovelier than she does this afternoon."

Derek nodded in agreement. "Red suits her, it looks fabulous with her hair. She's got great style, you know, that one. It's a special kind of chic only the French seem to have. Well, at least have naturally, and without having to make a big effort. I'm glad she's part of the family, she's been such a positive influence on Nigel."

"Yes, he's generally much pleasanter when Tamara's around, that's true. It's a marriage made in heaven, thankfully. She seems to have a soothing effect on him."

"She tempers his recalcitrant attitude. And makes him smile occasionally," Derek added succinctly.

Stevie threw him a quick look. "Please don't worry, no one is going to spoil the day. I won't let anyone. I know how hard Mom's worked. Incidentally, this room looks wonderful since she redecorated it."

"Your mother's very talented when it comes to design, but then I don't have to tell *you* that."

Derek once again swung his eyes, followed Stevie's gaze, seeing the drawing room of the Regent's Park flat objectively, through her eyes. And of course it *was* beautiful and grand and impressive, with its pale silk fabrics and fine antiques, the lovely old paintings gracing the cream silk walls.

So far from the Welsh valleys of his youth, the little back-to-back house where he had grown up, so far from the poverty and grind that had been his family's lot in life for generations.

The grand leap.

That was the way he thought of it. And even today, after so long, there were moments when he would stop whatever he was doing and survey this world where he now lived—and he couldn't help marveling at himself just a little. He marveled that he had been able to make that great leap from there to here. And the fact that he *was* here with a career, fame, success, wealth, and a title to boot said something for his courage, his nerves of steel, his strength of will, his drive, energy and desire to succeed.

It was a leap out of a place and out of a class . . . out of the working class, the underclass, and the underprivileged. The poor boy from Wales . . . now the toast of the town . . . of many towns and cities and villages the world over. An impossible dream achieved. And only by looking clearly at his beginnings could he understand how far he had come, and just how high that leap had been.

"Penny for your thoughts," Stevie said, touching his arm lightly.

"They're not worth a penny, since I was thinking of nothing in particular," Derek replied, tearing himself away from his thoughts.

He stood up, glanced at the champagne flute in her hand, and asked, "How about a refill?"

"I'm fine right now, Derek, thanks."

"Back in a minute." He excused himself and strolled in the direction of the dining room, where a small bar had been set up.

Stevie sat back against the cushions, looked around the room. Her entire family was present for once—her mother and stepfather, her three sons and daughter, her daughter-in-law and

192 ~ Barbara Taylor Bradford

two grandchildren, and her father-in-law. It was not such a big family by some standards; there were others she knew of that were much larger. For a small family, they had had their fair share of troubles over the years, and still had them.

Stevie instantly clamped down on this thought before it took hold, not wanting to spoil the day, knowing that the problems would still be there tomorrow and could be dealt with then. If they could be dealt with at all.

She lifted her glass and took a sip of Dom Pérignon. A split second later her eyes were focused on Tamara.

Her daughter-in-law was coming toward her; she looked as if she were walking on air, so graceful was she. Tamara had the longest legs Stevie had ever seen, and the slender, streamlined body of a model. Her hair was her most spectacular feature though, being neither silver nor gold but a mixture of both, and it was most arresting.

Tamara's face was narrow and elegant below her silver-gilt bangs. These stopped short of large jet-black eyes, a narrow nose, and a wide, generous mouth. She was beautiful in an offbeat way, and that was part of her charm and appeal. The red silk dress she wore swished slightly as she walked, its full short skirt fluid around those lovely long legs, the latter shown off by very high-heeled red silk shoes.

Her good looks aside, Tamara was a kind and considerate young woman who did not have a bad bone in her body, and Stevie had always adored her. Like Blair, Tamara had been a model before her marriage to Nigel, and both women shared certain characteristics, chiefly the desire to be a wife, a mother, and a homemaker more than anything else.

"Can you come to dinner tomorrow, Stevie?" Tamara asked, hovering in front of her mother-in-law. "I'd love it if you could."

"Are you sure, Tamara?" Stevie frowned. "Or perhaps I

should say does Nigel want me to come? You see, darling, he's been a bit odd with me lately."

"Of course he does! We both want you to come. And please don't pay attention to Nigel's temperamentality. He's been a bit snotty and irritable with me these last few weeks. I hope he's not sickening for something. And the Christmas rush always gets to him, you know that. Please come, Stevie, with Chloe. And perhaps Miles and Gideon will come too!"

"What's all this about Gideon?" Gideon asked, drawing to a standstill next to her.

"I want you to come to dinner tomorrow, Gid, well, supper really. A Russian supper on Boxing Day. Doesn't that tempt you?" She eyed him, laughter bubbling inside her.

"Ha! I knew *you'd* have to come up with a foreign meal at some point this Christmas," Gideon teased, looking at her fondly, putting his arm around her shoulders. "Why not a bit of good old roast lamb and Yorkshire pud for a change? Instead of all this foreign mishmosh."

Accustomed as she was to Gideon's teasing, she laughed and said, "Beluga caviar and Scottish smoked salmon a mishmosh! Goodness me, Gideon."

"How wonderful it sounds, my pet. And I'd love to come. What's the rest of the menu? Are you going to make that delicious borscht?"

"If you like. With piroshki. And what about your favorite, chicken Kiev?"

"That's great. But you're making me hungry." He turned to Stevie. "It's almost four o'clock, Ma. When's Grandma going to serve lunch, do you know?"

"In a few minutes. At four."

"All joking aside, I love your cooking," Gideon announced, turning back to Tamara. "I bet they didn't teach you how to make chicken Kiev at that snooty English boarding school you went to."

"You know they didn't, Gid. It was my Russian grandmother who taught me everything I know about cooking."

Suddenly Gideon swung around as a small boy hurtled across the room, calling, "Uncle Gid, Uncle Gid, look what Papa Bruce gave me!" As he came to a sudden stop next to Gideon, he opened his hand. "A little car!" he exclaimed, and showed it to his uncle, beaming up at him.

Gideon bent down to examine the new possession. "Aren't you the lucky boy. And it's a Jaguar, Arnaud."

The four-year-old's big blue eyes fastened on Gideon's face and he said carefully, "Jwagwar."

"Me. Look me," Natalie cried as she ran to join them, holding out her arm. "Papa give me."

"It's beautiful, sweetheart," Gideon said, smiling at her as he examined the slender silver chain with a heart, which Bruce had obviously just fastened on her wrist. That was a favorite game of his grandfather's, pulling surprises out of his pockets.

Natalie laughed and ran to Stevie. "Granma, look!"

"Oh, how lovely." Stevie put down her flute of champagne quickly as the three-year-old scrambled onto her lap unexpectedly. Natalie looked into her face and patted it. "Love you, Granma."

"I love you too, Natalie." Stevie hugged her vivacious little blonde grandchild closer and kissed the top of her head.

A moment later Blair came back into the living room and announced, "Lunch is ready at last, everyone. Shall we go into the dining room?"

Nigel suddenly appeared in front of Stevie, looking happy and lighthearted. He smiled warmly at his mother and said, "Can I relieve you of your little burden, Ma?" As he spoke he reached forward and lifted his small daughter out of Stevie's lap and placed her on the floor. Then he offered Stevie his hand. "Here, let me help you up," he said, and promptly pulled her to her feet.

Leaning into her, he smiled again, much to Stevie's astonishment, and then kissed her on the cheek. "I haven't had a chance to wish you a Merry Christmas yet."

"Thank you, Nigel," she replied. "And the same to you." She was relieved that he was in a friendlier mood than the last time she had seen him, in New York on her birthday.

Gideon said, "Let's go in, Ma, I'll escort you."

"Along with me," Miles said, joining them, taking her other arm.

Stevie laughed and allowed them to maneuver her across the floor.

Gideon said in a quiet, confiding tone, "Can I talk to you later, Ma?"

"Of course. But is there something wrong, Gideon?" she asked, quickly glancing at him.

"No, no. I just wanted to tell you something. It's nothing bad, honestly. Good, really. I'll drive you and Chloe back to Eaton Square after lunch, and we can have our little chat then."

18

"What did you wish to talk to me about?" Stevie asked later that evening, once she and Gideon were alone and settled in the small study of her flat in Eaton Square. She leaned back, crossed her legs, and focused her eyes intently on her son, who was seated opposite.

"The future, my future. Before I get to that, I just want to say something else. I know you've been concerned about me, Ma, and I'm sorry I worried you. But I am all right now. I've managed to sort out the things which were bothering me."

Stevie nodded, then asked curiously, "What was it you had to sort out, Gideon?"

"Margot Saunders. She was making a lot of trouble for me . . . because I broke off with her."

"If your mood was anything to judge by, she must have really been making your life hell."

"She was harassing me, and growing more hysterical as the weeks went by."

Stevie shook her head, looking regretful. "How awful for you. I'm sorry you had to struggle through something like that. It's frightening. I know that hysteria and irrationality of that nature can often lead to violence."

Gideon stared at his mother, and it struck him again how smart she was. There was very little she didn't know about people or about life. "You're right, Ma. I had to stop her before she went too far."

"How did you manage to do that?" Stevie asked swiftly.

"I said I would tell Jack Bellanger about the way she was behaving."

"It obviously worked. But *why?*"

"Margot hates the press. Don't you remember, her brother Julian was involved in some sort of scandal in the City a few years ago. He almost went to jail. The press coverage was pretty relentless. The minute I mentioned Jack's name, you'd have thought I'd held a loaded gun to her head."

"And she's left you alone ever since?"

"Yes."

"I'm relieved to hear it. It's funny, Gideon, how little we know about people really. The last person I would have suspected of being irrational was Margot. I always thought she was so down-to-earth and levelheaded."

"So did I. But I soon found out otherwise. She's really unbalanced, Ma. Well, that's all over and done with now, thank God."

Stevie said, "You've been lucky, Gideon. She could have hurt you—physically, I mean. But let's move on. You said you wanted to talk to me about the future, your future. I suppose I am right in thinking you meant your future as far as your personal life is concerned, and not your future at Jardine's?"

He grinned. "You hit the nail on the head, Mother. I wanted you to be the first to know that I'm getting married."

This was the last thing Stevie had expected to hear, and she stared at Gideon in astonishment. "I can't believe it."

"Believe it, Ma. It's true."

"Who are you going to marry?"

He didn't immediately answer her. Rising, he walked over to the window, stood looking down into the gardens of the square, wondering how best to explain the situation. There was only one way. He must jump in at the deep end and tell her everything. His mother would understand, he was quite sure of that.

When he did not respond, Stevie probed, "Is that the reason you broke up with Margot?"

Turning around, Gideon answered quietly. "Not really. I told you, the relationship wasn't working very well. When I realized how unbalanced she was, I became alarmed. However, I was . . . well, I *was* kind of getting involved with someone else by then."

"And it's this person you want to marry?"

"Yes. It's an old friend, Ma, someone you like, so I know you're going to be pleased."

"Who is it, Gideon?"

"It's Lenore, Ma."

"*Lenore. Our* Lenore?"

He nodded.

"But she's married already! Unless she got a divorce in the last week." Stevie was thunderstruck, and this showed in the expression on her face and in her tone of voice.

"She's going to get a divorce as quickly as possible. She's not been happy with Malcolm for a long time. The marriage is on the rocks."

"Oh, Gideon, are you *sure* about your feelings? Really sure? There have been so many young women passing through your life . . ." Her voice trailed off, and she looked at her son, filling with dismay. "And is Lenore sure? There are children involved here, and they must be considered. And what about Malcolm?"

"What do you mean?"

"He might not want to give her a divorce," Stevie ventured.

"The marriage has been over for a long time, Mother. Lenore is not at all happy with him."

"When did you realize you loved her?" Stevie asked, her voice low pitched and concerned.

"Years ago, just after she'd married Malcolm. It hit me then that I'd been such a stupid fool to let her get away, let her escape. You know how close we were. All of our lives, actually."

"Yes, I do, but—" Stevie cut her sentence off, stared into the distance.

Noticing the worry deepening on her face, Gideon said, "But *what*, Ma?"

"You can't build happiness on somebody else's *unhappiness*, at least that's my opinion. You must both think very carefully about this."

"Malcolm won't be unhappy, if that's what you're getting at. He wants a divorce."

"I see. But again, I ask you, are you really sure that you love Lenore, Gideon?"

"Yes, I am. Why do you doubt me?"

"It seems to me you've been . . . a bit fickle over the years. In and out of love at the drop of a hat."

"This is different, Ma. I really and truly love Lenore, and she loves me. It's going to be all right. Trust me. This love's going to last a lifetime. We were meant to be together."

Stevie was silent.

Gideon crossed the floor, sat down next to her on the sofa. Leaning into her, he took hold of her hand and squeezed it tightly. She turned her head to look at him.

"I love her so much, Mother, honestly I do. I know what you're getting at . . . the upset of the divorce, all of the problems involved, the children, their feelings and their young lives to be taken into account. But I'm ready and willing to shoulder it all, and take the children on too. Lenore will never give them up anyway. She wants custody, obviously."

"This is a big step," she murmured.

"It's a step I want to take."

"I hope you're both doing the right thing."

"Don't throw cold water on it, Ma, *please*," he exclaimed. He searched her face, his eyes as troubled as hers. "I know I don't have a very good record as far as women are concerned, but that's easy to understand, and explain now. It was always Lenore I loved, and that is the reason I soon became disenchanted with all the women I dated. They weren't her."

Stevie looked at him thoughtfully and slowly nodded. "I know what you mean." A little sigh trickled out of her mouth, and she said softly, "I've loved Lenore Philips since she was a little girl. And I love you too. And that's why I don't want either of you to make a mistake, do the wrong thing, and get hurt in the process. I've always believed Malcolm Armstrong to be pretty tough. Whatever you say to me to the contrary, it's not going to be *quite* as easy as you think." She bit her lip and finished in a voice so low it was almost inaudible. "I don't want you to cause others pain either."

"That can't always be avoided, Ma. Everyone gets damaged in a divorce. In my considered opinion."

Stevie merely nodded, but she knew he was correct.

"Aren't you happy for me, Mother?"

"Yes, of course I am, darling, if this is what you really want." Stevie forced herself to smile. "I suppose I just wish the situation were a little less complicated." Squeezing his hand, she said as reassuringly as she could, "I'm here for you, Gideon, for both of you, if you need me. Surely you know that."

"Thanks, Ma," he said, beaming at her. Pulling her into his arms, he hugged her to him.

Later that night, from the privacy of her bedroom, Stevie phoned Derek and recounted her conversation with Gideon. When she had finished, there was a silence at the other end of the phone.

"Are you still there, Derek?" she asked after a moment.

"I am, Stevie darling. Just thinking as I sit here, and wondering what to say to you."

"There's not much you can say, I suppose. After all, he is twenty-seven, he's going to do what he wants." As she finished speaking, Stevie laughed a little hollowly.

"What is it?"

"I always thought they would marry, you know. I hoped they would, actually. You must remember how close they were when they were children and teenagers."

"How could I ever forget it, Stevie? Your mother and I were always rather anxious about them. I for one held the strong conviction that he would get her pregnant. They lived in each other's pockets and behaved as if none of us existed. I was always very curious about what they did over at Lindenhill. They were alone so much, and let's face it, Jacquetta Philips had her head in the clouds. She wasn't much of a disciplinarian. They spent an awful lot of time there without any supervision."

"Except for Miles. He was often along, over there with them. But I know what you're getting at. To tell you the truth, I was startled when Gideon and Lenore stopped seeing each other. Even more startled when Lenore married Malcolm. That was probably a huge mistake, under the circumstances, and I can see why she and Gideon got back together again. Oh, God, more complications."

"They're really serious, then?" Derek asked.

"I'm positive of it. Gideon wouldn't have made the announcement."

"Then we'd better fasten our seat belts, we're in for a bumpy ride."

19

Stevie had not written very much in her journal of late, but once she said good-night to Derek, she took it out and entered the date and the place at the top of the page.

Christmas Day, 1996
London

I was startled earlier this evening when Gideon confided that he and Lenore were involved again, but only momentarily, given the circumstances of their lives. Because they were so extraordinarily close as children, and in their early teens, I'd fully expected them to marry when they were old enough to do so.

Something happened between them at one point, and they drew apart. Neither of them has ever spoken to me about it, but I was aware there was a rift. How could I not be? Gideon was like a bear with a sore head and gloomier than ever, and Lenore became withdrawn and remote. She eventually vacated our lives and was absent most of the time.

If only they had confided in me then, perhaps I might have been able to help them straighten it out, whatever IT was. Certainly I would have perhaps been able to prevent all these problems now.

I always thought it was rather sudden, the way Lenore married Malcolm Armstrong. He's never been a favorite of mine, and I've never grown to like him, not one iota, even though I've known him and his family for donkey's years. Too cocksure, arrogant, and tough, to my way of thinking.

I've often thought that part of Malcolm's attraction for Lenore at that time was his age. At twenty-five, he must have appeared more sophisticated and grown-up than Gideon, who was only seventeen, two years younger than Lenore. Yes, the older man would seem much more desirable, that's quite obvious to me now.

I don't dare write here that she was too young to get married at nineteen; after all, I was much younger when I married Ralph.

Stephen, my godson and namesake, was born a scant eight months later. A premature baby, Lenore said. But I've always had my doubts about that. Still do. If Malcolm got her pregnant, this might explain the suddenness of that unfortunate marriage. I think of it as unfortunate, because Lenore and Malcolm are as different as chalk and cheese, and ill suited.

Pansy was born a year after Stephen, and then came Thomas, Gideon's godson, just eighteen months after that. Three children one after the other in just under four years. But who am I to talk? I had three myself in a short span of time before I was even twenty.

I hope these children don't become pawns in this breakup of a marriage and the ensuing divorce. All are under ten. They will be Gideon's charges one day if he gets his way and weds Lenore. Quite a responsibility, taking on a ready-made family. Is he up to it? I don't even have to think twice about that. I know he is. Gideon has a great sense of responsibility.

And Lenore is strong, and in many ways she is like me. She's very down-to-earth, practical, and independent by nature. Thankfully, she didn't lose her wonderful sense of independence after her marriage.

As I think of that now, I realize it must have been quite a battle for her. Malcolm is a male chauvinist. Obviously, though, she really made her mind up not to become an appendage, a "yes" wife walking three steps behind her husband.

As I look back, Lenore was determined to be her own woman even when she was a young girl. And I know she always considered herself to be Malcolm's equal, which, of course, she is. How fortunate it is now that she went ahead and carved out her own life and her own career.

To me she has always been a clever girl; I think it is very clever of her, using her knowledge of old paintings, art objects, and furniture to her advantage the way she has, opening her own arts and antiques consultancy firm when she did.

I remember now how we used to laugh years ago, when she would take me on guided tours of Lindenhill, where her family has lived for centuries . . . one of the great stately homes of England.

Lindenhill is full of priceless objects that she knows everything about, right down to the last detail. All of this information, this knowledge, was force-fed into her by Allan, her father, before he died.

Lenore is twenty-nine now, and it has taken her ten years to come back to Gideon. Oh, dear, the trouble they are about to have. I can hardly bear to think about it. Derek was so right tonight when he said we're in for a bumpy ride. We are.

Whatever my son says, I know that Malcolm Armstrong is going to be a problem. I doubt very much that he wants a divorce. It would be inconvenient for him; in a sense, he would lose face. Lenore's aristocratic lineage was always of enormous importance to him. She was born Lady Eleanor Elizabeth Jane Philips, and her brother is the Marquess of Linden, and that is most meaningful to Malcolm, such a silly snob.

I suppose he thinks their impeccable background gives him stature, but he's wrong. He's an insignificant man and he will never be anything else. Anyway, I know he won't want to let go of her because of who she is.

Gideon asked me if I'm happy for him, for them, and I am. They are so right for each other, I know that. But I don't envy them the battle they will have to wage. I wonder how I can best help them. Just be here, I suppose, be a friend, help them however I can.

Well, looking back over this rather long day, I realize it was a day of confidences. Tamara drew me to one side after our long lunch and told me that she and Nigel are trying to have another baby. I hope it happens; she's so keen to have a third child. They want a big family, at least six, so she told me. Sweet Tamara, a mother-in-law's dream and so dear to me. I'm glad Nigel's made her happy, and vice versa; he's such a difficult man. Before he met Tamara, I thought he would never find a girl that pleased him. He's so critical.

He was much nicer to me today. That startled me too. Tamara softens him. He worships her, that's evident, and he adores the children. I'm thankful they're such a happy little family.

Everyone was so generous to me this Christmas. Bruce gave me a beautiful Nécessaire, a vanity case, made by Louis Cartier in the 1930s. It's a gorgeous little thing: black enamel decorated with tiny diamonds, rubies, and emeralds. He knows I love collecting these old signed pieces by well-known jewelers, and apparently he went to a great deal of trouble to find me a Cartier piece. This one he found in Rome, of all places. At least, someone found it for him.

My mother and Derek gave me a shagreen box; the shagreen is a lovely greenish-gray color. My mother said she thought it was meant for me, since an S made of gold decorates the lid. It will make a nice box for stationery on my desk. Chloe presented me with a lavender-colored cashmere shawl that's perfectly beautiful, and the twins gave me peridot earrings designed and made by Gideon, and paid for by the two of them. Their note said they chose peridots because they matched the color of my green eyes. They're all so loving. I'm a lucky woman.

The gift from Nigel and Tamara took me by surprise, because it's so obviously valuable, and not the kind of thing they usually give me. It's an icon, Russian of course, and exquisitely painted and intricately decorated with gold and semiprecious stones, and it's old. Very old. I'm quite certain it was Tamara's idea to get me the icon, and that she was the one who found it. But the note was loving, and Nigel seemed eager to know if I really liked it.

My adorable grandchildren gave me presents they had made themselves. Arnaud painted a picture of Natalie, not at all like her, naturally, but the intention was there. She gave me a small, fancy paper bag full of kisses, awkwardly drawn on a long sheet of paper, folded and tied with ribbon by Tamara.

All in all, it was a happy time, and there were no quarrels or disagreements for once. Everyone enjoyed the day, even Nigel, who was very amicable with us all. I hope his behavior today bodes well for the future.

On the way home from Regent's Park, Chloe started to talk about coming back to London for Easter. It's true that Brearley breaks for almost three weeks in March, and there's no reason she shouldn't come. I'm just reluctant to let her visit here on her own, and I don't really understand myself. After all, she is eighteen, and she would be staying with my mother and Derek. But something's holding me back from saying yes to her.

I'm so happy that Chloe has remained contented since Thanksgiving, that she hasn't gone on about working at Jardine's. She's sensible in that way. Having broached the idea to me, she's now waiting for me to make a decision.

She's so special, and in so many ways. She always was, too, from being a little girl. I'm blessed really. My lovely daughter has never given me any trouble.

Gideon didn't say too much when she said she wanted to have the Easter break in London, and spend time at Jardine's with him. His response was, "It's up to Ma." But he does love her, and he seems willing to take her under his wing. Well, we'll see. Tomorrow I'll talk to Gideon . . .

Gideon . . . Lenore . . . I understand only too well the pull between them, the overwhelming attraction that draws them back to each other. That kind of feeling is so hard to fight. I know.

On the other hand, it's wrong to build one's happiness on someone else's unhappiness. Doing that somehow always comes back to haunt you. It's like throwing out a boomerang that returns to hit you in the face.

It was a long time ago that I was faced with a similar kind of decision, and I knew I had to walk away, not look back. And, for the most part, I never have. There have been moments when a yearning for him has surfaced, the desire to see him blinding me to reason. But it was only ever for a moment or two. Sanity prevails. It always will. But how I've longed for him.

Stevie put down the pen, closed her journal, and returned it to the drawer. She had written enough.

Later, when she went to bed, she found it hard to fall asleep, she had so much on her mind. She tossed and turned for almost an hour until she finally dozed off.

And she dreamed of him.

It was a dream so vivid, it remained with her long after she awakened the next morning. As she lay in bed in her charming blue and white bedroom, watching the early light seep in through the curtained windows, she struggled through the residue of the dream. It still clung to her, enveloped her.

Stevie found it hard to shake off, so real had it been. It was as if he had actually been there with her in the room all night. She could feel his dominating presence surrounding her, could smell his cologne. Closing her eyes, she saw him again . . . . saw the dark, passionate eyes, the sensitive mouth, the wide and generous smile, the even teeth so white against the tan of his skin.

And she heard his voice, heard him telling her how much he loved her, and for a while she was transported back into the dream. For in it they had made love to each other, had been joined together in the perfect harmony that had once been theirs, and she longed to recapture it, just as she yearned for him at this moment.

Against her own volition she began to weep. Tears slid out from under her lids, trickled down her cheeks. She pushed her face into the pillow and she wept for the loss of him, for the life they could have had together, for all that might have been.

Eventually, when her tears had abated, Stevie got up, and after pulling on her dressing gown she went into the kitchen. As she pushed open the door, Chloe exclaimed, "Good morning, Mommy. I've made the coffee, do you want a cup? I'll—"

Chloe broke off, stared at her, then asked with a frown, "Are you all right, Mom?"

Stevie nodded. "Of course I am. Why do you ask?"

"You're so white, you look as if you've seen a ghost."

Stevie shook her head, thinking her daughter's choice of words was unfortunate. "I didn't sleep well; I'm a little tired, I guess. Too much on my mind," she improvised.

"I'm sorry. And you work too hard, Mom." Chloe stepped over to her mother, put her hand on her arm, and continued. "Sit down here, and I'll bring you a mug of coffee. Would you like some toast? I'll make it for you."

"Thanks, darling." Stevie smiled at her wanly.

Impulsively, Chloe grabbed hold of Stevie and wrapped her arms around her. "I love you, Mom." The girl hugged her tightly, clinging to her for a long moment.

"And I love you too, darling."

They finally drew apart, and Stevie, staring into her daughter's face, thought how much she resembled her father in coloring. She had his dark eyes, his hair. She was his child, even though she had a strong look of Blair.

"Let me get the coffee for you." Chloe hurried across the kitchen, suddenly filled with worry about her mother. She had dark rings under her eyes and she looked so sad this morning. Chloe wondered why, what had upset her.

A moment later, walking back to the kitchen table with the coffee, Chloe exclaimed, "I'm going to start *really* looking after you. That's going to be my New Year's resolution!"

Stevie laughed. "I'm perfectly all right, truly I am. As I said, I seem to have so many things on my mind right now. But you don't have to worry about me, Chloe. I'll be fine."

Chloe merely nodded and went back to make the toast. When it was ready, she brought it to the table along with her own mug of coffee. Sitting down opposite her mother she murmured, "You're not still angry with me, are you? I mean about wanting to work at Jardine's."

"I was never angry, Chloe. Just concerned about your education. I spoke to Bruce about it the other day, and he seemed quite tickled at the idea of you working in the company."

"He did?"

"Yes." Stevie saw the sudden excitement flashing on her daughter's face, the hope in her eyes, and on the spur of the moment she said, "You can spend the Easter break here, Chloe, if you like. It seems to mean so much to you."

"Oh, Mom, can I! Thank you, oh, thank you so much!" She jumped up and hugged Stevie, and showered her with kisses.

"But you have to stay with your grandmother and gramps in Regent's Park. You can't live here in this flat alone, you know," Stevie pointed out quickly.

"That's fine. Oh, I'm so excited, I can hardly wait."

Stevie took a sip of coffee, looking at her eighteen-year-old daughter over the rim. It gave her pleasure to see Chloe so happy. It had taken so little to bring that enthusiasm back. She fell down into herself for a few moments, her mind focusing on *him*. She had not dreamed about him for several years now, nor did her thoughts often dwell on him. But there had been so much talk about him since Thanksgiving, no wonder he was on her mind once more. The memories of him were painful. Long ago she had vowed to herself that she would not fall into the trap of wishful thinking, of dwelling on the past. And so she pushed aside thoughts of him. They were futile anyway.

Rising, walking to the door, Stevie said, "I'm going to get ready for work. Do you want to come to the store with me today, Chloe? You can spend some time with Gideon in the workshops if you want."

Chloe nodded and jumped up. "I'd love to come with you, Mom. I'll get ready too."

20

"AND WHAT EXACTLY DID THE SULTAN TELL YOU WHEN YOU WENT TO see him?" Bruce asked, leaning forward slightly, pinning his eyes on her.

Stevie was seated behind her desk in her office above the Bond Street store, and returning his steady gaze, she answered, "He said he thought I did not wish *personally* to handle his business anymore *and* that I was passing it on to my son. He had been wondering *why* this was so, *why* it had happened. He even wondered if he had offended me in some way, and this had worried him considerably. Mind you, Bruce, he couched all this in a most diplomatic way."

"I understand. How did he get this impression? Did he tell you?"

Stevie nodded. "Yes, he said his executive assistant, Gareth James, phoned me here at the beginning of December. The switchboard put him through to Nigel without any explanation. When Gareth asked for me again, Nigel told him I wasn't available, that I was abroad. Nigel then intimated he was now handling all of my clients for me. Gareth asked if I was in New York, and Nigel confirmed this. Once more he reiterated that he was looking after my clients, and he asked how he could be of assistance to the sultan. Gareth said the sultan was interested in seeing some of our newest designs. They made a date for Nigel to go over to Claridge's later in the week, to meet with the sultan. However, the next day Gareth called back and explained that the sultan had to leave unexpectedly for America. That's when Nigel suggested he could meet with the sultan in New York, at the sultan's convenience. And so they made a date."

"I see." Bruce steepled his fingers, sat staring into space, a reflective look on his face.

"It was for December the ninth," Stevie clarified.

Bruce sighed. "Nigel's being rather stupid, wouldn't you say? Playing these games. We could have lost a major client because of his manipulations."

"A mega client, as we say in New York."

"Well, we know what he's up to, don't we? First Gilbert told him he was courting your clients, and now we actually have it from the horse's mouth, so to speak. The sultan has given you all the ammunition you need. By the way, how did you straighten it out with the sultan? I'm presuming you did, since you sold him the yellow diamonds."

"I told him I'd taken some time off to recuperate from bronchitis, which, as you know, is partially true. I did take things a bit easier in late October and November, because I'd been so sick in September. I was very diplomatic. I explained that Nigel had been looking after things for me. *Temporarily.* You see, I didn't want him to think there was any problem within the family."

"Quite right too. The sultan wasn't insulted, was he? These chaps easily take offense, you know, especially if they think they're being slighted."

"No, no, he believed me. Why wouldn't he? And I told him I

was now available again, and whenever he needed me. I gave him my private number in New York, and I told Gareth James to call me there if I wasn't at the London store."

"That was a wise move."

"You don't have to worry, Bruce, the sultan understands. I think mostly he was terribly baffled, and whilst not slighted, perhaps he was a bit hurt."

"I'm relieved you've cleared it up, Stevie. When are you going to deal with Nigel?"

"I told you I would talk to him after the holidays, and since it's now the third of January, I'll have a word with him today. I have to, because I'm leaving for New York on Monday morning."

"I'm glad you're not wasting any time." Bruce rose. "I've got to go, I'm afraid. I have an appointment with my nutritionist." He paused at the door. "I wish you luck with Nigel, and don't be too soft with him, Stevie, he deserves to be on the mat for this. If he's difficult, unrepentant, do what you have to do."

Stevie got up, went around the desk, and embraced her father-in-law. "I'll phone you later."

Once she was alone, Stevie sat thinking for a short while, then finally coming to a decision, she picked up the phone and dialed Nigel's private extension.

"Hello? Nigel Jardine here," he said in his usual clipped, upper-class tone.

"Nigel, could you come to see me for a moment, please?"

"No, I can't. I'm very busy, Mother. Whatever you want to see me about will have to wait."

"It can't, I'm afraid. In any case, I think the Sultan of Kandrea is an important enough client for you to stop what it is you're doing and come in here. At once. We've rather a lot to talk about."

"Oh, all right," he mumbled, and banged the phone down.

Within the space of a few seconds he was barging into her office. From the doorway he asked, "What *about* the sultan?" His stance was angry and he glared at her, then he pushed the door closed with his foot.

It struck Stevie that his insouciant mood of a few days ago had completely vanished. She said slowly, "I just wanted you to know that I sold the sultan the yellow diamond necklace, with the matching earrings, bracelet, and ring."

"The set Peter designed and Gideon made?" he asked, looking slightly taken aback.

"Yes."

"When?"

"Yesterday."

"The sultan's in London?" His brows drew together in a frown.

"Oh, yes, Nigel, he is. And he sent me a handwritten note, inviting me to have coffee with him. You see, he was somewhat baffled at my behavior. He couldn't understand why I no longer wished to handle his business, after all these years of doing so, of being his personal consultant on stones." Stevie leaned back in her chair, and she did not take her eyes off her son.

Despite his arrogance and bravado, Nigel found himself flushing under her fixed scrutiny, and this mortified him. He loathed the idea that he had to answer to anyone, and most especially to her. He remained silent, for once in his life at a loss.

"Don't you have *anything* to say to me?" Stevie demanded softly, all of her attention focused on him.

"No, I don't, Mother."

"How *amazing* that you don't. After all, you're the one who created the situation with the sultan by telling Gareth James you were now handling my clients."

"You weren't in London when Gareth James phoned to set

up an appointment," he snapped at her. "I was only trying to help."

"A very lame excuse!" she shot back icily, her anger rising to the surface. "It just so happens that I know what you've been doing, Nigel. You've been courting my personal clients in an effort to take them over yourself. But it won't work. As long as I'm head of this company, *I* will handle all of our top customers."

When he made no response, she said, "Do you understand me?"

"Yes."

"There's another thing, I think you owe me an apology."

"For what?" he asked in an insolent tone.

"For lying to me."

"I've never lied to you!"

"Oh, yes, you have. You did so in New York. On December the ninth, to be exact, when you told me that Bruce had told *you* that I'd paid too much for the White Empress."

"You did."

"Maybe you mistakenly think so, but Bruce doesn't. Nor did he ever say to you that I had *always* paid too much for diamonds. That was pure invention on your part, and your grandfather is as angry about this as I am."

"Oh, who cares what he thinks? You said yourself he's retired now."

"I care what he thinks, and so should you. You haven't taken over from me yet, and as long as I'm here, you'll respect Bruce. He's still chairman."

"In name only," he sneered.

Ignoring this, she said, "Why did you lie, Nigel? You must have known you'd be found out."

"It wasn't a lie. Bruce might not have said it *exactly*, but he implied it. He's very forgetful now, he doesn't remember a thing from one day to the next," Nigel lied. "Anyway, it's true, you did overpay. You always overpay. You've no judgment." He walked farther into the room, drew closer to her desk, stood glowering at her.

How unpleasant he can be, and he's such a lovely-looking young man, she thought, gazing up at him, filled with sadness and regret. She knew now that he was indeed her enemy; he had just declared open warfare.

Quietly, Stevie said, "I don't like your tone of voice, Nigel, and you will not speak to me in this way. Furthermore, I don't appreciate your arrogant attitude either. Quite aside from being your mother, and therefore due some respect from you, I'm also your boss. Let's not forget that. You'd better adopt a different manner and tone immediately."

"The whole point is, you shouldn't be my boss!" he cried, suddenly losing all sense of caution. "*I* should be running this company, not *you*. By rights it's mine. Firstly you're a woman, and secondly you're not even a Jardine. This company has always been run by Jardines."

His last statement brought her to her feet. "I *am* a Jardine, and don't you dare say otherwise! I've been a Jardine for over thirty years, since the day I married your father. Don't you *ever* forget that, Nigel."

"I meant you're not a Jardine by blood," he cried, "and you know that's what I meant." He flushed, fighting a losing battle with his growing rage. "I hear you're leaving for the States on Monday. Stay there and do yourself and everyone else a favor. You're not wanted or needed here. And I'm perfectly capable of running Jardine's."

"No, you're not. Furthermore, you're not even going to get a chance to run it. You're fired."

Thunderstruck, he gaped at her. "You can't fire me!" he shouted.

"Oh, but I can. And I shall repeat it. You're fired."

He drew himself up to his full height and said in a cold, superior voice, "I'm a director of this company. Or had you forgotten that, Mother?"

"No, I hadn't, and you will remain a director. I can't take that away from you. However, I can fire you. And I just have."

"I'm going to see Grandfather about this," he spluttered, his face turning bright red. "He won't stand for this, he'll reinstate me."

"No, he won't, Nigel, you're quite wrong about that. Very frankly, I doubt that he'd want to, even if he could. And actually he can't. You see, as managing director of Jardine's, I have the last word."

"We'll see about that," he blustered.

"Hear me, Nigel. *You are fired.* Please vacate your office by the end of the day."

He stood looking at her stupidly for a split second, hating her more than ever, and then he shouted, "You're going to live to regret this!" And so saying, he stomped out.

Alone, Stevie poured herself a glass of water; her hand shook uncontrollably, and this annoyed her. She endeavored to calm herself, but it took her almost an hour to do so. Finally, just when she was settling down to do some work, there was a knock on the door.

As she glanced up and said "Come in," the door opened to admit Miles. Hovering on the threshold, he said, "Hello, Ma, am I intruding? Do you have a couple of minutes to spare?"

"Yes, darling," she said, smiling at him in relief, discovering that she was rather happy to see her favorite son. "Come in and shut the door. Do you want a cup of tea or anything?"

He shook his head and came into the room after closing the

door carefully behind him. "I came in to see Gid, and I couldn't leave the store without popping by." Seating himself in the chair at the other side of her desk, he peered at her intently, and then said, "You look as white as a sheet. Are you all right?"

She nodded, for a moment unable to explain. Finally, taking a deep breath, she said, "I fired Nigel."

"Good God! When?"

"An hour ago."

"Why?" He suddenly laughed. "Do I need to ask!"

Stevie took another deep breath, slowly explained what happened, told him everything, not leaving out any details. When she had finished, she shook her head sadly. "I'm sorry it's come to this, but there was nothing else I could do. He was so terribly rude to me, on top of everything else. He said I had no right to be running Jardine's because I was a woman, and also because I was not a Jardine."

"What a bloody nerve he's got, Ma. Talk about an ingrate, and after all you've done for him over the years. I'm glad you fired him, he deserves it. He's a bigger fool than I thought." Miles held her eyes for a moment. "Imagine how stupid it was of him to go courting *your* customers. They all want to deal with you, because you're the head of Jardine's. They view Nigel as a junior, your *underling*, albeit the heir apparent. Imagine if they'd taken offense, thought you were palming them off on Nigel. They'd be taking their millions elsewhere, like Cartier's, for instance. That would please Old Bruce no end, now wouldn't it?"

She half smiled. "Nigel certainly jeopardized an important area of our business, no two ways about that." She shook her head. "Anyway, that's that. Let's move on . . . Why did you come in to see Gideon?"

"I owed him some money." He laughed wryly. "For your earrings."

"You were both very extravagant. And you didn't have to buy me something so expensive, you know."

"We wanted to, Ma, and they came with a lot of love from us both. Gideon did spend a lot of time on the design of them with Peter. He wanted them to be perfect for you, and so did I." Stretching out his long legs, Miles went on. "Miss Chloe's all sweetness and light, and very happy today. She says you're letting her come to London for the Easter break, after all."

"It seemed rather mean not to, she wanted it so much."

"What about you? Will you be spending Easter here?"

"I don't think so, Miles. But she'll be all right, she can stay with my mother and Derek."

"I'm planning to come over around that time, so I'll bring her with me."

"Oh, Miles, that's wonderful, you'll be company for each other on the plane."

He nodded. "Gideon tells me he's confided in you . . . about Lenore."

"Yes. To tell you the truth, I was only startled for about half a minute. I always expected them to marry, you know."

"But without her having to drag herself through the divorce courts, right?" Miles grinned at her. "They really must love each other a hell of a lot. I wouldn't want to tackle that tough old bugger Malcolm Armstrong."

"He is tough, Miles, and I gather you don't like him any more than I do."

"I can't stand him, Mother. He's a phony. I'm actually surprised he's not come a cropper before now. He's another one, just like Julian Saunders, Margot's brother, always skating on thin ice in the City."

"Really," she exclaimed, sounding surprised. "I didn't know. But he was always sneaky even when he was younger."

"I don't know what Lenore ever saw in him," Miles muttered.

"Do you think Gideon and Lenore are going to make it work? The presumption being that they will marry once she is free."

"They will, Ma. You know they've always loved each other, and I for one never understood why she married Armstrong in the first place. After all, she'd had a crush on Gideon for years."

"What do you mean?" Stevie asked, raising a brow.

"Well, Gideon was about eleven, so she was thirteen. For all I know, it may have started even earlier. They were always messing around with each other, undressing each other when we played in the attics at Lindenhill. It began when Gid and I were about seven. They used to make me leave, so they could be alone, to play doctors and nurses."

"Miles, I never knew!"

"Well, I wasn't going to come and tell you then, but there's no harm you knowing now." He couldn't help chuckling. "Oh, Mother, if only you could see your face . . . you look so shocked."

"But they were just children."

"So they started their sex life when they were in kindergarten. What can I say?"

"Nothing."

"Do you know something, Ma, I've been thinking a lot about Nigel lately, and I believe he really changed when he was a teenager. The time you had that awful blow-up with Alfreda, when he took her side. What a lousy desertion that was. Gid and I have never really forgiven him for that. Choosing the old battle-ax Grandmother Jardine over you. Little sod, he was."

"I know. But I forgave him long ago. I put it down to extreme youth." Her private phone rang and she picked it up. "Hello?" As she pressed it to her ear, she went on, "Yes, Bruce, I did talk to him. And I had no alternative but to fire him."

She listened again, and then murmured, "Well, I could come over for a light lunch, but Miles is with me." She looked at her son questioningly.

Miles nodded, mouthed, "Okay."

"Bruce, Miles says yes. So we'll both come over to Wilton Crescent. See you at twelve-thirty." After she had hung up she said to Miles, "You don't have to come if you don't want to, you know."

"I do, Ma. I'm leaving tomorrow, and I would like to say good-bye to Grandfather."

PART THREE

Easter

21

CHLOE HAD BEEN VISITING THE BOND STREET SHOP SINCE SHE WAS A small girl, and she loved the marvelous old building which was a famous landmark in London. It was the epitome of elegance, its huge plate-glass windows filled with magnificent jewels and the finest of merchandise. "The best that money can buy," Bruce Jardine always said, and he was correct.

For as long as she could remember, everyone who worked at the store had made her feel special, from the uniformed door-men who smiled and touched their caps when they saw her, to the sales staff who never failed to have pleasant words for her.

She thought the interiors of the shop were the most impres-sive she had ever seen; these were a series of showrooms with soaring ceilings, crystal chandeliers, white marble staircases, and plush, dark blue carpeting stretching everywhere.

To her, the store was grand and stately, and perhaps this was what she loved the most about it. Jardine and Company had always been there, and always would be, and it was a symbol of prestige, dependability, and continuity.

She had been raised on family lore; she knew that Jardine's

had held the royal warrant to be Crown Jewellers since 1843, and that it was Queen Victoria who had given them the warrant. Years ago Bruce had explained to her that Jardine's had served six monarchs; he had also told her that the staff at Jardine's had one purpose, one aim—to do the best that could be done anywhere in the world.

It was her mother who had enumerated more about the royal warrants, explaining that they were granted to individuals, not companies. Gideon was the present holder and had the title of Crown Jeweller. This meant, among other things, that he had to take care of the Crown Jewels, which reposed most of the time in the Tower of London, in the new Jewel House which had been built.

As the Crown Jeweller, Gideon was the only person allowed to touch the jewels, and he was personally responsible to the queen for the upkeep of the great Crown of England, the Orbs, and the Sceptre, which Elizabeth II used on state occasions. As her mother put it, "Gideon is responsible for the symbols of the nation."

The size of Jardine's was surprising. It was much larger than most people realized, with many different workshops on the higher floors above the showrooms. It was there that some of the world's great master craftsmen labored on their extraordinary creations, producing objects of stunning beauty in silver and precious metals like gold and platinum. Lapidaries cut and polished diamonds and colored gemstones such as emeralds, sapphires, and rubies; designers created jewelry, the designs fulfilled by other craftsmen.

Last week, when she had come to work at the store, she had walked around the entire building with Gideon. "So that you can familiarize yourself with it, get the feel of it," he had said.

She had been impressed all over again as he led her through

workshops filled with these items, as well as antique clocks and watches, modern clocks and watches, and all manner of decorative objects.

Jardine's was an elegant store and it had an enormous variety of merchandise of the finest quality. Her mother took great pride in everything that was sold, as did her grandfather.

Chloe liked the store her mother had opened on Fifth Avenue in New York, but it was Jardine's in London that she really loved. She had grown up with the London shop from the time she was born until she was ten. It was to this store she had gravitated when she had decided she wanted to work in the family business.

A week ago, when Gideon had asked her what she actually wanted to do, she had been honest with him and told him she wasn't sure. For this reason, he had put her in the jewelry showroom, where some of the store's most magnificent pieces were sold. "Let's try selling first, see how you like that, see how you like dealing with people."

Today it was the Monday of Easter week. On Thursday she and Gideon were going to spend the long weekend in Yorkshire with Nigel and Tamara at Aysgarth End. For the next three days, she would work beside Gideon at his bench; he was going to show her in much more detail what he did as a lapidary.

She was waiting for him now, sitting on a stool next to his, wearing a white cotton coat, just the way he did. After a moment's absence, he returned, carrying a small packet. Putting it on the bench, opening the paper, he said, "This is a diamond I'm going to cut and polish." He glanced at her, adding, "You can cut a diamond only with another diamond."

She nodded. "But you don't use an *actual* diamond. You told me that a long time ago. You use diamond dust."

"Good girl, you remembered. And that's true, we use industrial diamonds crushed to a fine powder." As Gideon spoke, he reached for a glass jar and showed it to her. "This is it. Gray powder, but it *is* ground-down diamonds despite the way it looks. I'm going to mix some of it with linseed oil to make a black paste. You see, the diamond dust cuts the diamond, but it's the linseed oil that makes the dust adhere to the wheel."

Gideon focused his attention on the flat cast-iron wheel on his bench. "This wheel spins 3,200 rpm once it's turned on. If I simply put diamond dust on it, the dust would fly all over. That's why we need linseed oil—to make the dust stick to the wheel."

"I understand."

"I'm going to put the diamond in this tong, Chloe. Watch me now. As you can see, the tong itself is held in position by the arm, which is screwed onto the bench. That keeps it very steady. There, the diamond is now held in place by the tong, which I can move any way I want as I'm cutting the diamond."

After placing a ten-power loupe in his eye, Gideon moved the tong gently, held it over the wheel, and began to cut and facet the diamond.

She watched him, fascinated, not daring to say a word because he was so concentrated.

"So you're going to Yorkshire for Easter," Bruce said, looking across the luncheon table at Chloe. "Gideon tells me you're driving up on Thursday morning and coming back on Monday."

"That's right, Grandfather, but Mom knows all about it," she answered swiftly. "She said it was all right, she said that I could go."

A faint smile touched his mouth. "Of course it is. There's no reason why you shouldn't go to Yorkshire. Nigel behaved very badly, and he could have created quite serious problems in the business. But he's still a member of the family . . . still your brother."

Chloe nodded, her face suddenly very solemn. "Mom told me all about it. She was really upset, and angry, at first, but she's calmed down a bit now. Miles said Nigel's behavior was suicidal, and Gideon says he has a tendency to self-destruct."

"Quite," Bruce murmured, picked up his glass of water, and took a sip. "I must say, the twins have a rather dramatic way of describing events."

Leaning forward slightly, Chloe lowered her voice and said in a confiding tone, "Tamara's been very upset, you know, Grandfather. I mean about Nigel's foolishness. She loves Mom, and she told me she was ashamed of Nigel and the way he's behaved. She thinks he ought to apologize to my mother and ask to come back to work. I bet if he did so, Mom would have him back, don't you?"

"Perhaps," Bruce said cautiously, wondering if Stevie *would* let Nigel return to Jardine's. Would *he* if he were still running the company? He was not sure. Nigel's behavior had been extremely willful, and, as far as he was concerned, rashness was not a laudable trait to have, especially in business. Suddenly realizing that Chloe was staring at him, he cleared his throat and added, "Aside from being brilliant at what she does, your mother's a very compassionate woman, Chloe, and she still loves Nigel, despite the fact that he's behaved very badly toward her. So perhaps she will rehabilitate him. One day. Very much in the future, of course. But that's enough of that unpleasantness for the moment, my dear. Let's talk about *your* future at Jardine's. Do you really want to work in the family business one day?"

"Oh, yes, I do, Grandfather!" she responded enthusiastically. "And I've been fascinated by everything I've seen so far."

"And do you know what area of the business you would like to work in, Chloe?"

Chloe exhaled, then smiled at him, holding her head on one

side. "I know I don't have the talent to design jewelry, and I don't want to be a lapidary like Gideon. But I love stones, Grandfather. Especially diamonds. I'd like to be involved in buying diamonds, and other precious stones too. That's what appeals to me."

Bruce gave her the benefit of a huge smile. "That was always my area of expertise, and your mother's, Chloe. So, you're following in *our* footsteps. When you come back after Brearley's graduation, I shall ask Gilbert Drexel to take you under his wing. You can spend the summer in his department. You'll enjoy it and learn a lot."

"Oh, thank you, that's wonderful! Oh, here's lunch, Grandfather." She sat back in her chair and took a sip of water as the waiter placed the first course in front of them. They had both ordered the same lunch: Morecombe Bay potted shrimps first, to be followed by chicken pot pie, one of the specialities at Claridge's.

As she slowly ate the potted shrimps and the thin slices of buttered brown bread, Chloe did not say much, and neither did Bruce. When she had finished, she leaned across the table once more and said in a conspiratorial voice, "Nigel *resents* Mom working at Jardine's. He's not only a male chauvinist pig but totally out of date."

Looking at her alertly, Bruce agreed. "Yes, I think he is too. Women are involved in every type of business all over the world these days." A tiny amused smile flickered as he continued, "Why, even *I* have been properly educated to accept women as businessmen. You see, your mother always chided me about being old-fashioned, and years ago she decided to really straighten me out. However, it strikes me that she didn't do so well with her son, now, did she?"

"Nigel just slipped through the cracks," Chloe murmured, then added as an afterthought, "Or maybe it's yet another attitude he has developed for himself."

"What do you mean?" Bruce asked, frowning slightly, pinning her with his eyes.

"Well, he would always take a particular stance, when we were growing up, adopt a certain attitude. That's just the way he is ... *attitudinal.* And his attitudes change very quickly. Personally, I think he's mad at Mom."

Again Bruce looked at her with enormous interest, his eyes narrowing a fraction. "Why on earth would he be angry with your mother?" he probed, curious to hear what she had to say.

Chloe shrugged. "I don't know, Grandfather, maybe something from the past. He can be so touchy about things, *that* I'm really aware of."

Bruce merely nodded, thinking that she had turned out to be a very bright young woman. He himself had often thought Nigel was harboring a grudge as far as Stevie was concerned. As for Chloe, he felt a sudden rush of pride in her. She was such a beautiful girl with her glossy hair, shining dark eyes, and her faultless complexion. And she had a lovely, warm, outgoing personality that was very beguiling. *Sparkling* was the word that best described her, and her appearance as well. He suddenly wished he weren't so old, eighty-three next birthday, because he wanted to be around to watch her become a grown woman. She was so very special to him, and he loved her dearly. That was the trouble with dying, you missed so much of the future.

"What's the matter, Grandfather?" Chloe reached out, put her hand over his.

"Nothing, my dear. Why do you ask?"

"You looked so sad just then," she replied, sounding worried.

He smiled again and placed his hand over hers. "I was wishing I were younger, so that I'd be here to watch you growing up a little bit more, see you getting married, having children. Not to mention succeeding at Jardine's."

"But you *will* be here, Grandfather!" she exclaimed.

"I'm an old man now, Chloe."

"You're not to me."

"But you call me *Old* Bruce behind my back," he teased.

Her eyes opened wider and she flushed, then explained quickly, "But it's an affectionate nickname, it's not meant to be unkind."

He nodded and smiled, looking into her earnest young face, and his heart clenched. She was so very dear to him, this lovely young woman who had come into his life far too late. She touched the deepest part of him, brought out a tenderness in him no one else ever had. And it had been like that since the day she was born, since she had been a baby in her mother's arms.

22

I T WAS A BLUSTERY DAY.

There was a high wind that blew the trees, bending them backward and shaking free many of the new green leaves that were sprouting on the branches. These swirled around her feet as she walked along the narrow path across the moors, heading back toward the farmhouse.

It was a chilly morning, but the sky was a clear cerulean blue, filled with bright sunlight and puffy white clouds that raced across the great arc of the sky.

Chloe loved it up on these wild untenanted moors that rolled away toward the distant horizon. The awesome vastness had always appealed to her, held her in its thrall, and she loved coming back to this place where she had spent so much time as a child.

Aysgarth End dated back to the turn of the century; the rambling old farmhouse was built of local gray stone, and it stood on top of the moors in Coverdale, above the picturesque village of West Scrafton, near Coverham.

When she arrived at the gate leading onto the farm property,

Chloe paused, turned, and stood looking out at the panoramic vistas stretching in front of her. They were breathtaking in their austere beauty. Thrusting higher into the soaring blue sky were the great Whernside fells, massive formations that had an aloof majesty to them, and looked as if they had been sculpted by some almighty hand.

The farm itself was surrounded by green fields divided and defined by old dry stone walls built by the crofters long ago. These fields sloped down into the valley below, where the River Nidd was a shining silver thread against the green in the far, far distance.

Chloe squinted in the sunlight and shaded her eyes with her hand, staring down toward the river. After a moment, she swung around, opened the gate, and went along the dirt road. As she approached the farm, she realized how hungry she was. She took a quick look at her watch and saw that it was almost eight. Time for breakfast. She increased her pace. And a few seconds later she was pushing open the oak door that led into the small front porch.

Mingled aromas of coffee, warm bread, and bacon cooking assailed her as she took off her Barbour and red wool scarf and hung them up. Opening the front door, her nose twitched and her mouth watered as she stepped into the kitchen.

Tamara was standing at the big Aga stove, turning bacon in the frying pan.

Looking up, smiling warmly, Tamara said, "Did you have a good walk, Chloe?"

"It was great, thanks." Chloe laughed. "It blew the cobwebs away, that's for sure. And it's given me an appetite."

"*Good.* Is it cold today?" Tamara asked, turning more bacon with a spatula, glancing over her shoulder as she spoke.

"Brisk. But I think it'll warm up if the wind drops. It's lovely and sunny though, a nice day to be outside as long as you're well wrapped up."

Chloe walked across the large kitchen, which her mother had decorated so effectively years before. Nothing had been changed, and it always pleased her to see it looking the same. Standing at the counter near the refrigerator, she poured herself a mug of coffee, added milk and sugar, and carried the mug back to the big wooden table in the center of the room. This was covered with a green-and-white-checked cloth that matched the curtains at the windows; she remembered the day her mother had brought them up to Yorkshire and hung them at the windows herself.

Sitting down, Chloe asked, "Who's the bacon for, Tam? It smells so delicious, I can hardly bear it."

"Anyone who wants it. There're also some other grilled things . . . tomatoes, mushrooms, sausages, and scrambled eggs. And I've got a bread cake warming in the Aga. Would you like me to prepare you a plate, darling? Give you a bit of everything?"

"That sounds good, really yummy. Thanks, Tam. And where is everyone?"

"Nigel went upstairs to look for his wallet. He and the children have already had their breakfast. He's going to take them to Ripon with Agnes. To do some shopping for me. I need a few things. And Gideon's in the back parlor, phoning Lenore. He's driving over to Lindenhill later, to bring her back here for lunch."

"Oh, good, I've always liked Lenore. I'm so glad she's going to marry Gid, aren't you?"

"Absolutely. It's the best thing that's happened to him . . . I mean, that she came back to him. But that awful Malcolm Armstrong is throwing spanners in the works all the time as far as the divorce is concerned."

"Oh, I know. Mom says it's ridiculous."

"Somebody's going to have to pay him off, *I* think."

"I agree. Mom says everyone has a price, and it's not always money."

Tamara laughed at this pithy comment as she turned her attention to fixing Chloe's plate, enjoying mothering the eighteen-year-old.

Chloe sipped her coffee, glancing around the spacious kitchen. She had always loved this room; it was her favorite in the old farmhouse and very special to her, from its beamed ceiling to terra-cotta-tiled floor. There was a warmth and a homeliness about it that was most appealing and reassuring. Her mother had filled it to overflowing with comfort over the years, placing a big sofa and two armchairs covered in rose-colored linen at one end, near the big picture window facing the moors. She had included two pine chests within the seating arrangement, and these held charming old lamps; the large table in the center of the room was surrounded by eight wooden chairs with rose linen cushions, and it was there that they ate most of their meals, unless they had guests.

The huge stone hearth, where a fire burned brightly, was another addition her mother had made, and it was the focal point of the room. The many copper pots and pans that hung on the hearth gleamed and winked in the firelight, which gave the room a lovely glow on this cold March morning. Logs were piled on one end of the hearth; on the other there was a big copper bucket filled with dried flowers. Facing the fire were two old grandfather chairs with high wooden backs and rose linen cushions, the chairs linked by a colorful rag rug. At the other side of the room, the big Aga stove gave off additional warmth, making the kitchen the coziest of places, one where everyone loved to gather at all hours of the day. In a sense, it was the core of the house.

"Good morning, Chloe," Gideon said, striding into the kitchen, bending down and kissing his sister. Straightening, he added, "And don't you look bonny. Your walk on the moors has brought some color to your cheeks. Do you want to come with me later? I'm going to Lindenhill to fetch Lenore."

"Yes, I'd love to, thanks, Gid." Chloe rose, walked over to the oven, and took the plate from Tamara. "This is awesome, Tam. And so yummy-looking. Thanks."

Gideon went and got a mug of coffee and joined Chloe at the kitchen table.

Tamara asked, "Do you want something to eat, Gid?"

"A bacon butty, if you don't mind making it."

"A pleasure," Tamara answered, and flashed him a bright smile.

Chloe asked, "Is Lenore bringing her children to lunch?"

"God forbid, I'll never cope. Not with hers as well as mine!" Tamara cried, and made a face of mock dismay.

Gideon laughed. "Of course you would, you always cope with everything, Tam. But actually she's not bringing her brood. They've already gone riding with their Brindsley cousins, over near Middleham. Lenore said they wanted to go up on the gallops with the stable boys who exercise the race horses from the racing stables in Middleham. Apparently they really enjoy it, and have a lot of fun competing with the boys."

"It's the best place to ride," Tamara remarked, putting the thick bacon sandwich on a plate and bringing it to him.

"Thank you, Tam. Aren't you having anything to eat?"

"The same as you, Gid."

After serving herself a bacon butty, Tamara finally sat down and went on. "I'm sorry to bring up lunch when we haven't even finished breakfast yet, but I thought I ought to cook fish, since it's Good Friday. However, Nigel's not very fond of fish, so I'm going to make a shepherd's pie as well. I also have a baked ham which I brought up from London. I'll do vegetables and a big salad. What do you think?"

"Sounds fine to me," Gideon murmured. "But *I'd* prefer the shepherd's pie too, like Nigel."

"Fish for me, with a salad," Chloe said, glancing at Tamara. Then she asked, "Is Mrs. Entwhistle coming up from the village to help today?"

"No, I told her she didn't have to come. You see, her grandson's arriving from Portsmouth for twenty-four hours' leave. He's in the Royal Navy, you know. Well, anyway, I didn't want to spoil it for her, encroach on that special time. I can manage."

Chloe turned to Gideon. "I think I'd better stay and help Tamara make lunch."

"All right. And I'll come back from Lindenhill quickly, and Lenore and I will both pitch in."

Nigel said from the doorway, "We're all set to go, Tamsy darling." He walked over to his wife, kissed the top of her shining silver-gilt hair, and said to Chloe, "Good morning to you, miss. What's the weather like?"

"Morning, Nigel, and it's windy, chilly, but very sunny. A pretty day."

Agnes, the young nanny, followed him into the kitchen, holding Natalie and Arnaud by the hands. She greeted Chloe and Gideon; the children broke free and bounded toward Chloe, threw themselves against her legs.

"Hello, little ones," she said, and bending over, Chloe hugged them to her.

"Come with us, Auntie Chloe," Arnaud said. *"Please."*

"I'd love to, darling, but I can't. I'm going to stay here and help your mummy make lunch for us all. But I'll play hide-and-seek with you this afternoon. How does that sound?"

He nodded, beaming at her.

Natalie said, "Me too hide seek."

Chloe rumpled her hair, thinking how adorable they looked in their dark green loden jackets and matching pants worn with red sweaters and red Wellington boots.

"Let's go, Pumpkins." Nigel made for the door.

Tamara caught up with him, linked her arm through his, and accompanied him out to the Jeep parked in front of the farmhouse. "Try and find the hot cross buns if you can, Nigel, it's such a bother to have to make them."

"I will, darling, don't worry," Nigel answered, drawing her closer to him. "If they don't have any in Ripon, I'll pop over to Harrogate and stop in at Betty's Cafe. They're bound to have loads of them there." He looked into her eyes, his own full of love, and then he kissed her on the mouth.

"See you later, angel," he said as he strode over to the Jeep, opened the doors, bundled the children and Agnes onto the backseat.

"Good-bye, Pumpkins," Tamara called, blowing kisses.

They blew kisses to her in return, their small faces glowing with health and full of laughter.

"Drive carefully, Nigel," Tamara cautioned.

"Don't worry, I will. See you later, Tamsy."

23

Left to their own devices, Tamara and Chloe had another cup of coffee and chatted to each other in front of the fire for a short while. Mostly they spoke about Gideon again, and his involvement with Lenore. Both women welcomed her entry into the family, and they couldn't help speculating about the wedding.

Once they had exhausted this subject, they wondered out loud about Miles and *his* romantic entanglements. "Has he taken anyone to Paris with him for Easter?" Tamara asked at one point, eyeing Chloe, knowing how close she was to Miles.

Chloe shook her head. "I don't know, he didn't tell me on the way over from New York. But there was just the two of us on the plane. What I mean is, Allison wasn't with us, and he didn't make any reference to her. Actually, I have a feeling that's over now." Chloe shrugged and grinned. "Maybe he has a rendezvous in Paris. What do you think?"

"Could be," Tamara agreed, also chuckling.

It was Chloe who finished her coffee and jumped up first, exclaiming, "This isn't going to get anything done. I'm going to put the breakfast things away, then I'll set the table for lunch. Where are we going to have it?"

"Oh, in the kitchen as usual, don't you think? It's so cozy in here. Besides, without Mrs. Entwhistle to help, it's such a chore to carry things in and out of the dining room."

"I agree." Chloe set to work, moving swiftly around the kitchen.

For her part, Tamara put the leftover food in plastic containers, stacked them in the refrigerator, then filled the dishwasher. When she had finished, she took off her apron, replaced it with a clean one, shaking her head as she did. She turned to Chloe and muttered, "I get more mess on myself when I'm cooking than the children do when they're painting."

Chloe grinned. "I know what you mean, so do I. And I think I'd better have one of your aprons myself. This is a new track suit, and I don't want to get it dirty."

The two women, who were used to working together at the farm, soon had the kitchen shipshape and ready for lunch. Once they had cleaned up and set the table, Tamara took all of the salad ingredients out of the pantry and asked Chloe to wash the lettuce and the watercress, then slice the tomatoes. She herself set about cooking the ground lamb for the shepherd's pie.

"So, do you think you're pregnant yet?" Chloe asked at one moment, giving her sister-in-law a questioning look.

"I don't know, Chloe." She laughed and her eyes sparkled as she added, "Maybe it's happened this weekend. Certainly Nigel's romantic enough."

"He was certainly very sweet and loving with you last night, and in a good mood in general," Chloe commented. "I wish he hadn't done that awful thing to Mom, it's caused such a rift in the family."

"Yes, I know. But time heals everything, at least that's what my mother always says. I think she's right—" Tamara cut herself off, shook her head sadly. "I agree with the rest of you that it was foolish. I don't understand him sometimes, Chloe. I've no idea what gets into him. It's as if there's a demon inside him telling him what to do. And he can be so cantankerous, almost like an old man."

"On the plane coming over Miles told me that Nigel came under Grandmother Jardine's influence too much when he was about twelve or thirteen. Perhaps it's all to do with that. That's what Gideon thinks as well."

"Yes, perhaps they're correct about that." Tamara took a wooden spoon, pressed the meat into the pan, added a little water, and lowered the flame. Then she went into the walk-in pantry, looking for the condiments.

Chloe, who was washing the lettuce at the sink, smiled to herself as she heard Tamara whistling. *She* couldn't whistle at all, even though her brothers had tried to teach her many times when she was growing up.

Suddenly Chloe jumped, startled by the sound of someone moving around in the front porch. She swung around to face the front door just as it opened. A man walked into the kitchen, a man she had never seen before.

"Can I help you?" she asked, frowning, wondering who he was. Certainly he was not one of the locals from the village. She could tell that from his appearance, and from the clothes he wore. He could be French.

The man, who appeared to be in his early thirties, was good-looking in a dark, swarthy way, and extremely well dressed, very much in the continental manner. If he wasn't French, perhaps he was Spanish. He stared at Chloe without speaking.

Again Chloe asked, "How can I help you? Who are you?"

The man remained silent.

Tamara, hearing Chloe's voice, hurried out of the pantry holding the pepper mill, and stopped in her tracks. She gaped at the man speechlessly. Finally recovering herself, she exclaimed shrilly, "My God! *Alexis!* What are you doing here?"

The man called Alexis still did not speak. He continued to stand there as if frozen to the spot.

Tamara asked again: "Alexis, why are you here?"

"I've come for *you*," he said, finding his voice at last. "I've been looking all over for you, my Tamara. I've come to get you."

Chloe detected a distinct accent, and her startled eyes flew from Tamara to the man, and back again to Tamara. Her sister-in-law's face had turned sheet white, and there was a terrified look in her eyes. It was obvious to her that Tamara, usually so cool, contained, and fearless, was actually frightened of this man. Oh, my God, it's her ex-husband, Alexis Dumachev, Chloe thought, and immediately stepped forward protectively.

Moving closer to him, not in the least afraid, Chloe said in the firmest voice she could summon, "I think you'd better go. My brother's going to be angry if he finds you here. Please leave."

Ignoring her, rudely pushing past her, Alexis Dumachev walked across the kitchen and grabbed hold of Tamara's arm. Instantly, she dropped the wooden pepper mill.

He exclaimed angrily, "You're *mine*. You belong to *me*. And you're coming with *me*. Now."

Tamara tried to shake off his hand, struggling with him. But his grip was tenacious; his fingers bit into her arm, and she winced in pain. Swinging her head to face him, she said as evenly as possible, "Please let go of me, Alexis. This is silly, you're being silly. I'm—"

"*Silly,*" he yelled, his eyes bulging as he cut her short. "*Silly* because I *worship* you. My God, you are my life." He began to scream at her in Russian; Tamara shrank back, whilst still trying to break free of his hold.

Chloe ran across the floor and tugged at his coat, then his arm. "Leave her alone."

"Get away from me, you stupid little girl!" he yelled, turning to Chloe, pushing her violently.

Chloe staggered, but instantly steadied herself against the kitchen table. She lunged at him once more, tearing at his body, wanting to free her sister-in-law.

In an effort to fight Chloe off, Dumachev loosened his grip on Tamara. It was the opportunity she had been waiting for, and she struggled free at last. She leapt away from him, running to the far end of the kitchen.

Chloe dropped back, ducked him, and ran to join Tamara; shaking and scared, the two women huddled together behind one of the armchairs. "What are we going to do?" Chloe whispered, trying to catch her breath. "I wish Gideon would get here."

"I'll try to reason with him," Tamara muttered grimly, and took a few steps forward. In a conciliatory voice, she said, "Alexis, please be reasonable. You know I've been married to Nigel for five years, almost six. You and I were divorced so long ago. It's over between us, and it *was* over years ago, long before I met Nigel."

"You're mine! You'll always be *mine*," he cried, his handsome face contorting into an ugly mask. "And I am yours. You know you don't love *him*. I am the only man you love."

"No, no, that's not so," Tamara exclaimed. "You're wrong, Alexis. Please, leave me alone. Go back to Paris. Please, Alexis."

"If you will come with me, yes, I will go," he said in a most reasonable voice, suddenly, irrationally smiling at her.

"No, I can't. It's Nigel I love, and I belong here with him."

"No, no, you don't. I won't let you stay here. He's keeping you from me. Where is he? I'll kill him. I'll kill his children."

Tamara began to shake uncontrollably, and the fear rushed through her; it was more potent than before. Filling with dread, she gripped Chloe's hand and whispered, "He's not himself. I think he's gone crazy. We've got to get away from him, get out of here. Or we've got to get to the phone. Whichever's easier. Come on."

Chloe nodded, and the two of them slowly edged their way in the direction of the long countertop where the telephone sat.

Alexis was watching the two women like a hawk. He said finally, in a quieter tone, "You don't understand, do you, my Tamara? There is nothing for me without you. I have no life. No reason to live. I am going to kill myself." As he spoke, he pulled a gun out of his jacket pocket and waved it in the air. "Look, I have a gun! I will shoot myself."

"Please, Alexis, calm down," Tamara said softly, placatingly, even though terror was rampant in her now. "And put that gun away before someone gets hurt. This is not necessary."

"I love you" was his only response.

After a second, he did as she asked, and put the gun back in his pocket.

Tamara let out a breath of relief, inched her way toward the phone; Chloe stayed close to her. As Tamara picked up the receiver, Alexis jumped her, throwing both his arms around her in a bear hug, pulling her down to the floor with him. They struggled, grappling with each other, but he was the stronger.

Chloe flew across the room to help Tamara. As her sister-in-law strove to fight off her ex-husband, Chloe grabbed at Dumachev, pulled and pummeled him. Finally, Tamara was able to struggle free of his hold. But he was tenacious, and he still gripped the end of her apron. Then, unexpectedly, he let go of it and slumped, breathing hard.

Tamara stumbled, as she pulled herself upright, and hit the leg of the table. She regained her balance immediately and fled with Chloe, circling the table, trying to escape.

Dumachev was instantly on his feet, and he made it to the front door before they did. "If I can't have you, neither can he!" Dumachev screamed. The gun was in his hand and he pulled the trigger, firing wildly, then aiming at the women. He was a good marksman. He did not miss.

Tamara and Chloe were both struck by bullets. They fell instantly. Blood spurted from Tamara's chest and from Chloe's head. They sprawled near the sofa, only inches from the door.

Dumachev looked down at them, frowning, his glazed eyes suddenly registered puzzlement, as if he did not understand what he had done. Kneeling down, bending over Tamara's body, he began to sob, the tears pouring down his face. After only a moment he lay down next to her, put the revolver in his mouth, and pulled the trigger one last time.

He blew off the back of his head, his blood splashing onto the white kitchen walls and countertop, spilling onto Tamara, to mingle with her own blood.

Now all was quiet in the kitchen.

The only sounds were the sizzling of meat in the pan, the running of water in the sink, the crackling of logs in the fireplace.

In the background, the radio played softly . . . a love song.

24

As they drove through the pretty Dales village of West Scrafton, Gideon glanced at Lenore through the corner of his eye, and said, "After we're married, I'd like us to have our own house in Yorkshire. I don't really want to share Aysgarth End with Tamara and Nigel."

Lenore nodded, understanding how he felt. "We could use Lindenhill at weekends. Tony wouldn't mind. After all, the place is so big. Anyway, he's never up here much these days."

"I know, but—" Gideon paused momentarily, and then finished, "Let's think about it. I still might want to have our own place for the weekends, darling."

Lenore smiled and said, "By the way, talking of my darling brother, he wants to give the wedding. And he'd like us to be married in the church in Lindenhill, and have the reception at the house."

"How very nice of him, and it's a great idea." He laughed wickedly. "That's where I fell in love with you, after all."

"Me too, you, dearest one." Lenore also laughed, murmured

in her sexiest voice, "And it's there that you taught me all sorts of naughty things, you bad little boy."

"*You* taught *me*, you beautiful wretch," he shot back.

Still chuckling, Gideon drove on through the village, past the tiny village green and the huddle of ancient gray stone houses, pushing up toward the moors, and the road that would take them to Aysgarth End.

At one moment he said, "By the way, Chloe would love to be bridesmaid. When we were driving up from London yesterday she asked me to ask you if she could be."

"What a lovely idea, Gid, and I'd like that. However, I don't think we should have too grand a wedding, under the circumstances. That wouldn't be appropriate, because of my divorce." She sighed. "Whenever I get it, that is."

Glancing at her swiftly, bringing his eyes back to the road, he murmured, "Everything's going to be all right, Lenore." Suddenly coming to a stop, he waited as several sheep meandered across the road and went into a field; he then drove on up the hill.

"Do try not to worry. Malcolm's going to come around eventually," he reassured her.

"I hope so."

"As for the wedding, I agree it can't be grand. On the other hand, there's nothing very grand about one bridesmaid, is there?"

"No, of course not. And I *want* Chloe to be my bridesmaid. I also think we should invite Tamara to be matron of honor."

"She'd adore that, Lenore."

The two of them fell silent as they continued along the moorland road, lost in thoughts of their marriage which they both prayed would be soon. Just before they reached the side lane that branched off to the farm, Lenore said, "Oh, do let's stop for a moment near the big rocks. The view from there is spectacular. It's as if I'm standing on the roof of the world when I'm up here on the moors. I feel as if I have only to stand on my tiptoes to touch the sky, and grab a handful of cloud."

"I know." Gideon slowed down, then braked and turned off the ignition; the two of them alighted, linked arms, and walked over to the rocks. It was a sheltered spot, and they sat down on a flat rock, stared out toward the great Whernside fells soaring above the valley below. The view of the Dales from this vantage point *was* magnificent, and particularly so on this clear, sunny day. It was picture perfect and breathtaking.

"Look how the Nidd wends its way along the valley floor," Gideon said. "I remember the first time my mother pointed it out to me. It is so special here, just as you said. I feel as if we can see forever, don't you?"

Lenore nodded, pulled her Barbour closer to her body, shivering in the wind. "I'm so glad your mother found the farmhouse when she did, Gideon, and that you came to live here when you were little. Just imagine if you hadn't. We would never have met."

"Oh, yes, we would. I know that for a certainty. We were meant to be, you and I, Lenore. Fate would have found a way to bring us together."

Putting his arm around her, Gideon turned her to face him. Lenore was the most beautiful woman in the world to him. That morning her blonde hair was pulled back from her heart-shaped face and fell down her back in a plait, but there were fronds of hair and little wispy curls around her forehead and cheeks, and these softened the rather severe hairdo. Her fine complexion was scrubbed clean; she wore no makeup on her face today, and she looked like a young girl.

Gideon leaned closer, kissed her lightly on the lips, and then pulled away again, gazing into her misty gray eyes. They were large, luminous, and filled with intelligence. "You do believe it, don't you?"

"What?"

"That we were meant to be."

"*Absolutely.*" She paused, glanced at him, said softly, "You are more myself than I am. Whatever our souls are made of, yours and mine are the same."

"Stolen from *Wuthering Heights!*"

"Just paraphrasing Emily Brontë's words. I'd never steal from *her*, Gid. One of the great geniuses of English literature."

He smiled at her.

She smiled back.

And they drew closer together under the rocks, their arms wrapped around each other.

After a short while, he loosened his grip on her and jumped up, exclaiming, "Come on, darling, we can't sit here daydreaming forever. We'd better go. I told Tamara and Chloe that we'd be at the farm in plenty of time to help them prepare lunch."

Within minutes, Gideon was guiding the Land-Rover down the narrow road to Aysgarth End, and as they went through the gate, he said, "There's a car here, we must have a visitor. But I can't imagine who that would be on Good Friday."

"Maybe it's someone from the village."

"I doubt it, and I know Mrs. Entwhistle isn't coming today. Something about her grandson arriving from Portsmouth."

Gideon parked the Land-Rover in front of the house and the two of them went into the porch.

As Lenore struggled out of her Barbour and hung it up, she said, "Something's burning. I think Tamara must have left a pot on the stove."

Shaking her head and laughing, thinking that Tamara was as careless as she was when it came to cooking, Lenore pushed open the front door and stepped into the kitchen.

Instantly, she gasped, and the laughter fled her face when she saw Tamara and Chloe sprawled on the floor covered in blood.

She cried out in shock and fear. "Oh, my God! Oh, God, Gideon, there's blood everywhere! They've been hurt. Oh, my God! We've got to get help. They've been shot. Look, there's a gun over there next to that man." Shuddering violently, Lenore turned away.

Gideon was standing immediately behind Lenore, and he caught hold of her in an effort to support her as she swayed on her feet. He held her close, staring down at his sister and sister-in-law; he was horror-struck.

His face was ashen. All of his strength ebbed away; he thought his legs were going to buckle under him. There *was* blood everywhere. It was ghastly, horrendous. Surely they were dead. Oh, God, he hoped not. His heart was thundering in his chest, and he could hardly breathe. "Can you stand up on your own, Lenore?" he managed at last.

"My legs are a bit wobbly, I'll be okay. It's the shock. . . . "

"I know, I know. Lean against the door." Swallowing hard, Gideon moved nearer Chloe, knelt down, and took hold of his sister's wrist. "There's a pulse. Thank God she's alive," he gasped in a choked voice. "She has a head wound. All this blood. It looks bad."

"Don't move her," Lenore exclaimed, staring across at him. "That's the worst thing you could do . . . I just know you shouldn't move either of them, in case you injure them further." Lenore closed her eyes and gripped the door frame. Tears leaked out from under her lids. Then, pulling herself together instantly, knowing there was no time to waste, she snapped her eyes open and went to the stove. She turned off the flame and stopped the tap running in the sink.

Gideon was shaking inside as he knelt down and felt Tamara's wrist, seeking her pulse. "She's also alive. Thank God for that. I must phone for an ambulance, get help at once, Lenore. Time's of the essence."

Moving a bit unsteadily across the floor, but also getting a proper grip on himself, Gideon leaned against the counter, reached for the phone, and dialed 999. Endeavoring to control his voice, he swiftly gave the emergency service operator all the necessary details, and then hung up.

"Ambulances, paramedics, and the police will be here as quickly as possible," he said, looking at Lenore. Her face was drained of all color, but she seemed steadier now. "I'm going to call my mother," he added.

Joining him at the counter, Lenore took hold of his arm. "Don't you want to wait until help gets here? Hear what they have to say?"

He shook his head. "I think I'd better call Ma in New York immediately. We need her here, and she should be here for Chloe and Tamara."

"Yes, you're right." Lenore bit her lip, glanced quickly at the two injured women on the floor, and said to Gideon softly, "Who would do this ... this terrible thing, Gid?" Before he could answer, she murmured, "It was obviously that man. Who is he?"

"I've no idea. But he's dead, that I *can* tell you."

"Can I get you anything?" Lenore asked, touching his arm again, aware of the strain and tension in him.

"No, thanks." He pulled a chair up to the counter and sat down. He glanced at his watch. "It's almost eleven, nearly six in New York. Yes, I am going to call my mother now." As he spoke, he lifted the receiver, then put it back in the cradle. "Lenore, please keep an eye open for Nigel. He should be back any minute now, and I don't want him walking in on this ... especially with the children."

"God, you're right!" She moved to the window overlooking

the circular drive. "When he does get here, I'd better take the children and Agnes over to Lindenhill, get them out of the way."

"Yes, that would be best," he agreed, and lifted the phone once more. He dialed his mother in New York, steeling himself to break the news to her.

When she answered, he said in the steadiest voice he could muster, "Hello, Ma, it's Gideon."

"Yes, I know it's you, darling. And it's nice to hear your voice," Stevie replied. "You must be up at the farm. How're things?"

He did not answer this question; instead, he asked, "I didn't wake you, did I?"

"No, I've been up since five," she laughed. "I'm just having a cup of coffee."

"Ma . . . I've . . ." He stopped abruptly. Words failed him. He swallowed. There was a silence.

"Are you there, Gideon?"

"Yes, Ma, there's something I must tell you. There's—"

"What is it?" she asked, interrupting, her tone rising an octave. "Something's wrong. I can tell from your voice. What is it, Gideon?"

"Ma, you've got to come here today. To Yorkshire. When we hang up, you must call British Airways and book a seat on this morning's Concorde. The eight forty-five. I'll arrange for a private plane to meet you at Heathrow to bring you up here."

"Gideon, for God's sake, what is it? Tell me, please! Stop delaying the bad news. Because it *is* bad, I know that."

He cleared his throat. "Yes, I'm afraid it is. . . . There's been a shooting here at the farm. But they're alive . . . Chloe and Tamara are alive, Ma. I'm waiting for the ambulance."

"Oh, my God! What happened?" she demanded.

"Ma, I don't know. I wasn't here."

"Let me speak to Nigel."

"He's not here, Mother. He took the children and Agnes to Ripon. Shopping. Lenore and I just walked in on this, only a few minutes ago. *We* found Chloe and Tamara ... Nigel doesn't know yet."

"They *are* alive, aren't they, Gideon? You wouldn't lie to me, would you? Just to keep me calmer?" she asked, her voice shaking.

He could hear the tears in her voice, and he exclaimed, "Honestly, Mother, they are alive. They are, yes."

"Who did it?"

"I'm not sure," he hedged, "but the police are coming. They'll be here any minute. And Chloe and Tamara *are* going to make it, I just know they are."

"Oh, God, I hope so, Gideon! Oh, my little girl. My little Chloe. And Tamara, sweet Tamara ... They've got to make it." Stevie took a deep breath and tried to steady her voice as she finished, "I think I'd better hang up and get moving, unless there's anything else you want to tell me."

"No, Ma."

"All right. Phone your grandmother and Derek, Gideon, please. Tell them what has happened, and ask Derek to charter a private plane for me, for this evening. I'll be on that Concorde no matter what I have to do to get on it. And please stay in touch with Derek and my mother, let them know what hospital Chloe and Tamara are in, so that I know where to come. I'll be in touch with my mother—" Stevie's voice broke. She was unable to say anymore.

"They'll make it, Mother," Gideon reassured her again, praying that they would.

"Yes" was all she could say before she hung up.

Gideon's heart went out to his mother as he replaced the

receiver. He knew how much she loved Chloe, knew what Tamara meant to her.

From her stance at the window, Lenore said, "Your mother's a very strong woman, Gid, she'll be able to handle this, and better than most."

"I know. I'd better phone my grandmother in London."

"That might have to wait," Lenore told him. "I can see Nigel's car coming down the driveway. I think we ought to go outside to meet him, Gideon."

Together, Lenore and Gideon walked forward to meet the Jeep as it circled the urn in the middle of the drive and came to a stop.

Alighting, Nigel glanced at the parked car and said to them, "Do we have a visitor? Who's here?"

Gideon took hold of his brother's arm and drew him to one side, and Lenore ran to the Jeep. She stood talking to the children through the window, preventing them from alighting.

"Nigel, something's happened . . . there's been a shooting—" Gideon began.

"Oh, my God! Not Tamara? Not Chloe?" Nigel tried to pull away, to go into the farmhouse, his eyes flaring with fear. Holding on to him tightly, Gideon said, "They're alive. I've phoned for an ambulance. You must stay calm for the sake of the children."

"Let go of me, Gideon! I want to see Tamara!" he gasped, still trying to pull away, to move toward the house.

"No! Wait a minute. Listen to me. I think Lenore should drive the children and Agnes to Lindenhill, get them out of the way for the time being. Lenore will give them lunch, keep them busy. They can stay there with Agnes for as long as you want. There's staff over at the house."

Nigel stared at his brother, then his eyes flew to his children in the Jeep. Swallowing hard, he nodded. Summoning as much control as he could, he ran to them and said, "Auntie Lenore's going to take you back to her house with Agnes, Pumpkins. For lunch. I've something to do . . . with Mummy. Okay?"

"I want to see Mummy, show her my new ball," Arnaud said.

"See Mummy," Natalie repeated.

"Later. Be good, both of you." Nigel kissed them quickly, trying not to break down. He looked at the nanny, saw her bafflement. "Lady Armstrong will explain everything, Agnes. Take care of the children."

"Yes, Mr. Jardine. You can count on me," Agnes answered quietly, sensing trouble.

Nigel swung around and ran back toward the house.

Gideon ran after him.

Lenore called, "Phone me later, Gid."

"I will, darling," he shouted back without turning around.

As Nigel hurtled into the porch, Gideon caught up with him and grabbed his arm, restraining him. "Be prepared, Nigel, there's a lot of . . . a lot of blood."

Nigel nodded; his face was strained. "What the hell happened here?" he asked in a trembling voice, opened the front door, and went into the kitchen. Horror and shock at what he saw brought him to a momentary standstill, and a strangled cry escaped his throat. Then he hurried to kneel next to Tamara, taking hold of her hand. "Tamara, I'm here, darling. It's me, Nigel. I'm here."

Tamara was motionless. There was no response. He held her wrist, found her pulse. Lifting his eyes to Gideon, he nodded, and bringing his face close to hers, he strained to listen; he could hear her breathing. But it was shallow, faint. "She's alive."

Gideon was now checking on Chloe, and he also nodded. "Chloe's holding on too. There's a nasty wound on her forehead. She's been shot in the head, Nigel. It looks serious."

"Oh, God! What *happened* here?" Nigel asked, noticing the dead man. He looked Tamara's body over again, his eyes stricken. "I think Tam has a chest wound, but it's hard to tell with all this blood." Leaning forward, he moved a strand of silver-gilt hair away from her face. "Tam, oh, Tam, darling, please hang on, don't die. Please fight . . ." His eyes filled with tears; he struggled hard to keep his composure, and all the time he clung to her hand, kneeling next to her, praying silently, praying that she would live.

"Don't touch her, don't move her, Nigel," Gideon warned. "You don't want to hurt her, and you could without knowing it."

Nigel nodded. "What the bloody hell's going on? Where's that ambulance, Gideon?" he asked in a low, intense mutter, sudden anger and frustration rising to the surface.

"It should be here any minute." Gideon looked at his watch. "It's now eleven-thirty. I phoned emergency as soon as I got here. They said it would take about thirty-five to forty minutes. The nearest big hospital is in Harrogate."

Gently Nigel laid Tamara's hand on the floor and stood up. His face was white and taut, his vivid blue eyes dark with worry. He said to Gideon, "The chap next to her . . . I'm pretty sure that's Dumachev, her ex-husband."

Gideon nodded quickly. "I wondered if it was . . . I guess you can't be really sure . . . not even you can be."

"Why?" Nigel said hoarsely, staring at his brother, the tears springing into his eyes once more. "*Why*, Gideon? Why did he do it?"

Gideon shook his head. "I don't know. . . . " His voice trailed off and he thought of Margot Saunders and the potential for violence he had detected in her. He shuddered. Moving away from Chloe, he went to Nigel and drew him to the other side of the kitchen table. "Sit down, Nigel, the ambulance will be here any minute." He pressed his brother into the chair.

"I wonder what time they were . . . when do you think this happened, Gid?"

"I left here just after nine, a little bit after you, and I got back here with Lenore around ten-thirty, at the latest ten-forty. It must have been just before we arrived."

"Isn't it getting riskier by the minute?" Nigel worried aloud. "For them. They need help desperately." He got up and went over to Tamara.

"Yes, they do. And they're about to get it, Nigel. I can hear noises in the drive. Cars." Gideon hurried to the front door and ran outside.

Three ambulances and three police cars were tearing down the drive. They all slowed to a stop; police jumped out of the cars at the same moment paramedics leapt out of the ambulances.

"Are the injured people inside?" one of the paramedics shouted to Gideon as he and his partner hoisted a stretcher.

"That's right. My sister has a gunshot wound on her forehead, my sister-in-law looks as if she has chest wounds. There's a lot of blood on her—" Gideon stopped. The paramedics had already run inside the house.

One of the policemen came up to Gideon. "Mr. Jardine?" he asked, looking him over carefully.

Gideon nodded, thrust out his hand. "Gideon Jardine. My brother Nigel is inside with his injured wife and our sister, Sergeant." Gideon nodded to the parked car. "I think that must belong to the man who did the shooting."

"I see. Let's go inside, Mr. Jardine, and try to sort all this out," the police sergeant answered. "After you, Mr. Jardine."

25

THE BRITISH AIRWAYS CONCORDE FLIGHT FROM NEW YORK WAS A few minutes late when it landed at Heathrow just before six on Good Friday afternoon.

Stevie Jardine was the first person off the plane, the first in and out of Immigration. Since she had no luggage, only her briefcase, she went straight to the Customs Hall. Once again, because she was the first to enter, she was hurrying out into the terminal within a couple of seconds. As she emerged, her eyes scanned the crowd swiftly.

She saw her mother immediately. Blair was standing by the barrier, waiting for her, and she raised her hand in greeting. A moment later the two women were embracing.

As they pulled apart, Stevie stared at her mother worriedly, her eyes apprehensive and filled with questions.

Blair said, "She's alive, darling, they're both alive."

Stevie let out a sigh of relief. "Thank God for that. I'm sure I don't have to tell you that the flight over has been *torturous*. I'm exhausted from worry."

"I can well imagine," Blair murmured.

"Where's Derek, Mother?"

"Waiting for us on the private plane. You know how it is when he's seen in public, he tends to get mobbed. We thought it better for him to board. But let's hurry, Stevie, the plane's on the tarmac, ready to take us to Yorkshire. We can talk then."

Fifteen minutes later, Derek was greeting them as they came up the steps of the plane. After hugging Stevie and telling her not to worry, he showed them their seats. They all fastened their safety belts, and once the Gulfstream IV jet was airborne, the stewardess served hot lemon tea to Stevie and Blair, and a scotch on the rocks to Derek.

"How is Chloe *actually*?" Stevie asked anxiously, looking from her mother to Derek when they were alone. "I'm crazy with worry."

He said very quietly, "She's in a coma, Stevie, and she has been since she was shot. The bullet entered her brain, you see."

"Oh, *no*! Oh, my God," Stevie cried, and brought her hand to her mouth, stifling a cry of anguish. "What are they going to do?"

"They've already done it," Derek answered, putting a hand on her arm, trying to reassure her. "She had an operation on her brain this afternoon. To remove the bullet. And—"

"Were they able to take it out?" Stevie interrupted shakily. She felt as though all the strength had left her body.

"Yes, they did. It took almost three hours to do the operation. She was operated on by one of the best neurosurgeons in the country, in the world actually, Mr. Valentin Longdon. She's in the Brotherton Wing of Leeds General Infirmary. The private wing. In the intensive care unit. And so is Tamara. She was shot in the chest. Several times. They've managed to remove the bullets, but she's still unconscious, Stevie. Very weak. She lost a lot of blood."

Stevie swallowed hard, and her voice was a whisper when she asked, "Are they going to make it, Derek? Are they going to live?"

"We hope so, darling, we're praying they will."

Blair took hold of her daughter's hand and squeezed it. "It's going to be all right, I know it is. Try and have faith."

Stevie nodded, unable to speak for a few minutes. Then she murmured, "So they didn't take them to Harrogate District Hospital." She bit her lip. "It's closer . . . but then, Leeds is such a big medical center . . . "

Derek nodded. "True. And in fact, they *were* taken to Harrogate. But the doctors there wanted Chloe to be sent to Leeds Infirmary, where there's that crack neurosurgical unit. They wanted her to have the very best. From what I understand from Gideon, they decided to send Tamara to Leeds as well, because of the seriousness of her wounds. They were helicoptered from Harrogate to Leeds, and were in the operating theaters by two o'clock this afternoon. It was all handled very speedily, Stevie."

"I know Leeds General Infirmary is a good hospital," she acknowledged.

"And don't forget, it's one of the finest teaching hospitals in Europe, in the world. Bar none. So is St. James's hospital nearby. The Leeds medical complex is world renowned, so rest easy about their care, darling. They're getting the best, and every facility is available."

"I will try, Derek, but it's hard. I just can't help worrying—" She stopped, her voice breaking. Fumbling for her handkerchief, she blew her nose, tried to stem the tears that suddenly blinded her.

There was a small silence among them.

Eventually, clearing her throat several times, Stevie went on. "What about Tamara's parents? Did someone manage to contact them? I know they were supposed to go on a cruise this Easter. To the Far East and China, I think."

"They did go," Blair said. "Gideon had Bruce send a fax to the ship. Fortunately, Nigel remembered his father-in-law telling him they would be arriving in Hong Kong on Good Friday and staying there for the Easter weekend."

"How is Bruce holding up?" Stevie asked, glancing at Derek.

"Not bad under the circumstances. It's shaken him, of course, and he wanted to fly up with us today, but I told him it would be better if he came tomorrow. We've booked him a room at the Queen's. That's where we're all staying."

"Gideon found Miles in Paris. At the Plaza Athénée. He left immediately, and he's probably already in Leeds by now," Blair explained.

"Nigel must be distraught!" Stevie exclaimed, shaking her head. "He loves Tamara so much, worships her, really. He must be out of his mind . . . where are the children, Mother?" Stevie turned to Blair, her face taut with anxiety.

"Lenore took them to Lindenhill the moment they returned from their shopping trip this morning. They're there with Agnes. Apparently Agnes went over to Aysgarth End this afternoon, to get some of their things, and a few bits and pieces of her own. They're going to stay at Lindenhill indefinitely. Until we all go back to London, that is."

"Yes, that's the best solution," Stevie agreed.

"I spoke to Lenore at five o'clock," Derek said. "When your mother and I arrived at the airport. She's the one who told me about Chloe's condition and the operation, and about Tamara. Gideon asked her to stay next to the phone at Lindenhill. She's our base—the person we all call to get information and to whom we give it. That way she can keep everyone informed."

Stevie nodded. She moved slightly in her seat, crossing her

legs, then uncrossing them nervously. After a moment or two, she said to Derek in a low voice, "I guess nobody knows exactly what happened, why the shooting occurred. Or who did it?"

"Since the girls have remained unconscious, they haven't been able to tell Nigel and Gideon—or the police—anything. However, the man who shot them was Tamara's ex-husband, Alexis Dumachev. He's been identified."

"Oh, my God, no! But *why*? Why did he do a horrendous thing like this? I know Tamara hasn't heard from him for years. He went off to work in . . . Japan, I think."

"Yes, that's what Nigel said to Gideon, and it's true, they haven't heard from him for years." Derek sighed. "It seems as if he went berserk. *Why* we'll never know, I suppose."

Stevie inclined her head, and then she leaned back in her seat, closing her eyes. Chloe and Tamara might not make it, she knew that. Although her mother and Derek were being cheerful, she realized they were putting up a front. Derek made a good job of it; why wouldn't he? After all, he was a great actor. But her mother couldn't act, and it was Blair who gave it all away. Things weren't quite as rosy as they wanted her to believe, of that she was absolutely convinced.

The stewardess came and told them they were about to land at the Leeds-Bradford Airport in Yeadon. Opening her eyes, Stevie looked at her watch. It was twenty minutes past seven o'clock.

Miles was waiting for them in the Brotherton Wing of Leeds General Infirmary when they arrived at eight o'clock. As Stevie walked into the small private waiting room, accompanied by Blair and Derek, he leapt to his feet and hurried to his mother. Concern ringed his face.

"Hello, Ma," he said, wrapping his arms around her protectively, holding her close. Stevie clung to her son for a second, taking comfort from his reassuring presence before pulling away.

Looking into his eyes, she asked, "Tell me the truth, Miles, is Chloe going to live?"

"Yes, I think she is. From what I understand, the operation to remove the bullet from her brain was a success. But it's better that you talk to the neurosurgeon. He was just checking on Chloe a short while ago, and he's waiting in his office for you."

"Then let's go."

"Right away, Ma." Turning to his grandparents, he embraced them both before opening the door and leading them out of the private waiting room.

As Miles hurried them down the corridor, Stevie grasped her son's arm, asked urgently, "How's Tamara? Is *she* going to be all right?"

"They're hoping so. She's also in intensive care, and holding her own right now, Ma. Tam's in another part of the Brotherton Wing and Nigel's in a waiting room over there, to be near her. Gideon's with him, giving him support. Once you've talked to Mr. Longdon and seen Chloe, I'll take you to Nigel. The surgeon who operated on her wants to see you."

Stevie nodded. A moment later Miles was ushering them into the neurosurgeon's office.

"Valentin Longdon," the neurosurgeon said, rising, coming forward to greet them, his hand outstretched. "Mrs. Jardine, Sir Derek and Lady Rayner. Pleased to meet you." After shaking hands with them, he added, "However, I'm so sorry we're not meeting under different circumstances. Please, do sit down."

They did so, and Stevie said, "Thank you for taking care of my daughter, Mr. Longdon. I appreciate everything you've done to save her life."

The neurosurgeon inclined his head. "I would like to explain everything, so that you understand fully what has happened."

"Yes, that would be very helpful," Derek murmured, leaning forward slightly, pinning his eyes on the renowned surgeon.

"First let me tell you about the wound. The bullet entered the left side of Miss Jardine's forehead at a forty-five-degree angle, going in at the edge of the eyebrow. It hit the frontal lobe actually, and broke a bone in her skull. It remained in her brain." He paused and looked at Stevie questioningly, a brow raised.

She nodded. "Yes, I'm following you, Mr. Longdon."

Giving her a faint smile, the neurosurgeon continued. "I operated on your daughter immediately after she arrived here from Harrogate, in order to reduce the risk of infection. There was a large area of bruising, bleeding, and swelling. Great trauma in the brain. I operated down the track of the bullet, that is, I followed the track the bullet made as it went through her skull. I first removed the indriven bone, then the damaged brain tissue, then the blood clot, and finally the bullet. It was a three-hour operation, Mrs. Jardine, but she came through it well."

"Thank you for explaining, Mr. Longdon, but I'm not sure I quite understand why Chloe is still in a coma."

"Because of the great trauma suffered to the brain. We must wait for the swelling to go down. She is in an altered state of consciousness right now, as she has been since she was shot. She will come out of the coma slowly, over a ten-day period, or thereabouts."

"But she *will* come out of the coma, won't she, Mr. Longdon?" Derek interjected.

There was only a fractional hesitation on the neurosurgeon's part before he said, "She should, Sir Derek. I am very hopeful for her. And as I just said, she will emerge from the coma rather slowly, come into a lighter consciousness, a more stable state of being gradually."

"How long will she have to be in intensive care?" Stevie said.

"For the next forty-eight hours, at least, Mrs. Jardine. Perhaps longer."

"Is there the possibility that my daughter might not come out of the coma, Mr. Longdon?"

"Well, of course, there is always that possibility with every patient. I don't think this is the case with Miss Jardine, however."

"Could she be left with any brain damage?" Stevie stared at the neurosurgeon, biting her lip nervously now that she had expressed one of her worst fears.

"That is doubtful," he replied quietly.

Stevie continued to stare at him, detecting something in his manner she could not quite put her finger on. She wondered if he was making Chloe's condition sound less serious than it really was. She opened her mouth to ask him this, then changed her mind. Instead, she said, "Can we see Chloe, Mr. Longdon?"

"Of course you can, Mrs. Jardine. I will take you to the ICU now. Please, come with me."

The four of them trooped out after Valentin Longdon, and within several seconds they were entering the intensive care unit in the Brotherton Wing. "It would be preferable if you saw Miss Jardine one at a time," the neurosurgeon murmured. Opening the door to Chloe's room, he stood to one side, allowing Stevie to enter first. He followed her in and closed the door.

Stevie glided across the floor toward the hospital bed as quietly as she could, full of anxiety and apprehension. Her throat closed when she saw Chloe, and she had to fight hard to stem the tears that suddenly filled her eyes. It was with a sense of dread and a sinking heart that she came to a standstill next to the bed and looked down at her daughter.

Chloe was white-faced and motionless, her eyes closed. Bandages swathed her head and IVs were attached to her body.

There was one in her arm, another in her nose. A piece of equipment covered her mouth, and she looked so helpless, so vulnerable, Stevie's eyes welled; she fumbled in her jacket pocket for a handkerchief. After a moment, she composed herself and swung her head to look at the neurosurgeon. She was mute, unable to say anything, so choked up was she. She shook her head.

Understanding her state of mind, observing her anxiousness and worry, Valentin Longdon said quietly, "I'm pleased with her progress since the operation this afternoon. I feel optimistic she's going to be all right, Mrs. Jardine."

"Is she out of danger, Mr. Longdon?"

"I wouldn't go so far as to say that, but she's doing well. Let me explain something. Those are intravenous drips, as I'm sure you know. They give easy access to the bloodstream, just in case of any infection. And as you can see, I have her on a ventilator. Your daughter is being monitored for the blood gases and also for intracranial pressure. And so far so good."

"I know you're doing everything for her, and that she's getting the best of care."

Stevie gazed down at Chloe, the child of her heart, and took hold of her hand. Then she bent down and kissed it. Straightening, turning once more to the neurosurgeon, she murmured, "She doesn't know I'm here, does she?"

"She might, Mrs. Jardine, we don't know for sure." His eyes were full of compassion for her.

After a moment longer, Stevie tiptoed out of the private room; Blair went in to see her granddaughter. When she emerged, Derek entered, but he, too, stayed only for a few seconds.

Not long after this, Stevie walked into the private waiting room where Nigel was sitting with Gideon. Derek and Blair followed her. Both of Stevie's sons jumped up when they saw their mother and their grandparents.

Stevie went straight to Nigel, opening her arms to him. There was only the merest hesitation on his part as he searched her face, and then he stepped forward to take hold of his mother. Stevie put her arms around him and held him very close to her, the love she felt for him far outweighing her anger and disappointment of the last few months. "I'm here for you, Nigel, I'll do anything I can to help you, darling."

He clung to her, and unexpectedly his self-control shattered. He broke down and began to sob. "Oh, Mother, Mother, I don't know what to do for Tamara. She's lying there . . . so helpless. I love her so much, Ma. She's my life. I don't want her to die."

"I know, I know, darling. We must all be strong for her, pray that she pulls through this. I love her too, you know that, Nigel. Take me to see her now."

Finding his handkerchief, blowing his nose, and then pushing his hair back with his hands, Nigel pulled himself together as best he could. After greeting his grandparents, he took hold of Stevie's arm and led her out of the room. They all went to the surgical ward in the Brotherton Wing, where a nurse took them to the ICU and showed Nigel and Stevie into Tamara's room. Gideon waited outside with Blair and Derek.

Stevie's heart sank when she saw her daughter-in-law lying unconscious in the hospital bed, hooked up to so much equipment. She was so still. Stevie couldn't help thinking that Tamara looked ghastly, in a way, worse than Chloe did. The thought struck her that Tamara was at death's door, and she shivered involuntarily. Something inside her told her that it would be a miracle if Tam lived. She thought her heart would break as she leaned over her daughter-in-law, squeezed her hand, and lightly touched the lovely silver-gilt hair. There was a frailty about Tamara that frightened

Stevie, and she knew why Nigel was so distraught. He had detected this too, and it had alerted him to the worst.

Now Stevie turned to Nigel, took his arm, and led him out of the private room. Once again Derek, and then Blair, went in to see Tamara.

Stepping up to his mother, Gideon said, "Are you all right, Ma? Are you holding up okay?" He put his arm around her solicitously. Kissed her cheek.

"I'm fine, Gideon, and I'm glad you and Miles are here to help Nigel and me through this. Where's Lenore? Is she still at Lindenhill?"

"She's driving over to Leeds now. Natalie and Arnaud are just having their supper and then Agnes is going to put them to bed. I spoke to Lenore a few minutes ago. Don't worry about the kids, Ma, they're doing fine."

Nigel said in a hoarse voice, "She's not going to pull through, is she, Mother? Tamara's not going to make it, is she? I could see it written all over your face when we were in the room with her."

"No, you couldn't, Nigel, because I don't believe that at all. I'm just worried about Tam, obviously. That's what you're seeing, my anxiety and concern. And let's be positive, Nigel. Tamara's a strong woman, she's going to fight to live, I just know it. Now, take me to see the surgeon who operated on her."

"All right."

Gideon said, "I'll wait here for Grandma and Gramps."

Nigel and Stevie walked rapidly down the corridor, making for the surgeon's office, but as they turned the corner they ran into him.

"Mr. Jardine," he exclaimed, "I was just coming to see your wife, to check on her."

"This is my mother, Stephanie Jardine," Nigel said. "And, Mother, this is Mr. William Tilden, Tam's surgeon."

After they had shaken hands, Stevie said, "Thank you for everything you've done for my daughter-in-law, Mr. Tilden. From what I understand, her wounds were very bad."

He nodded. "Yes, very serious, Mrs. Jardine. She sustained bullet wounds in her chest and stomach. Unfortunately, there was a lot of internal bleeding, and she has lost a lot of blood. We've given her transfusions, naturally, and now we must wait to see how she improves in the next few hours."

"Is my wife going to die?' Nigel asked in a strangled voice.

"We don't know, Mr. Jardine. I personally think she has a reasonable chance of pulling through. She's a very healthy woman, and she's young."

"But she is in critical condition, isn't she?" Nigel said.

"Yes," the surgeon answered very softly.

26

It was a subdued, sad little group that sat around a table in the lounge of the Queen's Hotel in City Square, having a late night drink and snack: Stevie, Derek, and Gideon.

Exhausted from travel and the strain of the day, Blair had gone to bed. So had Nigel and Miles, who were equally worn out. Lenore had been with them until ten minutes before, but she, too, had now left to drive back to Lindenhill.

Stevie played with a chicken sandwich, not eating it; in fact, it was taking all her energy to force down a cup of tea. Finally, after a long silence, she looked at Gideon and said, "What in God's name made Dumachev shoot them?"

Gideon shook his head and let out a weary sigh. "We'll never know the answer to that, Ma. And I'm sure the girls won't be able to enlighten us either when they regain consciousness. All they'll be able to do is tell us what happened when he arrived at the farm this morning, tell us what he actually said, how he behaved."

"Personally, I think he was deranged," Derek interjected. "No one in their right mind walks into a house and shoots two women in cold blood. And, more than likely, he was obsessed with Tamara."

"Obsessional people can be extremely dangerous," Gideon announced, giving his mother a pointed look.

Stevie frowned, sat back in the chair, a reflective expression settling on her face. After a moment, she said, "Why would Alexis Dumachev be obsessed with Tamara? After all, they were married only a couple of months when they were very young. She was only eighteen, and she was divorced from him by the time she was nineteen. Anyway, Tamara hadn't seen him for years. Nigel told me that at the hospital." Stevie shook her head, bafflement edging onto her face. "Why would he suddenly come back into her life after all this time?"

"Who knows, Ma, and anyway, you don't have to *see* someone constantly in order to be obsessed by them. That is usually in the mind, and in a sick mind at that."

Derek nodded. "Gideon's right, Stevie." There was a little pause; he took a sip of coffee, then went on. "When I was speaking to Nigel earlier this evening, he said that Dumachev became engaged to a Japanese woman when he was living in Tokyo. Seemingly, over the years, Dumachev was in touch with Tamara's parents occasionally. They had passed this news on to her about two years ago."

"Perhaps something happened between him and the woman, something which triggered this," Gideon said, thinking out loud.

"We're speculating," Derek pointed out. "And that can be both dangerous and fruitless."

"You're right, Derek," Stevie agreed. "I'm glad Tam's parents received Bruce's fax and that they're flying to London tomorrow. It makes me feel better knowing they'll be here soon. Not that they can do anything either, but having them close to her will help Tam, I think."

Gideon remarked, "I believe that something made Dumachev snap, and then he fixated on Tamara in a very sick way. That's why he came looking for her. Incidentally, the police told me that he was in England only a couple of days before he came up to Yorkshire. The police found his airline ticket and passport, as well as the car rental papers, in the glove compartment of the car."

"So there's absolutely no doubt that it *was* Alexis Dumachev, Gideon?"

"None whatsoever, Ma." Gideon glanced at his watch. "It's ten-thirty, Mother, aren't you tired?" he asked in concern.

"Not in the way you mean. I'm on New York time, remember, and it's only five-thirty in the afternoon for me. But I must admit, I am a little worn out emotionally."

"That's not surprising." Gideon pushed himself up out of the chair; bending over Stevie, he kissed her on the cheek, squeezed Derek's shoulder, and finished, "I'm going to bed."

"Good night, darling." Stevie tried to smile at him. "Better news tomorrow, I'm sure."

"Good night, Gideon, and thanks for looking after us." Derek stood up as he spoke, and embraced his grandson.

Once they were alone, Derek looked at Stevie and shook his head. "You're not eating that sandwich, just toying with it. Shall I try to get you something else? Something more appetizing?"

"Thanks, Derek, it's thoughtful of you, but I'm really not hungry. I will have a drink though. A cognac. I feel a bit queasy. It might settle my stomach."

"I'll join you." Derek motioned to a waiter, who was hovering nearby, and ordered their drinks. Several moments later the waiter reappeared with a bottle of Courvoisier and two brandy balloons.

Stevie sat back in her chair, sipped her brandy, endeavoring to relax, but without much success. Eventually, she said softly, "Do you believe in premonitions, Derek? You know, of disaster, of trouble . . . "

"You ask *me* that? A Welshman, a true Celt through and through, and right to the very marrow of his bones. Of course I do. I'm very superstitious. I believe in presentiments of doom, and portents and signs. In spirits and ghosts and the supernatural . . . in Merlin's magic at Camelot . . . if it could happen then, it can happen now. It's atavistic, of course, it's in my Celtic blood. But why do you ask?"

"On the Wednesday afternoon before Thanksgiving, I went for a walk through the meadows adjoining Romany Hall. Quite suddenly the weather changed, a fog came down unexpectedly, and I kept thinking of Aysgarth End and the Yorkshire moors. In fact, for a second I thought I'd been transported back there, the two places were so similar. Anyway, I was cold, shivering, and I had such a terrible sense of foreboding, of impending trouble, I was actually frightened. And that's not like me."

"No, it's not."

"Later, back at the house, I experienced that same coldness, that sense of doom at one moment. I pushed the feeling away again, thought of it as being irrational. I even laughed at myself—" She broke off, staring at him.

He nodded. "Go on."

She could see he was taking her seriously, and so she explained further. "Ever since that day I've had nothing but trouble, one way or another. I wish I'd paid attention, done something about it."

Derek frowned at her. "There was *nothing* you could do, Stevie. You can't tamper with fate. What will be will be. You know I've always told you that."

"Yes, you have, and I suppose you're right."

Derek was thoughtful for a moment or two. He took several sips of brandy before he said slowly, "There are so many strange things in this world, so many things we don't understand, and which we cannot properly explain. . . . "

Earlier that day, Blair had gone to Stevie's flat in Eaton Square and packed a suitcase of clothes for her. Now, much later that evening, Stevie began to take her things out of the case, hanging them up in the bedroom of her suite at the Queen's Hotel.

Once she had put everything away, she telephoned Bruce in London, as she had promised she would.

"I'm sorry I'm phoning you so late, it's almost midnight, I know," she said when he answered. "I was hoping to have more news by now, but I don't."

"It's not a problem, Stevie, you can phone whenever you wish. I doubt I'll sleep tonight anyway. Since you've nothing to report, I'm assuming Chloe is still in a coma?"

"Yes, I'm afraid so."

"How is Tamara?"

"The same. In critical condition."

"I see. Well, at least they haven't deteriorated. Or have they?"

"No, they're holding their own, Bruce, and perhaps by tomorrow there will be some improvement, better news. I'll call you—"

"No, no, Stevie, you don't have to, I'm coming up there. I'm taking the Yorkshire Pullman from King's Cross tomorrow morning. There's one around eight. I'll arrive in Leeds in two hours. And it's the fastest way to get there."

"All right. I'll be at the hospital, of course. Take a taxi from the railway station to Leeds General Infirmary. It's only a few minutes, maybe eight at the most."

"I've arranged for a car and driver. I thought it was the best. Also, a car's useful to have on call. And a room has been booked for me at the Queen's."

"I see everything's taken care of, then."

"Yes, it is."

"What about Tamara's parents? They're flying in to Heathrow tomorrow night. Have—"

"Again, all that's been handled," he explained, cutting in. "There will be a car and driver waiting for them at Heathrow, and they've been booked into a suite at Claridge's."

"Thanks for doing that, Bruce, I know they must be devastated, and worried out of their minds. And they'll be tired after their long flight. Well, good night."

"Good night, Stevie my dear. I will see you tomorrow morning."

After she had hung up, Stevie took a bath before going to bed. Realizing she wouldn't fall asleep immediately, she went to the desk where she had placed her briefcase earlier.

Sitting down, opening it, she took out her journal, which went everywhere with her. She sat for a moment, staring at the page she had written last night in New York. How swiftly and drastically her life had changed since she had made that entry. It was about the trip she was planning to make to Paris next week. Now she made a mental note to cancel it, and to phone André tomorrow. He was her closest friend, had been through so many things with her, and he would want to know. He adored Chloe, who was his godchild, and he had a very soft spot for Tamara as well. Yes, he would want to know what had happened.

As she always did, Stevie wrote in the day and the place at the top of the page.

Good Friday, 1997
Leeds

Today has been the worst day of my life, a nightmare. I've been through many things in the past: Ralph's terrible, untimely death; giving birth to an illegitimate child alone, without her father. But nothing has been as difficult to handle as this.

My beautiful sweet Chloe is lying there in a coma which she may never come out of, and there is nothing I can do to help her. And lovely Tamara is in critical condition, also fighting for her life.

I am suddenly helpless. Me of all people, who is always in control of every situation. I'm usually so good at taking care of things, but I can't take care of this. I'm not a doctor. I need a miracle. An Easter miracle from God. I've never been deeply religious, but I do believe in God and I've always tried to be a good woman, to do good whenever I could, and I think I've succeeded in many ways.

I've prayed a lot today. I hope God hears my prayers. Perhaps He has already. Sometimes God needs a man to work His miracles for Him ... Valentin Longdon ... William Tilden. Good men, good doctors. God's surgeons. I hope they've managed to repair my two girls. My two lovely, and loving, daughters. I have always thought of Tamara as a daughter, ever since Nigel married her. And I've loved her from the start. Such a sweet, unassuming young woman, the perfect wife for Nigel, and the most wonderful mother. I have been blessed, having Tamara as a daughter-in-law.

All of our lives have been changed today ... and in less than a day. By a madman wielding a gun. It's unbelievable when I think about it. I always thought I was in control of my life, but I'm not. No one is, actually. We are all vulnerable, defenseless. We are targets. Anything can happen to us and we cannot stop it happening. We are victims of this violent age we live in, with guns available on street corners, and violence run amok. It's quite terrifying. I've never really thought about it before, but perfect strangers can destroy our lives through their own irrational acts against us. . . .

I must be strong. For everyone. Especially for my mother and Bruce, and for Tamara's parents when they arrive. And Nigel.

Stevie closed her journal, put it back in the briefcase, and locked it. And then she went to bed.

The phone rang shrilly.

Stevie picked it up immediately. "Hello?"

"It's Miles, Mother."

"What is it, Miles? And where are you?"

"I'm here in my room. Gideon just phoned me from the infirmary. Tamara's regained consciousness."

"Oh, that's wonderful!" Stevie exclaimed, feeling a surge of relief.

"But she's not great, Ma. I think she's still in critical condition."

"We'd better go over there, then."

"Yes, Gid wants us to come. He went to the LGI with Nigel at five-thirty this morning. Neither of them slept. Nor did I."

"I didn't either. Are you dressed, Miles?"

"Yes."

"I'll meet you in the lobby. I'm leaving the room now."

"All right."

Stevie hung up. She snatched a burgundy paisley shawl that matched her pants suit off the chair and threw it around her shoulders. Picking up the pen on the desk, she scribbled a note for her mother and Derek, put it in an envelope, and addressed it quickly.

She met Miles in the lobby. Her son greeted her affectionately and kissed her. After she had given the note to the front desk, he led her outside to the waiting taxi.

Nigel stood next to Tamara's bed, holding her hand tightly. He spoke to her softly, telling her how much he loved her, and he was positive she understood him. Earlier, she had opened her eyes and looked at him; he thought he had seen recognition in them, but he wasn't sure of that.

Suddenly, her eyes opened again and she stared up at him. He felt her fingers tightening slightly on his, and it was then he noticed she was trying to speak.

Bringing his face down to hers, he whispered, "What is it, darling? Tell me, Tamsy."

"Ni . . . gel . . . l . . . ove . . . y . . . ou . . ." Her eyes held his.

"I love you too, Tam, so very much."

Slowly, her eyes closed. A moment later her hand went slack in his.

Mr. Tilden, the surgeon, who was standing at the back of the room, glanced at the monitor. The lines had gone flat. He stepped forward, put his hand on Nigel's shoulder. "I'm very sorry, Mr. Jardine."

An anguished cry escaped Nigel's lips. "No!" he shouted. "No!" He clung to his wife. "Don't leave me, Tam!"

"She's gone, Mr. Jardine," William Tilden said gently.

"Leave me alone with her," Nigel mumbled.

The surgeon nodded to the nurse, and the two of them stepped into the corridor.

Stevie, who was waiting near the door with Gideon and Miles, looked at him intently. "Tamara has died . . ." she began, and stopped. Her throat choked up and tears rushed into her eyes.

"I'm very sorry, Mrs. Jardine," he murmured.

"Can I go in, Mr. Tilden?" Stevie asked in a shaking voice. "My son needs me."

"Of course," he answered, and opened the door for her.

Stevie went over to the bed. She gazed down at Tamara, bent over her and kissed her, touched the silver-gilt hair. My lovely girl, good-bye, she said silently. I'll never forget you, Tam, and I'll always love you. Her heart was full of sorrow; she thought it was going to burst. After a moment, endeavoring to marshal her swimming senses, her own grief, Stevie put her arm around Nigel and said quietly, "I'm here, Nigel. I'm here, lovey."

He turned his face to hers. It was wet with tears. "Why, Mam? Why, Mam?" he asked, reverting to his childhood name for her.

"I don't know, Nigel, I really don't. Sweet Tam . . ." She tried to comfort him, but he was inconsolable. His sorrow was unendurable.

A few minutes later Mr. Tilden and the nurse returned to the room. The nurse encouraged Nigel to leave, but he would not. He persisted in clinging to Tamara's hand, tenaciously. When Mr. Tilden attempted to escort him out, he became hysterical, his grief overwhelming him.

"I'll stay with him for a while," Stevie said to the surgeon. "Until he's a little calmer."

27

A WEEK AFTER THE SHOOTING HAD OCCURRED, CHLOE WAS STILL IN a coma. She had been taken out of the intensive care unit and put in a private room in the Brotherton Wing. There was no noticeable change in her state of consciousness.

Now that Chloe was out of the ICU, Stevie was allowed to stay in the room with her daughter, and for as long as she wanted until the early evening. At eight o'clock she usually went back to the Queen's Hotel, since there were no facilities for her to sleep at the Brotherton Wing.

Stevie had been keeping a steadfast vigil by her daughter's side, touching her constantly, holding her hands, talking to her, endeavoring to stimulate her, hoping and praying for a reaction from her. Any kind of reaction, even the slightest, would have been welcome. There was none. Chloe lay in the hospital bed pale and inert, as if she were in a deep, untroubled sleep.

Stevie was never alone with Chloe for very long. Members of the family were constantly in and out of the hospital room, underscoring Stevie's own efforts to stimulate Chloe, to communicate with her. Bruce, Derek, and Blair had been regular visitors, as had Miles and Gideon.

Nigel had gone to London on Monday, accompanying Tamara's body in the private ambulance. Lenore had driven the children and Agnes back to town the same day, and Gideon had followed in his own car on Tuesday morning. His main purpose for going was to help Nigel make all the arrangements for Tamara's funeral. This had taken place yesterday, and every member of the family had attended, except for Stevie and Derek.

Loving Tamara as she had, Stevie wanted to be present when her daughter-in-law was laid to rest. But she had been afraid to leave Chloe alone in case she came out of the coma. She wanted to be there for her daughter, to comfort and reassure her. Stevie's decision to stay in Leeds had been accepted, indeed endorsed, by everyone, Nigel included. Derek had insisted on staying with Stevie, in order to give her moral support, and also because he was so close to Chloe, like a father to her in so many ways.

Now, on this Friday morning at the beginning of April, Derek sat with Stevie in Chloe's room. Thinking out loud, he said, "It occurred to me that I might try reciting to her again. Bits and pieces from some of my roles, especially my Shakespearean roles. You know she loves Shakespeare."

"That's a wonderful idea, Derek. Her favorite role of yours is Hamlet. Why don't you recite the soliloquy?" Stevie suggested.

Derek thought for a moment, then he said, "I don't think it's appropriate, Stevie. There's something rather sad about it . . . Hamlet is talking about dying. The other day I recited some of the sonnets, but I know she likes Byron. We spoke about him at Christmas." Derek rose, walked over to the window, stood looking out for a few moments, composing himself, running the lines of various poems through his head. One of his great talents was his extraordinary ability to commit long speeches and reams of poetry to memory; in fact, he was renowned for this remarkable accomplishment. And like Richard Burton before him, he was able to recite Shakespeare and other writers virtually on request, so well versed was he in their works.

Turning around, he looked across at Stevie holding Chloe's hand, and nodded, smiled at her encouragingly.

Stevie proffered him a faint smile, sat back in the chair, ready to listen to him. But her eyes automatically swung to Chloe, and she gave her daughter all her attention, watching her closely and with enormous intensity.

Derek began to speak softly, his mellifluous voice carrying around the hospital room:

> "She walks in beauty, like the night
> Of cloudless climes and starry skies;
> And all that's best of dark and bright
> Meet in her aspect and her eyes:
> Thus mellow'd to that tender light
> Which heaven to gaudy day denies.
>
> One shade the more, one ray the less,
> Had half impair'd the nameless grace
> Which waves in every raven tress,
> Or softly lightens o'er her face;
> Where thoughts serenely sweet express,
> How pure, how dear their dwelling-place.
>
> And on that cheek, and o'er that brow,
> So soft, so calm, yet eloquent,
> The smiles that win, the tints that glow,
> But tell of days in goodness spent,
> A mind at peace with all below,
> A heart whose love is innocent!"

Derek finished speaking and walked over to Stevie, returning her smile. "My favorite poem by Byron."

"It was beautiful," she said.

"I thought of our lovely Chloe as I was speaking, and it fits her well, doesn't it?"

"Why, yes, it does." Stevie turned back to her daughter and examined her face intently; unexpectedly, she stiffened.

Noticing this, Derek exclaimed, "What is it?"

"I might be imagining it, but I thought I saw a slight movement under her eyelids." Stevie sighed. "But I was wrong. There's nothing, no reaction. She's just lying there motionless."

"Do you want me to recite something else, perhaps—" He cut himself off and glanced over his shoulder as Bruce Jardine walked into the room.

"Good morning," Bruce said. "I just arrived from London and came straight here from the railway station." He shook hands with Derek, and then went to kiss Stevie on the cheek.

Bruce stood looking down at Chloe, studying her carefully as they all did from time to time, frowning to himself. "No change, I suppose?" he said at last, addressing Stevie.

"No change. Although a moment ago I thought I saw an eyelid move. But it was just wishful thinking, I'm afraid."

"She's going to make it, Stevie," Bruce replied quickly. "I feel it in my bones. Remember, it has been only a week since she was shot. The fact that she's been out of intensive care since Sunday is very reassuring to me. What does Mr. Longdon say?"

"That she's basically doing all right, holding her own. He's optimistic."

Derek remarked, "Valentin Longdon has said right from the beginning that it might take ten days, perhaps even two weeks, for Chloe to come out of the coma." Derek walked to the radio and turned it on. "Let's have some music. Hopefully, that might stimulate her. Sounds *are* important. She needs sounds all around her. At least, that's what I've been told by some of my doctor friends."

"It's the swelling in the brain," Stevie murmured, glancing at Bruce. "That has to go down completely."

"Yes, so you told me before." Bending over the bed, he touched Chloe's shoulder, then sat down in a chair near her. Addressing Derek, he said, "How about a little Shakespeare, old chap? You're always so thrilling to listen to . . . it's that marvelous voice of yours. You could read the London telephone directory to me and hold me spellbound."

Derek chuckled. "Thanks for those kind words, Bruce. I just spouted a bit of Byron, so let me put my thinking cap on and come up with something else. Do you have any favorites?"

Bruce nodded. "Many. But mostly the Shakespearean tragedies, and I'm not sure they would be appropriate."

"Why not recite another sonnet," Stevie murmured. "They're gentle enough. Anyway, it's the sound of *your voice* that matters, not what you're saying. You know she's your biggest fan."

Later that afternoon, Gideon and Miles arrived at the hospital, eager to take over from their mother, Derek, and Bruce. They wanted to give their mother a respite from her vigil; they were also concerned about their sister, wished to be close to her.

The twins had just driven up from London, where they had been attending Tamara's funeral on the afternoon before. Taking Stevie to one side, Miles gave his mother a few details about the funeral, reassured her that Nigel was holding up despite the strain and his deep sorrow, and that her grandchildren were all right.

Stevie suddenly found herself weeping again for Tamara. Her death was a waste, senseless. She quickly took control of her emotions; her sole aim at the moment was to try and help Chloe, and she had to be very strong. She dare not give in to her feelings about anything.

It was Miles who said finally, "Come on, Ma, go out for a walk, take a break. You need some air, I'm sure of that. It'll do you good, even if you just walk around the city."

"And you ought to eat something," Derek pointed out.

"Let us go to the Queen's for tea," Bruce suggested, looking at Derek. "It'll do *you* good, old chap. You've been cooped up here all day too."

"That's kind of you, Bruce, but I can't join you for tea, I'm afraid. I'm aiming to catch the five o'clock Pullman back to London. I have a meeting tomorrow with the producers who are doing the revival of *The Lion in Winter*, and I must be there." Turning to Stevie, he explained, "Your mother's going to come up here tomorrow to be with you, love."

"Oh, why don't you spend the weekend in London together!" Stevie exclaimed. "I'm all right, really I am, Derek. Bruce is here, and the twins, I'll be fine. Certainly I'm well looked after."

"And Lenore's coming up tonight," Gideon announced.

"That's a nice thought, Stevie," Derek murmured. "But I don't think Blair will agree to it. She wants to be here with you and Chloe. But then, you know that. Shall we go? Shall we head back to the Queen's? I've got to finish packing my overnight bag."

Stevie became conscious of Bruce's eyes resting on her, and she put down her teacup and said, "You're staring at me, Bruce. Do I have a smudge on my face? Is there something wrong with my appearance?"

He shook his head, but continued to look at her thoughtfully, frowning slightly. At last he said, "Stevie . . . there's something I want to talk to you about—" He came to a stop, glanced away for a moment, and there was hesitation, even a kind of diffidence, in his manner.

"Bruce, tell me what's wrong."

"Almost nineteen years ago, something happened . . ." He coughed behind his hand. "I've never had the courage to talk to you about it before, although sometimes I've wanted to do so. I felt it was better to leave certain things unsaid. . . . But lately I've had the need to broach it to you."

Stevie stiffened, sat rigidly in the chair without saying a word.

Bruce cleared his throat, bent closer to her, and said in a low tone, "She *is* my daughter, isn't she? Chloe is mine?"

Not a muscle moved on Stevie's face, and her eyes were unblinking. She simply stared at Bruce. And she did not answer him.

Bruce went on swiftly, in the same low, intense voice. "What I did was unthinkable, Stevie, so very, very wrong. I don't know what came over me that time we were in Amsterdam, buying diamonds. I've never been able to forgive myself. Or forget it. I've been haunted and troubled for years. I behaved in the most unconscionable manner, and there's no excuse for my behavior. To take advantage of your . . . situation . . . vulnerability . . . to force myself on you that night . . . "

You mean rape me, don't you, Bruce, Stevie thought. Because that's what you did, you raped me. She did not say this. In fact, she did not speak at all.

Puzzled by her silence, Bruce said in a whisper, "I've loved her so much. Always. My Chloe. My lovely daughter."

"She is not your daughter, Bruce," Stevie said in a clear, firm voice.

Bruce gaped at her, his eyes suddenly filling with shock and disbelief. "But she is. She must be! I figured it all out. The timing, the dates. I thought she was probably born a little premature."

"No, Bruce, she wasn't. I was already pregnant by about eight weeks when you forced me to ... forced your attentions on me. And Chloe was actually born late. *She was late by two weeks.* I conceived Chloe in October of 1977, and she was born in July of 1978. My doctor confirmed my pregnancy of two months at the beginning of December. You and I were in Amsterdam a month later, in January of 1978. She's not yours. There's not even a question about it."

"I am not Chloe's father?" he said in a faltering voice that sounded unexpectedly anguished.

"No, you're not. It never occurred to me that you believed you were. I thought you were nice to Chloe and treated her so beautifully because you were grateful to me for running the business."

Bruce shook his head wonderingly. "I've hardly been able to live with myself all these years. There were even times when I thought I couldn't look you in the eye. I've been so dreadfully ashamed of myself. To do that to you ... my son's widow ..." His voice finally broke and he averted his head, stared off into the distance. His aristocratic face was bereft, etched with dismay and a terrible regret.

Stevie did not know what to say to him. Certainly she was not prepared to comfort him. She had never really forgotten that dreadful night at the hotel in Amsterdam. Or her anger and fear when Bruce had forced himself on her. Why mince words? she thought suddenly. He *raped* me; that is the only word for it.

Growing aware that her father-in-law was emotionally upset, and looked as if he were about to break down at any moment, she touched his arm, let her hand rest on it.

He covered her hand with his and brought his gaze back to

meet hers. "I've loved you for years, Stevie. I could not say anything to you about that either. I did not dare."

"Is that why you allowed me such freedom with the business? Gave me such leeway? Let me open the Fifth Avenue store? Because you thought you were Chloe's father?"

"No. Not at all. I gave you power in the company because you deserved it. I trusted you, and I had immense belief in you and in your enormous ability." He sighed heavily. "But I also cared for you." There was another momentary pause, then Bruce continued in a low voice. "When I first met you I disliked you most fervently, thought you were so wrong for my son and for this family. How mistaken I was, Stevie. You have been so *right* for this family, after all. You've become more of a Jardine than even I am, if the truth be known. As the years have gone by, you have truly earned my respect and my devotion. And my love. I care about you and your well-being." He looked at her intently, and his eyes narrowed. "I don't believe you know what a remarkable woman you are. Formidable, in so many ways."

Stevie sat back in the chair. She was startled by the things he had just said, and at a loss for words. She really did not know how to respond.

At long last, Bruce broke the silence. "Who *is* Chloe's father?" he asked, searching her face, longing to know the truth.

"I'm not going to tell you that." She stared him down, her gray-green eyes cool, unflinching.

Bruce took a deep breath. "You never forgave me for Amsterdam, did you?" Before she could answer, he exclaimed, "Why do I ask you that? It's a foolish question. How *could* you forgive me?"

"I didn't, not in the beginning," she responded. "But later on I did forgive you, although I've never *really* forgotten what happened. But, somehow, I managed to bury it so deep, it's never surfaced again. At least, not properly. I suppose I didn't want to deal with it. Or with you either. We had to work together. My sons are your grandchildren, your heirs. I had to find a way to operate around you. *Self-preservation*, Bruce, that was it really. Everybody is driven by self-interest, and I'm sure I'm no different. I think I deep-sixed the memory of Amsterdam in order to function in the family, and at Jardine's."

"I'm so very sorry, Stevie. Will you accept my apology now, after all these years?"

"Yes, I will. I do." She attempted a smile without much success. In a quiet voice, she continued. "You've been wonderful to Chloe, and I do want to thank you for that."

"I believed her to be my daughter. I made her mine in my head and my heart. And in many ways, she *is* mine, actually. I've loved her far too much, do love her very much, so that it would be impossible for me to stop loving her now. She is a part of my life, part of me, part of my soul."

Stevie couldn't help being touched by his words. After a moment, she acknowledged, "I know what she means to you, Bruce."

"I thought she was a Jardine by blood, and so I treated her as a Jardine," he said. "And she became one. A Jardine she will always be, Stevie. Nothing can alter that now."

Stevie sat alone in Chloe's hospital room, holding her hand, staring at her daughter's face, studying it closely. She knew she had done a most terrible thing.

She had denied two people the knowledge of each other. Chloe's father. And, more important, Chloe herself.

How Chloe had longed to know who he was. Only a few months ago, at Thanksgiving, she had been fussing about it, discussing it with Derek and Blair, and anyone else who would listen. How badly her daughter had *needed* to know who John Lane was.

I should have told her the truth then, Stevie thought. She has every right to know about him. Everything there is to know. I have been so wrong. How could I have done such an awful thing? Suddenly, she was awash with guilt, and she knew she would have to live with that for many months to come, perhaps longer.

She sat there for a long time, holding her daughter's hand, willing her to come out of the coma, willing her to live, willing her to flutter an eyelash or move a finger. *Anything* . . . just so long as there was a sign, however tiny, that Chloe's condition was changing, improving.

Imperceptibly, Stevie felt a sudden twitching of Chloe's fingers in hers. She looked down at her daughter's hand swiftly, but it lay there inert and still. She had only imagined that it moved.

Leaning back against the chair, Stevie closed her eyes. Silently she prayed: *Oh, God, please let her get better. Please let my beloved child come out of this. Let her be whole and well again.*

Stevie prayed for a long time. And then she made a silent promise to Chloe. She vowed to her daughter that she would tell her the truth about the man who had given her life. She owed her that. Yes, she would finally tell her who her father really was.

The following morning when Stevie returned to the Brotherton Wing with Miles, the neurosurgeon, Valentin Longdon, was waiting for them. The moment she saw the smile on his face, Stevie knew that the news was good.

"Chloe's come out of the coma!" she exclaimed, her eyes riveted on his face.

"Not exactly," Valentin Longdon answered. "But the nurses tell me there's been some movement. In fact, she's had a restless hour, moving around in the bed, and she has also moved the fingers of her left hand."

"I thought she did yesterday," Stevie told him, "but when I looked at her hand, it was still *lifeless*. I thought I'd imagined it."

"I'm sure you didn't, Mrs. Jardine. I was just about to tell you that when I went in to see her a few minutes ago, she opened her eyes."

"Oh, thank God for that! And thank you, Mr. Longdon, for all that you've done for my daughter."

"Let's go in and see her." The neurosurgeon opened the door, showed Stevie inside.

When Stevie reached the bed she immediately swung around and stared at the doctor. "Is she sleeping? Or has she fallen into the coma again?" she asked anxiously.

"Dozing probably. It's not likely that she'll fall into the coma again. She's now coming out of it."

Stevie touched Chloe's face, and slowly her daughter's eyes opened. They were still her beautiful dark eyes, but they looked glazed and unfocused.

"Chloe, darling, it's me, Mommy," Stevie said, squeezing her hand, holding on to it very tightly.

She loved this child so much, she wanted to weep with relief. But she took firm control of herself, said again, in a stronger tone, "It's me, Chloe, Mommy. I'm here for you. Everything's going to be all right, darling. I'm going to look after you, help you to get better."

Chloe's dark eyes stared back at Stevie. They remained blank and unfocused, and then, quite suddenly, she blinked. She did this several times.

Mr. Longdon moved closer to the bed himself, scrutinizing his patient. Looking up, he nodded, and said to Stevie, "I'm fairly certain she knows it's you, Mrs. Jardine. I believe she is coming back to her normal consciousness."

Miles said, "Once she comes out of the coma, what's the next step?"

"I told your mother a few days ago that your sister will have to go to another hospital for rehabilitation. Once she is no longer in an altered state of consciousness, she can be taken to London by private ambulance. I would like her to go to Northwick Park Hospital in Harrow for several weeks. Maybe even five or six weeks. She will be given physiotherapy, speech therapy, and occupational therapy, which will help her to get her strength back."

"Are you saying that she might be paralyzed? Or perhaps have a problem with her speech? An impediment?" Miles asked.

"That is a possibility, Mr. Jardine. But let us look on the optimistic side, shall we?"

28

"CAN YOU TAKE US ON A TRIP, GRAN?" ARNAUD ASKED, HIS SMALL, eager face upturned to hers. He leaned against her knee, his head on one side. "Please, Gran."

"Well, darling, that all depends on where you want to go," Stevie answered, smiling at him, touching his cheek gently with one finger.

"To heaven. To see Mummy."

Stevie's chest tightened, and she reached out for the child's hands, took them in hers. Softly, she explained, "I don't think we can go this week, Arnaud, you see—"

"I want to see Mummy," he wailed, cutting in. "Daddy says she's staying there. *Forever.*"

"Go to heaven. See Mummy," Natalie said, and patted Stevie's knee. She had been eating a chocolate biscuit and now the chocolate had been transferred from Natalie's sticky fingers to Stevie's pale blue skirt. Glancing down, Stevie stared at it absently for a second, and then turned her attention to her small grandchildren.

"Let's go see Mummy." Arnaud gave Stevie an imploring look. "I want to hug her."

"Me kiss Mummy," Natalie whispered.

Stevie swallowed hard, blinking. "Mummy couldn't see us if we went this week. She's very busy."

"What's she doing in heaven?" Arnaud asked, his delicate blond brows drawing together in a frown.

"Making angels' wings," Stevie improvised, not knowing how to answer them.

"*Oh.*" He looked at her through his big, round eyes. "Do angels fly, then, Gran?"

"Oh, yes, they do. They have lovely white wings and halos and they glide around the sky. I have a picture book of angels at home. Would you like it, darling?"

"Yes, please."

"Me a book, Granma?"

"Yes, you can have one too, Natalie."

Natalie stared at her and suddenly the three-year-old's eyes flooded with tears and she began to cry. "I want Mummy. Get her back, Gran!" she exclaimed hotly.

"Yes, get her back," Arnaud shouted, and his eyes welled. Tears ran down his cheeks.

Leaning forward, Stevie pulled them both to her, put her arms around them and held them close. "Why did Mummy leave us?" Arnaud asked through his sobs. "Doesn't Mummy like us now?"

"Oh, Arnaud, of course she does. And she loves you both very much, sweetheart," Stevie said. "Mummy didn't want to go away and leave you. But, you see, she got hurt and no one could make her better. God was very worried about her, so He decided she should come and live with Him. So that He could make her well again. But no matter what, Mummy's always going to love you both. You're her dearest children."

"Will she always love Daddy?" Arnaud gasped, the tears rolling down his cheeks, spilling onto his lips unchecked.

Wiping his cheeks with her fingertips, Stevie said, "Yes, Mummy will always love Daddy." She stopped, unable to continue, so choked was she. Taking the small tea napkin the housekeeper had given her, she wiped his face and then Natalie's.

Taking a deep breath, Stevie went on, "You must be brave and strong for Daddy. Mummy would want that, and she would want you to look after him."

There was a slight noise. Stevie glanced toward the arched entranceway of the living room in Nigel's Kensington flat. She saw her son standing there watching them, his face shattered, the pain in his eyes unbearable.

"Nigel!" Stevie exclaimed, trying to sound cheerful. "There you are, darling."

When they saw their father, the children pulled away from Stevie, ran across the floor to him, and flung themselves against his legs.

Nigel hunkered down next to them, put his arms around the two of them. "Hello, Pumpkins," he said, forcing a smile onto his ravaged face. "I hope you've been good for Gran."

"Yes. Gran says Mummy's making angels' wings in heaven, Daddy," Arnaud confided. "Angels can fly, Daddy."

"Oh, really, I never knew that," Nigel murmured, trying to hold his emotions in check. He looked over their blond heads at Stevie, and she gave him a faint smile.

Straightening, Nigel walked into the living room, holding each child by the hand.

Stevie rose to greet him, and he kissed her on the cheek, glanced at her skirt, and said, "A little person's ruined that."

"It doesn't matter. There are more important things in this

world than a skirt. Do you want a cup of tea?' she asked as she sat down again.

"A nice cup of tea," Natalie said, mimicking Melanie, the housekeeper.

"I'll go and ask Mel to make me one. Is Agnes back from the dentist?"

"She returned about five minutes ago," Stevie said.

He nodded and disappeared into the foyer, heading in the direction of the kitchen.

Agnes appeared a moment later. "Come on, children, let's go back to the nursery. Kiss Grandma good-bye."

"Can we watch *The Lion King*?" Arnaud asked.

"And why not," Agnes responded. She smiled across at Stevie. "Thanks for being here, for baby-sitting this afternoon, Mrs. Jardine."

"Anytime, Agnes."

Natalie ran and climbed onto Stevie's knee and put her small plump arms around her neck. She gave her grandmother a large, noisy kiss and whispered in her ear, "Gran stay. No go to heaven."

"Yes, Gran will stay with Natalie and Arnaud, darling. Don't worry."

The little girl scrambled off her knee; Arnaud came up to her, leaned against her knees, and kissed her cheek as Stevie bent forward. "Can I have a dog, Gran?"

"If it's all right with Daddy, yes. I'll get you a lovely little Bichon Frise puppy."

"What's that?"

"Like Lenore's two little dogs, Chammi and Beaji."

"Funny names. I'll call my dog Angel," he announced. "And Mummy will make it wings."

Stevie smiled but her heart was aching. She didn't answer her grandson. She couldn't find the right words.

After they had gone off to the nursery with Agnes, Stevie got up and put another log on the fire. Although it was the middle of May, it was a damp afternoon. The big living room seemed awfully cold to her, and dismal.

A few minutes later Nigel came back into the living room, carrying a cup of tea. "Mel wants to know if you would like another one, Mother."

"No thanks. I'm surprised I haven't floated away, all the tea I've drunk these last few weeks."

Stevie walked over to the sofa and seated herself on it. Staring at Nigel, she couldn't help thinking how ill he looked. He had lost weight, his clothes hung on him loosely, and his face was gaunt, drawn. His vivid blue eyes, always one of his best features, were pale today, and bloodshot. There was a cloak of sorrow and despair about him, and Stevie's heart went out to her son. Tamara had been dead and buried for just over six weeks, and it was obvious to Stevie—and everyone else—that Nigel was falling apart.

"You don't look at all well," Stevie began slowly, groping her way, wondering how to skillfully bring the conversation around to what she really wanted to say.

"I feel much worse than I look, Mother." He coughed behind his hand and turned away. When he suddenly brought his gaze to hers, he asked in a tight voice, "How did you manage to go on after my father died?"

"I don't really know, Nigel. I found the strength somewhere. But it was so hard. Extremely difficult. But I had you and the twins, my mother and Derek, and I just knew I had to find the will to continue living somehow. When I look back now, I honestly don't know how I did it, I really don't. I operated strictly by rote, like an automaton, for a very long time. I just got through the days."

Nigel nodded. "I know what you mean—" He paused and shook his head, his face crumpling up with emotion. "I loved her so much, Mam." Finally, his voice broke, but he recovered himself and went on. "Tam was so special, there was just no one like her. She was so sweet, so humorous, and she was such a loving human being."

"She *was* all these things, Nigel, everyone adored Tamara."

"I heard what you were saying to the children when I came in. Thanks for that."

"I didn't know what to say . . . they're so young. And children can ask the most terrible questions. It's hard for them to understand." Stevie let out a long sigh, wishing she knew of a way to help her son. But he could only help himself. That was the problem with grief, it was a heavy burden to carry, and also a lonely burden, in a sense. They were all grieving for Tam; obviously they would recover sooner than Nigel would. She must try to console him, give him what comfort she could.

Stevie spoke softly. "You know, Nigel, it does get a little easier as time goes by. I know that's cold comfort right now, just words, and words don't necessarily help when you're longing for the loved one you've lost. They seem so empty."

He stared at her, said nothing.

"I didn't believe it either, Nigel. But it's the truth. And then there's *work*. That helped me. Once your grandfather had agreed to let me work at Jardine's, my whole life changed. For the better. I found it took my mind off my pain and my longing for your father."

Without thinking twice, or weighing the odds, and speaking from the heart, Stevie went on. "And that's exactly what you need, Nigel. *Work*. There's not much to your life these days, hanging around the flat, seeing the odd friend for lunch. I think you'd better go back to Jardine's tomorrow."

Astonishment crossed his face, displacing the grief. For a second he was not sure he had heard her correctly. He frowned, his brows knitting together in the same way his little son's did. He was at a loss, hardly knew what to say. And so he said nothing.

It was Stevie who spoke again. "You need something to keep you occupied, busy. Work took my mind off my sorrow and the loss I felt. It will do the same for you. Do as I say. Go back to Jardine's tomorrow, Nigel."

"You're giving me my old job back, Mother?" he asked, his voice echoing with disbelief and surprise.

"Yes, I am."

"You would do that, after the way I behaved?"

"Of course I would, Nigel. I fired you for your insubordination, not because you were incapable of doing your job. As a matter of fact, you're wonderful at your job. Brilliant. And I've always said so. Anyway, the company's yours actually. When I step down in a couple of years, which I now plan to do, you'll be running Jardine's on both sides of the Atlantic. I just want you to get a bit more experience under your belt before I retire."

"I'm flabbergasted, I really am," Nigel murmured, looking at her intently. "Very few people would do that, take me back into the business."

"I'm not *people*, Nigel darling, I'm your mother. You're my eldest son, my firstborn child, and I love you very much. I've never stopped loving you, even when I thought you were working against me."

"Some people would hold a grudge."

"I hope I'm far too big a woman to do that. Grudges are petty. They're the tools of the weak and the small-minded in this world. But speaking of grudges, your Jardine grandmother had a grudge against me when she was alive. And lately I've been wondering if she implanted seeds of doubt and hatred of me in your head when you were much younger."

Nigel sat back on the love seat and closed his eyes. Finally, when he opened them, he said, "Grandmother Alfreda was . . . she was an old bitch, Mother. But I didn't know it then, when I was a teenager. And yes, you're right, she talked a lot about you . . . brainwashed me actually, now that I look back. Her poisonous stories about you, her innuendos and her accusations were all meant to kill my love for you."

"Accusations?" Stevie shook her head, looking puzzled for a moment.

"She said it was your fault that Dad died."

Stevie was taken aback. This was the last thing she had expected. "*What next?* But that's not true. And *you* know better than that. Your father died of peritonitis. A bungled operation by an incompetent doctor. Of her choosing, I might add. If anyone was responsible for your father's death, it was Alfreda, his own mother."

"She really chose the doctor?"

"Yes. He was the son of a friend."

"I didn't know."

"And what else did she say?"

"She questioned your morals . . . especially when you got pregnant with Chloe."

"That's typical of her." Stevie got up, went and sat on the love seat next to him. "*Did* she kill your love for me, Nigel?"

"Not entirely, no, Mother. But she did damage it, I've got to admit that. You see, she made me believe you wanted the business for yourself, for your own devious ends. She said that you'd kick me out one day. Take Jardine's away from me."

"And you believed her?"

"I was very young, just a kid."

"I know you were. And impressionable. She was wicked, Nigel, a really wicked woman."

"I'm so sorry, Mother."

"I know. And remember, my love for you has never changed, or altered in any way. I hope you realize that, realize how much I *do* love you, Nigel."

"I'm beginning to understand, Mam."

Stevie smiled hugely, and it was her first real smile in weeks.

"What is it?' he asked, frowning again.

"You probably don't realize it, but you keep calling me Mam, as you used to when you were a little boy."

He did not respond. Unexpectedly, he reached out for her, took hold of her, held her tightly in his arms.

"How will you ever be able to forgive me for what I did to you?" he asked against her hair.

"Oh, I already have, Nigel. Weeks ago."

"How can I make it up to you?"

"By going back to Jardine's tomorrow."

"I don't know how to redeem myself in your eyes," he said, drawing away, searching her face.

"By doing a good job at the store. By looking after your children and loving them well. By loving your brothers and sister. By loving Derek, Blair, and Bruce. By standing tall, Nigel, and being the man I know you can be."

"I will try. No, I *will* do it. I *will.*"

She smiled at him, her gray-green eyes spilling her love for her eldest son. She touched his cheek gently. "Love is so important in all of our lives . . . and I mean all kinds of love, Nigel, not just the romantic kind. Love has such tremendous healing powers."

"Yes, I know it does. I've witnessed it with you and Chloe. What progress she's made, and it's all because of you."

"And the rehabilitation hospital. And Bruce and Derek and Blair. And Miles and Gideon and Lenore. And you too, Nigel, and the children. The entire family has been part of her healing, as they will also be part of yours."

29

On Wednesday morning of the following week, Stevie drove to Heathrow and took a plane to Italy. The flight was relatively short, only an hour and forty minutes from London to Milan.

Now, as the British Airways jet approached the Linate Airport runway, Stevie moved her watch one hour ahead, in order to conform with European time. It was exactly ten-forty.

After leaving the plane, everything went very quickly; within twenty minutes she was sitting in the limousine she had picked up at the airport, heading into Milan.

She leaned back against the car seat, feeling relaxed, and much calmer than she had been for some time. Since the shooting, in fact.

Nigel had gone back to Jardine's the day after she had had her heart-to-heart talk with him, almost a week ago now, and already he seemed much better in spirits. Work had been important to him all his life, and just as she had predicted, being at the store again was helping him to adjust to the tragedy that had befallen him. It would take him a long time to recover from Tamara's death, but she knew now that he had a good chance of getting back on his feet. Work was a great antidote to sorrow; she had discovered that for herself. And he had his children. They, too, would help to sustain him, and, because of their need for him, give meaning to his existence, a reason to live.

As for Chloe, she was improving daily, growing stronger and healthier after her five-week stay at Northwick Park Hospital. The therapy had been necessary, had helped to bring her back to normal, and Valentin Longdon was pleased with her progress. He had seen Chloe only last week and pronounced her fit and well, but he had recommended to Stevie that they stay in England for another month. After that, he had said, they could travel back to the States. Or anywhere else they wanted.

I've been lucky, Stevie thought, staring out of the car window, her mind focused on her daughter. Chloe could have died, or remained in a coma, or been left totally paralyzed. God *did* give me an Easter miracle. For Chloe, at least, but not for Tamara. Whenever she thought of her daughter-in-law, her heart ached and she filled with sadness. She would miss Tam for as long as she lived; there would always be a hole in her heart now that her son's wife was gone.

Within twenty minutes of leaving Linate Airport, the car was entering Milan's Centro, the city center, where the hotel she had selected was located. As usual, the city center was busy with traffic, but within seconds the car was pulling up outside the Four Seasons on Via Gesù, near Via Montenapoleone. Once a cloister, the old monastery had been tastefully renovated, the fifteenth-century building updated to become a beautiful hotel, filled with sunlight streaming in through the large windows.

As she walked through the lobby to the registration desk, Stevie glanced around, liking the ambiance, the airiness, the sense of spaciousness that prevailed.

Once she was settled in her suite, she unpacked the suitcase she had brought and hung up her clothes. Seating herself at the desk, she called Jardine's. After speaking to her secretary, she then talked to Nigel and Gideon respectively before phoning the flat in Eaton Square to check on Chloe, make sure she was all right.

Her phone calls finally out of the way, Stevie refreshed her makeup and changed out of the black pants suit she had traveled in. For her appointment that afternoon she chose a dark gray flannel suit and a white silk shirt. Her only jewelry was her double strand of pearls, pearl earrings, and a watch. After glancing at herself quickly in the mirror, she picked up her handbag and left the suite.

Stevie walked to the Caracelli offices located on the Via della Spiga, enjoying being outside on this lovely May afternoon. It was sunny, the sky was blue and cloudless, and the weather was balmy, a nice bonus after the dampness of London.

As she walked she did a little window shopping, looking at the beautiful clothes and accessories in the chic boutiques. Milan was the fashion center of the world, and she decided she would do some shopping later if she had time. Perhaps she would find some pretty things here for Chloe as well as for herself.

When she finally reached the large Caracelli building, Stevie looked at her watch. It was a few minutes before two; she was exactly on time for her meeting.

As she sat waiting in the elegant reception area, Stevie leafed through a couple of fashion magazines to pass the time. Eventually, a pretty, young woman came to get her, made some pleasant remarks in English, and led her down a corridor. A moment later she was being shown into Signore Caracelli's office.

He was sitting behind his desk angled across a corner, facing the door. He rose at once and came around the desk to greet her, smiling broadly.

Stevie felt her stomach tightening. The calmness of earlier, which had so bolstered her self-confidence, instantly disappeared. She was suddenly tense and nervous, shaking inside as she stood in the center of his office.

Striding across the floor, the smile intact, he came to a stop in front of her, took her hand in his, and held it for a moment. Looking down at her, he said finally, in his slightly accented English, "Stephanie. How nice to see you again. Such a pleasant surprise when you telephoned me on Monday."

"It's nice to see you too," she replied, and she was surprised that her voice sounded so normal. "I'm glad you weren't away, that you were able to give me this appointment at such short notice."

He nodded, and, still holding her hand, he led her over to the seating arrangement near the window. "May I offer you some refreshment? Coffee? A drink? Tea, perhaps?"

She shook her head. "Thank you, no. I'm fine."

He smiled again, showing his perfect teeth, very white against his tanned complexion. Seating himself opposite her, he crossed his long legs and leaned back against the sofa, staring at her intently. His undisguised curiosity and interest in her was very apparent. Suddenly he made a sharp gesture with his hand, a chopping motion, and exclaimed, "Forgive me! I am being thoughtless. I should have asked you about your son. How is he?"

"He's doing better," Stevie responded.

"I read in the London *Times* that your daughter-in-law was fatally shot. Such a tragedy."

"It's been very difficult," Stevie admitted. "A painful time for him, for all of us. But he's . . . well, he's holding his own. He has two small children and they keep him . . . sane."

"Yes. I understand. . . ." There was a short pause before he continued. "To lose someone you love when they are so young . . . it is a terrible thing. And in such ghastly circumstances for you. Tragic, so tragic. I am very sorry, Stephanie."

"Thank you." Stevie bit her lip, hesitating, and then she said quickly, in a rush of words, "My daughter was injured in the shooting. I'm lucky she's alive."

A puzzled expression crossed his face. "Daughter?"

Stevie nodded. "She was with Tamara when the shooting occurred . . . at our house on the Yorkshire moors. A bullet lodged in her brain. She was in a coma for a week."

"Good God! She is all right?" He sat back, his expression sympathetic.

"Yes. She had a brain operation to remove the bullet. Thankfully, she recovered."

"I am glad." He had been riddled with curiosity about her since the moment she had arrived in his office, and now it got the better of him. He gave her an odd look and said, "I did not know you had a daughter." His eyes went to her left hand, then swung to her face. "How old is she, Stephanie?"

"Eighteen. She'll be nineteen in July."

"Eighteen . . . "

Stevie nodded.

"What is her name?"

"Chloe."

"*Chloe.*" He repeated the name so vehemently Stevie almost jumped out of her skin.

His eyes impaled hers and he said in a gentler tone, "She is eighteen, almost nineteen. Her name is Chloe. Is she . . . she is mine, isn't she? She is my daughter, Stephanie."

"Yes, Gianni, she is."

Stunned, momentarily floundering, he sat staring at her

speechlessly. Then he said at last, "Why didn't you tell me then, when we were together, all those years ago?"

"You were married . . . a married man with a family. And you were so well-known, a big industrialist. I also knew that as a Catholic, you could not divorce. I thought it better that I just end it."

"Oh, Stephanie." The look he gave her was reproachful, full of dismay, and he experienced a rush of sadness so acute, he was startled.

Stevie saw that he was emotionally affected, and this took her aback. She exclaimed, "I ended it, yes, but you accepted it—"

Interrupting her, he said somewhat heatedly, "Because I knew that to continue our relationship would cause you problems. I did not wish to make further trouble for you. With the Jardines. I knew what Bruce was like. And Alfreda. Tough. Hard. Difficult people. Without heart. I accepted your decision because . . ." He did not finish his sentence, but his eyes did not leave her face.

"Because *what?*"

Softening his tone, he replied, "Because I loved you very much, Stephanie. I could not bear your unhappiness. Your pain because we could not be together was like a knife in my heart. I was caught in a trap. A bad marriage. A dying father. A huge company to run. Two children dependent on me. I wanted you. But I could not have you. And so I let you go." A shadow crossed his face; pain lodged in his dark eyes.

Stevie could not fail to notice this, and she knew he was sincere in everything he said. He had always been a sincere and genuine man, and he had not changed. She moved slightly on the sofa, crossed her legs, but made no comment.

Again Gianni said, "It was wrong of you to keep it from me."

"I had to, Gianni."

"You did my thinking for me. That was a mistake, Stephanie. I can think for myself."

"I know you can. It was the best thing for me to do. Or so I thought then."

"How did you explain your child, *our* child?"

"I never did. I refused to name the father."

"The Jardines . . . did they accept this?"

"Yes. In fact, everyone did. I simply refused to budge from my stance."

"Amazing."

"There was nothing anyone could do, or say, Gianni. Besides, the Jardines had no choice. They needed me. At least, Bruce needed me to run the company."

"You've done a remarkable job with Jardine's. I've been proud of you as I've watched it grow." Leaning forward, his manner intense, he asked, "Why have you come to tell me about . . . our daughter? About Chloe? Now, after all this time. Because of the shooting?"

"Absolutely. When Chloe was in a coma, I made a vow. A vow that I would tell her the truth about her father if she recovered. I want to do that, Gianni, I want to tell her about you. And I want you to come to London to see her. It's very important to me that you do. Long before the shooting, she was desperate to know about the man who had fathered her. That's only natural now that she's reached young womanhood."

"It is. Of course it is. I understand that. You have still not told her about me?"

"No, not yet. I know it's a problem for you, and I don't want to intrude on your life and on your family. Look, I don't want to cause you problems of any kind, or—"

"I am a widower," Gianni said, cutting in peremptorily.

"Oh, I'm sorry . . ." Her voice faltered under his stern gaze.

He shook his head. "I am not going to be a hypocrite, Stephanie. You know what a terrible marriage I had. And we were separated when she died. Renata left me twelve years ago. For another man. When she died four years ago, she was still with him."

"I see. How are Carlo and Francesco?"

A sorrowful expression crept into his eyes. "Francesco is dead, Stephanie. My son was killed in a car crash five years ago. But Carlo is well."

"I am so very sorry, Gianni, truly. I know how you loved him." She shook her head. "You too have had your tragedies, your share of pain."

"That is so. But life is hard for everyone. In different ways." There was a brief silence between them, until he asked, "And tell me, who does Chloe think her father is? You must have put some name . . . on her birth certificate. What is the name?"

"John Lane." A smile stole onto Stevie's face. "I do believe you know him."

Gianni laughed, his passionate dark eyes so like Chloe's suddenly full of merriment. "I do. John for Gianni—Giovanni. And Lane because I always stayed at the Dorchester on Park *Lane*. My code name when I telephoned you at Jardine's."

She nodded.

"What is she like, this daughter of mine?"

Stevie reached for her handbag, opened it. As she pulled out a photograph of Chloe, the telephone rang.

"Excuse me, I must take this." He jumped up, hurried across the room to his desk, where he picked up the receiver and spoke into it quietly.

Stevie's eyes followed him. He had not changed much in eighteen years. He was fifty-four, seven years older than she was, but he did not show his age. He had thickened slightly, and appeared more muscular, but his face was relatively unlined, and tan as it always had been. He was a sportsman, loved tennis and skiing and sailing; he was a man who spent time outdoors. His thick dark hair had grayed slightly at the temples, but it was hardly noticeable. And he was still a very handsome man. Probably the most handsome man she had ever known. Tall and vital, he was full of energy, and it had been that energy that had appealed to her years earlier. No, he had not changed, not on the surface at least. But life had got at him, as it got at everyone, and in more ways than he had already mentioned. She could tell; there was a deep sadness in him, a sorrowfulness.

He had become, in the intervening years, Italy's greatest industrialist; he was known as the silk king, but he also owned fashion houses, manufacturing plants, shopping centers, real estate, and hotels. She knew all this because she had read about him over the years; he was frequently mentioned in the *Financial Times* and the *Wall Street Journal.*

As Gianni hung up and walked back to the seating arrangement, she could not help thinking how impeccable he looked in his beige gabardine suit, blue shirt, and yellow-and-blue-patterned silk tie. He had never been anything but beautifully dressed, from the top of his well-groomed head to the tips of his highly polished dark brown loafers.

"Is that photograph for me?" he asked, sitting down again.

Stevie handed it to him, explaining, "It was taken last summer in Connecticut."

Gianni stared at it for a long time. "She looks like me."

"Very much so. Especially the eyes and the forehead, and she has your strong jaw, Gianni."

"May I keep this?"

"Yes. But won't you come and see her for yourself?"

"You could not stop me. No one could." Gianni rose, came

and sat next to Stevie on the sofa. Looking deeply into her face, he took hold of her hands and said very softly, "If only you had told me then, Stephanie, perhaps I could have found a way." That sadness she had noticed before was reflected in his dark eyes once more. It made her catch her breath, so acute was it.

"Perhaps," Stevie murmured, returning his long, intense look. "All I want now is to introduce the two of you. I did a very wrong thing, keeping you apart. I want to make amends."

In the past Gianni had always driven his cars very fast. He had become a much more careful driver, Stevie noticed. As he drove his Ferrari out of Milan, heading in the direction of Lake Como, his speed was moderate.

Gianni chatted to her nonstop, or, rather, he continued to ply her with questions about Chloe, keeping up the continuing conversation, but he never took his eyes off the road.

At one moment he said, "I'm no longer a speed freak, as I used to be when I was younger. When I knew you years ago, Stephanie. Francesco's death cured me of that addiction. He was driving fast and talking to his girlfriend and he didn't see the truck coming. It was a head-on collision. Francesco and Liliane were killed instantaneously."

"I'm so very sorry," Stevie murmured softly. "I remember how much you . . . how much you loved him."

"Yes."

For the remainder of the drive to his house on Lake Como, Gianni was silent. Stevie sank down into herself, thinking about him. During their meeting at his office he had suddenly asked her if she would have dinner with him, and she had accepted. Now, here they were, driving along as if their eighteen-year separation had never happened. They had always been compatible with each other in the past, and incredibly that easiness, that sense of comfort, still existed between them. We're not much different now than we were then, she thought suddenly. Not deep down. Yes, we're older, and life has changed us both in certain ways; but essentially we are still the same people inside. Despite the ease which she felt existed between them, Stevie was tense inside. That acute feeling of nervousness she had first experienced in his office had persisted. And she was also very conscious of him as a man, conscious of his masculinity, his vitality, and his power. She had found him mesmeric when she had been younger; he had not lost his charismatic appeal for her. If anything, it was more potent than ever.

How she had longed for him over the years, longed to see his face, to hear his voice. She had never forgotten his voice. It was deep and resonant. Because he had been educated in England and America, his command of English was flawless.

She had given him up all those many years ago, and she was nothing if not disciplined. Once she had made the decision to cut him out of her life, she had not wavered in her determination. She had never again seen him, but the yearning had always been there.

She stole a look at him out of the corner of her eye, saw the strong set of his jaw, the well-defined nose, the shapely head. Chloe had his head, his eyebrows, his eyes.

Stevie could not help wondering about his life, about the women in his life over the years. And there must have been many, well, some . . . he was too sexual a man not to have been involved romantically. And he had told her he had been separated from Renata for twelve years. She clamped down on these thoughts, clamped down on other more dangerous thoughts of him that had been creeping into her mind for hours. She had come to Milan to see him because of Chloe, their daughter, wanting to bring them together at last. And that was her only purpose for being with him tonight.

When they arrived at the house on the shores of Lake Como, where many of the Milanese lived, Stevie was not in the least surprised at its size or its beauty. After he had parked in the courtyard, he led her inside to the large white entrance hall. It was elegant but somewhat austere, relying on its proportions and simplicity for its intrinsic beauty. Scanning it quickly, her eyes caught sight of a beautiful tapestry on one wall, a large gilt mirror on another. There was a huge crystal chandelier hanging from the high ceiling, a wide staircase flowing upward, and flowers everywhere.

A white-coated houseman greeted them, and Gianni spoke to him rapidly in Italian before taking her through a large living room. They came out onto a long terrace overlooking the lake.

"It's a beautiful house, Gianni," she said after a moment, glancing out at the water, then turning to him.

"Too big for one man, I think."

"Doesn't Carlo live here with you?"

"No."

"Is he married?"

"No, he's not. He lives in Rome. He has a flat there. Carlo runs my Rome office. He and I—" He broke off, shrugged lightly. "Carlo . . . was always his mother's son, hers more than mine. It is odd, is it not, the way one child will gravitate to one parent more than the other? And we never mean to make favorites, do we?" He smiled at her a little regretfully. A brow lifted. "You are a mother, Stephanie, you know how it is."

"I do, Gianni. Of my sons, Miles has always been a child of my heart, as Chloe is too."

"Francesco was the child of *my* heart, but now he's gone. Ah, life. It is difficult sometimes." He gestured to a chair. "Please."

The houseman returned with a bottle of champagne and two glasses on a tray, went to a small table behind them and opened the bottle.

Gianni smiled at her. "Veuve Clicquot for you, Steffie. You see, I have not forgotten."

A moment later they were clinking glasses. "Now. Tell me more about her. Tell me about Chloe." He began to chuckle unexpectedly. "If my grandmother were alive, she would be pleased to know my daughter was named for her. Thank you for that."

She spoke about Chloe for a while, telling him about her childhood, her relationships with her brothers and the rest of the family.

At one moment, when she paused to take a sip of the icy champagne, he asked, "When are you returning to London?"

"Tomorrow."

"Thursday. Mmmm." He regarded her over the rim of his glass, his eyes speculative. "I think I shall go with you. I want to see her."

"But it's too soon!" Stevie exclaimed. "I must prepare her. Explain everything." Stevie stopped when she saw the disappointment flashing across his face.

"How long is that going to take you? Fifteen minutes at the most. If that, Steffie."

There he was again, calling her by the name only he had ever used. Stevie looked across at him, found him suddenly irresistible. She glanced away, biting her lip. She said nothing.

There was a silence between them.

Gianni did not let it lengthen. He said, "That is true, isn't it? It won't take you very long to tell her about me ... about her father."

"I suppose you're right," she acknowledged without looking at him.

Gianni Caracelli sat back, studying her as she gazed out toward the lake. She had not changed at all. She was exactly the same as she had been twenty years before, when he had first met her in London. At a jewelry exhibition. He had taken one look at her and fallen head over heels in love. And so had she with him. It had been a *coup de foudre,* as the French called it, struck by lightning. It had been the most important and passionate relationship he had had with a woman in his entire life. His eyes narrowed slightly in the dimming light. Not a wrinkle on that lovely face, not a line. He smiled inwardly at himself. Of course there were tiny lines around her eyes and mouth; he had noticed them in his office earlier. But they had disappeared in an instant because he saw her as she had been then, not as she was now. In his mind she had never aged.

Clearing his throat, he said, "Let us go to London together, Stephanie. Tomorrow. On my plane."

Still, Stevie remained silent. She was afraid, if the truth be known. Afraid of him, of his power as a man, and of the appeal he had for her.

"I want to see Chloe," he insisted, although his voice was light. "And as soon as possible. Why wait?"

She turned to look at him.

His dark eyes were intense as they held hers. "So many years wasted, Steffie. Let us not waste any more."

30

"How do I look, Mom?" Chloe asked, coming into Stevie's bedroom. She stood in front of her mother, then turned around slowly. "Do you like this pants suit? Like the color?"

"Yes, I do," Stevie answered, the expression on her face approving. "The burgundy is wonderful on you. It's odd, but dark colors have always suited you, even when you were little."

"It's my olive complexion; I just look better in muted shades."

"I suppose so."

Holding her head on one side, studying Stevie, Chloe exclaimed, "You're very dressed up, Mom! Who did you say we're meeting for lunch?"

"Do I look too dressed up?" Stevie asked worriedly, and went to the mirrored closets that ran along one wall of the blue-and-white bedroom. She regarded herself thoughtfully for a second, then said, "I don't know what you mean. I'm not dressed up at all. I'm not even wearing much jewelry, just a brooch and earrings."

"I know, but that's your new suit. You told me you were saving it for a special occasion. And I've never seen that pin and those earrings before. They're wonderful sapphires, Mom. Are they new?"

"No." Stevie swung around, gave her daughter a careful look, and plunged in. "Your father gave them to me."

"My father! *When?*"

"Nineteen years ago." Walking across the floor to Chloe, Stevie took hold of her arm. "I want to talk to you. Let's go into the study for a minute."

"Okay. But what do you want to talk about? And why have you never worn those sapphires before?" Chloe eyed her mother curiously, wondering what this was all about.

"Come and sit with me" was the only answer Stevie gave her daughter as she hurried out.

Chloe followed her mother, sat down in a chair near the window, and focused all her attention on Stevie.

"When I was sitting at your bedside at the infirmary in Leeds, praying for you to come out of your coma, I made a promise to you in my heart and in my mind," Stevie explained. "I vowed that I would tell you the truth about your father. I am keeping that promise, Chloe, I want to tell you about him now."

Chloe nodded eagerly. She was on the edge of her seat in anticipation. Then before Stevie could say anything, Chloe exclaimed, "He's not dead, is he?"

Momentarily startled, Stevie gaped at her. Finally, she shook her head. "No, but how did you know that?"

"I didn't actually *know*, not for sure anyway. I just . . . well, I sensed it, Mom, I somehow *felt* that as a child. I always thought he was going to show up one day, just walk in and say, 'Hi, Chloe, I'm your dad.' I used to fantasize about it when I was little. I had an image of this tall, dark, handsome man walking toward me. My father. I thought he'd come looking for me, find me one day."

Stevie was speechless. After a moment she recouped and said, "Well, you're right. He's alive. And he *is* tall, dark, and handsome. Although I'll never understand how you knew that."

Chloe leaned forward. "And I bet his name's not John Lane either."

"No, it's not. That's not quite correct . . . part of it is."

"Why, Mom? Why did you hide the truth? Why didn't you tell me anything before?" Chloe asked in a small, puzzled voice, a hurt expression flickering in her brown eyes.

"I couldn't tell you the truth when you were old enough to understand, tell you who he really was, because of the circumstances of his life, his position in the world, his family. He was married, you see, and a very prominent man when we . . . when we were together—"

"Why didn't he divorce?" Chloe asked with a flash of vehemence. "Why didn't he get a divorce and marry you when you got pregnant with me? Didn't he want me?"

"He didn't even know about you. I never told him."

"Mom! Why not?" Chloe demanded, her voice rising.

"Because he was married. And he's a Catholic. I knew there would never be a divorce. There was no way he could get one. And he had children. I just made that decision not to tell him, and rightly or wrongly, I broke up with him before you were born." Stevie shook her head. "Perhaps I was wrong, but that's water under the bridge now. I never saw him again, once I had decided to end it."

"Didn't he try to keep it going? Pester you?"

"No, not when I said it must end because I couldn't live with the pain of it any longer. He respected my wishes, knowing how difficult everything had become for me. A love affair with a married man does become untenable. It's impossible, heartbreaking, Chloe."

A sympathetic note crept into Chloe's voice when she said, "It must have been hard for you, Mommy, not seeing him. I mean, if you loved him so much."

"I did. And it was. Very hard. But he lived in another country, which helped to some extent. He still lives there."

"Where does he live?"

"Italy."

"He's an Italian?"

"Yes."

"Wow! My father's Italian. *Awesome.* What's his real name, then?"

"Gianni ... short for Giovanni, which means John in English, you know."

"Gianni *what*, Mom?"

"Caracelli. Your father's Gianni Caracelli."

There was a small silence. Chloe eyed her mother in surprise, and said slowly, "Not the Italian industrialist? My father is *him*?"

"Yes."

Chloe stared at Stevie and then she got up and went and peered in the mirror above the mantel. "Do I look Italian, Mom?" She moved closer to the mirror. "My eyes do, I guess. But everyone's always said I look like your mother."

"You do. However, you also look like Gianni. You have his eyes, his brows, and forehead. And his strong jaw. And the shape of your head is the same as his."

"So I look like my daddy?"

Stevie nodded.

"That's why you went to Italy on Wednesday?"

"It is."

"Did you see him, Mom? Have you told him about me?"

"Yes, I have, Chloe."

"What did he say? I bet he was shocked," Chloe asserted.

"Stunned is a better word. I think a man like Gianni Caracelli is unshockable. And he was pleased."

"Was he really?" Chloe suddenly sounded anxious.

"Oh, yes. Thrilled really, and thrilled that I named you for his grandmother. Her name was also Chloe."

"*Oh.*"

"He wants to meet you, Chloe. In fact, he can't wait."

Chloe was suddenly feeling scared inside, yet excited and curious at the same time.

"He's here in London," Stevie announced.

"Is that who we're meeting for lunch?"

Stevie smiled. "It is. At the Dorchester. That's where he's staying. He always stayed there in the past, and I think that's where you were conceived, actually."

"Oh, Mom." Chloe stared at herself in the mirror again. "Are you sure I look all right? Maybe I should change. Oh, God, I look awful, Mom. I wish you'd told me about this before I got ready."

"You don't look awful. You're a lovely young woman."

All sorts of questions were suddenly jostling for prominence in Chloe's mind, and she exclaimed, "What happened to the wife? I mean, suddenly she doesn't matter?"

"Gianni's wife's dead, Chloe. She died a few years ago, but they were separated, and had been for a number of years."

"You said he had a family . . . "

"Yes, Gianni had two sons. Carlo and Francesco. Sadly, Francesco was killed in a car crash. Carlo lives in Rome, he runs the Rome office of Caracelli Industries."

"Does he . . . have a daughter?"

"You're his only daughter, Chloe."

Chloe was silent, digesting this, and then she asked, "Where did the name Lane come from, Mom?"

Stevie couldn't help smiling. "I told you a moment ago, your father always stayed at the Dorchester when he came to see me in London. He used the name Lane, as in Park Lane, when he phoned me. It seemed the obvious name to use on your birth certificate." Stevie rose, walked over to Chloe, and put her arm around her daughter. "I'm sorry I kept the two of you apart all these years, truly sorry. Can you ever forgive me?"

Chloe looked at her mother and unexpectedly tears filled her eyes. "*Forgive you?* Mom, for God's sake, there's nothing to forgive. You're the best mother anybody could ever have. You did what you had to do all those years ago, did what you thought was best for me. And I'm sure it was. I love you, Mommy, there's nobody like you in this whole wide world."

Stevie swallowed her incipient tears, and replied, "I think we ought to be going. To meet your father. He's waiting for us."

"Did he just arrive?"

"No, he came with me yesterday afternoon. Or, rather, I should say I came with him. I flew to London with him on his plane."

"He has a plane. Wow! Neat! Does he fly it himself?"

"No, he has a pilot. Mind you, he's quite the sportsman. You'll like him, Chloe, and you'll grow to love him very quickly."

Chloe hesitated before asking very quietly, "But will he like me, Mom? Will he love me?"

"He already does."

Gianni Caracelli stood up when he saw Stevie appear in the doorway of the Grill Room in the Dorchester Hotel. To his utter amazement, his heart began to thunder in his chest. And his throat tightened with emotion as he watched Stevie and Chloe walk toward the table. What a beautiful girl she was. She not only resembled him, she had a strong look of Francesco. For a split second he was so moved, he thought he would disgrace himself by weeping in a public place. His feelings were very strong; for his dead son, so beloved by him, for this young woman whom he did not know, and who was about to enter his life.

And then they were standing there in front of him.

His beautiful Steffie, the love of his heart, and his daughter. His only daughter. *Chloe*. He was unable to tear his eyes away from her face. They took in every detail of her appearance. She smiled at him, and without any hesitation stepped nearer to him, touched his arm, looked up at him. Her dark brown eyes were twin reflections of his own.

Automatically, Gianni drew closer himself. He embraced her, held her tightly against him. Flesh of my flesh, he thought. My child. He was thankful she was here.

Chloe clung to him for a second. He could not help thinking that he might never have known this extraordinary moment if she had not come out of the coma. She could have died without his ever meeting her.

His heart was suddenly full to overflowing. He thought: God takes so much away from us, but He gives back. And then he looked toward Stevie, filled with gratitude that she had come to see him in Milan. That action in itself had taken courage, for she had no knowledge of the circumstances of his life. Nor had she known how he would react. He was wrong there; of course she had known. No one in the world had ever understood him the way she had. What a fool he had been, never to have gone looking for her years ago.

Quite unexpectedly, Gianni experienced a feeling of peace flowing through him as he held Chloe in his arms. Oh, the blessed peace of it, to have this child. *His daughter*. It was the first peace he had known since Francesco had been killed.

Releasing Chloe, he turned to Stevie, took hold of her arm, kissed her on the cheek, then pulled out the chair for her.

The waiter saw Chloe into her seat and disappeared.

"I see that introductions are not necessary," Stevie murmured, and she smiled at him.

"No, they are not, Steffie." He smiled in return.

Chloe was as fascinated by Gianni as he had been by her. She stared at him quite unselfconsciously. "You look like I thought you would."

He glanced over at Stevie quizzically. And then his eyes swung back to his daughter. He frowned. "I thought you did not know of my existence."

"I didn't. But as I just told Mom this morning, I always *felt* my father was alive. I can't explain why. And I pictured him as being tall, dark, and handsome. And you are."

He laughed, amused by her forthrightness. "Thank you for the compliment. Unfortunately, I knew nothing about your existence, so you have the advantage. But you are lovely, Chloe. And a Caracelli. So like your half brother, Francesco. As he was at your age."

"Mom told me." She touched his arm. "I'm sorry."

He nodded. To Stevie he went on. "I ordered champagne. I hope that is all right. After all, this is a celebration. It's not every day that a man finds a beautiful daughter he did not know he had."

The waiter materialized with the champagne, and within minutes they were toasting each other. Gianni lifted his glass, beamed at them both. "To the two of you. I am so glad we are here together today. It's a happy occasion for me."

"And for us . . . to you, Gianni," Stevie said.

"To you . . . Father." Chloe said this hesitantly. "May I call you Father? Or should I call you Gianni?"

"No, not Gianni. I prefer Father. That is who I am."

"Yes, *Father*." Chloe looked at him closely, her head held on one side, her face reflective. "I've never called anyone that before . . . I never had a father. Only grandfathers."

Stevie stifled a gasp, and she looked stricken. "Oh, Chloe, I didn't—"

"No, Mommy. No," Chloe interrupted swiftly. "Don't be upset. I didn't mean it the way it came out. You know how much I love you."

Stevie realized Chloe was becoming agitated, and she said calmly, softly, "I know, darling, it's all right."

Turning to Gianni, Chloe confided, "She was a father to me as well as a mother. And she's always been wonderful. She saved my life, you know. She stayed with me night and day when I was in Leeds Infirmary. She never left me until I came out of the coma. I might not have lived if it hadn't been for Mommy. She's the best mother in the world."

"Yes, I know that," he answered. "I remember what a good mother she was to your brothers when they were small." Gianni laughed. "You do not have to tell me anything about Steffie. But I would like to know more about you. I understand you have been attending Brearley. Do you like it there?"

"Yes, I do," Chloe exclaimed, and in the same natural way she had greeted him, she began talking to him about school, regaling him with anecdotes.

Stevie interrupted her only once so that they could all order lunch. After they had done so, Chloe went on talking to Gianni nonstop. He nodded and listened, so obviously delighted with her.

Making up for lost time, Stevie thought as she listened to Chloe, surreptitiously studying Gianni Caracelli at the same time. There was no question in her mind that she felt the same way about him as she had eighteen years before. She could not help wondering how he felt about her. Did he, too, have a stomach full of butterflies when he was close to her, did he feel the electricity when they were together, as she did?

"I had a wonderful idea last night, Steffie," Gianni said, cutting into her thoughts.

"Oh, what was that?"

"I would like to invite Chloe and you to come to Lake Como. To stay with me at the villa. It would help her to fully recuperate, do you not think?"

Chloe's eyes widened. "It *is* a wonderful idea . . . Father. Oh, say yes, Mom. *Please.* I'd love to go."

"I'll have to speak to Mr. Longdon," Stevie replied, and explained to Gianni, "That's the neurosurgeon who operated on Chloe to remove the bullet. He did say she couldn't fly back to the States just yet."

"But this is such a short trip. Less than two hours to Milan. And she would be flying in a private plane. When can you speak with him?" Gianni asked.

"After lunch," Stevie responded.

"Oh, thank you, Mommy." Chloe pushed her chair away from the table and picked up her shoulder bag. "Would you please excuse me for a minute."

After she had gone, Gianni looked at Stevie intently, and said in a quiet voice, "My congratulations, you've done a wonderful job with her, brought her up so well. She is a credit to you, Steffie. Bright, self-confident, very natural, and not in the least precocious." He paused and shook his head sadly. "And you did it all alone. . . . "

"Not really, I had my mother and Derek, and her brothers. And thank you for the things you said . . . I'm so glad you like her."

"How could I not? She's lovely, so vivacious. I see you in her."

"And I see you, Gianni. I always did."

"Steffie?"

"Yes, Gianni?"

"There's something I wish to ask you." He hesitated, staring at her.

"What is it?"

"I wondered if we could . . . do you think we can be friends again?"

Stevie stared back at him, not sure what he meant, and she stiffened slightly in the chair.

He noticed this and exclaimed, "Please don't misunderstand me. I'm not proposing . . . that we . . . pick up where we left off eighteen years ago. What I meant was, could we be friends, platonic friends? We do have Chloe. I want to get to know her better." And I want to get to know you again, he thought. But you have not changed. You are still my Steffie, still the same inside. And a love like ours never dies. It only lies dormant when the two people involved are separated. *I need you both.*

Stevie had been watching him closely, and suddenly she understood. She knew with absolute certainty that he still loved her, and just as much as she loved him. Leaning across the table, she said softly, "Of course we can be friends, Gianni, I want that too."

He nodded. She was the only woman he had ever truly loved and, miraculously, she had come back into his life again. He was afraid to speak for a moment, so touched was he.

Stevie saw his love for her spilling out of his eyes, and she felt a surge of happiness like she had not known since she had left him. She touched his hand, which rested on the table. "Let's not waste any more years, Gianni. Let's be the *best* of friends." Her misty gray-green eyes held his.

Returning her steadfast gaze, he took hold of her hand. Bringing it to his lips, he kissed it lightly, and then he smiled at her. "Oh, yes, the *very* best of friends, my Steffie. My heart."